"MEDITATION WORKS BETTER IN SILENCE," MARISA SAID CALMLY.

"Seems to me your meditation isn't working." Rion's tone oozed charm. "There are better ways to relax."

"Like?" Marisa couldn't prevent a tiny smile from raising the corners of her lips.

His dark gaze flicked to her mouth, tracked it with hot male interest. He'd taken her smile for an opening. Of course, he would. She doubted anyone had ever told Mr. Irresistible no. Approaching with a long-legged saunter that made her eyes narrow with speculation, he sat on the mat behind her.

She should pull away until she knew what he was up to. But she couldn't. Not when he looked so damn good.

He went still behind her, drawing out a moment of silence that thrummed with tension. Her sizzling awareness of him seemed to fill the space between them with a rush of heat . . .

"Kearney is a master storyteller."
—VIRGINIA HENLEY,
***New York Times* bestselling author**

Please turn this page for more
praise for Susan Kearney . . .

PRAISE FOR
SUSAN KEARNEY

"[Kearney] combines sexy romance with spaceships, laser guns, psychic powers, and time travel."
—*Tampa Tribune*

"Susan Kearney takes you on a wild ride, keeping you guessing until the very end."
—*New York Times* bestselling author
KAREN ROSE on *Kiss Me Deadly*

"Out-of-this-world love scenes, pulse-pounding action, and characters who come right off the page."
—*USA Today* bestselling author
SUZANNE FORSTER on *The Dare*

"Looking for something different? A futuristic romance . . . *The Challenge* gave me a new perspective . . . love and sex in the future!"
—*New York Times* bestselling author
CARLY PHILLIPS

ALSO BY SUSAN KEARNEY

Lucan

RION

THE PENDRAGON LEGACY

SUSAN KEARNEY

FOREVER

NEW YORK   BOSTON

Copyright © 2009 by H.E. Inc.
Excerpt from *Lucan* copyright © 2009 by H.E. Inc.
Excerpt from *Jordan* copyright © 2009 by H.E. Inc.
All rights reserved. Except as permitted under the U.S. Copyright Act of 1976, no part of this publication may be reproduced, distributed, or transmitted in any form or by any means, or stored in a database or retrieval system, without the prior written permission of the publisher.

Book design by Giorgetta Bell McRee
Cover design by Diane Luger
Cover art by Don Sipley

Forever
Hachette Book Group
237 Park Avenue
New York, NY 10017
Visit our website at www.HachetteBookGroup.com.

Forever is an imprint of Grand Central Publishing. The Forever name and logo is a trademark of Hachette Book Group, Inc.

Printed in the United States of America

First Printing: December 2009

10 9 8 7 6 5 4 3 2 1

To my readers: You all are the ones who make my career possible. Thank you for your support. Thank you for telling your friends about my books. Thank you for joining me on this journey.

ACKNOWLEDGMENTS

First I have to thank Amy Pierpont for her terrific edits. And Alex Logan for her assistance during all facets of publication. I'd also like to thank Claire Brown and Christine Foltzer for yet another gorgeous cover, Anna Maria Piluso for the book's production, and of course Bob Levine and all his hardworking colleagues in sales.

And thanks to Holly Root for placing me at a wonderful publishing house.

RION

She who lives without taking risks dies without love.
—ENGLISH PROVERB

1

London, the near future

You call that relaxing?" A deep male voice reverberated through the exercise room, and Marisa Roarke opened her eyes. "Meditation is so overrated."

Rion Jaqard stalked with predatory zeal across the Trafalgar Hotel's workout room, flung a towel onto a chair, and whipped off his shirt before sliding onto the weight bench.

During the few times Marisa had run into Rion at her brother Lucan's apartment, she'd noticed Rion was built. But she hadn't realized he was so solid. Talk about walking testosterone. She'd bet even his sweat had muscles.

Rion always emitted a sexy aura. But tonight he seemed to have turned his charms up a notch. Almost as if his alluring appeal was a veneer. And beneath was an undercurrent of banked urgency. Intensity. She couldn't pinpoint exactly what was different about him but her tired mind was reluctant to question, preferring simply to appreciate his . . .

She had to stop looking.

Even if he was totally irresistible, she should have been immune. He may have been a first-rate flirt with other women, but he'd always treated her like a pesky kid sister. And who could blame him? A nasty divorce many years ago had left her with the expectation that most relationships were built on a mountain of lies.

Trying to ignore the size of Rion's very broad, very muscular chest, she frowned. "These days I find relaxing pretty much like trying to fly with only one wing."

Conversation over. She shut her eyes again. But the image of his ripped chest and totally toned, totally etched abs remained.

Marisa imagined those powerful arms around her. Strong, yet gentle. Warm and tight with a current of need. She imagined his eyes filled with desire . . . for her.

Stop it.

Stop imagining. She didn't imagine.

Not anymore.

She halted her wandering thoughts with hard facts.

Rion was from the planet Honor. The first chance he got to leave Earth, he'd be gone. But if all Honorians were built like him, Earth's women would be rioting for interplanetary travel visas. Of course, no such documents existed. Not since the United Nations had shut down travel from Earth to the rest of the galaxy.

For the moment Rion was trapped on Earth. She sneaked another glance. All that sculpted maleness was dazzling. Seductive. A woman could have a night to remember with a body like his. She suppressed a sigh. Too bad she wasn't that kind of woman. Since her failed marriage she'd become even more careful. Maybe too careful.

If he'd ever, even just once, shone any of his alpha sex-machine machoness in her direction, she might have succumbed to temptation and flirted. But he wasn't interested. He'd never been interested.

Stop drooling. Just look somewhere else. Anywhere else.

Marisa had thought herself past the age of ogling men who showed no sign of ogling back. She figured her reaction was due to work-related stress from her new career.

Just six months ago, Marisa had been a successful correspondent at the *St. Petersburg Times* in Florida. She'd covered everything from war in the Mideast to the story about her brother Lucan and his wife, Cael, who had brought back a cure from the planet Pendragon for Earth's fertility problems, which had been Marisa's last assignment.

While the cure had saved humanity from extinction, it had side effects, a genetic shift that required some people to periodically morph into dragons. But humans were not accustomed to their new dragonshaping abilities, which required controlling their more primitive side. So after discovering her own telepathic powers could be used to calm the dragons' highly sexed and predatory tendencies, Marisa had switched careers.

A fifteen-hour shift, exhaustion, and her not-so-successful attempt to erase the emotional aftereffects of dealing with her oversexed dragonshaping clients had clearly upset her equilibrium.

She closed her eyes. *Out. Out. Out.* Rounding up the

stray emotions, she corralled them into a tiny corner of her mind, then squashed down hard.

But she still couldn't block out the man across the room. The weights clinked as Rion raised and lowered them, and Marisa peeked again through her lowered lashes. The guy was gorgeous.

He slanted a glance in her direction. The gleaming interest in his eyes startled her. "Hard day?"

"Uh-huh." She looked away. The one-on-one telepathy she'd originally signed up for wouldn't have made her this susceptible to Rion's sexuality. But after Marisa had begun to work with the dragonshapers, she'd discovered she could simultaneously communicate with an entire group of dragons. Her unique ability to help many dragons at once made her a valuable asset to the Vesta Corporation. Unfortunately, the side effects subjected her to all of the dragonshapers' angers, fears, jealousies, and passions at once.

Don't think about work.

Left with residual sexual tension, all her cells hummed with need.

Let it go.

Unclenching her teeth, she forced her lips to part, breathed deeply through her nose, and told the muscles in her aching neck to loosen. Or at least to stop throbbing so she could go up to her hotel room and sleep.

"Maybe lifting would relax you."

She arched an eyebrow. Something had to be wrong with her hearing because his voice sounded coaxing.

"If you need help, I could spot you," he continued.

"No, thanks." Surprised by his persistence, she spoke without looking at him.

Why couldn't he just leave her alone? Surely by now even his oversized biceps had to be burning, his lungs aching for oxygen. But he didn't sound out of breath.

"Let me know if you change your mind." His tone held a hint of disappointment.

Disappointment?

No way.

Her tired mind had to be misinterpreting his signals. As much as she'd have liked to believe he was interested in her, she knew better. So she had to accept that the dragons' residual passions were affecting her judgment.

"Meditation works better in silence," she said calmly, pleased that her voice didn't give away how aware she was of the way his buttocks tightened and relaxed in a fascinating rhythm that made her mouth go dry.

"Seems to me your meditation isn't working."

He was right. She couldn't stop staring at him. A light gleam of sweat glistened on his skin, emphasizing his muscles as he set down the weights.

He straightened and raked her with a gaze that settled on the vein throbbing in her neck. "Your pulse rate must be over one thirty," he said.

Hell. Any woman within ten meters of him would have an elevated pulse. "Are you deliberately trying to annoy me, or do you come by it naturally?"

She expected him to take off, but he grabbed his towel, slung it over his shoulders, and wiped the sweat from his brow. And gave her a look brazen enough to heat every flat in London—for the entire winter.

Whoa. She might be tired. But not that tired. No way could she misread his male interest. Just what was going on here? He'd never looked at her like this before. What was he up to?

His tone oozed charm. "There are better ways to relax."

"Like?" Marisa couldn't prevent a tiny smile raising the corners of her lips.

His dark gaze flicked to her mouth, tracked it with hot male interest. He'd taken her smile for an opening. Of course, he would. She doubted anyone had ever told Mr. Irresistible no. Approaching with a long-legged saunter that made her eyes narrow with speculation, he sat on the mat behind her and placed his palms firmly on her shoulders.

She should pull away until she knew what he was up to. But she couldn't. Not when he looked so damn good.

He went still behind her, drawing out a moment of silence that thrummed with tension. Her sizzling awareness of him seemed to fill the space between them with a rush of heat.

At the first touch of his hands on her shoulders, she had to bite back a gasp of pleasure. Gently, ever so slowly, he kneaded her neck and caressed her shoulders with a sensual thoroughness that melted away the tension. Circling in on the tight spots with soothing caresses, he feathered his fingertips over her sore muscles.

Her pulse leaped. She swallowed hard.

Rion eased the heels of his palms into her tight shoulders with lingering, luscious strokes. After several mesmerizing minutes, he leaned forward and his breath fanned her ear. "You carry tension in the neck."

"I do?" She sighed and leaned into his hands, grateful for the relief.

He kneaded gently, gradually going deeper, until her muscles melted, until she felt as warm and pliable as taffy. His fingers were so clever, but as he released one kind of tension, a sensuous anticipation began to build.

"Am I too hard for you?" he asked, almost sounding innocent.

She jerked upright and made a choking sound. He was sitting behind her, but she could see his chiseled face reflected in the mirrors and caught a reckless I-shouldn't-be-messing-with-my-best-friend's-sister-but-I'm-going-to-do-it-anyway gleam in his eyes. "My hands. Am I rubbing too hard?"

"You feel great. And you damn well know it." She lifted an eyebrow and shot back her best I-know-what-you're-up-to look.

But she really had no idea what his intentions were. He might have been a first-class flirt with other women, but with her, he'd merely been friendly.

"I'm glad you like my touch," he murmured.

At his flirting, her heart fluttered, but she tamped down her excitement and cast him a curious glance. "From what I hear, you've had lots of practice."

Rion worked on a knot next to her spine, applying tension until the tightness ebbed. "You have an Earth saying, 'Practice makes perfect.' But I'm not certain if a massage can ever be perfect. After all, there are so many variations of where to touch . . . how to touch . . . when to touch . . ."

No one could accidentally be *that* suggestive—not even a man from another planet. And while she'd love to find out exactly where and how he would touch her next, all her caution signals flared.

Leaning forward, he whispered into her ear, "Did you know you have a very sexy neck?" His gray eyes met hers in the mirror, and she could have sworn they smoldered. When he brushed a wispy tendril from her nape, heat shimmied down her spine.

Damn, he was smooth. Real smooth. Although she'd already been burned by her ex-husband, she was long over the hurt. Yet when it came to men, she remained cautious, unable to trust her own judgment.

Ignoring the desire surging through her veins, she scooted from under Rion's hands and stood. "Thanks. It's been a long day. I need to hit the sack."

"Good night, Marisa." He stood, too, and grabbed his shirt. As she left the workout room, he called out to her. "Sweet dreams."

Sweet was out of the question. Sizzling hot was more like it.

He will speak at times of things yet to happen . . . for
he has the gift of sight.

—MERLIN

2

As always, Rion's vision flashed before his eyes without warning.

"You dare to defy me?" The Unari raised his
whip.

His victim, a man on his knees, bowed his head.

The Unari's lash swished, cutting the air and
biting into a back already scarred from too many
whippings, leaving yet another bloody welt.

At the vicious blow, the victim clenched his jaw
but didn't utter a sound. Eyes dulled by pain, head
down, his emaciated body trembled.

"Get up." The blasé tone of the Unari suggested
he'd beaten many men.

And then the vision widened in scope, like a cam-
era backing up and allowing a wide-angle view.
Bright orange Cuttees flapped their wings and soared
over the hellish Honorian desert. And Rion gasped in
horror. Beyond the two men were hundreds, maybe

thousands more starving Honorians, laboring to build a giant wall under the Unari lash.

"Get up, slug. There's work to do." The Unari landed a brutal kick on the man's hip.

Deep in a trance, Rion flinched. Willed the man to get up.

The lash descended again, this time shredding skin across the man's vulnerable stomach. With a primal howl, he pulled his knees into his chest.

As the man writhed in pain, Rion glimpsed a distinctive three-quarter crescent-shaped burn mark on his arm.

Sweet Goddess. Rion knew him. Avril had once been a giant, a palace guard.

"Back on your feet. Get up, slave."

"Slave?" Rion snapped out of his trance, head reeling. It took him a few moments to realize he'd had a flash, a gruesome vision of the future.

Currently a guest on planet Earth in the luxurious Trafalgar Hotel, where the Vesta Corporation had housed him for the last six months, Rion paced, clenching and unclenching his fists.

Ever since his arrival on Earth, Rion had been employing his diplomatic skills to convince the United Nations to join the Honorians' fight against the Unari. So far he didn't have the votes of enough delegates to swing a commitment from Earth. Hell, they wouldn't even agree to open the portal to send him back home, never mind pay for an army to fight the Unari.

But he was now done with diplomacy. Done pleading for Earth to help.

It was time to act. And his new plan was moving along nicely. Running into Marisa last night had been no accident. She'd been suspicious at first, smart woman that she was, but after the shoulder massage, he was pretty sure she now thought of him as more than Lucan's friend.

Sealing the deal might take longer.

His best friend's twin . . . annoyingly suspicious of him, downright intelligent, blessed with rare telepathic talent, she was definitely a woman with curves in all the best places. She deserved to be taken to London's best restaurant, wined and dined by a real gentleman.

His conscience stabbed, but he didn't have the luxury of questioning his scruples. Not after the horrors he'd seen.

By the Goddess, he'd had enough of political squabbling, indecision, and England. The visceral need to get home to prevent the disaster he'd envisioned flared hotly in his core. Only long years of discipline allowed him to contain his rage. But he'd do anything to save his people.

With communications knocked out on Rion's home world, Marisa was the key to his plan to free his people of the Unari invaders. A rallying cry sent to every dragonshaper on Honor would make it possible for Rion to organize a revolt. And Marisa had the rare talent to send that message.

Leaving his room, Rion strode down the hall to the suite next door and knocked on the door. "Lucan . . . you there?"

Marisa cracked open the door and slipped off the security chain. With her mass of chestnut hair—highlighted in various shades—vivid blue eyes, and slender body, she resembled a picture he'd once seen in a childhood book about a fiery mountain sprite.

"Enter at your own risk." Marisa's eyes sparkled with humor, as if he'd caught her at the tail end of a joke.

Tendrils of her luscious mane curled over her slender neck, and he was reminded of feeling that smooth, silky skin beneath his fingertips last night. She shot him a friendly grin as if their encounter had never happened. "Welcome to chaos."

"Isn't Lucan around?" Pretending to search for her brother, he forced his gaze from her provocative gem-studded earlobes to look around the hotel suite.

She hadn't been exaggerating about the chaos. Two baby dragons hopped across the carpet. Not yet strong enough for true flight, they took a few running steps, fluttered their wings, and toppled over, only to get up and do it all over again.

"Shut the door quickly before one of them escapes." Marisa scooted a baby away from the door.

Rion stepped into the turmoil of boisterous baby dragons, a barking dog, and a ringing phone, but Marisa seemed unfazed by the confusion.

Wearing high heels, jeans, and a snug tank top, Marisa swayed her hips with a sensual ease as she stepped between the furniture, the yapping dog, and the baby dragons' hopping test flights. "Lucan and Cael are out to dinner."

Watching the babies cavorting on the rug, Rion grinned at one major side effect of the sterility cure. Some people who took the vaccine now had the ability to morph from human to dragon and back. As did their children. And the babies shifted back and forth at will.

His smile faded as he recalled Earth's struggle to accept the dragonshapers. During the last six months, parents, governments, and schools had adjusted to a baby boom and three-month gestation periods. In order to adapt to the cultural changes, many people had made sacrifices. Marisa had given up her reporting job to work at a London university and now used her telepathic abilities to teach adult dragonshapers how to contain their powers and strength.

Thank the universe, the rambunctious little ones couldn't breathe fire yet. "You volunteered to watch the twins?" Rion asked, careful to simulate surprise.

"I must have been out of my mind," Marisa said with a laugh. Ignoring the ringing phone, she pivoted and leaned over to pick up a dragon. The pose drew his attention to her perfectly rounded ass, and he found himself battling the urge to yank off her jeans and nibble his way down to her panties.

She plucked one of the twins off the dog's back. "Condor, sweetheart, you can't ride Buster."

Rion laughed. "Why not?"

She set the baby dragon on the carpet and shook a finger at Rion. "Don't start." Her voice was stern, but her lips twitched into a smile. "Their claws might scratch him."

Rion raised an eyebrow. "Through his fur?"

"I don't know." Marisa shrugged. "Even their mother doesn't know. Cael says she didn't dragonshape until she was five and had a little common sense."

As baby dragonshapers, Rion and his cousins had often ridden the Honorian equivalent of dogs and horses. The young dragons' instincts were right on target. Lifting

Condor, Rion gently placed him on Buster's back. The dog wagged his tail. "See, he doesn't mind."

"But Nessie's throwing a fit. She wants up, too."

Rion patted the little girl's neck. "Nessie, you'll have to wait your turn."

Nessie squawked and flapped her wings.

"Uh-oh." Marisa reached for Nessie.

But the dragon dodged, evading her aunt's hands, and Marisa clenched empty air. She stepped forward to catch her balance, and her heel caught in a dog toy. Rion grabbed her shoulder and pulled her against his chest to steady her.

The sweet scent of her hair and the feel of her soft, toned body inflamed his senses and tempted his fingers to explore. He yearned to plunge his fingers into her hair, yank back her head, and taste her sweet mouth.

If she'd been unattractive, he still would have pursued her. But she was gorgeous, alluring, thank the Goddess, so lying, at least about his attraction to her, wasn't necessary. However, holding her this close had him all fired up. Both his hearts pounded out a rhythm. *Take. Take. Take.*

If Rion were here solely to slake his own needs, he would have slammed his mouth over hers and demanded what he wanted. But his people needed her help. He couldn't risk moving too fast.

Employing the utmost control, he held perfectly still.

She tilted her head back and smiled. "Thanks."

Rion didn't even attempt to control the huskiness in his voice. "I'm always happy to catch a pretty girl."

She blushed. Rion reluctantly released her, but not before he breathed in her scent once more . . . strawberry soap, with a hint of lime.

Eyes sparkling, Marisa spoke breathlessly. "Guess I should be wearing track shoes to keep up with this brood."

Kicking off her heels, she revealed bright turquoise polish.

At the sight of those toes, Rion sucked in a harsh breath. What other surprises did Marisa keep hidden beneath her clothes?

Were the dragon scales on the insides of her arms, legs, and spine deliciously thin, or intriguingly solid? When he'd held her so closely, had her scales undulated in response? Would she writhe with pleasure if he ran his tongue over them?

Buster banged into Rion's leg, and Rion reached down to pet him, glad for an excuse to move away from Marisa. This was not the time to come on to her. He had to hold back if his seduction was going to work.

The dog ricocheted off his leg and scampered around the couch, almost tripping Marisa again as he ran in a tight circle, barking and wagging his tail. Condor clung to Buster's back, flapping his wings, cooing happily. Nessie roared, spread her wings, and launched herself high enough into the air to settle perfectly atop her brother.

The scene was chaotic but also homey, cozy, and peaceful in a clamorous way. So different from the brutal violence in his vision. By the Goddess, he would do whatever was necessary to bring this kind of bliss to Honor again.

Patience. He couldn't come on too strong. While he'd have to wait until the babies were asleep to make a physical move, he could still put this time to good use.

Nessie's wing knocked over a vase of flowers. Rion

lunged and caught it, but not before water spilled onto the rug.

Marisa rolled her eyes and gave Rion a now-see-what-they've-done look. "Cael's going to scorch us."

"Your brother's put her through much worse, and she hasn't cooked him." Rion placed the vase in a closet and shut the door. He glanced up and spotted Merlin, Cael's owl, on the top shelf of the bookshelf by the fireplace, wisely settled high above the fray.

Rion turned to Marisa, his body back under control. "Cael loves your brother. Besides, he has more than enough fire to counter hers."

"I'm glad my brother and Cael found each other. They have it all—passion and friendship. They are true soul mates." She grinned.

Damn, she had a beautiful smile. "You aren't jealous?"

She shook her head, her chin at a jaunty angle. Marisa clearly couldn't have been happier for her brother. "The two of them give me hope. If they can be that happy . . ." Her eyes took on a dreamy hue that intrigued him. Floored him.

Sweet holy Goddess. He might have just enough scruples in him to stop his reaction to the smokiness in her voice or the vulnerable hope in her eyes. But his body reacted.

He shifted to hide his arousal.

Between Marisa's stunning looks and her quick mind, she was accustomed to men pursuing her. And accustomed to turning them down. That dreamy look in her eyes had told him she wanted the same kind of connection her brother had with his wife.

She wanted love. Commitment.

A decent man would walk away. A man with less responsibilities would do the right thing and leave her to pursue her dreams.

But Rion wasn't that man.

"I heard you set your own fire last week," he teased, turning the conversation in a safe direction. Marisa had dragonshaped, eaten platinum, and accidentally incinerated a tree.

"You heard about that?" Marisa laughed, not the least self-conscious about her actions. "I haven't had much time to work on my own dragonshaping control. The government's keeping me too busy calming everyone else."

New dragonshapers were required to go through Marisa's one-week training to learn to regulate their fire-breathing. Not so easy a task, especially since dragons lost most of their human intellect after shifting.

"How's it going?" he asked, careful to keep his voice casual.

"I'm getting the hang of group telepathy."

As twins, Marisa and Lucan had always been telepathic—but just with each other. However, after Marisa had taken the vaccine, she'd discovered she could communicate with multiple dragons, while remaining in human form. Selflessly, she'd given up her home in Florida and a job she loved as a reporter because Earth needed her unique talent. Not only could she train more than one dragonshaper at a time, she could draw on her full human intellect to cope with the primitive dragon brains.

The dog rounded a corner, and Nessie pitched sideways. Marisa bent to catch her, her jeans tightening again to give him yet another glimpse of the perfect shape of her ass. But the dragon righted on her own, and Marisa straightened.

"Excuse me a sec," Marisa told him, then focused on the babies.

Setting her hands on her hips, her face full of intense concentration, she moved her lips. While he heard nothing, the baby dragons did. They now used their front talons to cling to their ride.

Clearly, Marisa had given them instructions through a silent mental link. Impressive. And if his resolve had wavered, it was back in full force. It was too bad for Marisa that he needed her. But neither his genuine liking and respect for her, nor his own guilt, would deter him from carrying through with his plans.

Buster ran under a coffee table, scraping the babies from his back. Nessie and Condor tumbled, rolling and squawking, but weren't injured. Dragons were tough.

Marisa grinned. "I think that's enough rough stuff for . . ."

Buster barked at the dragons, circled them, then barked some more, as if ordering them to climb back on. This time, Nessie flew on first. Condor settled on top of her, and the three of them were off flapping and running again.

As if in unspoken mutual agreement, the adults gave up on conversation. They didn't have to wait long for the commotion to die out. A few minutes later, the dog lay panting on the carpet and the twins humanshaped. Stronger than non-dragonshaping children, Nessie at only three months could crawl over to Rion, and he lifted her onto his lap.

With a mischievous grin, Marisa handed him a baby

bottle, picked up Condor, and began to feed him. Looking lovely, she cuddled the baby close, in the easy pose of a natural mother. He followed suit, cradling Nessie in the crook of his arm and placing the nipple between her tiny pink lips, surprised at how good it felt to hold a child again. She smelled like powder and lotion. Sweet.

"Why so thoughtful?" Marisa asked, her face soft and happy.

He felt his neck flush. He'd just had a flash that implied imminent danger to his people, and here he was cooing over babies. He ignored her question. "Are you enjoying your new telepathic abilities?"

"Mm-hm?" She raised an eyebrow as if she knew his introspection had really been about the baby. "I'm still adjusting. I suppose we both have abilities that can be seen as advantageous as well as detrimental. Lucan told me how the flashes frustrate you." She crossed one elegant leg, reached for a soft cloth, and wiped a trickle of milk from Condor's cheek.

He kept his gaze on her eyes, although he really wanted to memorize the curve of her leg. "For me the worst part is when I don't have a clue if my vision is from the past, present, or future. What's worst for you?"

"The residual emotions. When I'm open and sending messages, I'm also receiving. I'm not so good at filtering them out." Marisa might have looked maternal, but her eyes sparkled with a sexy-as-hell curiosity. "Are your flashes like a waking dream?"

"Sort of." Rion rarely spoke about his flashes. But to gain her confidence, he had to give a little. "When a trance hits, I'm still aware of what's going on around me. If I have to I can move, but only slowly, since I'm so distracted. Like being caught up in a good book, only more so."

"Can you make yourself—"

He shook his head. "The flashes come at random. Sometimes I see a one-second snapshot. Sometimes I see an entire scene. It's rarely complete, and I don't even know if it's the beginning, middle, or end."

"Does everything you see in the future come true?"

"Unless I do something to alter that future." He hesitated to say more.

Her gaze, suddenly sharp and curious, locked with his. "You can alter the future?"

"That's what my father and grandfather believed."

She pursed her mouth as if she'd figured out a puzzle. "So like the telepathy I share with Lucan, your flashes run in the family. But . . . you don't like them?"

Her perception surprised him. "They are my birthright. I've learned not to ignore them. The good visions can be very useful. Three years ago, I got a visual warning to escape just before the Unari invaded Honor. That one saved my life."

"The Unari? Who exactly are they?"

"No one knows for sure. But my people believe the Unari race are one of the most powerful partners in the coalition of evil that makes up the Tribes."

"And you saw Lucan in a vision before you two met?" she asked.

He nodded. "Before I'd ever heard of Earth, I saw myself and your brother battling the Tribes."

Marisa frowned. "The Tribes? King Arthur's ancient enemy? Isn't that who you and Lucan fought on Pendragon?"

"Yes and no. It's true we fought the Tribes on Pendragon."

"But?" she prodded, her gaze burning into his, her body tensed.

"My vision of your brother and me fighting the Unari Tribes together hasn't happened yet."

Marisa's gaze pierced his. "Oh, my God. Are you certain?"

"Yes." Rion nodded. "While we were on Pendragon, we found hints that King Arthur's ancient enemy, the Tribes, might be rising again. Not just on Honor. Not just on Pendragon. But all across the galaxy."

3

"And one of the Tribes, these Unari, has invaded your world," Marisa said, putting together all the information Rion had just given her.

"You can bet your sweet oxygen my people will fight for their freedom," Rion said, his tone fierce with pride. "I expected Earth to do the same."

Marisa admired Rion's passion and understood his frustration. And she'd always been a sucker for causes. That was why she'd become a reporter. She, too, had wanted to make a difference.

"I'm damn tired of Earth's politicians jerking me around."

"Give Earth a chance. We've been through a lot." Condor sucked hard on his bottle, but Marisa gave Rion a long look. "You can't blame Earth for keeping the portal closed. Or for not jumping into a war that would help your people. We fear that what happened to your world could happen here. And now that we can have children again, families don't want to be split apart by war. I hate the idea of my brother heading into danger again. He's done his part. He's got a family to take care of now."

His tone remained soft, but his eyes hardened. "Closing the portal won't make Earth safe."

"But it'll make it more difficult for anyone to attack us. Besides, the expense of fighting a war on another world on the other side of the galaxy would be astronomical."

"The consequences of *not* fighting will be worse," he promised, his eyes flashing a bold gray challenge.

Condor had fallen asleep, and Marisa gently eased away the bottle, her mind thoughtful. Had she actually found a decent guy who could respect her opinion, even if it was different from his own? In her experience, men who had enough confidence in themselves not to feel intimidated by another point of view were rare. To find that trait packaged in such spectacular wrapping was a bonus and had her second-guessing herself.

If she'd stuck around longer last night, she might have found out exactly how good he was. And she probably wouldn't have spent the night tossing and fantasizing about how good he could have made her feel.

She eyed Rion, still testing. "If the situation were reversed, would Honorians use their own resources and risk their lives to save a people they didn't know, against an enemy they'd never met?"

"I'd like to think so." He glanced down at the baby in his arms. "The Unari Tribes' brutality doesn't merely extend to soldiers. They don't distinguish between civilians and the military. They make war on women and children, too."

"Children?" She couldn't imagine. On Earth, children

were not just their most precious commodity, but their hopes, their dreams, their future.

How ironic that by the time Lucan had returned with the fertility cure and children became a possibility for her, her marriage had ended. Afterward, she'd closed down tight, unwilling to risk another mistake, unwilling to risk hurting like that again. Yet losing her husband to another woman hadn't been as bad as her shaken confidence in her own judgment. For years she couldn't trust anyone. But she'd healed. There were good men out there. She just had to find one.

Sure, she'd be more cautious this time. But she was no longer holding back. "You have a family on Honor?"

"I have parents and a . . . cousin. Erik. I pray to the Goddess that they're still alive. That my own people didn't—"

"Didn't what?"

Pain filled his eyes. "That they didn't hurt my mother."

She bit back her gasp. "Why would your own people—"

"She wasn't born on Honor." The words poured out of him as if he'd kept the worry bottled up too long and had to release the pressure. "My people never really accepted her as one of us." Then he clamped his lips together as if he'd said too much.

"Why not?" she asked softly, her heart going out to him.

She resisted the urge to go to him, place her arms around him. She might intend to give comfort, but she didn't trust herself. At the moment the conversation was serious, but the underlying sexual heat from last night remained. And like an unlit fuse in need of a match, one touch from Rion would light her up.

"On your world, when things go bad, it's often the foreigner who's blamed. It's not so different on Honor."

She could see that not knowing about his family's safety tormented him. That he cared so much proved he was capable of love. That he so easily revealed his worry made her feel special. "Your visions haven't shown you—"

"Nothing, except that the situation back home is deteriorating." He thrust his fingers through his hair. Then, as if realizing what he was doing, he stilled completely.

His stiffness warned her he might shut down, that something terrible was bothering him. Back in her reporter days, she'd seen soldiers with the same glazed look in their eyes. "What did you see?"

"Unari flaying my people with whips."

She grimaced. "But you didn't see any of your family"—she tried to offer hope—"so maybe they are all right."

He stared at her, unseeing, looking inward, his voice flat, yet all the while he tipped the bottle at the perfect angle so Nessie wouldn't suck in air. "It was daylight. The man I did see . . . he was so emaciated, I would never have recognized Avril, but he had a distinctive scar on his arm from a childhood accident."

"Watching and being able to do nothing must be horrible."

"I saw hundreds. Maybe thousands of people brutalized. Unless I find a way to prevent it, it's going to happen . . . soon."

"How do you know?"

He spoke with a methodical precision that she now

knew masked the pain beneath the surface. "Avril looked
as though he'd aged a few years since I'd seen him last.
But I also saw a Cuttee in the sky."

"A Cuttee?"

"It's a bird that changes from tan to orange when it
goes into mating mode about once every five years. The
last time the Cuttees mated was about a year before I left
home."

"So how long until your vision comes true?"

"Weeks. Maybe days."

Nessie spat out the bottle's nipple. Deftly, Rion placed
her over his shoulder and rubbed her back, waiting for
the burp.

Marisa's eyes widened. "You've taken care of a baby
before?"

"I've watched Cael care for these two." He glanced toward the bedroom where the young boy Cael and Lucan
had adopted usually slept. "Where's Jaylon?"

"Staying over at a friend's." Marisa frowned, her eyes
burning into him. Something wasn't right. Rion couldn't
be that comfortable or knowledgeable about a baby just
from the few times he'd watched Cael take care of the
twins.

"I'm sorry I missed Jaylon. He's a fun kid."

Nessie burped, and he moved her back onto his lap to
feed her the rest of the bottled milk. She suckled for a
minute or two more and her eyes closed.

Rion looked up at Marisa, a Marisa who no longer hid
from the hard questions. Ten years ago she wouldn't have
confronted him or said, "You didn't get this comfortable
taking care of baby dragons from watching Cael."

He didn't deny it. "Why don't we put Condor and Nessie in their cribs. Then we can talk some more."

What was he up to? Without a baby in her arms, she could focus on him. Decide how much closer she wanted to get. His story tugged at her. The sight of his big hands gently burping the baby had shaken something loose inside her. Rion had passion for his people. He had tenderness for a baby. He was her brother's best friend, too, and that complicated everything.

Was he worth the complications?

Yes. The answer came so fast, so hard she halted midstride. She peered down at the baby in her arms. For so many years, she'd yearned for one of her own. She still wanted kids, but it had to be with the right man.

Was Rion that man? She didn't know. But she'd never find out without taking a few risks. So she would learn all she could about him, not just his history and plans for the future. She would learn what made him laugh, what made him happy. She wanted to know it all. His taste, his touch, what made him tick.

And there was only one way to do that: get closer. Much closer.

The idea excited her. Pleased her. Her step light with certainty, she gazed at his broad back, wondering about the possibilities.

After placing the babies in their cribs, she led him into the kitchen. With a steady hand, she poured them each a glass of wine. She sipped, savoring the rich flavor as it rolled over her tongue. "So how did you get so good with babies? Especially dragonshaper babies?"

"I'm a dragonshaper."

She jerked her head to stare at his wrist. She saw no

scales, just a thick wrist, the skin bronzed, the forearms ripped with muscle. "You're a dragonshaper?"

Rion turned over his wrist, exposing his skin to her curious gaze. "Honorians aren't marked by the dark purple scales that Cael has passed on to Earth's dragonshapers."

"Does my brother know your world has dragonshapers? That you're a dragonshaper?" Her own double hearts skipped a few beats as she waited for his reply.

He took her hand, laced his fingers through hers, and squeezed. "Lucan knows. So does Cael, but I asked them to keep my secret."

And now he was telling *her* his secret, too. "Why?"

He made tiny, enticing circles with his thumb over her hand. "During my travels, for my own safety, I've learned not to talk about myself. I've visited many worlds and am not always certain who is friend or foe. If rumors spread back to the Unari Tribes about an Honorian dragonshaper, they might come after me."

"Why?" she asked again.

"Because the Unari creed is total domination, total darkness. Part of their tactic is to crush all hope. The mere idea of anyone escaping is total anathema to them."

"So you don't speak about your dragonshaping?"

"Or about my visions, either." Life had etched composure and dignity into his face.

She cocked her head to the side, not totally buying that he trusted her, but not pulling her hand away, either.

"It's difficult to predict what will upset others," he continued. "People fear what is different, what they don't understand. And what they don't understand, they don't believe."

She shot him a thoughtful look. "Are you talking about

your visions? Are you saying that we don't believe in them the way you do?"

"That's really the core of the problem." He released her hand and stroked his fingertips up and down her arm, his touch feather light. "Because if your people believed me, they'd marshal every resource to fight the Unari Tribes."

The guy was complicated, fascinating, and determined. She tipped up her glass, sipped the last of her wine, then rested her hands on his shoulders and looked him straight in the eyes. "My brother believes you."

He held her gaze, the gray in his eyes darkening. "Do you?"

She didn't look away, but her stomach fluttered. "My brother has an inherent faith that goes beyond what he can see, taste, and touch. I'm a bit more hands-on. I like proof. I'm cautious."

Yet she was leaning into his chest, her fingers inching over his shoulders to his neck, enjoying the feel of him. She couldn't seem to help herself.

"Aren't you curious?" Rion asked, his voice low and husky.

"About what?" All his muscles bunching between her fingertips had a way of distracting her as much as his sexy tone.

"Other worlds." He stared at her mouth, and she could have sworn she felt the heat. "Wouldn't you like to use the transporter?"

He tangled his finger in a lock of her hair, and she cuddled into him, the movement feeling natural and right. As much as she enjoyed having him here, she sympathized with his eagerness to go home. "I'm sorry you're so worried about your family and friends. But we can't risk all of our safety by opening the portal. Surely you can understand that?"

"That's not all I understand." Wrapping his arms around her, he pulled her against his broad chest, his eyes searching hers. "That's not all I want."

She saw herself mirrored in his eyes and knew she was desired.

—LADY GUINEVERE

4

Oh, God. Rion was about to kiss her. She could see the hunger in his gray eyes. The tension in his neck that held him rock steady.

Was she going to kiss him?

It wasn't every day that Marisa could have all that male sizzle wrapped around her. Hell, she wasn't dead—and that's what she'd have to be, not to appreciate Rion's attractiveness, or the power in his ripped muscles. But what really drew her in was the purposefulness beneath the suave charm. Rion was a doer. Passionate about his cause and his people.

She raised her gaze from his long, calloused fingers to his shoulders that were as broad as the English Channel, to his fascinating lips, to his bold gray eyes. Eyes that seemed to pierce straight to her core.

"Kiss me," he demanded, his voice a sexy rumble.

There was nothing safe about his request. Nothing safe about the way she felt, all jumbled raw nerves, all excited and eager to take a risk. And Rion was Lucan's friend, honorable and trustworthy. Besides, she'd never felt desire this powerful. The combination of his rugged good looks and the heat radiating from his body was sweeping her away in a perfect storm.

She let her fingers drift over his commanding shoulders to the cords on the back of his neck and threaded them into his thick hair. Then ever so slowly, she tugged his head down, until she could distinguish tiny flecks of dark green in his gray eyes.

Stomach clenching in delicious anticipation, she rose on her tiptoes, leaned toward all his magnetic male hardness. Another inch. And then his lips met hers.

His mouth brushed hers with a soft, teasing graze that left her aching and craving far more. Parting her mouth, she used the tip of her tongue to trace his full lips. He tasted of red wine, plus an erotic tang uniquely his own.

His tongue tangled with hers, giving and taking. Dancing and arousing her with a smooth rhythm that made her feel light and supple. And then he kissed her forehead, her eyelids, her nose, her ears.

"That tickles." She squirmed and nipped his shoulder right through his shirt.

"Are your scales ticklish, too?" he asked with a mischievous grin. Then before she could answer, he lifted her hand and pressed his lips to the inside of her wrist, right on her sensitive scales.

Wondrous sensations undulated up her arm and down her spine, then spread to her limbs. Rion nuzzled his way over her flesh, his lips nibbling and licking. Every scale on her body quivered in an electrifying chain reaction that escalated with each lick. And the scales that crossed at the apex of her thighs had her squirming.

She let out a soft moan of pleasure as her dragonblood pulsed through her like a crisp burst of wind, leaving no part of her untouched. Her nipples hardened. Moisture seeped between her thighs.

Pure erotic sensation had her swaying on her feet. Rion scooped her into his arms and carried her to the sofa. Kneeling beside her, he leaned forward and kissed her mouth. "Are you all right?"

"Very all right." With a grin, she grabbed his collar and pulled him on top of her. His weight settled nicely between her legs, his sex hard and firm against her thigh.

To avoid crushing her, he lifted onto his elbows, but she didn't let his lips escape hers. She needed more. More of him. Her fingers burned to explore all his powerful male flesh.

Bunching his shirt in her hands, she yanked it over his head. Up close, his chest was broader, smoother, harder than she'd expected and all deliciously bronzed by wind and sun. She ran her hands over his hot flesh, wishing she could touch all of him at once. Damn. He was ripped.

She skimmed her hands along his tapered sides and muscular back. He sucked in his breath, then let it out slowly, the air rasping her ear. "How long until your brother gets back?"

"Long enough if you hurry." She wriggled her hands between them to his zipper.

"Easy." His hand closed over hers. "Our first time, shouldn't be rushed."

"Damn it." She didn't want to stop and think. Right now, at this moment, she knew exactly what she wanted. Him. "If you're afraid of my brother—"

He snorted.

"There's a chain on the door." She pulled off her own shirt, unhooked her bra. And then boldly lifted her breast and puckered nipple toward his mouth. "Kiss me."

With a soft growl, he lowered his head, sucked her nipple into his mouth. Hard. But his tongue swirled the tip with delicious, delicate circles that had her clutching his back, digging her fingers into his muscles.

As he sipped and sucked, her breath came in pants. Her flesh slickened with sweat. Her hearts threatened to beat their way out of her chest.

Marisa hadn't made love in years. Not since she'd become a dragonshaper. So she didn't know if her fierce response to Rion was due to her new blood. Or to him.

At the moment, it didn't matter. Nothing mattered beyond feeling, touching, kissing. All her senses focused on him. His hands on her body, his scent in her lungs, his tongue on her nipple.

Arching her back, straining, she offered him her other breast. He lavished it with the same hungry skill, until she thought she might come from that alone. But he rolled from the sofa, his big hands guiding her to her feet, and then he peeled down her jeans.

He explored her belly button with his tongue, swirled lower until he licked the edge of her panties. Oh, God. She swallowed hard as the dizzying heat from his mouth made her breathless with desire.

Inch by inch, he tugged down her panties, kissing, nipping, until he blew softly on her curls. When he nuzzled apart her thighs, she quivered in anticipation. And then he began to lick his way up the scales on her legs.

Her scales rumbled in wave after wave of pleasure,

leaving her panting, needy, aching. "Rion. Hurry. Please, hurry."

He licked her ankles, her calves, the insides of her thighs. And just when she thought he was about to place his mouth where she desired him most, a key grated in the front door's lock.

The door opened, but the chain held.

"Oh, my God," she whispered. "Lucan and Cael." She started to reach for her jeans.

Rion held her in place. "They can't see us from the door."

Between his hands spanning her butt and his knees preventing her from closing her legs, he'd made it impossible for her to move, never mind dress.

Her voice choked on exasperation and disappointment. "Give me my clothes."

A smile played at the corner of his lips. "No."

"No?" Panic shot through her. Followed by a tiny thrill of excitement. She was standing there naked in her brother's living room.

"Marisa," her brother called out, "the chain's still on the door."

Rion caressed Marisa's soft folds. At the same time, he spoke calmly to Lucan. "Come back in ten minutes."

"Rion, is that you?" her brother asked. "Where's my sister?"

"Occupied." Rion's big hands tightened on her bottom, and he replaced his finger with his tongue.

Oh . . . my. She couldn't think beyond wanting more. Rion's tongue flicked wickedly. She began to shake. Couldn't hold back a moan. "Ah . . . Oh . . ."

"Marisa." Lucan's tone sharpened. "Is everything okay? What's going on?"

"Nothing," Marisa whimpered. Rion's tongue flicked faster, making it almost impossible to speak. But somehow, she forced words out. "Go awayyyy," she told her twin, barely keeping a moan from her voice.

Cael laughed. "We'll give you ten minutes."

"We will not," her brother protested. "And don't think this silly chain will prevent me from—"

"We're leaving now," Cael called out. "I'll keep him busy."

The door shut.

Rion kept stoking the heat between her thighs. He felt so good. Her legs trembled. Her scales vibrated, and pressure built and built.

"Please," she whimpered.

He increased the tempo. Upped the friction.

She exploded right into his mouth and had to clamp shut her lips to deaden the scream. Pleasure strong and sharp consumed her, shook her, racked her with spasm after spasm. And she rode the wave to the end, taking in every last rift and eddy.

When she opened her eyes, Rion grinned and with a sparkle in his eyes he shoved her clothes into her hands. "You've got two minutes."

"But"—she glanced at the bulge in his pants—"what about you—"

"I can wait."

His words implied there would be a next time, and warm, happy heat flowed over her. "You sure?"

"The first time I'm inside you isn't going to be a rush

job." His gray eyes glinted pure silver. "I plan to take my time."

That sounded like a very good plan. A plan she could look forward to. Who would have thought that after years of being alone, she could feel so alive again?

She might have felt like skipping and singing, but she dressed quickly, then opened the door, bracing for her brother's wrath. But to her relief, Lucan and Cael still hadn't returned.

Good. She and Rion would have another few moments of privacy.

"You were wonderful." Standing on her tiptoes, she threw her arms around Rion's neck, fully intending to kiss him.

But before her mouth touched his, he staggered sideways. Had he stumbled? No. Rejected her? No.

He clutched his arm almost as if it were broken, his face racked in terrible pain. His lips twisted into a grimace, and she suspected that if he hadn't clutched the wall, he would have fallen.

"Rion?" Totally baffled, she placed a hand on his shoulder. "What's wrong? Are you all right?"

"I'm fine." His voice raspy, his eyes glazed with pain, he yanked from her touch, staggered toward his room. "I have to . . . go."

The truth lies somewhere between Earth, Pendragon, and Honor.

—ANONYMOUS

5

With the sting of a million wasps, fiery pain burned through Rion. His tormented muscles jerked. The pain-induced blindness had him certain he was about to pass out, but he staggered into his room and closed the door before he collapsed.

Agonizing jolts of energy ripped through his system. Blinding blasts of purple fired his optic nerves. He jerked on the floor, his limbs spasming. Sweat broke out under his arms and across his chest, then streamed down his neck.

Sweet Goddess. He gritted his teeth.

"Are you okay?" Marisa's voice trembled with concern from the other side of the door. When he didn't answer, she pounded on the wood, tested the knob. "Let me in."

"I'm . . . fine." He spoke between gritted teeth. "Go back to the babies."

"Lucan and Cael just returned. And if you don't open this door right now, I'm going to get Lucan."

He winced. "Hold on."

Shoving to his knees, he gasped as more needle-like pains stabbed his optic nerve. He dragged himself to his feet and yanked open the door. "Told you. I'm fine."

And with that emphatic statement, he fell backward and cracked his head on the floor. Tiny red stars exploded behind his eyes, and bolts of pressure made his head feel like his skull would explode.

Marisa leaned over him, her cool palm pressed to his forehead. "You're burning up." Her clothing rustled, and he blinked hard to see that she'd shoved back to her feet and hovered over him, her tone worried yet calm. "I'm calling for help."

"No." He grabbed her ankle and groaned as pain shot up his neck and into his brain. "Give me . . . a . . . minute."

"You need a doctor." She yanked her foot to get away.

"No." He gripped her ankle, refusing to release her, his anchor in a world of pain. "Don't . . ."

Her tone softened. "At least let me bring you some water."

He watched her hurry to his kitchen, grab a bottle of water from the fridge. As promised, she returned and twisted off the cap.

Sitting beside him, she scooted under him, until his head rested in her lap. "Drink."

Cool fluid trickled down his parched throat. He'd never tasted anything so delicious. "Thanks."

Worry radiating from her every pore, she demanded, "Tell me what else to do for you." Her voice was hard, but her hands smoothed across his forehead in tender circles.

Ignoring the pain, he focused on her gentle touch. Enjoyed the softness of her thighs cradling his head, her sweet female scent. Her concern for him.

Slowly, finally, the searing pain faded.

"I'm recovering." He paused. "Pain's fading fast."

"Good." Questions burning in her eyes, she ran her hands through his hair.

He used the silence to gather his strength. To regroup. Guilt stabbed him, and he quashed it. Now more than ever, he had to stay on plan.

She offered him more water. Lifting his own head this time, he sipped, then lay back in her lap, letting her thighs pillow his head.

Biting her lip with worry, she peered into his face. "So was that one of your flashes? Because if so, you forgot to tell me about the part where you look like you're frying from the inside out."

"It wasn't a flash." Thank the Goddess.

"Then what happened?"

"The Unari invasion took us by surprise."

She tensed in concern, and the furrows between her eyes deepened. "Rion, you aren't making sense. You aren't on Honor. This is Earth."

"I know." He had to get a grip. "You need a bit of history to understand what just happened." He continued, "During the first days of conquest, the Unari destroyed Honor's communications and closed down our transporter, preventing Honor from asking our allies for help. With the transporter down, I had to try and escape the Unari in a creaky spaceship left over from the old days."

"What does that have to do with the pain you just went through?"

"I'm getting to that." He paused. Distilling his four-year quest into a neat explanation took some doing. "My spaceship needed repairs, so I flew to Tor, the closest planet to Honor in our solar system. While engineers ret-rofitted my ship, I had a vision that suggested I might not return for many years."

"Are you saying Tor wouldn't help?" she asked.

He shook his head. A mistake that he paid for with a residual slicing pain. "Our worlds have been enemies since the time of King Arthur."

"But then why did you go there?"

"My ship wouldn't fly any farther. And though I couldn't use Tor's transporter, Honorians have some friends on Tor."

"I'm not sure I'm following."

"The conflict between our worlds is an old one. According to legend, long ago, a man named Gareth had two sons—one ruled Tor, the other Honor. During an ancient war with the Tribes, the father had the resources to save only one world. He chose Honor, a world of dragonshapers, over Tor, a world of people who couldn't morph. Since then, there have been many wars between our planets. To this day, Tor both covets and fears our dragonshaping abilities."

"So while you were on Tor, you couldn't dragon-shape?"

"Luckily, the Toran engineers rebuilt my ship before morphing became necessary."

"Did you convince the Torans you were one of them?"

He shook his head. "Some of them, like Phen, my con-tact on that world, want peace between our planets."

"I see." She wasn't certain she did, but she allowed him to tell the story in his own way.

"But with communications out on Honor, I still needed a way for my people to contact me."

"In case of an emergency?"

"Exactly. So Phen found a doctor to implant a communication and translation device into my arm." He touched the lump on his forearm and placed her fingertips there. "This is why I can understand and speak your language."

Blue eyes curious, she gently traced the bump. "The device sends messages to you from home?"

"I wish." He sighed. "We modified the language translator to receive a simple onetime alert. We weren't sure it would even work. The device was never engineered to be more than a last-ditch effort to contact me. The situation on Honor must have gone critical." His gut churned. He had to go home.

She caressed his arm. "Maybe you should have one of our doctors remove—"

He rubbed away the last of the stiffness from his arm. "I wasn't supposed to experience that kind of pain. The transponder must have malfunctioned, but it's now harmless."

"Good." In direct contradiction to her words, her eyes suddenly narrowed with suspicion, and she removed her fingers from his arm. "But if that device translates language, and it just died, then how come you're still speaking English?"

Did her suspicions stem from dealing with her ex? Or did she suspect Rion's motives?

Rion recalled her passionate kisses, her warmth, her taking care of him while he'd been in pain. No. She couldn't suspect his motives, or she wouldn't be with him now.

His guilt was making him anxious. And his worry over the deteriorating situation back home had him off balance. Still, he'd give everything he had not to hurt her again. At least this question he could answer honestly. "After being immersed in your language for six months, I know English."

She accepted his explanation with a simple nod. As the tautness in her shoulders eased, she resumed playing with his hair. "So this contact, Phen, I assume he wouldn't panic for no reason?"

"Exactly. The transponder's activation just confirmed my vision might already be coming true. I have to get home. The sooner the better."

"You still don't have proof," she insisted softly. "Maybe a design flaw set off the transponder."

"That's unlikely."

"But if the Tribes jammed all communications, and Phen is on Tor, how does he know what's happening on your world?"

"Phen's resourceful. If anyone can find a way to stay in touch, it'll be him." Rion swiped a hand over his face. Clearly his vision and the transponder's emergency signal weren't enough proof to convince Marisa of the coming disaster.

Tamping down his sense of urgency, he forced himself to move slowly. He shifted to the side and pulled Marisa into his arms until he was close enough to see her eyes sparkle. Ever so delicately, her nostrils flared, encouraging him closer, until he was breathing in her crisp strawberry scent.

She placed a hand on his chest. "You're thinking about kissing me again."

"Oh, yeah." He allowed a slight smile to play over his mouth.

"Good." She grinned saucily. "Because for a minute back there I thought that overloaded circuit must have fried your brain. But now I can see you're back to normal."

She lifted her head, and their eyes met and locked. Her pupils dilated, and a rosy flush rose up her neck.

He slid his hand to her nape, and a soft tendril of her hair tickled his wrist. Tingling with anticipation, he wanted to get her naked all over again and finish making love.

And yet he needn't go that far. Satisfying his own needs wasn't really necessary. But there was nothing wrong with satisfying his lust, either.

Angling his head, he looked straight into her eyes. And while his fingers delved into her hair, he brought her closer. Close enough to breathe in her sweet exhalation.

He dropped his head until his lips were within an inch of hers. Catching a dangling tendril of hair between his thumb and forefinger, he played with it, grazing her cheek, her neck, her ear with his fingertips.

"Stop. That tickles."

"Whatever you say." But he swirled the curl around his finger, watched the pulse in her neck leap.

Her lips softened. "Quit playing around. Are you certain you don't need a doctor?"

"Yes." Nuzzling aside her hair, he whispered in her ear. "And I'm not playing. How about dinner?"

She blinked, licked her bottom lip, and frowned. "Dinner?"

"You know, when two people sit down together for a meal, share a bottle of wine, and talk over food," he teased. "How about tomorrow night?" He'd have suggested something sooner, like breakfast, but he couldn't arrange everything that quickly.

Her gorgeous eyes sparkled with happy confusion. "You're asking me out?"

"We'd have food. Good food. And excellent wine." He wriggled his eyebrows. "And then for dessert, I'm going to kiss you again. Only this time I won't be rushed."

Turning, she placed her hand on his shoulder, slid her palm up his neck, and slipped her fingers into his hair. "I like to have my dessert first," she said with a breathy sigh. "That way, we won't be losing sleep wondering . . ."

He didn't know about the not-losing-sleep part, but he wasn't arguing. He'd given being noble a shot. This was her choice. She was offering her sweet mouth to him. And she tasted smooth and rich and heady, kissing with a red-hot heat that almost succeeded in driving his mission from his mind.

A pounding on the door broke them apart. "Marisa!" The hard edge in Lucan's voice shot her scrambling to her feet.

Rion swore under his breath.

Lips bee-stung from Rion's kisses, she flung open the door. "What's wrong?"

Lucan, still in a dark suit, black shirt, and white tie, burst into the room. "Marisa, we need you. The dragon-shapers are going wild."

Relief washed over Rion. He didn't want to have to deal with an angry Lucan.

"What are you talking about?" she asked Lucan.

He tugged his sister into the hallway and kept walking. "The females are drawing blood over food. The males have gone berserk. They're biting and clawing and ripping one another apart to get to the females."

"I don't understand," Marisa muttered, hurrying to keep up with her brother's longer stride. "This has never happened before."

"Hurry. You have to calm them down before the guards shoot them out of the sky or they kill one another."

Beware the man with the gift of sight, for knowledge is a dangerous thing.

—HIGH PRIESTESS OF AVALON

6

According to Marisa's schedule board, the crowded sky should have been empty. But overhead, dragons bellowed fire, their mighty wings maneuvering them to take tactical advantage of deadly claws and razor-sharp teeth.

Marisa stood beside Rion on the university's grass field, trembling with the effort of sending her telepathic message to over a dozen dragons. *No biting. No fighting.*

Lust blasted her through the telepathic link. Primal fury ricocheted down the connection. With three giant males fighting over one female, blood dripped from beaks, claws, and necks.

So far, the guards had refrained from shooting the dragons with tranqs, but their trigger fingers were ready, the weapons aimed. Marisa spoke to the guards over the radio. "Stand down. I'll deal with them."

The guards lowered their weapons but remained alert. Wary.

Marisa turned her attention back to the dragons. *Calm*

yourselves. Control the primal urges. You are dragons, but you are also human.

To her right, four females battled. This time over turf and platinum pellets. The females were about Marisa's age but they outweighed her by twenty tons.

Share the platinum. There's enough for all.

Marisa kept her messages short and simple. In dragon form, their brains were primitive, and more complicated thoughts became difficult to process. At least the females sheathed their claws.

But the males flew straight up, then engaged in a deadly air battle filled with squawks of pain, flapping wings, and bellows of fury. They weren't listening to her. She wasn't getting through.

Two dragons shot fire at each other, and the air reeked of burned flesh and roars of rage. If Marisa didn't stop them, the dragons were going to kill each other.

Stop it. Stop. Stop.

The male dragons broke apart. Had her own fear gotten through? Relief filled her.

But then three males dived straight at Marisa, their deadly mass targeting her.

No.

She held up her hand, signaling the guards to hold. At the same time, she closed her eyes as the dragons flew at her in attack formation. *I am your friend. Friend. Friend.*

As a huge roar rolled like thunder across the sky, she opened her eyes and gasped. The largest dragon she'd ever seen had placed his body between the three angry males and Marisa.

She recognized the clothes on the ground beside the

massive dragon. That dragon was Rion. He'd dragon-shaped. And now, rearing up on his hind legs, he trumpeted his fury.

But even with his tremendous wings and fierce bellow, he couldn't defeat three blood-hungry dragons. Not if he stayed rooted to the ground. An easy target.

Fly. She shot him a message.

Not leaving you.

The guards fired tranqs at the three attacking males. And missed. Their darts fell short, unable to reach the dragons barreling down on them. No way could Rion stop them; it was like a semi-truck trying to stop a freight train.

While the guards reloaded, Marisa pleaded with Rion. *If you don't fly, you'll die. We'll both die.*

Rion roared fire, his flames flaring across the sky in bright reds and fiery oranges, singeing the attacking trio.

Fear sliced Marisa until she trembled with it. *Fear. Fear. Fear.*

Just as the guards fired again, one of the attacking dragons swerved right, the other left. The third pulled up short, tumbled.

Thank God. They'd broken off the attack.

Still shaking, her fear easing, she sent soothing praise. *Good work. You did well. We don't fight. We are friends.*

Marisa sighed with relief. "That was close."

"Too close." Rion humanshaped and tugged on the clothes he'd left behind.

She flung herself into his arms. "You idiot. You could have died."

His arms closed around her, warm and powerful. She

felt safe as he gathered her close and murmured, "You're shaking."

She stared at Rion, marveling that she hadn't been roasted alive, that he'd risked his life to save hers. "If you hadn't been here . . ."

He placed an arm over her shoulders. In the distance a dragon roared. With a puzzled glance at the dragon, Rion removed his arm from her shoulder. "You would have found another way to calm them. That's some skill you have."

While she appreciated his admiration, she immediately missed his touch. "I still don't understand what set them off."

"I have a theory."

Several of Marisa's team members approached, their faces filled with awe and fear. "Ma'am, we need you."

"I'll be right there." Wishing she didn't have to work, Marisa turned to Rion. "I have to give instructions and fill out reports."

Rion nodded, his tone warm and understanding. "I'll see you later."

Marisa arrived back at the hotel to find Rion had left her a message, saying he'd take her to dinner tomorrow at someplace casual. After being up all night, Marisa slept most of the day. When she woke at six, she showered, then dressed comfortably in jeans, layered tank tops, and a soft jacket.

She took extra time with her hair and makeup. Humming happily, eager to see Rion again, she remembered his sexy kiss, his sexier touch. How he'd saved her life—by risking his own. She was so looking forward to seeing him again.

Sure her hormones were in overdrive, their chemistry amazing. But he'd shared so much with her, talking about his family, his past, his flashes.

Reminding herself she still didn't know him that well did no good. Her hopes were high. She hadn't felt so filled with eager anticipation in years.

At exactly seven, Rion knocked at her hotel room door and handed her a bouquet of stargazer lilies. Dressed in jeans and a black V-necked T-shirt, he looked sexier than ever.

"Hi." His greeting was casual, but his gray eyes reminded her of thunderclouds filled with heat lightning.

Surprised to find herself slightly uncomfortable under his intense gaze, she dipped her face into the flowers and breathed in one of her favorite scents. "Thanks."

On street level, a rental car with a driver and a huge picnic basket on the front passenger seat awaited them. Wonderful aromas wafted through the vehicle, and she appreciated that Rion had planned a romantic evening for them.

The car took them to the London Victoria railway station. After less than an hour's train ride, they were back in another car with another driver. Having lived in England only a few months, Marisa didn't know British geography that well. But when she glanced out the window and saw the Salisbury sign, she looked at Rion in surprise. "We're picnicking at Stonehenge?"

"I have special permission."

Marisa was impressed. The ancient site was a political hot potato, and until the United Nations decided who should gain admission, no one was supposed to be allowed near it.

The car stopped. Rion retrieved the basket of food and escorted her from the parking lot to Stonehenge. As they walked the path toward the site, the megalithic stones towered out of the rolling hillside.

As she stood staring at the site, she had no difficulty imagining primitive people coming here to worship, thanking their gods for the end of winter or celebrating the spring planting or autumn harvest. However, the idea of people using Stonehenge as a spaceport thousands of years ago seemed like something out of a science-fiction movie.

When she and Rion reached a grass knoll, he stopped, pulled a green-checkered cloth from the enormous basket, and floated it over the ground. "I was hoping we'd arrive in time to watch the sunset."

For an instant, a bird with outspread wings was silhouetted against the setting sun, and Marisa wondered if Merlin, Cael's owl, had followed them, but she dismissed the possibility. England had thousands of owls.

She gazed across the open fields. The tourist buses were long gone. She didn't see any guards, although how Rion had arranged that she wasn't sure she wanted to know. With the sun setting, they seemed alone here—except for the ghosts of ancient Druids and the shadows of knights from ages long past.

He uncorked a bottle of Merlot. "Have the dragons all calmed?"

"Yes." She held two glasses, and he poured. "But I still don't understand what set them off."

"You did." He tipped his glass to her.

"Me? It's my job to settle the dragons. How would I set them off?"

"Right before the dragons' chaos, you were enjoying my touch."

"And your point?"

He grinned into his glass as if he couldn't help himself, as if he knew his theory would both irritate and intrigue her. "You're telepathic, and you projected your feelings."

Her feelings?

Right before Lucan had come to fetch her, she and Rion had been talking in Rion's hotel suite. Then they'd kissed. She'd tasted the wine on his tongue. His clever fingers had caressed her scales, driven her wild. He'd made her feel good. Better than she'd ever felt. But had she actually projected her desire and arousal onto strangers?

Stunned, she sipped her wine. "You really think . . . that I affected the dragons?"

"Yes."

"Even if that's true, I wasn't sending violent thoughts. The males were fighting."

"Over a female."

"My thoughts weren't vicious. You saw the dragons. They were tearing each other apart. After you left, the docs gave them massive doses of antibiotics."

"Which probably weren't necessary. Dragonshapers heal fast." He peered at her over the rim of his wine-glass. "To a dragonshaper, fighting is . . . foreplay. Your lust stirred their hot dragonblood. And then they couldn't control themselves."

The implications rocked her. "Are you sure?"

"Later, the dragons calmed. But then do you remember when you flung yourself into my arms?"

"Of course." Marisa sucked in a short breath.

"One of the dragons roared." He spoke gently as if he understood how shocking she'd find his theory. "And it happened again when I placed my arm over your shoulders. It's why I pulled back so quickly."

Her hand shook so hard she had to set down her wine before she spilled it. "So kissing you, what we did together, was a mistake."

"Not for me." Again he kept his tone gentle, almost playful. "I rather enjoyed it."

So had she. And yet . . . "Damn it. Unless I learn to control what I project, I can't kiss you." Or feel passion. Or make love. Yikes.

"Or you could practice kissing me and keeping control." His words were sexy, low and husky, and very suggestive.

"Is that possible?"

His hair ruffled in the breeze and he chuckled. "I'd be more than willing to help with the experiment—for scientific purposes."

"This isn't funny, Rion. Those dragons could have died. If I hadn't calmed them, the guards would have shot them with tranqs. They'd have fallen out of the sky." Earth's non-dragonshaping population was already leery of dragonshapers. And what sane person wouldn't be wary? The dragons were huge and powerful, lethal when they blasted fire from their throats.

"Relax." Rion gestured to the setting sun. He dug into the basket and removed fresh bread, pickled onions, roast chicken, Cornish pasties, corn on the cob, and gooseberry trifle. "We'll figure this out."

"How?" Disappointment washed over her. And

yet . . . she reminded herself he'd gone to all this trouble *after* he'd known they wouldn't be doing anything physical. Surely that meant he felt more than a physical attraction. "I'm afraid to even think . . . about us."

"I'm not going to let a bunch of dragons stop me from having you." His eyes gleamed with heat. "We'll think of something."

She unpacked dishes and utensils. "At least you're honest."

That he'd openly admitted having seduction in mind made her very aware of him. She looked down to watch his long fingers fist, then relax. She recalled those fingers teasing up the insides of her legs, caressing her slick folds. And she'd been so looking forward to making love. But now they couldn't—and disappointment flooded her. To distract herself, she took a piece of bread and bit into it, tried to enjoy the setting sun. "Why did you choose this place?"

"I didn't want your brother interrupting this time." He handed her a napkin. "And I want to show you something, but let's eat first. I'm starved."

She nibbled, sipped her wine, and enjoyed the pink and gold streaks of the dying sun. Most of all she enjoyed the anticipation of what he'd do next.

She would have liked to kiss him again, out here under the stars, encircled by mystical ancient stones, surrounded by history. The rugged megaliths, rough and weathered, lent a raw excitement to the air. But she didn't dare give in to emotions that might set the dragonshapers off. "Do you think the people who placed the stones here were dragonshapers?"

He ate the last bite of his pasty and licked a crumb from his finger, then froze, his face expressionless.

"Rion?"

He didn't answer.

She reached for him. "Rion? Are you okay?"

THE FLASH CAME on Rion fast and hard. He could see and hear Marisa asking him if he was all right, but at the same time his vision showed him another Marisa.

This Marisa's face was white, her eyes wide with fear. Her hair stuck to her damp face. A streak of dirt smudged one cheek. Shots fired. Bang. Bang. *With each shot, Marisa flinched.* Bang. *The third shot struck Marisa right above the bridge of her nose, slamming directly into her forehead.*

"Rion?" Marisa's worried voice broke into his consciousness.

Sweet Goddess. He'd just seen her death.

Shaken, Rion stared at her beautiful face. Was his being near her going to get her killed? Rion tried to think clearly. Should he tell her what he'd just seen?

Last night the subcutaneous communicator had almost rendered him unconscious. Marisa had dealt with the alien technology without seeming too put off, but she didn't need a nightly display of his peculiarities. And even if he told her what he'd seen, what good would it do except upset her? So he said nothing.

But he memorized the bullet pattern he'd seen. Tried

to brand that cheek smudge's shape into his memory. And yet he might not be there to protect her when she died.

He had so little information. But he'd long since quit damning his visions. He had a piece of something important. More than most people got.

Marisa was staring at him, concern in her gaze.

"Sorry." Rion poured more wine into their glasses. "These stones are quite spectacular. It took either levitation skills, antigravity machines, huge cranes, or the strength of dragonshapers to set the stones here."

She smiled with her mouth, but her eyes remained thoughtful. "It's difficult for me to remember that dragonshapers have been around for a long time. Their presence seems new . . . not as old as Stonehenge."

"You keep saying *they*—as if you aren't one of us."

"It's kind of like changing my hair color."

"Excuse me?"

"My hair's naturally dark. Every time I go to the salon, they add another color."

That explained the multitude of shades from copper to wheat to golden. What color exactly had her hair been in the flash? It had seemed darker, but it could have been the lighting, or perhaps her hair had been damp with sweat. He must have looked confused.

Marisa chuckled. "I still think of myself as a brunette. It's not until I glance in a mirror, or hair blows in my face, that I remember I've changed. It's the same with dragonshaping. I still think of myself as pure human . . . until I shift."

"I suppose that makes sense. Like anything new, it takes time to incorporate a change into one's core thinking processes."

"You sound so scientific. What was your career on Honor?"

He scratched his chin. "I was trained in astrophysics. My father believed that might help me date my flashes."

"Does it?"

"Occasionally. But I work for the government. I'm a diplomat." The partial lie rolled off his tongue easily enough. Yet he resented the need for dishonesty. She deserved better.

"What did you like best?"

"Meeting new people. Learning their culture. Finding out what's important to them. No matter how different we all appear, when I go deep enough, I find we want the same things." At least that was true. He gazed into her open face and wondered what about her made him want to tell her everything.

"Such as?"

"Peace. Security. Hope for a better future for our loved ones." He leaned back, laced his hands behind his head, and looked at the stars, enjoying this moment.

He knew all too well the peace wouldn't last, and neither would Marisa's contentment. As much as he'd have liked to be the man she wanted, as much as he'd have enjoyed exploring their new closeness, he had obligations. The needs of his people came before his own. And if that meant Marisa ended up hating him, he would have to live with the consequences.

Wrapping up the leftovers, she neatly repacked them into the basket. "You ready for trifle, or do you want to walk off this meal first?"

"Whatever you like." She looked content. Happy. Guilt warred with his responsibilities. Fighting his very real attraction to her while he tried to do what was required tore at him, forcing him to reconsider his options. But no matter how he added up the parts, his conclusion always remained the same. He could never have her permanently, but he needed her.

Resigned to carry through with his plan no matter how upset with him she was going to be, he took her hand. They strolled around the megaliths. This sightseeing expedition gave him an excuse to check the perimeter. Thanks to his well-placed bribes, the guards had retreated to the security trailer. But cameras still had them under surveillance.

Rion knew exactly which angles the lenses covered. Last week he'd done a test run and had taken the opportunity to stash a carefully packed bag inside a hidden cavity within one of the stones. The Earth officials had no idea how to make Stonehenge function as a transporter. But Rion did.

When they rounded one of the largest megaliths, he stopped, reached out, and placed his finger into a crack. Marisa held his other hand but watched, curious. "What are you doing?"

"I thought I saw a glint of metal." He pressed a stone. A click activated a hidden panel, and the stone, about as wide and high as a door, slid sideways with a soundless swish.

"Oh . . . my . . . God." Marisa raised her hand to her mouth.

Beyond the door was a stone chamber about the size of an elevator. The air smelled stale and dusty. An owl flew inside. Rion tugged her into the chamber and reached for a lever.

Her eyes widened. "Don't—"

He pulled the lever. The stone panel closed behind them, leaving them in total darkness.

Marisa gasped, and her hand tightened on his. "We're trapped."

"Don't move."

With his free hand, Rion grabbed the backpack he'd stored last week. He slipped one strap over his shoulder, then flipped on a penlight and shone it on Marisa. Her eyes were wide, but when Rion quickly punched coordinates into a metal faceplate embedded in the stone, Marisa jerked backward, distrust sharpening her tone.

"You just activated the transporter, didn't you?" Her voice snapped with fury. Her entire body shook with stress. If her anger could kill, he'd be dead. And he deserved every bit of her rage.

From above, Merlin hooted softly. Cael's owl had followed them to Stonehenge.

Rion's gut tightened, but his resolve hardened. "It's going to be all right."

"You don't even know if the transporter still works." She lunged for the lever.

He stepped in front of her, clamped his arms around her. "It works."

Marisa fought like a wild woman, trying to break free. But he held on tight, trapping her against his chest and pinning her arms to her sides. "Easy. Don't hurt yourself."

"Let me go." Her entire body trembling, she twisted and jerked sideways, trying to yank free.

Guilt stabbed him. "I'm sorry. I need your help. I can't let you go."

"You mean you won't." Anger, hurt at his betrayal, and panic rolled off her in unmistakable waves. If any dragons were nearby, they'd soon be in a killing rage. No doubt she'd already sent a frantic telepathic message to Lucan. But her twin would receive her call for help too late.

Within seconds, the ancient stones began to heat. Pressure built. His ears popped. Sweat broke out on his forehead. Marisa shook so hard her teeth clicked.

"Damn you." She tried to bite him, but he shifted back an inch. "You have no right to kidnap me."

"The situation's gone critical, or I would never—"

She glared at him. "What if I can't return?"

"I programmed this transporter to accept your imprint when it's time to send you home."

The stones rumbled louder. The ancient mechanisms gathered energy and heated.

"Where are you taking me?" she demanded furiously.

"The Unari have closed the portal on Honor. We have to go to Tor first."

She went rigid, her tone raw with horror. "But that's an enemy planet."

This had happened before—going farther and farther into the mists until one could no longer see the way home.

—LADY OF THE LAKE

7

Marisa couldn't believe Rion was kidnapping her.

One moment she was standing inside Stonehenge's vault, the next she'd arrived in a blinding burst of light. The air seemed too thin. Although it was crisp and clean, she couldn't suck enough oxygen into her lungs. Had they made it to Tor?

Could she find a lever to pull to send her back home?

The metal platform they stood on vaguely resembled Stonehenge, but the proportions were wrong, the materials peculiar. Instead of a huge ring of rocks, she and Rion stood surrounded by glowing green granite.

She didn't see a control panel. Or a lever.

They'd landed on a platform inside a busy bronzed metal dome where people in unusual styles of clothing strode by. Many wore makeup that covered half their faces. Men and women had skin that was neon pink, sparkling silver, gold, or blue, their hair wired with blinking crystals that changed color, too.

She'd landed in a bizarre dream—only she was fully awake. This couldn't be happening. But it was. She was far from home. And it was all Rion's fault.

"Why did you kidnap me?" She kept her tone low but couldn't control the edge of anger.

"I need your help."

"You could have asked."

"You would have said no. And if you'd known how badly I needed you, you'd never have gone on a date with me—not to Stonehenge."

Now she knew why he'd suddenly started treating her differently. To set her up. The bastard had flirted with her, kissed her, given her a spectacular orgasm . . . all to lure her out to Stonehenge so he could kidnap her.

Damn it. She'd thought she'd finally found a man she could trust, a gallant knight. But he'd been deluding her from the start.

"Look, I'm sorry I brought you here against your will. But I have to save my people." Rion's tone pleaded for her understanding. She wasn't in a forgiving mood and said nothing, so he continued, "In my flashes, the conditions on Honor are brutal. Men are whipped until they can't work. They kill women and children." His face hardened. "I know taking you was wrong, but I'd do anything to save my people."

Was he feeding her another story? More lies? She spoke between teeth gritted with anger and embarrassment over how foolish she'd been. "What exactly do you want from me?"

"Once we get to my world, I need you to send telepathic messages to Honor's dragonshapers. Help me organize a revolt."

A revolt? "That sounds dangerous."

"I'll protect you."

Like she could believe a word he said after he'd lied to her? Kidnapped her? She snorted. "I'm not interested. Send me home."

Rion pressed a microchip into her forearm.

She jerked back too late. The device had already sunk painlessly through her skin. Although it didn't sting, she frowned and rubbed the spot. "What did you do to me?"

"I placed a subcutaneous translator under your skin. Now you'll understand any language. And when you speak English, others will understand you."

"You could have asked first," she muttered, a chill icing her blood.

The public square was unfamiliar territory, but Marisa had traveled to many different countries on Earth. Humanity had basic needs. People required food, shelter, transportation. Most civilized societies had police or the equivalent.

When a group of people surged past, she pointed. "Hey, that man's waving to you. Is he your contact, Phen?"

When Rion turned to look, she slipped into the group of people passing by. Within moments, the crowd swallowed her. Her nerves yelled at her to run. But blending in was the best way to hide. So she kept walking at the same pace, but at the first opportunity to change direction, she slipped into a new group.

Behind her, she heard shouting and footsteps slapping

the pavement. Had Rion called her name? She couldn't be certain, but she didn't dare turn back and look.

Pulse racing, Marisa kept walking, feeling as if she were being chased through a nightmare. Overhead traffic vehicles looked as if they were about to crash but never did. Kids pulled behind them shiny red balls on leashes, which could have been toys, pets, computers, or a place to store their personal belongings. She had no idea.

When a hand clamped onto her shoulder, her knees went weak. She turned to see not Rion, but a man wearing an official-looking gray uniform with piping on the collar. A black helmet with blue Plexiglas hid his face. Metal plates protected his chest. Between the chrome baton that hung from the holster at his hip, the knife strapped to his sleeve, and the throwing stars at his belt, he looked dangerous, deadly.

"Come with me." His voice, rough and mechanical, shot a shiver of fear down her back. Had she fled from a kidnapper to someone even worse?

"What do you want?" She tried to step away, but he kept a firm grip on her shoulder.

The crowd around them parted and kept swarming, paying no attention.

"You have broken many laws."

"I have?" She glanced anxiously from the official to the crowd. Even if she could break his grasp, he might shoot her before she could hide.

He ticked off regulations. "Landing without a permit or a license. Failure to pass through customs or decontamination. Trespassing. Evading Enforcers."

"I can explain." She wished she could stop the dread rolling through her. Would he believe her if she said that this wasn't her world? That she didn't belong here? While she had no knowledge of Tor's legal system or the consequences of breaking so many laws, her arrest seemed imminent.

She should flee.

As if sensing her rising panic, the Enforcer gripped her shoulder harder. "Let's go."

"Where?"

He didn't answer. He simply marched her down the sidewalk. All around her, life went on. No one stared. No one shot her a sympathetic glance.

Foreign smells hit her in a mélange of spicy perfumes, citrus fruits, cleaners, antiseptics, paint, and industrial fumes making her gut clench. Meat and vegetables, speared on shish kebabs and fried in oil, had a sugary-sweet aroma that made her stomach roil.

Oh . . . my . . . God. She'd never felt so completely alone in her life. She had no friends or family here. She didn't even know where this Enforcer was taking her.

"How long before I can explain to someone in authority what happened?"

"There's nothing to explain. You broke the law. You are guilty. According to law 154 of the broken stone, the sentence is death."

"Death?" This Enforcer was dragging her to her execution? Her mind reeled. "You don't understand. I was forced to come here."

"You broke the law. You will be punished."

"But I had no choice. I was brought to Tor against my will. Surely there are exceptions?"

"None." The Enforcer's fingers tightened into an iron lock on her shoulder.

Marisa began to shake with fear. She'd been in tough spots before. Covering a war in the Mideast, she'd once been caught behind enemy lines. This was worse. Her government wouldn't be demanding her release. No one besides Lucan even knew she was gone, and although she'd gotten off one last telepathic message to him, even if he'd heard her, she hadn't had the chance to tell him where Rion had taken her.

She was going to die. Alone. On an alien world. And no one would ever know what had happened to her.

WHERE THE HELL was Marisa? Rion searched the crowd but she'd disappeared. A bit of movement snagged his attention. There. She'd tried to blend into the crowd but her Earth clothing gave her away. Already an Enforcer had found her. With a leap off the platform he followed. He'd promised to protect her, but he hadn't known he'd have to protect her from herself. He'd expected her to be furious that he'd tricked her. He'd anticipated that she wouldn't easily accept her new circumstances. But he'd never expected her to flee. Not from him.

Yes, in his flash, he'd seen her shot. At the time, he'd assumed she'd died in a gunfight, not execution-style.

If the Enforcer shot her . . . Sweet Goddess. Rion wouldn't let that happen. He had to save her.

Rion peered through the crowd at the Enforcer marching Marisa to her death.

Shifting position, he followed closely. Enforcers always worked in pairs. Another one had to be nearby. But if he could take out this Enforcer in one blow, before he could radio his partner for help, before he could hurt Marisa, he might be able to rescue her.

Damn it. He shouldn't have been so careless.

Her ploy had taken him totally by surprise. And her actions scared the life out of him. Who would have thought she'd make such a bold move when she didn't know the terrain, or the laws or the customs? She'd never even set foot off Earth. For her to boldly take off on her own . . . amazed him.

But she was Lucan's twin. And her life in danger had Rion on edge. Not only because she was his best friend's sister. Not only because of her telepathic talents. Above that, she was Marisa. If anything happened to her . . . it would affect him in ways he couldn't explain.

She would not pay for his mistake. Every cell in his body focused on getting her back.

When the crowd thickened, Rion closed the distance, sneaking up behind the Enforcer and Marisa. Protected by helmet and body armor, the Enforcer had few vulnerable areas exposed.

Rion struck hard and fast, slashing his knife into the neck, slicing the carotid artery. Hands going to his bloody neck, the Enforcer released Marisa. She immediately jerked away.

Her face was dirty, a new smudge on her cheek. Yet Rion had seen that smudge before. From somewhere the Enforcer's partner fired two shots. *Bang. Bang.* There was a pause. Another shot.

The exact same smudge and weapon pattern from his flash. Marisa was about to take a fatal bullet.

As the crowd screamed, ducked, and panicked, Rion dived and tackled Marisa, and they rolled, knocking into people who were trying to scramble out of the line of fire. Rion used their momentum to keep rolling. They ended up behind a garbage bin.

"You found me?" Marisa wiped her hair out of her eyes, which speared him with defiance. "Of course you found me. You need me."

"There's no time to talk." Rion grabbed her hand. "Come on. More Enforcers are on the way."

RION POINTED OUT a group of Enforcers headed in their direction. "Keep your head down. By now, they know what you look like."

"They do?"

"They took our pictures the moment we arrived on the platform. By now, every Enforcer in the city must be looking for us."

The Enforcers' deliberate march through the parting crowd and toward them made Marisa's mouth go dry with fear. Police in any country looked much the same, but the difference here was that the populace practically tripped over themselves to avoid their own Enforcers.

Something swooped at her. She staggered, and a small projectile whizzed by her ear. "What was that?"

"Tracers. If one of them tags us, it'll make it easy for the Enforcers to keep tabs on us."

She caught a flash of wings. Between Rion's kidnapping and the Enforcer's capture, she'd forgotten that Cael's owl had also flown through the portal.

"We have to move out. Now." Rion placed his arm over her shoulder to steady her. "They have the exits covered." He urged her forward, and she didn't pull away.

Rion might have forced her here against her will, but it was in his best interests to keep her alive. Going it alone had almost gotten her killed.

"If Merlin hadn't flown right at me, the tracer would have gotten me." She craned her head back and searched for Merlin but didn't see him among the monorail vehicles that swished in and out of the terminal. Overhead, more moving cars traveled through the air and disappeared into tunnels. She saw no tracks, no wings, and wondered how the moving trains stayed aloft. The immense geodesic dome had several windows. Outside, the sky was blue, a deeper blue than on Earth, and wisps of silver clouds floated by. But Merlin had vanished. "Where did he go?"

"Someplace safe, I hope."

From his tone, she knew she and Rion were far from safe. She glanced back longingly but could no longer see the platform with the transporter.

With eyes sharp and wary, Rion glanced over his shoulder at the Enforcers hunting through the crowds for them. Together he and Marisa dodged into thick foot traffic, and he pulled her with him behind a food station, where they merged with a group of singing youngsters.

Rion took a right, then a left, leading her past stores and fruit stands, then maneuvered them onto a moving walkway. They stood between a janitor pushing what looked like a phone booth full of cleaning supplies and two men who had to be over seven feet tall.

"Where are we going?" she asked.

"To meet my contact."

"To get the charges dropped?"

"To hide us until we can leave for Honor." He steered

her around a copper-colored puddle on the pavement. But it couldn't rain inside this building, could it?

She needed to focus. On the important things. "I want to go home."

He raked a hand through his hair, face weary. "I'm sorry I had to drag you into this. But if you help me, I'll make sure—"

"I don't make bargains with kidnappers," she snapped.

Rion glanced over his shoulder. "Keep your voice down."

She spotted a large squad of Enforcers coming toward them and jerked her thumb. "They've already spotted us."

"Come on." Rion dragged her to the side of the moving walkway. He leaped onto the railing and hauled her up beside him. She looked down. They were balanced ten stories above another level. Below, the people were tiny. The ground was steel or concrete. Whatever. It was hard.

"Trust me." Rion squeezed her hand and yanked her over the edge.

She would have screamed. But her vocal cords froze. Automatic reflexes kicked in, and she tried to dragon-shape. But the morphing didn't happen. She remained fully human, with no wings to stop her fall. Her stomach swooped up into her throat. Her hair whipped back from her face, and her eyes watered, giving her a blurred view . . . of death. She squeezed her eyes closed, all the while thinking, *No, no, no.* This couldn't be happening.

She was going to wake up in her bed, her pulse racing, and laugh at this insane nightmare. But slowly the wind stopped plucking at her. The swooping sensation faded.

And she dared to crack open her eyes. The world was still alien, but they'd stopped falling. Some unknown force floated them down gently toward a crowded square.

People sat eating, drinking, and playing games on spinning cubes. One man walked a six-legged canine. The diners acted as if they hadn't noticed Rion and Marisa's crazy fall and subsequent landing.

"Antigravs caught us," Rion explained. "Throughout the city they also prevent dragonshaping—something to do with electromagnetic changes on a cellular level."

Her feet touched the metal decking and her legs shook. "What are antigravs?"

"Safety devices. You're okay now."

"No. I'm not okay." She was shaking so hard she had to hold on to Rion to keep from falling. "I thought I was going to die. Again."

He gathered her into his arms and cradled her against his chest. "I'm sorry. There was no time to explain."

Her teeth chattered. Sorry wasn't good enough. The Enforcer could have executed her. During that fall, she could have died of fright. But she bit back the complaints. Rion's warmth settled her. His solid strength was an anchor of familiarity in this strange new world. She breathed in his scent, closed her eyes, and told herself that she'd been in tight spots before. And there was nothing wrong with clinging to Rion if that righted her world.

He murmured soothingly, "Just hang on a little longer and we'll find a safe place to hole up."

"All right." Her shaking subsided, and she stepped away from him. Taking comfort was one thing, but she couldn't let herself forget that he'd gotten her into this mess in the first place.

He half led, half carried her behind a slowly rolling automated cart that whistled and rumbled on metal wheels. After boosting her onto the cart's seat, he climbed up to sit beside her. "We can rest here for a bit. But not for long. Sooner or later, they'll figure out we jumped levels and are out of the grid pattern."

She rubbed her temples, trying to understand. "What are you saying?"

"Isn't the translator working?"

Struggling to control her fear and anger, she told herself that screaming at him wasn't going to help. "I understand . . . your words, not the concepts."

Rion nodded and slung his arm over her shoulders, until their hips and thighs touched. "You're suffering culture shock and jump lag—like jet lag, only worse. The Enforcers will canvass the entire level up there before they search down here. But with our pictures on their monitors, it's only a matter of time before one of them spots us."

"How long have we got?"

"Maybe ten minutes."

"How long will it take to reach Phen?"

"An hour."

"Then we need a disguise."

"Good thinking. How do you feel about blue skin and silver hair?"

She blinked, recalling the people she'd seen with blue-and green-tinged skin. She'd assumed they'd been born that color. "You can change my skin color?"

He winked. "We can change you from the top of your head to the bottom of your feet. But it's expensive, and I don't have any credit chips." He slung his pack from his shoulder and removed two hats, handed her one and donned the other. "However, if you can walk a bit farther, I brought some barter items."

Marisa forced herself to tamp down on the fear. Instead, she made herself think about the safety of a disguise. Taking a deep breath, she twisted her hair up on her head and put on the hat. "I'm good to go."

She wasn't, of course. Any moment she expected a tracer to tag her. Or for the Enforcers to swoop down and surround them. But adrenaline kept her on her feet, kept her careful.

A few minutes later, Rion led her into a booth that housed a machine that looked like a four-sided ATM. After opening the zipper on his pack, he removed five Krugerrands and placed the gold into a bin. The bin ate the coins, and credit chips came out.

He handed her almost half the chips and pocketed the rest. "Gold's even more valuable here than on Earth. Of course, after the Enforcers examine the gold, they'll figure out it came from offworld. They'll try to find us here. But we'll be gone by then."

Just knowing the Enforcers might once again be tracking them down made her antsy. She didn't plan to linger.

He led her through a maze of stalls that reminded her of a flea market, with vendors selling carpets, machines, clothing, and dozens of items she couldn't identify. But despite her fear, what interested her more than the items for sale were the aliens themselves.

While all were humanoid, with two legs and two arms, some had extra eyes in the middle of their foreheads. She saw men who were tiny and slender, perfectly formed and very beautiful. And women with locks so long that to keep their hair off the ground, tiny carts trailed behind to support it.

"How many races live here?" she asked.

"Tor has always encouraged commerce. Import and export taxes are low. Hundreds of races pass through this trading center daily."

Hundreds? It appeared the galaxy was teeming with life—not so surprising when one considered the billions of stars. Still, the sights amazed her. If she hadn't been on the run, she'd have longed for a camera.

Rion took her into an establishment that seemed more substantial than many they'd passed. The outside window was painted with beautiful images of humanoids, but the holographic images kept changing to display a variety of options in facial features, bone structure, and even eye color.

"We don't have time for more than a superficial make-over," Rion told her.

"Thank God." She preferred to at least recognize herself in the mirror.

"That's the female side." Rion pointed to an arch on the left. "Order new clothes, a skin tint, and a hair color option."

"How long will this take?"

"Five minutes. I'll meet you back here."

Marisa walked through the door he'd indicated. She paused for a moment, wondering if she should take this opportunity to escape. But where would she go with the Enforcers after her? She didn't even know if she could find her way back to the transporter. After she used the credits he'd given her for her disguise, she'd have no money. She'd already run from Rion straight into the Enforcers.

Before making a move that might place her life in danger again, she needed to learn more about this world. So for now, she'd stay with Rion.

Marisa expected someone inside the establishment to greet her. But as she stepped through the door, a mechanical voice issued instructions. "Please follow the orange light."

Trying to breathe evenly, she followed the orange neon light on the floor into a room with a tub. The automated instructions continued. "Remove all clothing and jewelry before stepping into the tub."

She did as instructed, feeling very vulnerable as she stood naked in the tub. Now what? Did she sit, stand, or lie down?

"Choose your preference."

A panel in the tub opened, and a screen popped up. She picked silver skin with a slight blue tint and shiny silver hair. She also got a choice of clothing that was more appropriate for clubbing than for a fugitive. But blending in with the general populace was her immediate goal. She ended up wearing a minidress with a halter top and strappy sandals that made her think Manolo Blahnik was an alien.

"Please insert five credits."

She placed the chips into a blinking slot. Marisa had no idea what to expect. She should have asked Rion more questions. But when silver flakes began to fall from the ceiling, then spun around her before adhering to her skin, she held out her arms and watched in amazement. Her skin turned silvery blue, the flakes drying on contact. Other flakes stuck to her hair and turned it silver.

Wow. She could make a fortune with this machine

back home. Talk about the end of prejudice. When anyone could change skin color or features, ethnicity and race based on looks became irrelevant. This machine alone could have stopped wars and saved millions of lives. When the flakes stopped falling, she climbed out of the tub and dressed. Her shoes were now dyed to match her new clothing, which looked way too large, but after she put it on, it shrank to fit her perfectly. Nice technology.

Still, reluctant to leave her own clothing behind, she scooped up her Earth things and tucked them under her arm.

Rion stood waiting for her in the lobby, and she handed him her old clothes. He took in her hair, her skin, her short dress, and he whistled. "You look . . . amazing."

She almost thanked him for the compliment, before she bit back the words. Damn him for making her feel good. She shouldn't care what the hell her kidnapper thought about her appearance.

Rion shoved her clothes into his pack, which gave her time to check him out. He'd also chosen silver skin tint, and his hair was now navy blue. He wore a dove gray shirt with royal purple piping and charcoal pants. Somehow the clothing suited him more than his Earth clothing ever had. His shoulders looked broader, the cords in his neck thicker, his chest more powerful. Despite his effort to blend, Rion would draw attention wherever he went.

He escorted her out the door. "We haven't much time."

"How do you know?"

"An Enforcer squad is sweeping the area."

With her silver-blue skin and hair, she felt less conspicuous. But Merlin had no trouble finding them. Out of the corner of her eye, she glimpsed a flutter of Merlin's wings as the owl dropped onto an overhead ledge.

Keeping an eye out for Enforcers, Marisa stayed beside Rion as they threaded their way between slower groups of people, traveling at the same pace as the fastest pedestrians. Breaking into a run would draw attention—or so she assumed.

"Enforcers, ahead," she whispered.

"Stay calm." Rion held her tightly and she ducked her head, letting the hat shade her face.

Marisa held her breath until the Enforcers strode right by them. Thanks to the disguises, they didn't stop.

"That was close." After the encounter, Marisa couldn't stop shaking. "How did the Enforcers get so much power?"

"It's complicated. But the bottom line is that people on Tor were fearful of an invasion. In exchange for the safety and protection they wanted, they gave away too much power and freedom. Eventually the Enforcers took over, dominating . . . everyone. Now they are too powerful for the citizens to abolish them. But what is worse is that some of us suspect that the Enforcers are covert members of the Tribes."

That old saying that absolute power corrupts absolutely seemed to be a universal constant, not just a pattern on Earth. Marisa kept walking, her mind spinning from one angle to the next. "If the Torans feared a Unari invasion, wouldn't it have been to their benefit to have helped you after you escaped your world?"

"The Torans fear Honor's dragonshapers as much as they fear the Unari."

"Why?"

"They believe Honor wants to take over Tor. That's why the antigravs in the city prevent dragonshaping."

Her mouth went dry and she licked her bottom lip. "Are you telling me that—"

"Yeah, if they find out we are dragonshapers, they shoot on sight."

So much for eliminating prejudice. She pressed her arms against her sides to hide the scales on the insides of her arms.

"It's doubtful anyone here will recognize you have the scales of a dragonshaper."

She recalled him saying that the dragonshapers on his planet didn't have her telltale marks. "So everyone on Honor can dragonshape, and none of these Torans can?"

He nodded. "Our ability to fly and breathe fire has kept us at war for thousands of years. We've had an uneasy truce for the last few centuries. Since my people can't dragonshape here, they don't like to visit."

"I understand." To stay alive, dragonshapers needed to feed periodically on platinum and hydrogen in dragon form. Being in a place where she couldn't morph was akin to being a fish out of water.

"We'll have to leave before it's time to feed."

She gave him a hard look. "How are we going to leave?"

He smiled. "Phen and I have a plan to retrofit a spaceship."

If the land comes under disaster or perilous times, we must be willing to die so the land may live.

—HONORIAN LEADER

8

Cranky, footsore, and in desperate need of sleep, Marisa gritted her teeth and followed Rion around another corner.

Rion noted her flagging pace and took her hand. "Just a little farther through the spaceport and we'll reach the rim."

He'd said the same thing over an hour ago. "Is Phen on the rim?"

"Yes. But it's farther than the last time I was here."

Since she'd already noticed how the buildings around the city's rim moved from place to place on silent air sleds, she nodded and forced one foot in front of the other.

Beside her, Rion stiffened, and his gaze darted past two Enforcers. Suddenly he stopped, spun her around, and planted his lips on hers.

Reality kicked in. This kiss wasn't for the usual reasons. They had to hide their faces. Fast. When she didn't try to pull away, Rion eased up his hold but kept her tucked against his chest.

She hadn't forgiven him. She shouldn't want to lean closer into his hard muscles. She shouldn't want his powerful arms wrapped around her. She shouldn't want him to make her feel safe.

She told herself her heart pounded with fear—not arousal. But already the Enforcers' footsteps were fading from her awareness, replaced by the sound of Rion's breathing.

His kiss was hot, hard, and a haven against the outside threat. Fiery need ignited, and for a brief moment she sank into the safety of his arms, gave way to the strong sanctuary of his protection.

His hand fisted in her hair.

An Enforcer shouted. Footsteps pounded past them.

Rion groaned and tore his mouth from hers, grabbed her hand, and dragged her down an alley to sweep her into a building and through a set of double doors.

Damn it. What was wrong with her? Rion had kidnapped her, put her life in jeopardy. How could she have just melted in his arms as if he were her gallant knight?

"Let's hope Phen is here." Rion moved into a dimly lit chamber. Merlin flew inside with them and settled on a hanging light fixture.

She shook her head. "Where did he come from?"

"I have no idea," Rion said. "But on Pendragon he proved very helpful. He's always welcome."

Within the chamber, solemn people sat in rows facing a fluted column that held a dish of green fire. They swayed in unison, apparently praying. Music tinkled softly in the background. Burning incense floated in a dome-like pattern around the flames.

Marisa hoped they'd entered a sanctuary, a holy place

the Enforcers wouldn't violate. But Rion's shoulders remained tense. He led her to one side, past carved statues of men, women, and children in assorted poses that depicted daily life. Gilded wall murals represented scenes from space—exploding suns, asteroids, planets.

Rion hurried her through an alcove and opened a door. She glanced over his shoulder. This room consisted of a bed, one chair, a bookshelf filled with dusty magazines, and a tiny bathroom.

He led her inside, and again Merlin followed before Rion shut the door behind them. "We can rest here. The deacon allows those in need to use this place for shelter."

"You've been here before?"

"Yes."

The owl perched on the bookshelf. Marisa stepped into the tiny bathroom, taking the opportunity to freshen up. She'd no sooner washed her hands and rejoined Rion than a man barged into the room.

Merlin hooted.

Rion reached to his side, where a weapon glinted, and took a protective step in her direction. In the tiny room he didn't have to go very far to place his solid body between her and the stranger.

The intruder wore a brown cloak and a silver pin on his collar. His eyes were sharp, very brown, and wary. He held a flat metal rectangle in his hand, consulted writing on it, and frowned. "You aren't on my schedule. Who are you people? And how did that creature get in here?"

Rion closed his fingers over the hilt of his knife. "We're friends of Deacon Phen."

"I see. Wait here and I'll tell him you've arrived." The man glowered at the owl and left in a hurry.

"Something's wrong," she told Rion.

"Yeah. I got that, too." Rion eased his hand off his knife.

"He could be reporting us to the Enforcers right now. Shouldn't we go?"

Before Rion answered, the door swung open again. Another large man wearing a brown hooded cloak stepped into the room. The moment he saw Rion, he tossed back his hood to reveal a weather-beaten face, a full silver beard, a bushy mustache, and twinkling blue eyes.

"Phen, you old space dog." Rion grinned and wrapped the larger man in a bear hug.

Phen clapped Rion on the back. "Come back to save Honor, have you, boy? It's about time."

"I was hoping it wouldn't be necessary." Rion gestured her to come forward. "Marisa, I'd like you to meet Deacon Phen, my mother's brother and my uncle."

Phen bowed, lifted her hand to his lips, and kissed it. "Pleased, my lady. Welcome."

"Hello." Marisa liked the man immediately, although she wasn't sure why. "Sir, while I'm pleased to meet you, from the way your associate greeted us, I fear we should not stay long."

"Of course you're staying. Just not here. The man's not to be trusted."

Rion turned to Marisa. "Phen believes in keeping his friends close and his enemies even closer."

"Now, don't be giving away all my secrets." Phen shot Rion a glance, and Rion shook his head slightly.

She wasn't sure what silent question had just been asked and answered, but it told her one thing—Phen and Rion had more secrets they hadn't revealed. What didn't they want her to know?

Rion smoothly changed the subject. "Our stay won't be long. I have to get back to Honor," he said.

Phen frowned. "Come, we need to talk. Besides, the Infinity Circle is still closed."

"Infinity Circle?" Marisa asked.

Phen explained. "The Infinity Circle is Honor's ancient portal. For thousands of years, Honorians used the Infinity Circle as a way station to the stars."

Marisa guessed the rest. "And the ancient builders disappeared into antiquity?"

"Yes. The science behind the portals vanished with the builders, but their machinery has survived floods, wars, erosion, and time. Let's hope it survives the Unari."

CONVERSATION ABOUT THE Infinity Circle triggered one of Rion's visions. He could still hear Marisa and Phen's conversation, but he was also seeing the distinctive monument.

Massive rounded boulders sat on the hillside overlooking the river Kai. Rectangular cross-stones spanned the tops of the boulders to link them together.

Unari guarded the control panel, preventing any Honorian travel onto or off the planet. Unari guards patrolled the Infinity Circle's perimeter. Unari skimmers watched from the skies.

Rion sucked in a breath of surprise.

On the side of the hill, a group of Honorians worked in secret silence. They were digging a tun-

nel into the sloping area, a tunnel aiming directly for the control panel.

Stars. They were taking the offensive.

The plan to retake the portal was bold.

His vision narrowed to follow one man as he crawled into the blackness. The rebels used planks to brace the ceiling, the narrow passageway wide enough for only two men to slide by each other. They worked a bucket brigade, the men at the front of the tunnel digging the earth, then sending it back in buckets, where others carefully dumped it into the river, the water carrying away the evidence.

Rion's vision flashed back outside to the Infinity Circle. The Unari patrols suddenly ran for their vehicles and drove away. Even the guards abandoned the critical control panel. Every skimmer took to the sky.

Although he saw no reason for the retreat, Rion's hopes rose. If the Unari fled, if Honorians took control of the Infinity Circle . . .

The skimmers formed a line in the sky and circled over the river. They turned back, heading straight for the tunnel.

No! They were lining up a bombing strike.

And they knew exactly where to aim.

The skimmers dropped their deadly bombs from the sky and blasts shook the hillside. One of the upper stone links connecting two boulders crashed to the earth with a thunderous thud and shot up a cloud of dust.

Suddenly Rion was back inside the tunnel. The planks of wood snapped like twigs. The tunnel col-

lapsed; tons of earth and rocks crushed the men. The lucky ones died immediately. The unlucky ones lasted until their air ran out.

No one survived.

PHEN MOTIONED MARISA and Rion closer, then pulled a lever, and the room began to move smoothly straight down—like an elevator. She had no idea how far they fell, but when Phen reopened the door, instead of going out into the house of worship they entered a huge open space with designated areas for work, sleep, and food preparation, all in pinkish-gray steel. Merlin flew into the loft-like space, and Phen hit a button, sending the smaller room back up to the surface.

"Come, eat, rest. Make yourselves at home. You should be safe here for a while. Your bird, too." The deacon shot Rion a significant look and frowned. "And we need to talk."

"I'm in dire need of news. I've had no word from Honor for almost three years." Rion didn't change the tone or volume of his voice, but she picked up on his anxiety.

Marisa damn sure didn't approve of how Rion had kidnapped her. But she couldn't help admiring his commitment to his people. He hadn't risked just her life but his own, too. And the reporter in her understood just how heroic and brave he was—even as the woman in her resented his assumption that she would go along with whatever he wanted.

"You've been gone so long, I feared you might not ever return." The deacon gestured for them to sit. He brought a tray with fizzy blue drinks and a heavy platter of food from an oven. The assortment he was providing on such short notice amazed her. Sweetmeats, casseroles, breads, vegetables, and crunchy crackers were a veritable feast. Either Phen had been cooking for hours before they'd arrived, or the machine always kept hot food ready.

She was hungry again after all that walking. Of course, Marisa recognized none of the vegetables or meat. But the spices and sauces smelled delicious, and her mouth watered. She filled a plate and began to eat with a spoon-like utensil with tines on the end.

"Merlin. Food." Rion tossed a piece of meat upward, and the owl snatched it out of the air and took it to a rafter.

"Tell me of my parents." Rion sipped his drink and braced himself, as if expecting the worst. "Is there news?"

Phen dropped his head and stared at the floor. "They may still be alive, but if they are, they are now Unari slaves."

Rion didn't change expression, but shadows of pain clouded his eyes. "I feared as much."

If Marisa had been told that her parents were enslaved or dead, she wouldn't have been able to hold in the pain. Or the sobs. But Rion stilled, going so stiff and silent that the air around him seemed brittle. And despite her anger with him, she couldn't help but feel sorry for him, too.

He'd lost . . . everything. His home. His parents. His world.

Rion went inside himself, but very aware of his pain Marisa yearned to touch him, hold him. And, she admitted to herself, she wanted to drag him back into her arms again.

A low voice in the back of her mind whispered it was about time. It had been many years since her divorce.

As if sensing Rion needed time to pull himself together, Phen raised his head and looked at Marisa closely, especially interested in the scales on her arms. "Where are you from?"

She glanced at Rion. He squared his shoulders, raised his chin, and eyes still bleak, he nodded. "I'm from Florida, in the North American States." At Phen's blank look, she added, "Planet Earth."

The deacon's brow furrowed. "Earth? It's on the Unari list. A very long list."

"What list?" Marisa asked.

"You must understand, it's not just Honor that the Tribes seek to dominate," Rion explained, his tone bitter. "Every world that falls to the Tribes gives their empire more resources and a wider base from which to spread their madness. They hate dragonshapers and intend to enslave all free men under an absolute dictatorship. They replace enlightenment with fear and darkness."

Marisa kept her tone mild, but her pulse escalated. "You didn't answer my question."

Phen took a drink, settled into his chair, and looked at Rion. Again Rion nodded as if giving his uncle permission to speak. "One of the Honorian rebels smuggled out a list of worlds. We believe this list is composed of planets the Unari plan to invade. Earth is near the top of the list."

Marisa gasped. "If the Unari are planning to attack my home, I should warn them."

"They didn't believe me. Would they believe you without any real proof?" Rion asked, his voice skeptical.

To her dismay, Marisa already knew the answer. Lucan had come back from Pendragon with the same supposition. And after all he'd done for Earth, the authorities had questioned his sources and had demanded genuine evidence.

"Let me be clear," Phen added, his demeanor serious. "We don't know for certain if the list *is* an invasion plan. Maybe it's a travel itinerary."

"But you don't think so?" Marisa pressed him, her hearts heavy. Earth could be facing the same fate as Honor.

Her parents, her brother, her sister-in-law, and their babies, everyone Marisa knew, could be in danger. Sickened, desperate to warn them, she pressed her lips together to keep back a gasp of helplessness. But what could she do?

Her eyes met Rion's. He'd kidnapped her to help free his people. She still couldn't condone his actions . . . but she understood. Because she, too, would do whatever she could to save Earth.

And while she could distract herself with everything going on, the kidnapping, the Enforcers, the Unari threat to Earth, Rion was the one she looked to for help. She couldn't deny that whenever she was near Rion, her hearts beat faster, that she was more aware, more alive. Couldn't deny she wanted to know him better.

Phen softened his tone. "It's more likely the Unari are already on Earth. You see, the actual invasion is usually the last stage of their domination plan."

Rion pushed aside his untouched plate and poured another drink.

Marisa frowned. "What do you mean?"

"The Unari send moles in first. Spies. They do whatever they can to weaken a world, bankrupting strong countries, starting wars, devaluing currencies."

Rion spoke softly. "Chivalri was once the strongest and most prosperous country on all of Honor. Like England, Chivalri had both a king and a representative democracy."

Phen nodded. "The Unari worked from the inside on many levels to bring down the strongest first. They are patient and relentless. Their plans can take decades."

"They infiltrate the military?" Marisa asked.

"And the government," Rion said. "The Unari are brilliant strategists. They penetrated both sides of Honor's political system, pushing an agenda of global unification, one currency, one government, one world order. Those who spoke up against them didn't stand a chance against their giant propaganda machine."

"Once they controlled the media," Phen said, "they could sway the way people thought." He held up a cube and tossed it to Rion. "These images were taken by robotic spy cameras and smuggled to me two days ago. As soon as I viewed them, I triggered the microchip for Rion to come home."

In Rion's hands, the cube turned into a six-sided video screen. On one side a chained dragon bellowed in pain, blood running down his neck. Marisa gasped in horror at the sickening image. The other sides of the cube showed dragons dragging huge stones up steep inclines, their masters whipping them, their backs scarred, their scales shredded. Midsized dragons shivered in mud, their wings broken. At the baby dragons cowering in tiny cages, a tear slipped down Marisa's cheek.

"I'm too late. I'd hoped to get there before—"

"Your flash came true." Marisa wiped away her tear and shot a glance at Rion. So he hadn't lied to her about his flashes. These images matched the vision he'd described. No wonder he was so determined to go home. No wonder he'd kidnapped her. No wonder he'd risked their lives. No decent person could see those terrible images and fail to act.

"The whips have two settings," Phen told them, "agony, or heart-stopping lethal pain."

Oh . . . God. Marisa momentarily squeezed her eyes shut but couldn't rid herself of the sickening images.

Rion's face was bleak. "Is anyone still free?"

"Rebels are down there. But food is in short supply and . . . every day, their numbers are less." Phen turned off the cube.

Rion's face hardened with determination. "Have you found a ship to fly us to Honor?"

"Sir Drake at the military museum has a ship, but it needs work, and you may have to steal it. I'm not certain where his allegiance lies. But don't even think about trying to use the transporter to reach Honor. Elite Unari squads guard it. Attempting to go near the site is an automatic death sentence."

Rion gripped the arms of his chair, his fingers digging deep into the padding. "Tell me about Erik, please."

"The Unari have him."

"They torture him." Rion slammed one fist into another. "Erik's fate should have been mine."

Marisa slipped her hand into his, not just to give comfort but to take some. It was the only answer to subduing the pain at hearing such terrible news.

Phen shook his head. "Erik did what any good man would do. He saved his friend."

"Erik's your cousin?" she asked, recalling Rion mentioning the name back on Earth.

"My father's brother's son. Without Erik's help, I'd be dead."

The deacon's expression turned grim, and sympathy flickered in his eyes. "They torture all captured Honorians."

Rion pressed his lips together so hard they turned white. A muscle ticked in his jaw. "What information could Erik have that the Unari need?"

Phen sighed. "They don't torture to gain information."

"Then why . . ."

"They torture dragons to induce pain. Then a machine called a Tyrannizer captures their agony and projects that pain onto the other dragons. Everyone suffers."

Rion swore. And bowed his head.

"I don't understand," Marisa whispered, and clung tightly to Rion's hand.

"The Unari use dragons as their labor force. To keep them docile, they make them work while they endure great pain. The less they resist, the less pain they experience."

Marisa almost choked on her food and had to force herself to swallow.

Rion released her hand, stood and knocked over his chair, and paced. "This pain prevents even our warriors from rebellion?"

"Yes."

"How far does this pain project?" Marisa asked, wondering how much more horrible news Rion would have to hear.

"Dragon pain now blankets all of Honor," Phen said.

"Once the Chivalri capital fell, the Unari took over the rest of the planet in one massive swoop."

Phen's communicator clicked and he stood. "Please excuse me. One of the brothers needs me, and I may be gone for some time. Make yourselves at home."

Phen departed, and Rion stopped pacing. Eyes locking with hers, he stood very still, yet he radiated tension. "I was wrong to bring you here against your will. But now that you know what's happening on Honor, I hope you'll join my cause."

"And if I say no?"

"Then I'll find a way to send you back to Earth."

Her heart skipped a beat. "Would you really do that?"

He kneeled and took her hand in his. "I swear it."

But who was the man kneeling before her? Gallant knight, or lying scoundrel?

Rion's bringing her here against her will had been wrong. But how could she hold that against him now that she understood the stakes? And he'd admitted his mistakes. Plus, he'd given her an out and offered to send her home.

He'd been desperate. Forced to kidnap her so he could free his people from slavery.

Gallant knight? There was only one way to find out. Only one way to help Earth.

"So what's our plan?" she asked.

Marisa had doubts. But she no longer believed her initial instincts about Rion were wrong. He had goodness in his heart. He was passionate about his people, and perhaps one day, one day soon, she'd let him drag her into his arms again.

"We break the Unari hold on Chivalri and find enough

proof to convince every intelligent race the Tribes are rising again." Rion placed his hands on her shoulders. "With your help, we just might stop them."

She closed the short distance between them and placed her hand over his. Touching him seemed to be the only relief they had. And the ache in her hearts told her it was the only answer to the need in her body whenever he was near. "I'll do what I can."

Rion shot to his feet, yanked her into his arms. The sparks in his eyes burst into flames and fired her senses. Her hearts jolted and her pulse pounded.

His mouth found hers and their lips locked. His need brought her to a slow burn. His tongue set her on fire.

"You won't be sorry," he whispered, his voice husky. "I thank you. And my people thank you."

Marisa sighed into his mouth and prayed she wasn't getting in over her head.

Comfort can come in many strange forms . . . so can friendship if one keeps an open mind.

—KING ARTHUR

9

Rion had apologized for kidnapping Marisa and his offer to try to send her back home had been genuine. But he was grateful that after seeing those horrible images from Honor, she'd agreed to stay and help. Warmth had returned to her eyes when she looked at him, and the tension between them had diminished. While she might not have totally forgiven him, he still wanted to prove that he was worth her trust—even if he hadn't told her who he truly was.

Yet that didn't change the fact that he wanted to please her. She'd had a rough journey. She'd almost died. She should have hated him. Instead she'd promised to help. He was humbled by her courage, terrified of her bravery.

With a touch of a button on a control panel, Rion materialized walls to form a private room within Phen's spacious hideout. He ordered beds and several chairs, everything in soothing white.

Looking exhausted and shell-shocked, Marisa wandered the room, fingered the soft cream coverlets, then kicked off her shoes and wriggled her toes in the thick carpet underfoot. "Would it be possible to take a bath?"

Pleased he could fulfill such a simple request, he adjusted the program to insert a large spa tub into the room. But this time he used his imagination. He added flower petals to the tub's steaming water, and globes with candles that drifted through the room for scent, atmosphere, and pregnancy prevention. Soft music filtered in, and he dimmed the overhead lighting.

He turned from the control panel. She plucked one of the drifters from the air and slowly inhaled the vanilla scent of the floating candle.

"Anything else you'd like?" He wished he could take her to the Isle of Laniap on Honor, where the emerald sea washed across pink sand beaches and trade winds rustled the palm trees. He doubted the Unari appreciated the pink sunsets with the lavender-streaked clouds—at least not the way he did. His family had always escaped the summer city heat for the cool island breezes and healing waters of the sea. Cousins played in the pink sand, and parents admonished and taught the children, no matter who had sired them. Those were carefree times, fun times, times he hoped might one day come again.

"This is cool." Marisa released the drifting candle and watched it soar into the flight pattern, its tiny antigravs keeping it airborne. "And to answer your question, yes, there's something else I'd like—walls for the bathroom."

"Of course." He materialized partitions to give her privacy, and she entered the cubicle and shut the door.

He could have used a bath himself—anything to drain the tension of waiting for Phen to return. He could call up vids or text readers, but he doubted his tortured mind could concentrate on anything, especially with Marisa behind those walls, taking off her clothes.

When she'd come out of the store with her skin and hair tinted, wearing that short dress, he'd had difficulty keeping his gaze off her. Yes, he'd seen her naked, but between that sexy halter top that teased him with the curved shadows between her breasts and her long, toned legs, he'd had to fight his overwhelming desire.

And now that she was getting naked, he imagined the water lapping around her skin, sensuously seeping into her every pore. He couldn't stop thinking about how inviting she'd look with her hair piled atop her head, tendrils curling softly around her face as scented steam drifted from the hot water.

He hadn't realized how much he craved her. But if he wanted to earn her trust, he couldn't go barging in there. No matter how much he desired her. No matter how much he ached.

Something between a groan and a grunt rumbled up his throat.

Marisa called out to him. "Rion?"

He opened the door and strode into the bathroom. She looked even lovelier than he'd envisioned and not a bit surprised to see him. A soft smile played at her mouth. With her hair slicked back against her head and water trickling over her shoulders, she stretched out naked in the tub.

Thank the universe they didn't have bubble bath here. He could see every delectable inch of her sweet flesh. From her secretive smile to her delicate collarbone to her silky-soft breasts, she was lovely.

His gaze searched her face. *He* wanted to be what she

sought. "Rion." Her tone was soft and sensual and her eyes held a hint of challenge. "I was going to ask you which of these containers was the shampoo. But now that you're here, maybe you could wash my hair?"

"I'll be happy to do anything you ask."

"Thank you. Soaping up and rinsing seems like so much effort." She closed her eyes, tilted back her head, and left the rest to him.

Had she deliberately raised her breasts out of the water so that her nipples rested just under the surface? Rion bit back a grin and strode around the tub, thinking that the best way to pamper her was to make her ask for exactly what she wanted.

"We have three different scents of soap." He opened them one by one and placed them under her nose. "Would you like the sweet, the floral, or the star scent, my lady?"

"Star scent, please. It reminds me of the crisp smell of autumn leaves, when they're all vibrant golds and reds before they fall off the trees."

Rion wet his hands, then scooped some star scent into his palms and rubbed up a good lather. Taking care not to let the soap drip into her eyes, he worked the thick lather into her hair. "Would you like your scalp rubbed, too?"

"Yes, please."

Rion massaged her head with his fingertips, noting how much she enjoyed his rubbing over and behind her ears. She leaned into his hands, and the tension seeped out of her face and neck.

"You feel wonderful."

"Keep your eyes closed. I'm going to rinse you now." Employing a spray hose, he tipped her head back and rinsed the shampoo from her hair. With her back arched, her breasts rose completely out of the water. When a water droplet clung to her nipple, distracting him, he dropped the hose. Water sprayed everywhere—including all over him.

Marisa surveyed his wet shirt and chuckled. "Since you're already soaked, you might as well come in and get clean, too."

"So we're okay again?"

Their gazes met. And in her eyes he saw acceptance.

"Yeah. We're okay."

Rion didn't wait for a second invitation. He shucked the clothes but climbed into the tub behind her, settling so that his back rested against the side of the tub, and her back settled against his chest.

"Lean against me," he instructed. "I'm not done with your hair."

She scooted down a bit and her breasts disappeared beneath the surface. He gulped and applied the Toran equivalent of conditioner and perma-shine rolled into one, smoothing his fingers through her hair from the neck up to the roots.

"Umm. That feels so good that I think you should wash the rest of me."

He'd been hoping she'd ask. His chest tightened. Her lovely dragon scales, winding along the insides of her arms and down her spine and her silver skin, made his mouth water. There was something very beautiful about Marisa, not just her stunning looks, but the way she opened her-self to new experiences, the way she could take joy in small pleasures.

"Star soap?" he asked.

"Whatever you think," she murmured.

Again he lathered his hands, then spread the soap over her shoulders and along her arms. The soap wouldn't immediately dissolve in water like Earth soap. Instead, it clung to the skin, the soap nodules bubbling away to leave the skin clean and buffed.

"Oh . . . my." Her eyes popped open. "That tingles."

"Uh-huh. Lean forward." He spread the soap over her back, all the way down to her shapely ass. "Now lean back again so I can do your front."

His hands closed over her breasts. She gasped. "How long does the tingling last?"

"That depends."

"On what?"

"Your chemistry and hormones. The more aroused you are, the more you tingle."

"But the more it tingles, the hotter I get."

"Umm." He nuzzled her neck with his lips, fondled her breasts with his hands. "Such an interesting dilemma. What would you like me to do?"

"You've missed a few spots."

He nipped her earlobe, tweaked her taut nipples. "Have I now?"

She moaned softly. "I didn't know I could feel like this."

"I haven't even begun to make you feel good," he promised, lathering up his hands again. He spread the soap over her belly and down her thighs. "Raise your legs, please."

He leaned forward and ran his hands over her thighs, her knees, her calves. He took particular care with her feet. And then he repeated the process with her other leg.

When he finished, she trembled against him and parted her thighs. "More."

Dipping his fingers between her legs, he swirled the soap into her triangle of curls, then dipped lower. She moaned softly, and he carefully coated her delicate lips with soap. Her sexy ass got the same treatment. And when he slipped his lathered fingers into her from two angles at once, she panted. Squirmed.

"I can't . . . hold still. It's tingling everywhere."

"Not everywhere." His finger moved to where her scales joined between her thighs, the delicate bud where her nerve formed a pulsing nexus.

"Oh . . . my." She jerked. "I think . . . I'm . . . going to explode."

He shook his head, mouth dry as all her bare skin rubbed against his. "You won't."

"Why not?"

"The soap has smart technology. It will only let you get so aroused."

"That doesn't sound very smart to me." She raised her hand to trail up his neck. The other clutched his hip.

His erection pressed against her bottom. She tried to take him between her legs.

He shifted slightly to the side. "Not yet. I promised you I wouldn't rush, remember?"

"But I'm ready."

"According to Earth standards that may be true. But Earth standards aren't my standards."

She gasped again. "Ah . . . sweet . . . stars. What is happening to me?" She tried to shimmy closer to take his erection inside her, but she got his hand instead. "You don't . . . play fair."

"This is more fun." He kissed his way down her back. At the same time his fingers stroked between her legs, his other hand teased the crease of her ass. "Does that feel good?" he murmured, flicking his finger slowly over her clit.

"Faster," she demanded. "Harder."

She was lighting up his every nerve ending. Raw need poured through his system. Marisa had always charmed him. Intrigued him. Attracted him. But now he could breathe in the star scent, mixed with a delicious female mustiness. She wanted him.

He wondered how long he could hold back. Already on the edge of control, he felt his breath grow tight in his chest.

Marisa leaned forward onto her hands and knees, raising her hips out of the water. The sight of her set off his primal need. He wanted to ram into her like some wild animal.

Heat cascaded over him, engulfed his chest, making breathing difficult. And as the heat swirled lower, his sex drew so tight he was certain he'd never been this huge. Or in such need.

His thoughts swam in a sea of passion until he was drowning in the moment. It was as if every drop of testosterone in his body had fired. Lust clawed at him deeper, harder, hotter than ever before.

"Take me, Rion."

"I will." He'd had difficulty speaking at all, but he'd forced words past lips that wanted to taste her flesh and embed this moment into his memory.

There was no reason not to take what she was offering.

*   *   *

WHAT WAS TAKING him so damn long? Marisa didn't get it.

Her body was demanding release. Between the incessant tingling and Rion's damned clever fingers taunting and teasing her soft flesh, tiny goose bumps of need rose everywhere.

She wanted him inside her. Her body was saying *now, now, now.*

He bit her, and God help her, she lost it.

Holding back was madness. She had to have him. Could think only of him. And the aching hollow between her legs that needed filling. A hollow only he could fill.

When she reached for him, he moved his fingers faster over her flesh. Her skin prickled, her dragon scales undulated, and her nipples drew even tighter. The damp, sensitive folds between her legs ached.

She jerked her hips up. "Rion . . . please."

She glanced over her shoulder. His nostrils flared, and he smiled. His grin was feral, primal. His eyes burned, and he rose to his knees. His greedy fingers kept demanding.

He was primed to take.

But he kept nibbling her butt, his hands taunting her until she had to bite her lip to keep back a soft moan. Her hips gyrated wildly; her body surged to and fro, seeking release.

Just when she thought her muscles couldn't clench tighter, when she couldn't yearn for more, when she couldn't stand another moment without taking him deep inside her, the door burst open.

She sank low, hiding behind the lip of the tub, her hearts still pounding, her face hot and flushed. Rion leaped naked from the bath, flung a towel at her, and wrapped one around his waist.

Phen bolted inside, one hand pressed over a bloody chest wound. "Enforcers."

Phen took a step forward and toppled into Rion's arms.

Fingers shaking, Marisa scooped up her clothes and slipped them on. At the sight of Phen's terrible injury, she rushed to the outer door to lock it.

Rion carried Phen from the bathroom and lowered him to the bed. "Hold on. Let me place a pressure band—"

"No time. Leave. Now." Phen pointed to a panel on the wall. "Third button. Push it."

Rion's eyes went cold. "Your wound . . . if we leave . . ."

"I've lived"—he coughed up blood—"a good life. Besides, it's not my time . . . to . . . die."

Rion ignored Phen's plea. Instead he materialized a bandage and ripped open Phen's shirt. Marisa placed her ear to the door and, over her rush of fear, listened. "I hear shouting. Lots of footsteps."

She glanced over her shoulder. Rion worked with a humming orange wand to close Phen's wound. The sounds of boot steps increased in volume. "Rion, we don't have much time." She headed to the panel and found the button. "Should I press it?"

"Not yet." Calm, efficient, Rion kept working. "I need to stop Phen's bleeding first."

"Push the damn button," Phen ordered.

"Not yet."

A boot slammed into the door, and the vibration sent

a shock wave through her system. "They're here." She raised her finger over the button. "Rion?"

"Five seconds."

The door shattered.

"Four seconds."

Her mouth went dry. Her gaze focused on Rion. "We don't have four—"

"Now. Now."

Choose your friends as if your life depends on it.
                                        —KING ARTHUR

10

Marisa pressed the button. That's when Rion realized she had no idea that the building was about to lose its gravity and fly above the city as part of the sky grid's traffic pattern. Without looking up from the wand he held over Phen, he ordered, "Marisa, hang on to something solid and close your eyes."

"Why?" she asked, instead of obeying.

"When you pushed that button, you severed this room's connection with Phen's house. We're traveling like an uncoupled train car, except instead of following tracks, we're free-floating through the city."

Rion swore as she floated to the ceiling. Eyes wide with curiosity more than fear, she waved her arms and legs. "Where are we going?"

"Toward the outer rim. Just hang on to something. I need a minute." Rion finished sealing Phen's wound and injected the man with pain-no-more. Phen closed his eyes and eased into a deep and hopefully healing slumber.

With his hands still covered with Phen's blood, Rion

found talking difficult. He'd lost too many people who were close to him. He couldn't lose another friend.

Rion tucked a blanket around Phen to keep him from floating, and then, reaching up, he seized Marisa's foot and gently tugged her back to the floor. Of course, the term *floor* was relative. Without gravity, there was no up or down.

"Thanks." She set down on her feet and held on to a chair. All the furniture in the room had been automatically fastened to the floor when she'd activated their flight.

Rion adjusted their directions on the control panel. He turned part of one wall clear, allowing a view of their progress. But he wasn't watching the view.

He stared at Phen. "The Enforcers who shot him will be on our trail. We don't have much time. Perhaps just a few minutes."

Marisa peered out the window. "What do the Enforcers up here look like?"

Rion pointed. "See those tiny capsules? Those are singles darting in and out between the buildings. The Enforcers will come for us in a black one of those. Keep an eye out." He returned to Phen and placed a finger over the man's pulse.

"A black single's coming right at us." Her voice was tight but not panicked. "Never mind. It flew on past."

"Keep watching." Rion placed his ear to Phen's nose and mouth. His breathing was steady, the bandage already soaked with blood. "Phen should be in a hospital."

She glanced at his uncle. "If we take him there, will the Enforcers arrest him?"

"Yes." Phen coughed an answer. He opened his eyes. "You two must go. Get to Drake."

Rion took Phen's hand. "I'm not leaving you."

"Yes"—Phen squeezed his hand—"you are."

"After I left Erik, I swore I'd never leave another man behind." Rion's throat closed. "I still can't believe I'm free and he's not."

Phen raised Rion's hand to his lips and kissed it. "I'm glad you're here. Now pull the fire alarm and go. The fire officer's an old friend. He'll protect me from the Enforcers."

"I said I'm not leav—"

"You can't delay." He coughed again. "To escape, you need to dragonshape, and I'm not strong enough to morph."

"You're a dragonshaper, too?" Marisa's eyes widened.

"It runs in the family," Phen muttered, then glared at Rion. "So does hardheadedness."

Rion's lips tightened. "You can ride me."

"I'm too weak to hold on. I won't be the reason—"

"Enough." Voice stern, Rion tried to cut off this conversation.

"Look, either you go or you'll be captured. You owe the Honorians—"

"You don't need to remind me of my duty," Rion snapped.

Gut churning, furious and frustrated that he had no other choice, Rion floated over to the wall. Punching the alarm, he broke the glass with his knuckles, welcoming the pain that couldn't match the agony in his heart.

Phen might be his last living relative.

Shutting down his emotions, he turned to Marisa. "Phen's right. We need to dragonshape. And we're almost at the hub. It's a colossal storage sector of swirling debris, forgotten rooms, and antiquated machines."

"We can lose the Enforcers there?"

"I hope so. We have to find Drake at the space museum. The trick will be getting there."

"Trouble's coming," Marisa said from her position at the window. "Six Enforcers are heading our way from three directions."

Merlin flapped his wings and flew down to Marisa. At first Rion thought the owl meant to hitch a ride on his backpack, which she wore, but the bird began to peck frantically at a tiny piece of dull black metal embedded in the material.

Rion shooed the bird aside, plucked the metal object from the pack, and swore. "It's a tracer. The Enforcers must have hit my backpack when they were shooting at us in the space station. That's how they're homing in on us."

Phen coughed, drawing their attention. "Since you left Tor, the Enforcers have improved the damn things. They not only pinpoint your location, they monitor your conversations."

"They've been listening to everything we say?" Rion asked in horror.

"It's been recorded. How much they listen to—is anyone's guess."

Marisa scrambled to her feet. "The Enforcers' vehicles are almost here. Do something."

Rion kicked out a tiny window. Glass shattered. He planned to drop the tracer onto another building, setting a false signal for the Enforcers to follow.

But Merlin hooted, flapped his wings until he hovered over Rion's hand. With a quick dip of his head, the owl plucked the tracer from his fingers and flew straight through the broken window, his wings spread in graceful flight.

"The Enforcers are turning," Marisa said. "They're following Merlin."

"Thank you, my fierce little friend," Rion said under his breath. "I hope we meet again."

RION STAGGERED. SWEET dragonblood. Not now.

Light zapped across the heavens, the deadly beacons aiming with lethal accuracy. Silver shiny balls, killers, spewed their death rays, hunting their prey, firing at will at two dragons.

Rion and Marisa.

They flew for their lives, their wings tucked tight to their bodies as they plummeted, zigging and zagging between lethal beams of light. But no dragon could survive that deadly barrage of firepower.

And neither did they. In one silent moment . . . they disintegrated.

Rion emerged from the vision in a cold sweat. Hoping he hadn't just seen their own deaths, Marisa didn't ask about his vision. But even if he hadn't started to pull C-4 and wires from his pack, the grave tightness in his jaw would have told Marisa that whatever they were about to do would be dangerous.

Her mouth went dry with fear. "What's the risky part?"

"Getting shot down by the DKs. Dragon killers."

Dragon killers? Rion's expression was grim. If he was worried, likely she should be terrified. Going on without Phen was leaving a bitter taste in her mouth, and she'd known the man only a few hours. For Rion, who'd treated the man like a second father, the abandonment must have been far worse.

While Rion pulled out a second pack of C-4, Phen glanced at a wall monitor. "Good thinking. The Enforcers won't follow that bird for long."

Ignorance might be bliss, but it wasn't her bliss. She'd rather know what she was facing. "Dragon killers?" Marisa prodded Rion. "What are they?"

Rion twisted wires together. "The city has antigravs that prevent dragonshaping with electromagnetic waves. But that technology won't work on the rim. So out here, they have DKs. They look like flying silver balls, and the DKs are programmed to shoot dragons. We'll have to avoid them."

"How?"

"We're going to keep buildings between us and the DKs."

Rion's flat tone scared her. "Has anyone ever done this before?"

Phen warned, "You'll have to do some tricky flying."

Eyes dark and determined, Rion glanced at her. "Once we fly out there, you stick close to me. Don't deviate, don't think. Just do what I do . . ."

Or the DKs will disintegrate me.

Anxiety slithered down her back. His plan was crazy. Desperate.

Outside, a maze of buildings moved up, down, and

sideways, all on different levels. And between the buildings she could see the shiny silver balls. Dragon killers.

My God. They were everywhere.

Rion pointed to a building. "That one will pass right under us. Just stick with me. And remember the DKs won't shoot at the buildings."

She couldn't exhale. The air seemed lodged deep in her lungs. "That one's moving too fast."

Rion handed Phen the detonator and squeezed his forearm. "Bye, Phen. Heal well, old friend."

"Thank you for your help and your hospitality," Marisa added softly.

Rion placed his hand on her shoulder. "Get ready. It's going to be extra noisy after I break this window."

Several well-placed kicks and another window shattered, tiny pieces of glass blowing everywhere. Her hair whipped her eyes, but she could still see hundreds of buildings and vehicles outside, all moving in a pattern that looked like pure chaos to her.

They both removed their clothing and stuffed it into their pack. Marisa placed the strap in her mouth, supporting the weight with her hands.

Rion dragonshaped and dived from the building. She morphed, too, the backpack dangling from her mouth, its weight now insignificant. Within moments her eyesight sharpened. The dragon killers twinkled a deadly silver, spinning and whirling toward them. Taking aim.

A DK's beam suddenly shot and struck a stray piece of wood floating between building lanes. The wood glowed and disintegrated.

Dive. Rion's telepathic order urged her on.

She spied another silver DK shooting down at them

from above. A third one shot up from below. Marisa tucked her wings into her body and focused on staying on Rion's tail.

Behind them, an explosion rocked the air, battering them with giant pressure waves that threatened to knock her out of the sky.

She glanced over her shoulder at the building they'd just left. It was easy to spot. The fire inspector's vehicle was landing on the roof, its lights flashing yellow and orange.

Enforcers positioned themselves in a tight net around the building. But the fire inspector waved them back.

Rion must have seen, but somehow he flew on, his pace relentless, jogging right, zooming left. She followed his weaving and darting between the moving vehicles and buildings, which kept them hidden from the deadly beams slicing the sky.

Stomach rising up her throat, she flew. Any moment she expected a flash of light, followed by the pain of her cells disintegrating.

The threatening silver balls maneuvered as one, coordinating their attack. Clearly picking up the dragons' movements, the DKs spun, aimed their disintegrating rods at them. Beams of light flashed close enough for her to feel the heat.

She held her breath, bracing for pain.

Land. Rion deployed his massive wings. She did the same. Her wings were strong but not made for this kind of sudden stopping. Wind pressure tore at her straining limbs. She banged down hard on another roof, skidding, dropping, and rolling but finally came to a sliding halt on a slick cool surface.

She couldn't keep plummeting and crashing from

building to building. Her wings felt too heavy to lift. How long since she'd slept? Or fed on dragon food? She was no superhero.

At least the DKs had stopped shooting, but they flew in closer, began to surround them. If they trapped them, they'd be dead.

We can't stay here, she told Rion.

Don't move.

But the DKs—

Let them come. All at once. His determination and certainty came through with his thought.

Primal fear zinged down her scales, and her pulse spiked.

But Rion, who had been through as much as she had, stood tall and proud. His nostrils flared. His eyes gleamed with a predatory fury.

The DKs flew closer. She trembled at the sight of hundreds of the silver disks closing in.

Rion opened his mouth, displaying huge sharp teeth. He bellowed, roaring fire. As his flames streamed over the DKs, the silver disks to the right exploded. Marisa breathed fire on the disks to the left, until the sky twinkled with their deaths.

Rion had turned the trap back on them. *That was brilliant.*

Fly. Rion spread his wings and soared. They flew past the heaviest traffic toward the rim. He didn't stop until he spied a skimmer, a lightweight flying craft, parked on the roof of a building.

After they humanshaped and dressed, Marisa flung herself into his arms. "I don't know how you avoided the

DKs for so long. It's almost as if you knew where they were going to shoot before they aimed."

His arms closed around her. "I had a flash."

"And you memorized the pattern so we'd be safe?"

Rion's gray eyes darkened with shadows and he pulled her close. "In the flash, we were killed."

"You saw us die?" Marisa gasped. "Then how did you know we could . . ."

He caressed her back, his voice even, firm, and confident. "I have faith that I can change the outcome of my flashes."

She wrapped her arms more tightly around him. "But if you hadn't changed our future . . ."

"I told you I'd protect you. I won't let you die." He nuzzled his cheek against the top of her head. "I finish what I start."

"Promises. Promises." She squeezed her arms around his waist tighter, savoring his warmth, the feeling of being alive.

Reluctantly, Rion pulled away and opened the skimmer's hatch. "Let's hope the Enforcers are now looking for dragons, not humans."

"But if they listen to the tracer recordings, they'll know we're heading to the space museum. It's not safe to—"

"We'll just have to get there before the Enforcers do."

She was about to climb into the skimmer's passenger seat, when she heard a soft fluttering. Her pulse leaped and she jerked around, fearing one of the DKs had escaped their fiery breaths and caught them.

"Relax." Rion climbed into the pilot seat. "Merlin's back."

She slid into the passenger seat. "How did he find us?"

Merlin settled between them. From his beak, he dropped a chrome object into her lap.

Marisa picked up the shiny metal piece, peered at it in confusion. "What did you bring us?"

She didn't expect an answer.

But Rion's voice rose in excitement. "Be careful with that. It's the key to our survival."

In a world of conflict, during the fight for survival, it is the job of thinking people not to be victims, nor to be on the side of the executioners.

—KING ARTHUR

11

Marisa looked down at the crystal and metal object, then back at Rion. "This is the key to our survival?"

"Over the last few years, I've had three flashes about that key." Rion steered the skimmer in a wide arc toward the museum. "Every flash was exactly the same, which is unusual. My flashes don't often repeat."

"What did you see?"

"A man's hand inserted the key into a lock. Then this solid rock wall opened into what appeared to be another dimension."

Marisa tried to keep the skepticism from her tone. "Another dimension?"

"Inside the rock was a room filled with switches, lights, and monitors, a huge wall-to-wall instrument panel."

Marisa carefully zipped the key into the backpack. If Rion believed the key was important, she wouldn't argue. While she didn't understand his flashes and wasn't willing to take their importance on mere faith like he did, she couldn't discount them, either. Not after he'd just saved their lives by flying safely through the DKs' pattern.

Ten minutes later, Rion parked the skimmer outside a huge building sadly in need of renovations. A sagging roof, cracked cornices, and peeling paint didn't inspire her confidence.

Upon their arrival, a docking tube extended from the museum to their skimmer's hatch and attached with a clang of metal on metal. A pressure lock hissed, and she expected Rion to escort her through the tube to the museum.

Instead, the hatch's iris opened. Four Enforcers aimed weapons at them.

They were trapped.

Someone must have listened to the tracer recordings and sent word ahead to these Enforcers. Was their mission over before it had begun? Were they about to be executed?

Beside her, Rion didn't move, giving the Enforcers no reason to fire. The faceless shiny helmets shot a shiver of terror down her spine. Their complete silence reminded her these guys didn't negotiate. You broke their laws and they executed you. No trial. No judge or jury.

She braced for pain. Death.

But the leader simply motioned with his baton-like weapon for them to enter the docking tube.

A dark swath of feathers flew before them, and Marisa averted her gaze from the owl. That the Enforcers took no special note of the bird comforted her a little. At least Merlin might escape.

The Enforcers pressed weapons at their backs, forcing Rion and Marisa to march through the metal passageway.

While she and Rion hadn't been shot on sight, they'd broken enough laws for sweat to bead on her forehead and under her arms. That the officials hadn't bothered to even search them for weapons was a measure of the Enforcers' intimidating confidence.

But Rion's knife was no match for four armed men. Fighting would only get him hurt or killed. Dragon-shaping inside the tubing or museum wasn't an option, either—not with the probability of an I-beam ending up embedded within their dragons' large masses.

When the docking tube ended, the men herded them into the museum and down a series of brightly lit hallways, painted dull gray, with lots of closed doors. Marisa saw no one except their captors.

Mouth dry, she risked a glance at Rion. Very slightly he shook his head, his signal not to do or say anything.

She'd seen him under pressure before. He'd been calm, but tense. Now he was filled with . . . stillness.

Moments later, the Enforcers stopped, opened a set of double doors, and gestured them inside. Behind them, the doors clanged shut. Frightened, she twisted her hands together. Rion reached out to steady her.

For that brief instant, she clung to his strength. Clung to the realization they were still breathing.

When she looked past him into the room, she saw a man standing by a large window. Tall and whipcord lean, he had gold-tinged skin, blond hair, hollowed cheeks, and an aristocratic nose. He turned the greenest eyes she'd ever seen on them, his gaze speculative. "You are Sir Rion from the land of Chivalri, sector of Camelot?"

Sector of Camelot? As in King Arthur and Queen Guinevere's Camelot? Marisa sucked in a breath and forced it out slowly. She supposed if the transporter at Stonehenge had worked fifteen hundred years ago, she shouldn't be so shocked at references to Camelot on this side of the galaxy. For all she knew, travel fifteen hundred years ago through the transporter between Earth and other worlds had been common.

The man turned his attention to Marisa. "And you are from Earth?"

"You've been eavesdropping?" she asked, her stomach sinking.

The man nodded. "After you destroyed the tracer, we could no longer track your progress, but I'm pleased you came here."

"Really?" She couldn't get a bead on him. Despite his civil welcome, she sensed he was making a great effort to appear cordial. But why? In her experience, men in power didn't treat their captives well unless they wanted something.

Rion nodded curtly. "And you are?"

"Sir Drake. Head of the Enforcers in this quadrant and a loyal Toran citizen who should execute you." He frowned, his eyes hard and brilliant.

"But you aren't going to." Rion folded his arms over his chest. "Why?"

Drake gestured for them to sit. "Because I am the last native-born Toran in charge of Enforcers." His words hadn't answered Rion's question, but maybe the picture cube Drake was handing Rion would explain what was going on.

Rion shook the cube and videos showed on every side. At first Marisa didn't understand what she was watching. She saw Enforcers shot by what appeared to be other Enforcers. As far as she was concerned, she wouldn't mind if they all killed one another. Good riddance.

Rion frowned and tossed the cube back to Drake. "The Unari Tribes are taking over Tor?"

Marisa kept back a gasp. Drake had said he was the last *native Toran Enforcer* in charge. She'd missed the implication of Drake's statement that offworlders were now Enforcers, but Rion hadn't.

Drake's hand closed around the cube. "I believe the Unari have taken over every single position of power among the Enforcers—except mine."

"And that's why you aren't executing us?" Rion searched the man's eyes with calm deliberation. "Because the Unari are a bigger threat to Tor than we are."

What was Rion thinking? That the enemy of his enemy was his ally?

Sir Drake stood and paced, his hands clasped behind his back. "We cannot fight the Unari without help."

Their help? Was Sir Drake asking them for help to rid Tor of the Unari? She held back a frown. What could she and Rion possibly do to help?

"I can tell you what they did to Honor." Rion's voice was grim. "The Unari pick planets with a centralized power base, where it's easiest for them to plant moles and weaken the infrastructure from within."

"I'm not sure I understand," Drake said.

"Tor has one supreme ruler, correct?" Rion waited for Drake to nod before he continued, "Suppose the Unari placed their own man here as supreme ruler? Or as the supreme ruler's chief adviser?"

"They could cripple us from within."

"And when they invade, there's no organized resistance."

"The Unari may have already replaced some of our politicians with their own people," Drake admitted.

Rion frowned. "With one central government on Tor, with consolidated power at the top, you make an ideal Unari target."

The concern in his eyes matched Marisa's deepest fears for her own people. She had grown up believing that unity created strength. That it was a good thing to sacrifice national priorities for the well-being of the world community. It bothered her that the earth she'd left behind was well on its way to forming a global government.

Back home, Europe had gone to one currency decades ago, and Asia, Africa, and North America had followed suit. The United Nations had blurred the old lines between borders. The soldiers of many nations fought for the Peace Alliance.

Had Earth also consolidated too much power in one place? Were they ripe for a Unari takeover, too?

Drake turned and faced Rion. "If we decentralize, form different countries of Tor, with separate governments, would it make it harder for the moles to infiltrate us? Make it harder for the Unari to conquer us?"

"It would. If you can get your politicians to listen. But you don't have much time," Rion warned. "If the Unari are already here, it won't be long until they cut off communications and close down your transporter."

Marisa watched Drake's lips tighten. He hesitated.

Finally, he leaned forward and glowered at Rion, as if the threat to Tor was Rion's fault. "*You* agree that power should be spread out and shared?"

Rion calmly stared the other man down. "I do."

Drake's eyes narrowed. "I find that very hard to believe."

Rion spread his arms. "I once thought Chivalri had the best system of government on Honor. That all Honorians would be better off under one central ruling body. But I've lost my home. I see things . . . differently than I once did. If I could return to Honor, I would make sure each realm is ruled by its own leader and governed by independent legislatures."

Tension between the two men arced through the room. Clearly, there was no love between them. No friendship. No trust. Their only bond was a hatred of the Unari. Would that be enough for Rion to form some kind of agreement with Drake so she and Rion could complete their mission?

Rion was speaking as if he was negotiating from a position of strength. Yet as far as she knew, he had nothing to offer. What was he up to?

Refusing to undermine Rion's bargaining position, she kept her face blank, her eyes staring out the window. She didn't know what Rion was planning, but she trusted him to think fast on his feet.

With their lives on the line, taking a backseat wasn't like her. It had been such a long time since she'd trusted a man. But at the moment, letting Rion take the lead seemed natural. He bore the weight of the negotiation well, without so much as a flinch of emotion.

He appeared steady, in total control. "Is there a spaceship in the museum I can use to fly home?"

She didn't move. Didn't breathe. Was the ship here? Would Drake actually allow them to go free?

Ever so slightly, Drake nodded.

Rion's voice remained businesslike. "In return for your looking the other way, I'm prepared to offer something valuable in return."

"What?" Drake asked, eyebrow raised.

Rion leaned over the desk, his face intense. "Dragonblood."

Marisa sucked in a breath. Tor and Honor had fought for centuries over their differences. And for over a thousand years, Honor hadn't given up the biological advantage.

The sheer beauty of Rion's plan, strengthening the Torans so they could fight the Unari, was not only brilliant, it would become a galactic legend—if it worked. Yet there were parts to this exchange she didn't understand. She and Rion were prisoners here. There was nothing to stop Drake from taking their blood by force and giving it to the Toran people.

Drake scowled at Rion. "What trick are you playing?"

"None." Rion's face remained open, honest.

Marisa found herself holding her breath and had to remind herself to relax.

Drake eyed Rion with cynicism. "For centuries Tor and Honor have been either at war or vicious competitors. Dragonshaping gave Honor the advantage. Why would you give that up?"

"If Torans become dragonshapers, you can out the moles. You can kick out the Unari."

"But if they are already here and they also become dragonshapers—"

"The Unari can't dragonshape. Their genetics won't allow them to morph."

Marisa expected Drake to accept immediately, but the man remained cautious.

"And how would our becoming dragonshapers help you?" Drake asked.

"You fear Honorian dragonshapers, and as long as you fear us, you won't help us, and we won't become true allies. For us to have a real alliance, we need to be equals. Genuine equals."

"You think after centuries of mistrust, your dragonblood will unify us?"

"It would be a start. As a gesture of good faith, I will give you our dragonblood—no matter whether you decide to give us the spaceship or not."

"No matter if we help Honor or not?" Drake leaned forward, his eyes intent. "Why would you do that?"

"Because you'll fight the Unari here on Tor. And anyone who fights my enemy helps my world. Any Unari foothold in this solar system will eventually hurt Honor. But you can't effectively fight the Unari without dragonblood. You don't even know who they are."

Marisa realized the problem of outing Unari spies on Earth would be much more difficult. Every Honorian could dragonshape. Apparently, so could every Toran. But on Earth, only ten percent of the population had the correct genes. And a chill skimmed down her spine as she imagined the frightening scenario where Unari infiltrated Earth's governments, military, and conglomerates.

Drake nodded. "Dragonshaping would help us secure our world."

"Still, the battle won't be easy," Rion warned. "But if you understand what those Unari bastards do . . . you'll fight to your last breath."

"You'll really just give us—"

Rion lowered his voice to a harsh whisper. "Do you want the blood or not?"

"Yes." Drake rubbed his brow, as if his temple ached. "And the ship—such as it is—is yours."

Rion stood and held out his arm. "Thank you."

Drake clasped his forearm. "I've heard you're a man of honor."

Rion smiled. "I would like my grandchildren to grow up free from the Unari, knowing true peace between our worlds."

"Goddess willing, the dragonblood will allow us to find the Unari moles. Once we rid our world of Unari, we can use Tor as a base to kick the Tribes out of the solar system for good."

Marisa hoped he was right, that this alliance would last.

"I will do what I can," Rion agreed. "Now, will you take us to that ship?"

"You actually lucked out. As part of a joint project with a local university, my best engineering team has been making extensive renovations on the ship."

"How far have they gotten?" Rion asked.

"It's a work in progress." Drake grinned and gestured to his door. "Come on. I'll show you."

The greatest conqueror is he who overcomes the enemy without a blow.

—SUN TZU

12

Marisa and Rion followed Drake through the museum, and Marisa caught sight of Merlin several times, always from the corner of her eye. Drake didn't seem to notice the bird, possibly because Merlin was adept at staying in the shadows and merging into the backgrounds of the interactive displays.

Rion strode beside her, his pace relaxed, yet he remained vigilant, constantly scanning rooms and people as they passed through a series of exhibits. She recognized some displays, basic astronomy or geology in holographic presentations, but others, like a series of floating cubes that changed colors and shapes, baffled her.

"So you are in contact with other Enforcers in the city?" she asked Drake. The question had been burning in her mind ever since he'd admitted to knowing they were coming to the museum.

He glanced sideways at her. "Not all Enforcers are in league with the Unari."

"You've organized a secret network?" Rion asked.

"Yes. We've been watching and monitoring transporter traffic in an attempt to figure out who the Unari are and who's working for them. We're especially interested in anyone who comes through the transporter illegally."

Rion raised his eyebrow. "It happens often?"

"More than you'd think. Most illegal traffic is sophisticated smugglers trying to avoid paying import taxes. But every once in a while, someone comes through that I suspect is a spy or a mole. So I keep tabs on them. But it's frustrating, because the Unari are very good at hiding among us."

Marisa was surprised Drake had acknowledged so much and wondered if his underground network might be even more elaborate than he'd just admitted. And once again, she had to consider why Drake trusted Rion at all.

The next display they passed demonstrated cooking techniques, complete with the delicious scent of food and free samples. From there Drake led them into a domed area the length of three football fields. Hundreds, maybe a thousand flying machines of every shape and size rested on pedestals, hung from the ceiling, or floated on antigravs.

"These machines look really old." Marisa craned her neck, looking for something that wasn't rusted, pitted, or corroded.

Drake nodded. "They're ancient. My people used these machines before the portal opened two thousand years ago."

Marisa looked at Rion and tried to suppress her shock. "Are you telling me we're going to travel to Honor in a spaceship that hasn't worked for—"

"We can fix, renovate, and modernize the ship." Drake pointed to a flurry of activity around one of the ships.

A crane lifted a small capsule, about half the size of a car and shaped like a child's spinning top. Talk about cramped. She wondered if she and Rion would even fit inside.

But even worse, men in dark lab coats were pulling wires from the machine and tossing them into a coiled stack. Black oily metal that stank like old cheese had her breathing through her mouth. Worst of all, rusty cracks crisscrossed the spaceship's hull.

"That machine's a death trap," she whispered to no one in particular, then realized how ungrateful she sounded. "I'm sorry," she said to Rion and Drake. "I know you think this is the best way—"

"It's the *only* way," Rion interrupted.

The capsule didn't look any stronger than a tin can. She wasn't a rocket scientist, but she understood basic physics. "But that structure won't hold pressure or air. Even if you fix the leaks, what's going to keep us from burning up as we enter the atmosphere?"

Drake told her, "We're cannibalizing parts from these other machines."

The other machines were just as old. Decrepit. She'd seen better metal in a junkyard.

She didn't want to insult these people or upset the new alliance. She reminded herself that Rion hadn't gone to all the trouble of bringing her here to get her killed. She had to trust him. Still . . . "We'll test it before we—"

"I'm afraid not," Drake said. "We have only one booster."

Marisa shook her head. Every brain cell was calling

her a fool to trust her life to the dilapidated capsule. As the men inside worked, light shone outward through penny-sized fissures in the hull. That capsule had no more chance of flying than her Lexus.

Rion must have followed her stare. "I'm sure Drake's men can weld the holes."

She tried to keep her tone reasonable. "I appreciate what you're trying to do, but your people have traveled by transporter for so long that I'm concerned you've forgotten the basics of space travel. For us to breathe, the ship needs to hold air. And stand up to huge pressures and heat. We need protection from radiation, shielding from space dust. A braking system when we land. Computer systems to navigate. A decent engine to boost us away from Tor's gravity."

Rion turned and placed his hands on her shoulders. "It's going to be okay. We won't go until you think it's safe."

"WHILE YOUR MEN work on the ship, could you take us to a medical lab?" Rion asked.

Drake turned and led them down another corridor. "This way."

The medical facility consisted of a tiny room with little more than a few cabinets stocked with basic medical equipment. It would do. Rion entered the room and turned around. "Do you have a physician on staff?"

"We have a nurse." Drake sent an Enforcer to fetch the nurse.

Marisa took a chair near the door.

Rion sat on the exam table and rolled up his sleeve. "We'll need to draw my blood."

Drake frowned. "And then what?"

Rion grinned. "That's all you need."

"Out!" Drake dismissed the Enforcers. And he slammed the door shut behind them, leaving only Marisa, Rion, and Drake in the room. He lowered his voice to an angry hiss. "We are not stupid. Don't you think that over the centuries we've taken blood from dragonshapers? A simple blood transfusion will not alter our genetics."

"*My* blood will," Rion assured him.

As a male nurse came inside, Rion looked up. "Can you take blood from my arm and place it into a sterile container?"

"Yes, sir." The nurse looked at Drake for permission.

"Do it." Drake folded his arms and leaned against the door. "What's so special about your blood?"

"My father is from Honor and my mother is from Tor. My blood carries the genes you need."

Drake's eyes lit with hope. "How can you be so certain?"

"I've done it before." There was no need to reveal that his uncle Phen could dragonshape.

The nurse wrapped his upper arm in tight tubing. Rion made a fist. The nurse inserted the needle into his vein.

Rion focused on Marisa. Sweet Goddess. The approval shining on her face humbled him.

"You are not to speak of what you've heard here," Drake told the nurse.

"My lips will never speak of the sacred gift. But if this is dragonblood, I'm willing to volunteer for the experiment." The nurse looked at Rion. "How much blood must I infuse into Toran veins to allow us to dragonshape?"

"Three drops."

"How long until the Torans will be able to make their own dragonblood?" Marisa asked, her tone casual. He understood her concern. If the Torans held him here to keep producing more blood, they could delay his journey for way too long.

"The gene replicates quickly. If you inject my blood into Drake's veins today, in thirty more days, he can give dragonblood to your people."

Tears of gratitude shone in the nurse's eyes, and his hands shook as he removed the needle from Rion's arm and held the precious packet of blood. "I will pray to the Goddess for your safety."

Drake appeared mesmerized by the blood. "Go ahead. Inject both of us."

While the nurse went about his work, Drake asked Rion, "Is there anything more we can do for you?"

"You mentioned you had contacts in the city. As you know from the tracer recordings, Phen helped us and was injured. Could you find out his condition for me? And if possible, could the recordings where he is mentioned by name be destroyed?"

"I will do what I can," Drake agreed.

The offer sounded genuine, and Rion's hopes soared at the thought that there might someday be a brotherhood between their two worlds.

Love is like water. We can fall in it. We can drown in it. We can't live without it.

—UNKNOWN

13

Marisa paced in the quarters Drake had assigned, an apartment reserved for visiting museum lecturers that consisted of a living area and sleeping quarters. She'd tried to nap, but between overexhaustion and residual adrenaline, she was too unsettled to sleep.

Rion had gone off with Drake to check on Phen and bring back food. What was taking him so long to return?

She was watching the starscape of the city floating in the clouds when the door opened and Rion walked in with containers of piping-hot food. Bless him. The scent of sweetmeats made her salivate.

Rion seemed quite pleased with himself and answered one of her questions before she could ask. "Sorry it took so long. Drake's a busy man, and we had to wait until his Enforcer contact in the city got back to us. But Phen was making a good recovery in the medical center before he disappeared."

"He escaped?"

"Looks like it." Rion grinned and set the food containers on a table in front of the sofa. He tossed her a shirt and slacks. "See what else I brought us." From his backpack he pulled out a small bottle of red liquid—a bottle that couldn't have held more than eight ounces.

"Wine?" She plucked a piece of meat from one of the containers and popped it into her mouth. A burst of flavors curled on her tongue, a crisp sweet-sour with a hint of apricots.

His eyes sparkled in obvious pleasure. "Not just any wine. This is Alazon, a gift of the Goddess—well, actually a peace offering from Drake." He twisted a cork from the bottle and placed the neck under her nose. "Breathe."

She sniffed. "Nice." The wine had a very distinctive scent that reminded her of chocolate-covered strawberries that had been soaked in rum.

"Nice?" He chuckled to take the sting from his objection. "This bottle is over three centuries old. The grapes were grown during the year of the eclipse on Albarin IV, a planet in the Waycom System, and harvested by hand, then transported at exactly the right temperature with no more than half a degree variation, and it has been stored in darkness with not even a hint of light shed on the bottle. Until now."

He poured the wine with care, filling her glass about halfway. She didn't want to spoil his enthusiasm, but, in truth, she was much more interested in the food. Telling her gnawing stomach pangs to wait, she picked up the glass and breathed in the bouquet. This time the scent shot directly to her brain. For lack of a better word, she was already intoxicated. And she had yet to take a sip. The aroma opened her senses. She became much more aware of Rion's smile, the way one side of his mouth curved just a tad higher than the other, of the sexy stubble of beard on his jaw, of her own pulse's increased rhythm.

"Are you trying to take advantage of my empty stomach to get me drunk?" she asked.

He threw back his head and laughed. "You can't get drunk on Alazon. In fact, it has no intoxication properties at all."

She frowned at her glass. "Then what exactly am I feeling?"

"Your true feelings. With none of the doubts, none of the worries, none of the complications that hold us back. After we eat, when I kiss you and make love to you, you'll simply feel, sense, hear, and see details that you usually overlook or block."

Wow. He'd just given her a lot to process. His intent to make love to her had to go to the top of the list. Wine and the promise of making love sounded good to her. Between the danger stalking them and the danger that awaited ahead, tonight would be for them.

Rion clinked his glass with hers and then drank. He helped himself to fruit and some cheese.

Marisa sipped the wine and began to eat the food he'd brought. At first, she didn't notice anything different. The food tasted really good. But then she was really hungry. She swallowed more wine and noted her fears dropping away. She didn't forget the Unari invasion of Tor, or the spaceship that would never fly safely without a major overhaul, but she didn't allow it to sour this moment. She was solidly in the now, more than she'd ever been. She still knew that Drake could break down the door and arrest them, she just didn't care.

No, that was wrong. She did care. It was just that her

thoughts didn't focus on her worries. Instead, she appreciated the flavors of food, the strange mix of textures and tastes.

And she couldn't take her gaze from Rion. He looked larger-than-life, extraordinarily handsome, extremely comfortable in his own skin, warm and open. Attentive to her every need.

He handed her a napkin, then fed her a tidbit from his plate. "Taste. It's an orangeberry, spiced with cinnamon."

His fingertips stroked her lips, the sexiest caress. She opened her mouth, and he slipped the orangeberry onto her tongue. When she closed her mouth, the pad of his thumb smoothed her lips, leaving an aching trail.

She chewed, then swallowed the delicious juice, and without hesitation sucked his finger into her mouth. Used her tongue to lap at his flesh. And all the while she locked gazes with him, a heat swooping deep into her belly.

Excitement poured straight into her core. Her nipples tightened. Anticipation, adrenaline, and desire surged through her system. She wanted Rion. That this passion was stoked by her growing feelings for him left her breathless. If she could have been anywhere in the universe right now, she would have chosen to be here. With Rion.

She accepted that while the wine had enhanced her senses, she was clearheaded. It didn't matter that Rion was from another world. That he'd kidnapped her. That they might die tomorrow. They had now. And she intended to make the most of this moment.

She'd just finished a gourmet meal. They were alone. As safe as she'd been since she'd arrived.

"Mm." She sipped the last of her wine and kissed Rion, aching to press her body against his. He placed his hands on her hips, splayed his fingers over her buttocks, his fingers drawing slow and sensuous strokes that shot a tingle of heat between her thighs.

His mouth angled over hers, and his tongue on her lips sent a shiver of anticipation through her. His lips were soft and tasted of wine, and she wanted this kiss to last and last and last. But at the same time, she ached to press her bare skin against his. She needed a stronger connection. Fumbling with his clothing, she finally removed his shirt, then his pants, pleased to find that he wore nothing beneath.

Then he was standing there naked, kissing her while she remained fully dressed. A zing of feminine power flowed through her. Yet even as she appreciated his wide silver-toned shoulders, his broad chest, flat stomach, straining sex, and lean thighs, she appreciated the kind of confidence he possessed to allow her to have her way.

She wanted him. What could be more natural?

She kissed his neck, nibbled a path over his collarbone, and breathed in his male scent. At the same time, she tried to memorize the feel of his muscles. His skin was firm, almost hot to the touch, his muscles flexing under her exploration.

"Enjoying yourself?" he murmured into her ear, his tone low and husky.

"Oh, yeah." She tugged gently on one of his chest curls. Then she licked away the pain and enjoyed the goose bumps of pleasure that rose on his skin. She tugged more curls and again licked away the sting, letting him imagine where she'd go next and enjoying that he was allowing her to do whatever she wished, explore for however long she liked.

Lazily, she nibbled his chest, trailing her lips down to his stomach and over his hip. She bit his skin, just hard enough to sting.

With a grunt, he threaded his hands into her hair, massaging her scalp. She swirled her tongue into his belly button, a cute little inny, and he sucked in his breath hard.

She mischievously ignored his gorgeous silver sex. Instead, she trailed her fingers along the insides of his thighs, taking delight as he released a low groan.

"Turn around," she said.

His eyes widened, his nostrils flared, but a smile softened his face. He nodded and did as she asked.

"Part your legs for me."

Again he complied, leaving her free to play with his tight ass, skim her fingers between his legs. She couldn't resist a few tiny bites along his cheeks, followed by soothing caresses.

Never had she been so bold. Or enjoyed herself more. The idea of all that coiled power beneath her fingertips, just waiting for her next touch, turned her on. "God. You're beautiful."

He whirled suddenly, like a tiger uncaged. "I can't . . . wait any longer." He swept his hands into her hair. His fingers fisted and he yanked back her head, taking total control.

Another spear of pleasure shot through her. Here was a man who knew how to give. And he knew how to take. He held her on tiptoe, her back arched, her breasts tipped upward. Fire in his eyes spread through her. Still holding her hair, he ripped off her shirt and unsnapped her bra. In moments she stood in her panties. Then, still holding her, he eased his grip and his gaze raked her.

As if his searing look was a kiss, the heat inside her burned hotter. Every inch of her flesh seemed raw, tense, drawn tight. The dragon scales along the insides of her limbs fluttered, the sensation shooting tingles of delight through her.

And he had yet to touch her.

Was her dragonblood making her hot? Needy? The rush of sensation was leaving her weak in the knees.

The Alazon wine alone couldn't be wreaking all this havoc, making her breath come in gasps, her scales undulate, her pulse rush in her ears.

"Touch me, damn you." She barely recognized her own voice, so tight, so deep and needy.

He released her hair and then gently touched her nipples, and only her nipples, with his fingertips. At the exquisite sensation, she released her breath, and it came out a soft sigh. She so needed more. More pressure, more skin. More Rion.

Her breasts tingled and ached. She wanted him to touch more of her. But maddeningly, he kept right on teasing her nipples. She closed her hands into fists, trying to hold still, determined to enjoy every second.

Talk about sweet torture. There seemed to be a direct line of nerves from her breasts to her tingling core.

Could she have an orgasm just from what he was doing to her breasts? Or was she simply going to die from frustration? She licked her lip. "I . . . can't take . . . much more."

"Sure you can. You will." His tone was low and rough. He kept the same light pressure, the same infuriatingly slow and tender tempo. "You like this, don't you?"

"Yes . . . but . . ." She wanted to place her hands over

his to stop the torment. Or reach out and draw him against her. Her desire to feel his heat directly against her bare flesh intensified. Yet, wondrous heat and tension curled through her and she didn't want him to stop.

"If you can hold out, I'm going to give another of your sweet spots this same treatment." He was full of hot promises, his words silken threads that captured her in his web.

When she didn't think she could last another second, he dipped his head and took her nipple between his lips. And sucked hard.

She would have lost it then. But he clasped his hands on her hips to hold her. Very slowly, he closed his teeth around her nipple. While his tongue flashed over the tip, his hands dipped beneath her panties, down past her curls, between her moist folds.

The instant he touched the right spot, she exploded and saw stars. Her bones melted, as if all the tension that gripped her flared and burst, her nerve endings firing in one vast and mighty blast.

Vaguely, she felt herself falling, Rion catching her. Then the bliss of his flesh against hers had her clutching him. One moment of pleasure was not enough. She needed more. She needed him inside her.

He scooped her into his arms, carried her to the bed, and laid her on soft sheets that smelled like spring rain. After slipping off her panties, he parted her thighs. And this time he placed his lips there.

Right there.

Exactly where she craved.

All the tension that had exploded and burst contracted back in on itself. Only this time the edge was sharper. The flames burned hotter. Panting, desperate for him to fill her, she tugged on his shoulders, but he kept his mouth firmly on her sweet spot, his tongue flicking maddeningly.

When she tumbled over the edge the second time, her legs jerked, her arms flailed. Her hips arched off the bed. And still he didn't release her.

He gave her no time to recover. No time for her pulse to slow or her lungs to catch a breath.

Her pleasure was like a series of waves, each one crashing a bit higher than the last, then withdrawing, then peaking ever higher. And she just kept cresting.

He seemed insatiable, and she let herself go. Let herself enjoy every moment, every stroke, every kiss and caress.

When they finally joined flesh to flesh, it was all the bliss she'd craved. He filled her completely, and as his hips pumped, as she raised her legs to take him deeper inside, she reveled in how good they were together.

Finally, she'd met . . . the right one . . . the right man.

A lover for her. A lover for . . . forever.

Danger can come from any direction.
—FIRST HONORIAN WARLORD

14

O pen the door," Drake shouted.

Marisa awakened slowly. To chaos and pounding on the door. Rion leaped out of bed, where they'd fallen asleep just a few hours ago after making love yet again.

"We've been betrayed," Drake shouted. "Unari Enforcers are on the way."

"Give us one minute," Rion muttered, his tone deep and determined.

"Don't take two."

Pulse accelerating, Marisa leaped from the bed. Rion was three steps ahead and tossing clothing at her. She recalled him ripping off her tunic last night, but the nanobots had repaired the tear.

They dressed quickly, and Rion slipped his backpack over his shoulders and jerked open the door. Drake's green-tinged skin had turned grayish; his voice was high-pitched and anxiety-filled. "Come on. Come on. If we can launch the capsule, we can get you away before they arrive."

"Can you claim I stole the ship?" Rion suggested as they sprinted down the hallway that led to the spacecraft.

Drake didn't answer Rion directly. "My welfare isn't as important as yours." Rion shot him a questioning look, and Drake continued, "The Unari Enforcers know you are the crown prince of Chivalri."

Marisa stumbled. Crown prince of Chivalri? Rion? What the hell?

"Keep your voice down," Rion muttered to Drake but glanced at her. "Most of my own people don't know my true title."

She'd heard his secret. Rion had lied to her. And his lack of trust in her stung.

Last night she'd almost told him she had deep feelings for him. How could she have been so stupid to let passion overrule her judgment? Somehow she'd let him slip past her defenses, allowed her hopes and dreams to convince her that he was the man she wanted.

Assessing her situation right now made her head spin. Even worse, she couldn't decide if she was more disappointed with Rion's lack of trust in her, or with herself for believing they had more going for them than just a common enemy and hot sex.

They sprinted up to the capsule. She didn't want to look at Rion, much less talk to him.

"Get inside. Hurry." Drake's demand pulled her out of her funk.

The spaceship was still a rusty mess. She could see through part of the hull, and the rubbish pile was now larger than the capsule itself. The bundle of wires, tubing, and assorted metal parts spilled into the aisles and flowed like a river of garbage across the massive warehouse. No way could they have rebuilt the interior while she and Rion had . . .

She'd think about it later. Right now she had to focus.

"Let's go." Rion beckoned her to follow.

She fisted her hands on her hips and planted her feet. "Are you insane? That capsule's a death trap."

Merlin soared from the rafters, circled the capsule, flew in and back out, then inside once again. So much for the bird's intelligence.

Rion lowered his voice and clamped his hand over her wrist. "I had a flash. We'll be okay. Besides, staying here is not an option."

They didn't have time to argue. Damn him. He didn't trust her with his identity, but he expected her to trust him and his flashes—enough to lay her life on the line.

A communications unit on Drake's arm beeped. "Yes?"

"Five minutes before Unari Enforcers arrive."

"Understood." Drake glared at her but spoke to Rion. "Leave her, or knock her out if you must take her with you, but you need to launch now."

Before she could step into the capsule, Rion lifted her into his arms and carried her inside.

"This isn't necessary," she said.

"Hurry," Drake urged.

It would have been dark inside the capsule, except beams of light leaked in from outside. If the engines were in the same dilapidated condition as the hull, they'd never start, never mind launch them into space.

When Drake and his men used a machine to secure the hatch, the metal shrieked in protest. No doubt over thousands of years it had warped. The sharp clang of the hatch made her feel even more trapped.

Dust kicked into her lungs and she coughed as her eyes teared. Rion coughed, too, set her down on an oily and corroded floor, and slipped the pack from his back. Even Merlin made odd choking noises.

When the dust settled and Marisa could breathe again, she looked around. There was no instrument panel. No seats. No controls. For all she knew, there was no engine. The capsule was like a hollow metal eggshell cracked in dozens of places. A few rusty bolts held the metal skeleton together—but everything else was missing: engineering, navigation, stabilizers. They had no oxygen, food, water, or bathroom facilities.

From outside, Drake issued orders. "Spread out. Don't reveal which ship they're in."

Marisa and Rion were locked in, wrapped up like a tidy present for the Unari Enforcers. Crouching low, Rion contorted his body, touching every crack, every indentation.

"What are you doing?" At the sound of shouting, she peered through a hole in the hull. "Unari Enforcers are marching into the museum and securing the perimeter."

"Do they know where we are?" Rion asked.

Her heart pounded. "Not yet, but it won't be long."

"Drake will stall them as long as he can." Rion ran his fingers along the cracks.

"They're working a grid pattern through the room, searching the ships one by one. It's only a matter of time—"

"According to my flash"—Rion kneeled on the floor,

dug grime out of a crack—"there's an indentation in the hull for the key Merlin brought us."

"An indentation?" She tipped her head to look at the ceiling. And that's when she spied a triangular impression in the hull connected to a straight rod with a rounded end.

The Enforcers started searching the ship next to theirs. She and Rion had less than a minute before they were discovered.

"Is that it?" she whispered and pointed.

"Good work." Rion reached for his pack and unzipped a compartment and pulled out the key. "Got it."

Enforcers strode over to where they hid. One of them pounded on the side of the ship. She winced as dust flew into her eyes again.

Another Enforcer peered between the cracks. "They're in here."

"We've got them." Enforcers swarmed from all directions.

Whatever Rion was going to do, he needed to do it fast. "Hurry."

Reaching up, he inserted the key into the matching indentation. She heard a click, and then the world . . . changed. The capsule disappeared. The room vanished. So did the smell of old dust and spilled oil.

She looked around in shock. Rion, Merlin, and Marisa now sat on the bridge of a modern starship.

Only the key was now embedded in a shiny black plate high above their heads on a semicircular starship bridge with giant view screens that showed the vessel already traveling on course for Honor.

"Am I dreaming?" She stood and spun around to take

in the starship, a vessel so large it couldn't have fit in the museum.

Rion grinned and placed his fists on his hips. "I think we're in multidimensional space."

"I don't understand. This ship was old. Now it's new and shiny and huge."

"The ancient ones had secrets we can't duplicate—like the transporters. This ship and the key may be from ancient times."

She folded her arms across her chest. "Well, wherever we are, it's way better than where we were." She squinted at him with suspicion. "You didn't hide your knowledge of this technology, did you?"

"No." He looked her straight in the eyes. "I only hid my birthright. I am the crown prince of Chivalri."

"And you didn't tell *me* because . . ."

"I tell no one. Ever. Even when I served as a military commander, my men didn't know of my royal blood. That's how I've survived my entire life. Not even my own people know my title."

"But I've agreed to stay and help you."

"And you could change your mind again."

His words hurt. "Is that what you think I'd do?"

"I don't know you well enough to be certain you'd keep your word. It's possible that you only stayed with me to learn my plans."

"Why would I do that?"

"Maybe you'd try to bargain with the Enforcers. Turn over the information on me in exchange for their promise not to invade Earth."

She stared at him. "I'm not that conniving."

"I'm sorry. I couldn't take the chance. If I'd trusted you

and then you'd gone and told the Torans who I was, you could have stopped me from going to Honor. I couldn't risk that."

"Phen knows who you are. And so did Drake," she said sadly, realizing Rion had lied to her yet again by telling her no one knew his identity.

"Phen's my uncle. Drake figured it out—"

"And what am I to you?" Hurt slammed her, but she wanted to understand. "And why don't even your own people know that you're in line for the throne?"

"The deception started before I was born. A flash revealed to my father that I was targeted for assassination. To save me, he had my cousin Erik and me trade places. We kept our own names. But back home, everyone believed Erik was heir to the throne. I was a free man. But once I claim my title as a prince, I'm an assassin's target. A threat. A negotiation piece. Take your choice." He paused, then spoke quietly. "I've also had flashes about a traitor—a man who may be the same man my father saw assassinate me in his vision. I haven't seen his face, but he's responsible for killing a rebel group who tried to dig a tunnel to retake the Honorian transporter. And he possibly gave intel to the Unari that will prevent dragonshapers from going to the hills for platinum. I kept secrets to protect not just myself but my people."

"What else haven't you told me?" she asked softly.

She expected him to make denials. Instead he took both her hands in his, holding them tightly. "There's something else you should know."

"What?" Marisa swallowed hard, realizing that whatever he had to say wouldn't be easy for him. And that whatever it was, he knew she wouldn't like it.

"I can never marry an offworlder."

She didn't understand. "But your mother was from Tor."

"When the Unari invaded, my mother was an outsider and Honorians blamed her. The charges were unfair. But that didn't matter. The resulting discord weakened my country and helped tear us apart. I won't repeat my parents' mistakes. I need to bring my people back together. I have no choices in this. My people need stability. Unity. I have to marry an Honorian."

An outsider, her, would cause strife. Distrust. Well, he'd certainly answered her question about what she was to him. A fling. With no chance for more.

Eager to put distance between herself and Rion, she strode toward the view screen and gazed out at the stars. The view was dark, cold. Infinite emptiness.

Between what Rion had just told her, her disappointment, and the sudden change in the space-time continuum, her head ached. She rubbed her temples.

Still confused by the sudden turn of events, she turned around and caught sight of Merlin. She wandered over to the owl. His talons gripped the console. He pecked at the controls, as if he were steering the ship.

No wonder her head hurt. Marisa was losing it, attributing paranormal powers to a bird. But why shouldn't she be thinking insane thoughts? She was flying with a man she had feelings for to a world she knew little about, one occupied by Earth's most ancient enemy.

Why was she risking her life for a man who had just told her they couldn't have a future together?

It is almost as good as bringing good news not to bring bad.

—CELTIC PROVERB

15

Awed and stunned by the sleek spaceship, Rion looked around, taking in the helm. He yearned to use the navigation instruments to plot their heading, to make sure they were on course for Honor.

But Merlin had settled by the controls, and a glance out the view screen at his home world told Rion they were on course.

Rion's curiosity and elation over evading the Unari Enforcers dissipated when he looked at Marisa. She wouldn't meet his eyes. But he didn't have to see her face to recognize her anger.

With any other woman, he would have shrugged off his lies. Keeping his identity hidden was more important than hurt feelings.

But this was Marisa. The woman he'd kidnapped and who had still offered to help him. A woman who could put a higher cause before her own interests. Marisa, who was willingly risking her life and agreeing to use her telepathy to save his people.

And he'd hurt her. Deeply. He could see it in her stiff posture, in the way she refused to look at him.

Taking a deep breath, he moved closer to her. "I'm sorry I couldn't be truthful."

"Your apology doesn't make me feel better." She raised her eyebrow, the sadness in her voice yet one more indication of her hurt.

"Will you hear me out?" He headed to a padded bench in the hopes she would join him.

"Why?" She looked at him with big eyes full of sorrow. "I really don't see the point."

He ignored her statement. Ignored her refusal to join him on the bench. "When my father saw me die in the flash, he couldn't see the murderer. His only clue to help save me was my age, which he estimated between three and five."

"Since you're still alive, I'm assuming your cousin taking your place as prince changed the future."

"Yes. Erik and I were born within three weeks of each other. My father switched us shortly after birth. Erik was brought up as a prince, and he lived at the palace with my parents."

"You were sent to live with your aunt and uncle?" she guessed. "So how did Erik survive?"

He shrugged. "We don't know. Maybe the switch changed our fates. It's happened before, flashes that allow us to alter the future. But although Erik seemed safe, my father still refused to let me return to my rightful place."

"Why not?"

"He saw many flashes, all leading to my death." Rion had long since accepted the necessity of his father's action. "If I hadn't had flashes, my parents might not have told me who I really was until I'd reached adulthood. But my gift is well known to pass only through the royal line of Chivalri. So I was trained from the time I could walk to never speak of my flashes, to never reveal my true identity."

"Your aunt and uncle . . . were they loving people?" she asked.

Odd how she speared straight to the difficult part of his past.

"I was well fed, clothed, and educated. I wanted for nothing—including love. My aunt and uncle could have resented the bargain they'd made. Giving up their own son couldn't have been easy."

His aunt and uncle had done their best by him. And he missed them with all his heart. He couldn't bring himself to speak about his last day at home, the day someone had betrayed him, and the Unari had come searching for the Chivalri prince. Because of him, his aunt and uncle had died screaming in pain, sacrificing themselves so he could live. "Raising me . . . was not easy."

"Why am I not surprised?" She cocked her head and folded her arms over her chest. "Did you lie to them, too?"

"Sometimes," he acknowledged, recalling how they hadn't understood his curiosity about the world, how they had sought to keep him safe from all things, how the boy in him found their overprotectiveness stifling. "I often escaped to the palace to play with my cousin. My real parents treated me as a beloved nephew. It was difficult for us. Perhaps most of all for Erik. Raised as Chivalri's future king, he was brought up with wealth, power, and privilege, yet he knew that when my father died or abdicated, it would be me who took the throne." Rion paused. "But that time never came. Erik saved me. And the Unari took over and . . ." So many good people had died that day. It would not be in vain. He'd promised his dying uncle that he would return and set his people free. "You know the rest."

"Why did you keep up the deception after you left Honor?" She paced in front of him, her steps quick and furious.

"When I landed on Pendragon, survival was my primary goal. I didn't speak to anyone until I'd healed from the crash and hiked to civilization. As an uninvited alien, I was uncertain of my welcome. To survive, I went even deeper undercover and hid not just my heritage, but my ability to dragonshape, as well as my planet of origin."

"But you told my brother you came from another world. Why not tell him your position, too?"

He shrugged. "Telling him could have put him in danger. I suspected that the Unari have advance teams already in place on Pendragon and Earth. And if those advance teams had known I lived, that your brother knew, the Unari wouldn't have hesitated to come after him to get to me."

Anger and understanding flashed in her eyes. "You kept your secret because it was to your advantage to do so."

"I did." He should have known she'd accept nothing less than the entire truth. "I may be the only surviving member of the royal family. It's up to me to free my people."

"I get it." She shook her head. "You must put the safety of your people before everything else."

He lowered his voice. "There won't be any more lies. I'm all out of secrets." He shot her a contrite look. "I really am sorry."

Her expression didn't soften. She didn't say anything.

He sighed. "I'm going to tell you something that I've never told anyone."

Still she said nothing.

"While the needs of my world must come before my own, and the needs of my people must come before my own honor, I don't have the luxury of taking the high road—not when that decision means billions of my people are at risk." He leaned back and closed his eyes. "Choosing between duty and honor is a choice no man should have to make. In truth, Erik might have been more cut out for the role of king than I will ever be."

"Because he was raised in the palace?"

"Perhaps."

"If you weren't born to be king, what would you have chosen?"

"As a kid?" He grinned. "I wanted to be a planetary explorer. As I grew up, any career where I didn't have to spend hours in school studying diplomacy, protocol, leadership skills, and military tactics held major appeal."

Her tone was soft but threaded with thoughtfulness. "So you don't covet power?"

"Power is merely a tool, which can be used for good or evil. But I would prefer to be a leader of peace, not war."

Marisa sat on the bench, kicked off her shoes, and tucked her legs under her. Her spine was straight, her blue eyes thoughtful yet steely with determination. "If you lie to me again, I won't help you."

"I understand." He had to be grateful for small blessings. Yet he could see that she'd retreated on a personal level, and he was truly sorry for that.

But this withdrawal was for the best. He was becoming too attached.

He stood and located the ship's head, where he quickly turned his skin back to its normal bronze. When he returned to the bridge, Marisa stood staring out the view screen. "On Honor, we don't tint our skin. And when we land, I'd rather we didn't look like Torans."

With a nod, Marisa disappeared into the head. A few minutes later she came out, wearing her Earth clothing—jeans, layered tank tops, a loose jacket, and shoes. Her skin was once again flesh toned, her hair its natural chestnut. It didn't matter what color she was, Marisa was beautiful, regal. Even when disappointed, she handled herself with intelligence and grace.

Merlin hooted shrilly, pecked the touchpad, and fluttered his wings, drawing Rion's attention. A computer voice came through the speaker system. "Captain, I'm picking up a message."

"Play it," Rion ordered.

Another low-pitched voice shrilled through the speaker. "Warning. Warning. Any violation of Honor's planetary space shall be considered a hostile invasion. Turn back or prepare for disintegration."

With a curse, Rion lunged toward the controls. "Computer, are all systems voice activated?"

"Yes, sir."

"Where did that warning originate?" He checked the view screen for signs of an approaching attack.

"A space buoy sent the warning," the computer replied.

Marisa joined Rion and faced the view screen. "Can we retreat and navigate around the buoys?"

"No," the computer replied. "There's a protective ring of buoys around the entire planet."

"Do we have weapons to shoot down a buoy?" Rion asked.

"Yes."

"Will destroying a buoy instigate a counterattack?" he asked.

"Uncertain. If we destroy a buoy, it could trigger an attack from other buoys, from the planet below, or from hostile ships."

"What are our options?" Marisa asked.

"Turning back would be safest," the computer said.

Rion had not come all the way across the galaxy to turn back now. "What else? Give us more information."

The computer said, "Without knowing their weapons capabilities, I can't suggest countermeasures."

"What countermeasures?" Marisa asked.

"We could increase power to the shields," the computer replied.

"Do it," Rion ordered. Beneath his feet the vibrations hummed, and the lights dimmed, but their speed stayed constant.

"We can also increase speed," the computer said.

"When this ship left Tor, our initial jump into space seemed almost instantaneous," Marisa commented. "Can we land on Honor that fast?"

Rion shook his head. "When we left Tor, empty space was a big target. Our destination didn't have to be precise. But landing takes much more precision and requires deceleration time." Rion leaned over his monitor. "Perform evasive maneuvers. Release warm chaff to fool the heat seekers into latching on to our tail dust."

"Commencing evasive maneuvers," the computer said. "Release chaff as necessary. Do you wish to employ the blinding device in the hull?"

"Elaborate," Rion demanded.

"I can alter the hull's cell structure to avoid radar, sonar, and psionic detection."

"Are you saying that we'll become invisible?" Marisa asked.

"Only to their computer instruments. Not to the naked eye."

Rion grasped the concept. Knock out a submarine's instrumentation and the sub went blind. But that didn't stop a man with a periscope from spotting an oncoming missile.

"Why didn't you suggest the blinding tactic first?" Rion asked.

"There's a huge power drain," the computer said. "I'll have to cut life support back to the minimum. And we'll still be a target to any pilot who sees us."

Rion glanced out the view screen. Bright flashes on the planet warned they'd soon have company. "Do whatever it takes to get us down there in one piece."

"That's the problem," the computer said.

"What?"

"With power diverted to other systems, we're going to come down . . . hard."

"So find a soft place to land. An inland waterway. A mud slide. Quicksand. Give us a chance to survive the crash."

"More trouble's on the way." Marisa leaned into the

view screen, staring at the ships blasting off from the planet, leaving huge streaming tails in their wake. "There are hundreds of them."

Unari ships were launching from every continent. The Unari invasion had spread across his world. The bastards.

The bridge lights dimmed, an indication they had only auxiliary power. A red emergency light blinked. The air didn't go stale, but it no longer tasted crisp and clean. The engines strained and roared through the hull.

Marisa spoke quietly. "Computer, I'd like to send a message to Earth."

"Earth?" the computer asked.

"My world."

The computer said, "Lock in the coordinates and I'll transmit a message."

Rion pulled down webbing from the ceiling. "Web in. The harness will help protect us during a battle or a hard landing." He buckled himself in, then continued, "I have Earth's coordinates. But what would you say?"

"I'd warn them about the Unari invasion."

"That's not a good idea. The Unari might trace the message."

She stepped toward the webbing and halted. "Even if they decipher my message, what would be the harm?"

"If they know you've warned Earth, they might move up their invasion plans."

Marisa clenched her hands and sank her fingers into the webbing. The red emergency light flickered over her face. He could see the agony of indecision in her eyes. And yet she stayed calm.

He said softly, "Even if the message gets through, will they believe you without proof?"

"I don't know."

"It's your decision." He spoke quietly, gently. "But whatever you decide, you haven't much time. Those ships will be in shooting range soon."

The computer chimed in. "Thirty seconds."

Marisa stared at the ships, a thousand of them. "God help us."

The spaceship and the planet are subject to the same laws of gravity.

—HONORIAN SCIENTIST

16

Incoming missiles," the computer blared. "Web in for evasive maneuvers."

"Get into your harness," Rion urged Marisa.

Ignoring his warning, she veered toward the console. "I have to warn Earth."

She took two shaky steps. A tremor shook the ship. Rion, already webbed in, grabbed her, twisted the webbing around her, and hung on tight. A second later, the ship quaked and streaks of pink light burst across the view screen. The engines whined, revved up, and accelerated.

G-forces slammed them. If not for the webbing, he'd have been flattened against the hull. He strained to hold Marisa, the tangle of partial webbing aiding his efforts. Her cheek ended up plastered against his chest, and her fingers gripped his shoulders. Sweat dripped down his forehead. He gritted his teeth, and his vision blackened to a narrow tunnel.

"Systems report," he requested.

If the computer answered, he couldn't hear it past the blood rushing through his ears. His vision went black.

Moments later, when he could see again, the ship had slowed. Marisa was still in his arms, unconscious. Merlin was gone.

With no one flying the ship, Rion struggled to untangle the webbing.

His arms locked around Marisa, he fought to regain his footing. Then she lifted her head, opened her eyes. "What happened?"

"Computer, status report?" Rion asked.

"We sustained a hit to the starboard engine. Hull breach is contained. Life support is on the backup generator. Communications are down."

Marisa raised her fist to her mouth. "Oh, God. Earth. I didn't warn them."

"There's nothing you could have done." He gave her a quick hug.

Marisa's eyes were full of regret. "The moment we were in space, I should have used the communicator."

"Stay here." He webbed her in, and she didn't protest.

Lurching to the control console, he glanced at the instrumentation. Enemy ships lit up the screen. Yet their vessel, apparently undetected, appeared to be flying right through the fleet.

The hull's invisibility shield was preventing the Unari computers from targeting them. But once they hit the atmosphere, the pilots would use their own eyes instead of instruments for visuals, and the invisibility shielding would be useless.

"Land on Chivalri," Rion instructed the computer. "It's on the eastern seaboard of the northern continent."

With his soul hungry for sight of home, he wished he had better visuals, but the weather was proving uncooperative. A huge storm had moved in from the sea, and the cloud cover over his homeland didn't allow him to make out the coastline. But it might offer them protection.

"Can we hide our descent in the cloud cover?" he asked the computer.

"Affirmative. According to my sensors, there's fog even at sea level. Unless you have landing coordinates, the lack of visibility will make us dependent on instrumentation for landing."

"Pull up a geographical survey," Rion ordered. He leaned over the console, staring at the map, considering options. If they landed too close to the capital, Unari forces might immediately spot them and take them prisoner.

Rion pointed to a mountainside beside a lake. "This is a private royal hideaway and hidden by mountain peaks. The lake is deep. Can you set us down here?"

"That depends."

"On what?"

"The first strike may have damaged the hull's invisibility screen. It appears the Unari can see this ship from one angle. They've shot five missiles at us. I can avoid three."

"Rion. Web in," Marisa called out.

He pulled down another harness. He had just tightened the last buckle when a missile struck a glancing blow against the stern.

The bridge console sparked bright reds and dark purples. Smoke hissed out of a broken pipe. Then automatic systems snuffed out the fire, creating a white mist that smelled like burned oil.

For a moment, the ship seemed to hang in the sky. Then the vessel tilted, slid sideways, and rolled.

"Are we going to die?" Marisa asked.

Rion reached out and seized her hand. "I don't know. But . . ."

"But?" she prodded.

"I've seen many things that have yet to happen."

He wanted to give her hope. He didn't mention that the flashes often allowed him to see into the future far beyond his normal life span. If his tiny omission of truth could give her comfort, he could live—or die—with that.

The ship rolled stern over bow. The gravity system shut down. Bright orange flashes flared off the hull. But unless he looked out the view screen, he had no sense of the out-of-control somersaulting.

"Where's Merlin?" Marisa peered through the smoke. "Is he steering?"

"We're on autopilot."

"Brace for impact," the computer warned.

"Just once, I'd like to land on a world without crashing," he muttered.

Marisa didn't say anything. She closed her eyes. Her lips moved as if in prayer.

"Give me updates," he ordered the computer.

A missile swished by.

"We just avoided number two. Number three is off the port . . ."

Metal screeched. Fires flared. A roar of wind snuffed out the flames. Their craft had dropped out of space and into the atmosphere like a rock.

"Apply antigravs," Rion commanded.

"Compliance not possible. Deploying the emergency chute."

The canopy snapped open with a jolt, caught air, and jerked them into a spiral as it braked the ship. Slowing down before they crashed was necessary. But it also left them an easier target for missiles four and five.

A gust of wind swerved them sideways and missile four missed. Mountains rose through the clouds. Rion could make out trees and a clearing growing in size as they plummeted.

"Missile five has a lock."

Rion closed his hands into fists. "Evade."

"Evasion is no longer an option. Engines are down. Chances of survival are less than one percent. Missile trajectory is heading straight at us."

He couldn't change the missile's path. He couldn't shoot it down. He couldn't evade.

"Cut the chute," Rion ordered.

"What?" Marisa clung to her webbing. "We're going to crash."

"Better to crash than take another missile hit," he explained.

"Chute cut." The ship plummeted. "Brace for impact. Warning. Warning. Impact in five. Four. Three. Two. One."

MARISA AWAKENED WITH a terrible taste in her mouth. She turned her head and spat out dirt. Dirt? She sat up, stunned, confused. She was sitting in a heap of wreckage in the middle of a forest.

She blinked. And it all came back. She and Rion had crashed on Honor. "Rion?"

Her voice came out a croak. She spat more dirt and raised herself from the pile of smoking debris, metal fragments that had once been a magnificent spaceship. She had a dozen scrapes and cuts. Her entire body was one giant bruise.

Oddly, the scrap metal began to move as if an animal was scavenging among the wreckage for food. Was it Rion? Was he buried and trying to get out from under a mountain of debris?

If he were buried under there, he'd be incinerated. "Rion?"

She tried to scramble toward the parts, determined to pull him from the wreckage. Her head swam, and she was so dizzy she clutched a nearby branch to steady herself. Swaying on her feet, she gulped the thin air, tried to keep her balance.

But her legs collapsed. She sank into the dirt. She was hurt. Really hurt.

"Rion!"

Silence was her only reply.

If she was this hurt, he could be dead. But she didn't want him to be dead. She wanted him to come walking out of the burning wreckage with that charming grin of his and a remark about how she should have faith in his flashes. Damn it. He'd told her they would survive.

"Rion?"

Again there was no reply.

"No!" It didn't matter that they couldn't be together again. It didn't matter that they couldn't have a future together. Or that they couldn't wed. He couldn't be dead.

The wreckage moved, began to reassemble. She couldn't be seeing what she was seeing. But the pieces crawled together as if they were alive and seeking other parts of themselves. Metal fused with metal.

Was she losing her mind?

If this insane machine could fix itself, why hadn't it done so back on Tor? Marisa jerked backward and watched the wreckage in amazement. This really was happening. The ship was growing back together.

She should be more frightened. Her mind was fuzzy, as if the world were coming to her filtered through a gauze-like curtain. She must have been in shock.

But she had to pull herself together. Find Rion.

She took a deep breath. Closed her eyes, willed the dizziness to go away.

Something sticky slid down her cheek. She raised her hand and her sleeve came away bloody.

Her head throbbed. Her mind was clogged, not working properly.

Or she wouldn't be seeing snow. Only the snowflakes weren't like the tiny ones on Earth. These were fist-sized flakes that clung to her clothing and quickly covered the ground. Within minutes the snow had hidden the debris.

If Rion was lying somewhere hurt, he would now be covered, too. God. Was he even alive?

17

Not now. Damn it. Why did his flashes have the habit of arriving at the most inconvenient times? Like after a spaceship crash that had left him dangling in his harness upside down. With his straps caught in the tree, and his arms tangled in the webbing as tight as a straitjacket, he could barely move.

Even if the Unari were on the way to take them prisoner, he couldn't have freed himself and begun his search for Marisa. He had to outwait the series of images in his flash.

A man making love to his woman.
The woman's belly full and round with child.
The woman holding the baby boy up to her lover.

Before Rion could assess details, his flash changed locations.

A soldier united with his mother.

Again his vision switched images, so fast his head spun.

A blue-eyed man called out for "Pendra."

What did it mean? The people were unfamiliar. Yet from their manner of dress and language, he recognized they were from Chivalri.

Rion had too much respect for his gift not to try to remember the details. So he committed what he could to memory—even if all the blood in his body had rushed to his head.

He'd thought the flashes were over. That he could cut himself from the webbing and climb from the tree. But yet another flash hit.

Marisa, wearing clothing from Earth, sat on the ground, her back against a tree. Snow crusted her hair.

Rion hadn't been able to see her face. Hadn't seen if she'd been breathing.

Had she been sleeping? Hurt? Dead?

Sweet Goddess. She needed him, and he must find her, help her. He wasn't going to let her die. Not this woman. Not Marisa.

Rion swore. He twisted in his bonds, straining for his knife.

But the webbing bound him tight. He had only one way out. Dragonshaping would require using precious energy reserves, but he had no choice. His body expanded to twenty times his human size, and his arms extended into powerful wings. His skin thickened and changed color until dark purple scales covered his body.

The straps popped as if they were no more than string. His clothing shredded. Free of the harness, he plunged toward the ground. Spreading his powerful wings, he employed an updraft to stop his deadly fall.

He'd dragonshaped every six weeks during his lifetime to feed on the platinum that maintained his energy reserves. But this time the dragonshaping slammed him with sickening pain. Smoke poured from his nostrils.

He bellowed in fury.

Terrible electric shocks zigzagged down his spine and over his wings. Agony cramped his stomach, pounded through his skull.

He barely landed safely on the ground before he humanshaped. Almost instantly, his shredded clothing repaired itself and, more importantly, the pain disappeared. He gasped in huge breaths, stunned. In dragonshape, every nerve ending had felt as if it had been bathed in acid. His mind took a few moments to clear.

Then he swore.

That terrible agony he'd suffered had been due to the Tyrannizer. And the machine projected that pain onto every dragonshaper on Honor. No wonder his people couldn't break free of the Unari domination.

Holy Goddess.

The dragonshapers who'd had to bear that agony for three endless years would have been better off dead. He prayed his parents had not had to withstand such torture. But if any man could endure such agony without going insane, that man would be his father. He couldn't bear to think of his mother . . .

A Unari drone flew overhead and snapped him out of his grim thoughts. Had the search cameras spied him? Would they spot Marisa?

Staying under the cover of the trees, he battled through the drifts, backtracking to the crash site. He had to find Marisa before the Unari did. Before she tried to dragon-shape.

Rion sprinted through the forest. Thorns scratched his face and tore through his clothing to his flesh, but the discomfort was nothing compared to dragon pain. Nothing compared to his people's suffering. Or his fear for Marisa's safety.

He couldn't have lost Marisa in the crash. If he'd survived, she could have, too. Dread spurred him on. He recalled the blue heat in her eyes when they'd made love, the sparks that sizzled through the air when she'd stood up to him, the way her skin felt soft and silky smooth under his fingertips—and he redoubled his efforts.

She could be lying on the ground in the cold snow. Alone.

He'd brought her here. She was his responsibility.

He ran through the forest without stopping. Once, he saw movement in the trees. "Marisa?"

He spied a darthog rooting through the brush. No sign of Marisa.

Ignoring his tired legs, he got his second wind. He leaped over a stream, climbed past a fallen log. He had to find Marisa and keep her safe.

She had no one else here but him. His people had no

one who could help them but him. His fists clenched in anger. If that meant making war, he would make war.

His own preference for peace didn't matter. If it meant sending men into battle to their deaths, he would give those orders. Some things were worse than death—like living under Unari domination. Like losing Marisa . . .

"Rion?" Marisa's soft call sounded close by.

Thank the Goddess. She was alive.

"I'm coming." He headed in the direction of her voice. "Are you okay?"

"I'm not sure."

She didn't sound right, and her flat tone scared him more than her words. Again, he increased his pace and scrambled uphill past rock outcroppings, toppled trees, and thick underbrush. "Don't move. I'll find you. Just keep talking."

She didn't answer. Fear crawled down his spine. He'd told her he would look out for her and that she would go home after they freed his people. He'd promised himself that he'd win back her respect. He'd lost his aunt and uncle, perhaps his cousin and his parents. He would not lose her, too.

His breath came in harsh gasps as he struggled up a steep incline. "Marisa?"

Again she didn't answer.

The sight of snapped treetops clued him in to the general crash site's location. He'd been flung far away. He climbed a rock cliff, using his fingers and his boot tips to scale the mountainside.

After he cleared the lip, he didn't pause to wipe the sweat off his brow. The sight that met his eyes rocked him back on his heels. His spaceship's debris lay scattered in a huge field of grass. Snow floated over the grass and debris, and smoke fluttered in the light breeze like a shroud.

The ship's automatic systems had attempted and failed a self-repair. The task had been too great. This ship would never fly again.

But he saw no sign of Marisa.

"Marisa?" He shouted and sprinted through the burned wreckage. He looked right, then left, and remembering his own plight, his webbing caught in a tree, he looked up at the few remaining trees.

He spied another drone.

Had he really heard her call? Had he imagined her voice because he'd wanted to hear her so badly?

He turned around full circle and glimpsed a movement at the edge of the tree line. "Marisa?"

Whatever he'd seen move didn't move again. He bolted that way. It was as good a direction as any.

When he spotted her, sitting with her back against a tree, looking wonderfully alive and unhurt, his fear rumbled into aggravation. Why hadn't she responded?

Head up, her shoulders braced against the tree trunk as if she didn't have a care in the world, she sat in the snow between gnarled roots. She'd pulled her knees to her chest. Eyes open and staring straight forward, she didn't glance in his direction.

Something was wrong. She was breathing. But still. So still that he curbed his anxiety, lowered his voice, and spoke gently. "Why didn't you answer me?"

She didn't react. Not to his presence or his voice. Since she'd responded earlier, the crash hadn't damaged her hearing. But now she acted as if he wasn't there.

Had she injured her head? Had the stress finally gotten

to her? She didn't have a scratch on her perfect profile. Not one bruise. Yet, something was off and his stomach tightened.

He placed a hand on her shoulder. "Marisa?"

She turned her head, blue eyes unfocused and vacant. He gasped as the other side of her face came into view. Blood caked her face. Her scalp was loose, a flap of skin and hair hanging from her skull. Blood and snow matted her lovely hair and oozed from the ghastly wound.

She seemed to have no idea of the extent of her injury. Or of the reaction he'd failed to hide. He slipped an arm under her and eased her onto her side, facing her wound toward the sky. "Marisa, your head's cut. Don't move. I'll be right back."

He needed water to clean the wound. Thread to sew her scalp. As a military commander he'd had rudimentary first-aid training, and he'd need all of those skills to stop her bleeding and close the wound.

The cold had slowed her bleeding. But if she caught an infection that close to her brain . . . she could . . .

No. He would not let her die.

At least she didn't seem to be in pain. But if her shock wore off and the feeling returned before he patched her up . . . he would have to hurt her even more.

He hurried to find supplies.

The wreckage didn't look promising. Finding a first-aid kit in the strewn ship parts was too much to hope for. However, he did find plenty of sharp splintered metal—nothing with a needle-like hole in one end, but he spied a sliver of metal with a notch that might hold thread, and slipped it into his pocket.

He glanced into the sky. The drones were gone. How

long until they returned to base? He had no idea how much time he might or might not have. Surely the Unari would send someone to investigate the crash site, and he wanted to be long gone before they arrived.

Rion found no water, no alcohol, no cotton gauze or antibiotics. Instead he trudged past burned plastic, engine pieces, bits of hose, gears, and many objects so badly damaged he couldn't identify them. He was about to turn back when he heard water trickling.

There must be a stream nearby. Quickly, he scooped up a broken pipe, ignored the heat to his fingers, and bent it into a U shape. Then he hurried to the stream, where the water ran swift and clear. Kneeling, he drank. It was sweet and clean. He washed out the pipe and turned his attention to his own hands, filthy from stumbles in the forest, climbing the rock face, and searching through the debris. Dipping his hands into the water, he scrubbed his flesh with sand from the creek bottom, then soaked them some more. Then, careful not to get his hands dirty again, he filled the pipe with clear water and hurried to Marisa.

"I'm back," he said softly.

She lay in exactly the same position. But now her eyes were closed. She didn't appear to have heard him.

He took comfort in her steady breathing. Holding the water-filled pipe in one hand, he kneeled beside her, then wedged the pipe between a root and the trunk to avoid spillage.

Quickly he gathered tree moss, kindling, and firewood and stacked these around the pipe. He left her once again to retrieve a burning ember from the wreckage, scooped it into a metal tray he'd found, then fed the ember with moss until it burst into flames. Finally, he transferred the burning moss to his collection of dry kindling and coaxed the tiny flickering flame into a full-fledged fire.

While the water heated, he shredded the hem of his tunic with a sharp-edged piece of metal, then carefully separated the longest thread from the others. He thrust his makeshift needle into the fire for a few seconds and waved it through the air to cool it.

These conditions were far from sterile. But he didn't know what more he could do with the supplies at hand.

After the water had boiled, he waited for it to cool. Finally, he dipped more cloth he'd torn from his shirt into the water and began to clean her wound. The cut was jagged. Dirty.

His gentle dabbing reopened the wound, and more blood flowed. But he kept cleaning, eventually resorting to trickling water from the pipe directly onto her scalp.

She sputtered once, opened her eyes, then closed them again. But at last, the wound looked dirt-free. As gently as possible, he fitted the palm-sized flap of scalp into place, satisfied he saw no major gaps. Then he began to sew.

"Ow. Ow. Ow." She swatted at his hand and thrashed.

"Easy. Easy." He straddled her side, using his knees to trap her hands but keeping most of his weight from pressing her down. "This is going to sting a little."

"It hurts!"

Her cry tore at him. "I know. I'm sorry. But I have to patch you up." He kept murmuring a steady patter as he sewed. "The wound is clean, and you're going to heal as good as new." Unsure if she was conscious, he prayed she'd passed out and couldn't feel the needle going in and out of her scalp.

But when he sat back to study his handiwork, she opened her eyes. "Are you done?"

"Yes."

"Thank God." She released a long breath. "Get off me, please."

"Of course." He'd been so focused on the wound, making sure he'd closed all the flesh and left no hair in the gaps, that he'd forgotten he was still holding her down.

She glanced from the bloody cloths to his fingers covered with her blood. "If you're done performing brain surgery, we should probably get out of here."

Marisa didn't sound quite like herself, but her attempt at a jest cheered him. Still he felt compelled to warn her, "When the shock wears off, your head's going to hurt like hell."

"But I'll be okay?"

"Your brain's fine—as far as I know. You just had a surface cut."

She scowled. "I thought you weren't going to lie to me anymore?"

"A large surface cut," he amended with relief. If she felt up to arguing, he figured she'd be fine. "If infection doesn't set in, you should heal quickly. And your hair will hide the scar."

"Thanks. Sorry, I'm not a good patient. Next time I have stitches, I'd prefer it was under anesthesia."

"Let's hope there is no next time." He helped her to her feet. She leaned heavily against him and he wrapped an arm around her waist. "How're you feeling?"

"Dizzy. Light-headed. Cold."

"Maybe we should rest." He looked at her tawny skin.

She was pale, but her jaw gritted with her determination to stay on her feet.

"We can't stay here. Look." She pointed toward the sky.

Damn it. He'd been so focused on her he hadn't noticed the squad of aircraft heading their way. Unari. Six aircraft with guns forward and aft.

"Let's go." He kicked the fire apart, hiding all traces of their survival, except their footprints. However, it was still snowing, and in a few more minutes their tracks would fill in. "If we stay out of sight, perhaps we'll luck out and the Unari will assume we died in the crash."

She picked up a branch to use as a walking stick. But even with the extra support, Marisa required his help. Weak from loss of blood, she needed food and rest. Antibiotics and a doctor would be even better.

She didn't complain and stepped forward gingerly. But as he slipped an arm around her waist, he could feel her trembling against his side. "We need to move away from the crash site as fast as we can."

The hum of the aircraft grew louder.

"Can they see our heat signatures from the air?" she asked.

"They didn't have that kind of technology when I left. But the smoking debris should provide cover."

She nodded, then winced in pain. "But once we leave the area . . ."

"We have no choice." Rion half carried her from the crash site. "If we stay, they'll find us."

"Which way?" she asked.

"Toward the trees."

If Chivalri dies, then Honor is without her heart and will die, for the Goddess has withdrawn her soul from all the realm.

—CHIVALRI KING

18

Each step pounded like a hammer blow to Marisa's head. Hot and cold flashes hit her at random. The drone of Unari ships grew louder. It seemed as though someone had been hunting her ever since she'd left Earth.

Rion hurried her through the forest, and the alien landscape lent a nightmarish edge to her pain. She didn't think the taste of the smoke that made breathing painful would ever leave her mouth.

She had a hard time recalling when her head hadn't throbbed, when the vegetation had smelled familiar, when the gravity under her feet didn't make her unsteady. She wouldn't have made the first hundred yards without Rion's help. They kept a steady pace for at least an hour and finally stopped to drink from a stream. Rion helped lower her to the bank, then cupped his fingers so she could drink from his hands.

His kindness and the cool water revived her sagging energy. He'd sewn her wound, then half carried her from the crash site, their bodies pressed tightly together. Despite her need to protect herself and keep an emotional distance, intimacy was growing between them again. She'd wanted to drink in his strength. Lean into him for comfort.

She had to remain vigilant. Remind herself that he was helping her for his own reasons. That they could have no future together. Nevertheless, she would have been rude and ungrateful not to acknowledge he was half carrying her. "Thanks."

He studied her with concern. "If I remember correctly, it's not much farther."

"Where are we going?"

"To the royal mountain house—Winhaven."

Her pounding head didn't prevent her from objecting to his plan. "Won't Winhaven be the first place the Unari will look for survivors of the crash?"

He shrugged. "Not if they believe we died."

She tied her fear into a tight, controllable knot. "But when they don't find our bodies . . ."

His response was gentle yet firm. "You need food, rest, and shelter. I won't have you sleeping on the ground."

"Better the ground than a cell or a grave." Battered or not, she couldn't let his need to protect her from the elements ruin his mission. Trying to hide her weariness, she shot him a hard look. "If I weren't injured, you'd never go there, would you?"

"But you are injured."

She couldn't refute his logic. Besides, arguing taxed her strength. Thinking was hard when her head felt like someone was using it for drum practice. She'd kill for an aspirin.

Rion wet a scrap of cloth in the stream, wrung it out, and placed it on her forehead. "Better?"

"Yeah—" She nodded, then winced as more pain flooded through her. Closing her eyes, she mumbled, "Note to self. No extraneous head movements."

"We should move on."

She agreed, but a five-minute nap would do wonders. "Just a few more minutes, okay?"

Sitting in the sun, the cool cloth on her brow, she felt her body grow heavy. Eyes closed, she rested her forehead against her knees and listened to the tweeting of birds, the fluttering of small squirrel-like creatures, and dozed off.

When she opened her eyes, Rion was carrying her, striding through the forest as if she weighed nothing. A warm tingle spread through her and into her core. After that crash, who would have thought her battered body could even produce such a hormone? Even her fear of the Unari catching them couldn't mitigate her attraction to Rion.

She watched the sun setting low on the horizon, trying once more to maintain an emotional distance. There was no snow. She estimated several hours had passed. Several hours with her breasts snuggled against his chest and her cheek cradled by his shoulder.

"Feel better?" Rion asked, his voice a silky male purr.

"The rest helped. You don't have to carry me. I'm awake now."

"I didn't mind." He set her down as if she was cherished, priceless. As if he feared she might still topple, he kept a hand on her waist.

His tenderness overwhelmed her. She refused to meet his eyes. Didn't want him to see the desire coursing through her.

Get a grip. She took in a deep breath and let out the air on a long sigh. "Any sign of the Unari?"

"None. But I haven't heard their ships fly off the mountain, either."

Which meant the Unari remained on the ground. Probably searching for them. "It's been a long time. You think they're still combing the wreckage for our bodies? Or are they now hunting for us?"

"If they're trying to track us, they won't find signs of our passing. Or pick up our scent." He grinned down at his wet boots, clearly pleased. "I walked downstream for a few miles."

If she had to be stuck on an alien world with an enemy hunting her, she couldn't have asked for a more skilled or caring companion.

"The royal house—Winhaven? How much farther is it?" She tried to keep the weariness from her voice.

"I'm not sure." His brows narrowed. "I've only been there once, a long time ago, and we flew in."

"Are you saying we're lost?"

He peered at the setting sun, then over his shoulder at the highest mountain peak, getting his bearings. "I know where we are. I'm not sure where Winhaven is."

"Maybe we should head for civilization."

"We're in the Jalpani Mountains." He pointed toward the setting sun. "If we walk that way, we'll enter the capital city of Chivalri."

"How far would that be?"

"Twenty miles. Maybe twenty-five."

She bit back a groan. Her stomach rumbled with hunger. But she'd been sleeping all afternoon while Rion, who'd expended large amounts of energy carrying her, had been walking for hours.

He pointed to a distant outcropping of trees. "I think that bluff might be the western edge of Winhaven."

She looked in the direction he'd pointed, hoping it wasn't far. Her gaze picked up a familiar silhouette against the sky. The owl had survived the crash, but like Rion could have been flung far away. Or like Marisa, could have been injured. Yet Merlin looked fine, and she was happy to see him again. "Hey, there's Merlin."

The owl swooped toward them, circled over their heads, and then flew off about twenty degrees to the right of Rion's familiar bluff. When they continued to stand and watch him fly, he returned and circled them again before repeating his flight path.

"He wants us to follow him," Marisa said.

"Let's go." Rion handed her a walking stick. "After he gave us the key to that spaceship, then steered it, I'm thinking there's more to Merlin than we know."

Marisa followed Merlin's flight. "I wish I'd asked Cael or Lucan more about him, but I thought he was just a pet." Watching Merlin fly and cover so much ground with so little effort, she longed to do the same. "If we dragon-shaped, we'd be at Winhaven in minutes."

"No. Don't even think about dragonshaping." Rion's voice turned harsh.

Surprised, she looked at him, but kept walking, following Merlin. "Why not?"

"If the Unari are around, we'd be too easy to spot as dragons. And"—he hesitated, as if there were something he didn't want to say, then continued—"after the crash, my webbing tangled in a tree. I had to dragonshape to free myself. I got a taste of the Tyrannizer's pain."

His face turned hard, and his eyes blazed with anger.

"I'm sorry." What in God's name had the Tyrannizer done to him? She couldn't bring herself to ask about the pain.

"It's not something I want to ever experience again. No one should have to bear that agony. It's savage."

She placed her hand in his and squeezed. "We'll stop them. You, Merlin, and I will find a way to stop the Unari."

"Goddess help us if we don't."

Marisa's stomach knotted. She could do this. Stay strong. "To use my group telepathy to communicate with the dragons, I'll have to link minds with them. I won't just feel my own pain, I'll feel theirs, too."

Rion stopped walking and looked at her. "Back on Earth, you remained in human form when you communicated with the dragons."

"And my efforts failed." If not for Rion's dragonshaping and placing himself between her and the angry dragons, she wouldn't have survived. "I can get through to small, receptive groups of dragons in human form. But to send a message worldwide or to deal with fighting dragons or ones in terrible pain, I need my full telepathic powers. I have to dragonshape to communicate effectively."

"You'll feel all their pain?" he asked.

"Yes." She hoped she had the courage to do what was needed. Because if she didn't, not only his people but all of Earth might be doomed, as well. "The link—and the pain—won't be as intense if I remain in human form, but

I can communicate with larger groups and with more authority if I dragonshape."

He shook his head. "In dragon form, the pain is unbearable." He spoke briskly, without inflection. "You can't dragonshape until after we find and destroy the Tyrannizer."

"Are you sure?" she asked, even as relief slid through her.

Eyes gentle, he cupped her face between his hands. "I wouldn't ask that of you . . . or of anyone. Because it's impossible. No one can endure that much pain."

Up ahead, Merlin hooted, clearly growing impatient with their slow pace. She gazed into Rion's eyes and saw his fear. For her? Or fear that she would fail his people? Or both?

Her doubts lingered. She wondered if she would ever completely trust him again. After her failed marriage, it had taken her a long time to think she would ever love again. She'd lost faith in herself, in her own judgment.

At the moment, she was already up to her neck in indecision. And yet she couldn't deny she had feelings for Rion.

He was resourceful, caring, and gentle. He was the kind of man she admired. Even considering whether to trust him again was dangerous—especially after he'd told her they could have nothing permanent together. Ever since the crash and his learning how his people were suffering, he seemed more responsible, more determined than ever to free them, which made him even more attractive.

Perhaps that knock on her head had skewed her perceptions. In her experience, people's character didn't change. Yet who would have thought her adventure-loving brother could happily marry and settle down? Lucan's domestication had proved anything was possible.

"Where's Merlin?" Rion interrupted her thoughts.

She'd been focused on putting one foot in front of the other while avoiding thornbushes and hadn't been paying attention to the owl. She peered through the trees, and her hopes rose. "Is that a fence?"

A stone wall about waist high meandered between thick shrubs and towering trees along the steep hillside.

"It's Winhaven's perimeter. We've found it. Merlin led us straight here, but he's disappeared." Rion slowed his pace. "Why don't you rest and let me check out—"

"No." She recalled when he'd left her behind in the space museum and the time she'd spent worrying. She didn't like him leaving her behind. "We'll go together."

"Don't move," a voice called out. A group of men, wearing ragged camouflage clothing, stepped from behind the trees, weapons aimed.

Rion stepped in front of Marisa. She held her breath and peeked around his broad shoulders.

These men had the chiseled angles from living hard and lean. Rion couldn't defeat all of them, especially with their blasters pointed right at him.

Icy fear rooted her feet, and she could only stare at the collection of massive chests, powerful arms, and long, lean hips and wait. If these guys were the Unari, then she could understand how they'd infiltrated society from the inside out.

"Who's Merlin?" The stocky leader with the glinting baby blues moved forward, a ring of command in his tone. He stared at them over the barrel of his weapon, suspicion and hostility in his eyes.

Before Rion had an opportunity to answer, the blue-eyed leader fired orders to his men, his voice low and deep. "Find their friend, Merlin. He must not escape, or we're all—"

"Lexiathon," Rion called the man by his name, "there's no need to waste energy chasing an owl."

At Rion's words, the men paused and looked to their leader. Lexiathon frowned, stepped closer, and stared at Rion, his eyes wide open and direct. "How do you know my name?"

"I am Crown Prince Rion Jaqard of Chivalri."

"Lies. Our king is Shepherd Jaqard."

"Shepherd is my father."

"If Sir Shepherd resigns or dies, then the throne goes to his son, Erik."

"Erik is my cousin and not the direct heir."

"That's impossible."

"Please hear me out. You've heard that King Shepherd Jaqard has flashes?"

"What of it?"

"In one of his visions he saw that his infant son would die from an assassination. So shortly after my birth, he had Erik and me switch places."

Lexiathon didn't lower his weapon. His stance widened and his back snapped straighter. "Erik wasn't assassinated."

"My father changed the future by his actions." Rion stepped forward and held out his hand. "I have seen you by my side in the future many times. I am happy to finally meet you, Lex."

Lex didn't budge. "I'll need more proof than your word."

Marisa swallowed back a hysterical laugh. Rion had finally revealed his true identity, and his people didn't believe him. If the Honorians had DNA records, she supposed that, in time, Rion could prove his claim to the throne.

Rion dropped his hand, but he kept his smile. "You are Chivalri's rebel leader."

Lex held Rion's gaze, his stare level. "You could have heard that anywhere."

"You protect children in Winhaven's basement."

The rebel leader narrowed his eyes. "So one of my men talked."

"You dream of a woman. Pendra. She's the leader of another rebel group, and you admire her—"

"Enough," Lex snapped.

Rion didn't smile. "I don't think you've told anyone about her, have you?"

Lex remained silent, doubt in his eyes.

"Darian," Rion called to another man, with short blond hair shaved close to the head and the body of a world-class wrestler. "Your lady is pregnant. You'd best marry her soon."

Darian's perfect square jaw dropped open. "She just told me this morning."

"It's a boy, and he'll become a man of whom you're proud." Rion faced another of the men, the tallest and most powerful of the bunch. "Mendle, your mother—"

"Is dead."

"When the Unari burned her house, she fled. You will see her again . . . but it may be some time before you reunite. That vision is still in your future."

Mendle gasped. "I buried the Unari arsonists in the

backyard and told no one for fear of reprisal. But I didn't know my mother . . . still lives." Tears of happiness shone in his eyes.

Lex lowered his weapon, dropped to one knee, and bowed his head. "Sire, only direct descendants of the royal line have such an ability."

His men kneeled, bowed their heads.

Rion reached down and grabbed Lex's forearm. "Rise. All of you. My flashes are snapshots of the past, present, and future. However, the more I share, the less control we have over those events. Sometimes change is good. Sometimes it's not. This time the goal is clear—I would join you to rid Honor of all Unari."

"Yes, sire."

Rion rarely mentioned his gift. It was the longest explanation she'd ever heard Rion give at one time. His commitment to these people was set in stone.

"Until all are free," Rion continued, his tone regal, "I would swear you and your men to secrecy about my identity."

"You have our word, sire," Lex agreed.

"I ask that you address me as Rion. No titles, no special deference should be given to me—except as a rebel leader."

"Understood . . . sir."

Rion placed his arm over Marisa's shoulders. "This lady has come from far away to help us."

Marisa nodded a greeting, pleased the men's attention remained on Rion. In wartime, people didn't take kindly to outsiders. If she hadn't arrived with Rion, these people would never have taken her in.

"Is there a place the lady can rest?" Rion asked. Before anyone answered, he continued, "It's possible that

Unari are looking for us." As they walked along the fence, Mendle taking the point, Darian covering the rear, Rion explained how they'd crashed and had been on the run ever since.

"You haven't seen any Unari on the ground?" Lex asked.

Rion shook his head. "And I hid our trail, walking for miles through a creek. I would not bring trouble into camp."

"Trouble can come from any direction," Mendle mumbled, then clamped his lips tightly shut.

"Sir," Lex said hesitantly, "your cousin Erik has recently joined us."

"Erik's here?" Rion broke into a wide smile. "I was told he was a Unari prisoner."

"He escaped. We usually don't accept recruits, but with his claim to the Chivalri throne we allowed him to stay."

"Praise the Goddess, this is good news." Rion stepped forward, clearly eager to meet his cousin. "The day I escaped Honor, Erik was captured in my stead. I owe him a debt I can never repay."

The men wound through the woods, choosing their steps with care not to snap branches or leave a trail. With their movements skilled, graceful, and easy, they made good time.

Marisa was determined to keep up. So what if her head throbbed? She didn't want these men or Erik to think her weak. Or helpless.

Lex walked at Rion's right shoulder. He glanced at Rion and raised an eyebrow. Clearly, he had questions but was unsure of protocol. While the men treated Rion with deference and respect, they were obviously uneasy around him.

"Sir, why haven't you come forward before now?" Lex asked.

Rion clapped Lex on the shoulder, his mood cheerful since he'd heard news of his cousin. "We're going to work together. There's no need to stand on ceremony."

Lex's men looked down, as if they realized the question carried a hint of disrespect, but they also seemed curious.

Rion sighed. "The day the Unari invaded our capital, my aunt and uncle gave their lives so Erik and I could escape. We fled through the city toward the museum. I thought if I could fly the spaceship—"

"That old relic?" Lex whistled. "It's a wonder you didn't kill yourself."

"Thanks to Erik, I got away. I lifted off and made it to Tor, where I made some hasty repairs but again had to flee before Enforcers caught and imprisoned me. Later, I ended up crashing on another world, called Pendragon. I've been trying to return ever since."

"I'll bet you have some adventurous tales to tell." Darian grinned and pulled aside a branch so it wouldn't whip Marisa's face.

She walked past. "Thanks."

"What's amazing is that you've all remained free." Rion returned the compliment.

Mendle shook his head. "None of us are free. Not when we must dragonshape to eat . . . and the pain . . ."

"We're also running out of platinum," Lex told them.

Rion's eyes widened in surprise. "You aren't mining the mountain platinum?"

"I've sent men up to the mountains," Lex told him. "None have come back."

*   *   *

RION'S VISION TOOK him to a place he didn't recognize. A man sat in a chair, his arms chained behind his back. Rion couldn't see the prisoner's face; his view was only of his back. And before him, a Unari torturer shone a brilliant light into the prisoner's eyes.

"How many rebels are there?"

"I don't know." The man's voice was low, racked with pain.

A whip descended and the prisoner shrieked.

"Where do the rebels hide?"

"I don't know."

The whip descended again. "Tell me what you do know."

"About what?"

The whip descended repeatedly. "Tell me how to kill the rebels."

"I've already told you. Take away their food. Don't let them reach the platinum in the mountains. There is nothing more I can tell you."

"Nothing?"

"I've told you everything." The man raised his head and spoke defiantly. "It's you who doesn't keep your word."

"Why would we keep our word to a traitor?"

Traitor? The vision faded. But Rion's mind kept sifting the new information.

It didn't surprise or shock or even disappoint him that men under torture would give up information. But was the man really a traitor?

And if so, was he a Unari traitor? Or an Honorian traitor?

MARISA KEPT A careful watch on Rion. He'd just had this glazed look in his eyes that she recognized as another flash. But he said nothing, and Lex didn't seem to notice.

Lex kept speaking, his voice even and thoughtful. "There are other rebel groups besides ours scattered around the capital. You were lucky we found you before the Unari did. It's possible they know we're at Winhaven, but so far they haven't made forays out here."

"Why not?" Marisa asked.

"Likely they know all they have to do is wait another season and we'll starve."

"You stay in small groups to avoid detection?" Rion asked.

"Yes. There's some communication back and forth between us, but we don't have the resources to feed and hide more than a few in this place. Your flash was correct. We've converted Winhaven's basement into a giant nursery."

"The poor babies," Marisa said. "How do they endure the pain?"

"Fortunately," Lex explained, "they feel it only when they dragonshape to feed on platinum."

Rion swore. "But babies and children must feed more frequently than adults."

Lex nodded grimly. "They have to dragonshape more often, but, thank the Goddess, only for the briefest of times."

"Are there women at Winhaven?" Marisa asked.

"Not many. Sometimes, people who have escaped Unari enslavement beg us to take their children. But we don't have enough food to feed everyone and must turn away most adults. We wouldn't have let Erik stay, except he's the king's heir—or so we thought until you arrived."

"How do the babies' parents find you?" Marisa asked.

"There's an underground network in the city, and rumors abound. Many parents stumble around in the woods blindly, and we find them like we found you."

"Are there rebels in the cities?" Rion asked.

"Every building in Chivalri's cities has been leveled. Disintegrated with giant lasers."

Rion winced. "All of them?"

"Nothing is left. No cities, no towns, no villages, no farms. Only the royal palace in the capital and this lone building out in the country, and a few isolated others like it, have escaped destruction."

"So where are the Honorians and Unari living?"

"Captured Honorians live outside like fenced-in animals. The Unari may live in parts of the old palace. There are rumors it still stands."

"What about other countries beyond Chivalri?" Marisa asked.

"There are more rumors of rebel groups—but nothing solid." Lex paused. "Let's get you some food and a place to sleep, and tomorrow I'll get you brought up-to-date."

"Sounds good." Rion spoke quietly. "Have you any word of my parents? The last I heard was they were in the palace when the Unari invaded Chivalri."

"If they're alive, it's likely your father's been enslaved by Cavus Prime."

"Cavus Prime?"

"The Unari leader." Lex spat into the bushes. "We've heard unsubstantiated reports that Cavus keeps our strongest warriors, including your father, right next to the Tyrannizer. It's said Cavus enjoys watching the torture of our best leaders and warriors."

Rion scowled. "Our first task is to find the machine that broadcasts pain."

"Then what?"

"We'll mount a mission to shut down the Tyrannizer."

Lex shook his head. "Sir, I'm afraid you don't fully understand."

"Explain."

"No Honorian can pass through the great walls the Unari have built around the city—not without giving up their freedom."

"Are the Unari planning to annihilate us, then colonize Honor with their people?" Rion asked.

Lex shook his head. "We don't think so. The city no longer has living accommodations, except for the palace. Dragons work as beasts of burden, building high walls, but no one knows their purpose."

"What else can you tell me?" Rion prodded.

"After the Unari capture our people, they don't give them food or water until they dragonshape. After we take dragon form, they force us to work. The more a dragonshaper resists, the worse the pain grows. The Tyrannizer is so debilitating—even our strongest warriors succumb to Unari orders. Also, the closer one gets to the machine, the worse the pain and the more difficult it is to disobey orders."

"But if dragonshaping is so painful, why do they stay

in dragon form?" Marisa asked, an ominous shiver making her cold.

"When dragons are starved for platinum, we don't have the energy to humanshape."

Rion stilled. His eyes darkened, and his voice threaded with steel. "We have to destroy the Tyrannizer."

Babies are cuddles and kisses on toes, the sweet scent of dragon's breath, and a kiss on the nose.

— LADY GUINEVERE

19

After a meager meal, Lex showed Marisa and Rion to their quarters in Winhaven. The royal home had been looted of furnishings, and a fire had destroyed most of the main building, but one of the guest wings had survived partially intact. Here the resistance, such as it was, had made its headquarters. She and Rion would sleep in the same room. The sensual awareness that had dogged her ever since he'd carried her through the forest rose on a gentle ripple of heat.

Rion had been silent since Marisa and he had left the others in the dining area. Apparently Erik was off on a foraging mission with several of the rebels and not expected back until dawn.

Standing at the bedroom window, Rion gazed past a shredded curtain toward the capital, his potent male presence dominating the room. "When I was here last, the city's lights brightened the sky for miles. Now it's so dark, it's as if we've regressed to another age."

"But the knowledge to rebuild is still here," Marisa said softly.

She ached for him. Yearning to give him comfort, she joined him by the window and placed her hand on his arm.

He stood stiff and tense, his head high, his eyes alert. She suspected his thoughts were gloomy and began to run her fingers lightly up and down the sculpted ridges of his forearm. Retaking this world from the Unari might be an impossible task. And although they were now stuck on this world, with no means to depart, every time she breathed in, her lungs filled with the delicious scent of his male musk and her thoughts turned to being with him again.

Now was not the time to feel any attraction. He had to bring his people together, and she would cause strife. But that future seemed impossibly far away. And Rion was here right now. Totally within her reach.

He turned from the window. His voice was low and filled with gravel. "How's your head?"

The throbbing in her head matched the beat of her heart. "The medic who looked at me after our meal said you did a good job. There's no sign of infection."

"Good." Rion walked her to the bed, the only piece of furniture in the room besides a broken table someone had propped in the corner. "You should rest. Tomorrow, I'll talk with Erik, and Lex will show us a secret passage to the city walls."

"You should rest, too." She patted the bed next to her, but he remained on his feet, every muscle rigid.

She didn't have to ask what was wrong. She knew. Conditions here weren't just bad, they were terrible. Tomorrow he would see Erik, but he might also have his worst fears about his parents confirmed.

Wrapping her arms around him, she said, "We'll find a way. The Unari didn't take this planet in a day. You can't take it back overnight, either. Your people need you. And if you wear yourself ragged—"

"You didn't feel that pain . . . it's like your bones have been dipped in acid. We'll have to take out the Tyrannizer before you can dragonshape and use your abilities. And before that, you must feed on platinum."

She twined her fingers into his hair and rested her cheek against his chest. "You've found your cousin. We'll find the machine, too. We'll destroy it. Maybe we can do it from a distance, blow it up or something."

"While you were with the medic, Lex told me that he believes the Tyrannizer is kept running by the torture of Honorian dragonshapers."

She leaned back to look into his face. Moonlight filtered through the window and reflected in the hard blackness of his eyes. "You'll find a way to save them."

"If Cavus Prime keeps our best warriors near the Tyrannizer"—he held his head high, but his voice choked—"if we have to knock it out from a distance, we'll have to sacrifice our best people . . ."

Oh, God. Lex believed Shepherd Jaqard, Rion's father, was kept near the Tyrannizer. If Rion could take out the Tyrannizer only from a distance, he might have to sacrifice his own father.

She tried to be optimistic. "Maybe I can use my telepathic skills to urge the dragonshapers near the Tyrannizer to break the Unari hold and fly away. I'd only have to link for a minute or two . . ."

"No." His tone was harsh. Firm. Sure. "We have to find another way."

Talking about it was stressing him out. And she knew only one way to distract him.

She slipped her hands under his shirt, up his warm chest, and onto his broad shoulders. Beneath her palms, his flesh was smooth, firm, muscular.

He hissed in a breath, and then, as if all that pent-up emotion sparked, his eyes glowed with the promise of raw sensuality. He brought his lips to hers and poured molten heat straight into her.

He tasted of coffee and sweet cream, and as his tongue slipped into her mouth and danced with her own, she melted against him. He clutched her shoulders, not roughly, not with finesse, but with hot need. They fell backward against the wall, and he eagerly began to re-move her clothing. She did the same as they shared an urgency to give and take pleasure. An urgency to banish the Unari for a few hours. At least here, at this moment, they had the freedom to do as they wished.

And she wished for release from painful truths and an uncertain future. It meant shoving aside the past and her distrust, forgetting about the future, and living right now. Right here. Taking what this moment offered. Taking what Rion offered.

And he offered a lot. He was a giving lover. Sensual. Erotic.

Living in the present meant kissing him and touching him and breathing in his masculine scent. She focused on the taste of his tongue against her lips, sipped his fire, breathed in his eager murmurs that tingled like the electricity in the air before a summer storm—until the very air around them crackled with heat.

His kiss was hypnotic, calling to her, pulling her into him, until she couldn't think of anything but him. Or his kiss. Or his hard flesh against her softness.

She shimmied out of her clothing, yanked off his. Naked, she pressed herself against his male heat.

Her blood simmered, and she breathed in huge gasps. Drawing him against her, she arched her back, enjoyed his chest hairs tickling her breasts until her nipples hardened to tight nubs.

He dipped his hands between them, skimmed his fingers up her waist until his hands cupped her breasts. His thumbs twirled around her areolas, and he used the pads of his fingertips to draw maddeningly exquisite circles that had her standing on her tippy toes to get more. More pressure. More friction. More Rion.

He obliged, tweaking her nipples, and the zing of pleasure burned straight to her core. A soft moan tore from her throat.

She clutched his shoulders, moving her hips in an urgent shimmy. She didn't require more kisses. She didn't require more caresses. Already moist and ready, she felt fire roar through her core.

"Take me." She parted her thighs. She was hot. So hot.

He grabbed her buttocks and lifted her. She straddled him, took him straight inside, until he filled her while she brimmed with delicious desire.

He was pure molten heat. And the wild passion in his eyes matched the frenzied thrusts of his hips. The taking was savage, reckless, and natural.

He ravaged her mouth. She was ready, slick, tensed to explode. Hunger and a fierce possessive yearning lent her strength to ride him, hold on tight, and take what he offered.

Like a cleansing wildfire, the flames burned so hot she exploded in a streak of molten gold with slashes of scalding scarlet. For long seconds the pleasure took her outside herself to a heavenly place where there was only Rion.

When she finally found the strength to slide down his body and place weight back into her limbs, she opened her eyes and realized that someone was pounding on the door.

Outside the closed door, Lex's voice rose to a frantic shout. "Rion. There's an emergency with the babies. We need everyone's help."

"Just a minute." Rion scooped up their clothes.

"Hurry."

Quickly they sorted out their clothing in the darkness and dressed. Marisa was certain that Lex would know what they'd been doing, but at the panic in his tone she didn't waste time straightening her hair, barely pulling down her top, and tucking it into her slacks.

When Rion opened the door, she was still breathing heavily. Lex was already down the hall, running with a flashlight aimed toward steps that spiraled downward. Rion grabbed her hand, and together they sprinted after him. As they raced through the hall in the darkness, she could hear the squeals of baby dragons, and dread poured through her.

Back on Earth, Rion had theorized that their intimacy had caused her to inadvertently send out telepathic waves of passion, thereby upsetting the adult dragons. She now feared his theory might have been right.

"Rion," she whispered. "I shouldn't have been so careless. I didn't even think about how my telepathy might affect the baby dragons."

"Why would you? You couldn't have caused permanent damage."

"We don't know that." Fear drilled her as they ran down the stairs after Lex.

Lex held open a set of thick wooden doors, and bright lights made her blink several times. With the basement underground, the rebels didn't have to worry about the Unari spotting the lights. This giant underground cavern must have extended beneath all of Winhaven. Although cribs and playthings lined one wall, most of the room was empty of furnishings, large enough for the young dragons to fly.

The purple dragon babies were racing along the floor in frantic circles as if intoxicated. Some of them were too tiny to escape their cribs. Others took their first clumsy steps and flapped their wings, while toddlers ran and toppled, hopped and skidded, attempted to fly and failed.

The oldest dragons had managed flight. Most struggled to stay level, and a few crashed into walls. Others barely avoided colliding into one another. The eldest children flew near the ceiling in uncoordinated circles.

They were all snorting, shrilling, and flapping so loudly, Marisa could barely hear herself think. Two babies flew into each other and flopped to the ground. Neither appeared hurt, but this was her fault. And she couldn't calm so many of them in human form. She had to dragonshape.

Marisa had only to think and her body morphed.

"Marisa—no!" Rion shouted at her to stop.

His warning was too late. Her sight sharpened and her mass grew, until her head reached halfway to the ceiling. With babies everywhere, she didn't dare take a step.

Thank God, she wasn't in pain. But she didn't question her good fortune. Marisa sent out a greeting of happy calm. *Hello.*

She received back a cacophony of excited answers, the children's delighted thoughts flying at her.

Hi.

Fun.

Play.

Fly.

Up. Up. Up.

She'd braced for anger. But oh, my goodness, the babies were . . . happy.

The youngsters sent excited and cheerful thoughts at her. Light and jolly. Filled with joyous laughter. And with all that happiness coming at her, she took it in, magnified it, and sent it back out to them. The emotional loop happened automatically, without thought or effort on her part.

The baby dragons floated and dived, played tag, ran and flapped their wings. A few shoved their snouts into platinum food and hungrily chowed down.

"This hasn't happened before?" Rion asked.

"Sweet Goddess." Lex grinned. "They are flying, carefree, and curious, the way the Goddess meant for them to be."

Darian stared in wonder. "This is the first time most of them have experienced dragonshaping without pain."

Two dragons almost crashed in midair. Rion frowned. "Too bad it's so crowded they are a danger to themselves."

Marisa agreed. The babies might have been giddy, but they could still get hurt. Flying into a wall or another dragon could break bones.

Marisa went to work, toning down the happy excitement and sending calming thoughts to the entire room. *Good babies. Nice flying. But you all need to eat. Need to rest. Come on, little dragons, fly down and eat. Rest your wings.*

At first, they refused to listen. But as they slowly tired, they walked, crawled, and flew toward the food that Lex and his people held out to them.

After the dragons ate, they humanshaped. The caretakers placed the children back into their beds. Even Rion tucked one of the babies in.

Eventually the nursery settled down. Just in time.

Pain began to pulse through Marisa. Fiery pain. Nerveshocking pain that caused her to roar and wake a few of the children.

She, too, humanshaped. Her throat had swollen shut. Her lungs seized. *Breathe, damn it. Don't pass out in front of everyone.*

Marisa fought down the pain, willed herself to stay on her feet.

Her knees buckled.

Rion caught her in his strong arms and gathered her close to his chest. "I've got you."

"Thanks." His embrace steadied her. Gave her a moment to regroup.

He carried her to a sofa and pressed a glass of juice into her hand. "It's laced with platinum. Drink it."

She hesitated. "I don't want to take someone else's share."

Rion lowered his voice. "Marisa, you need your strength to help us. Now drink."

"How did you hold out against the pain?" Lex asked her, his gaze cool and assessing.

What was he talking about? "I caved—the very second it hit." So much for courage. All her good intentions had flown out of her mind the moment that pain struck.

Hands shaking from the residual agony, she sipped. While she could ingest platinum in human form, it wasn't a real meal, more like a snack. But she was grateful to replenish her energy and take a moment to collect her thoughts, pleased that the clothing had immediately reassembled around her when she'd humanshaped.

She drank the juice, and when she looked up, she was shocked to see Lex and his people surrounding her, odd expressions she couldn't read on their faces.

"The babies are okay? They're happy . . ." Her gaze flicked to Rion.

He didn't seem to be listening. His eyes were hard, his face grim. "I told you not to dragonshape."

"You brought me here to use my skills. With so many babies flying at once, it was dangerous. I had to end the chaos."

"But you resisted the Tyrannizer," Lex said.

"No. I only felt the pain right at the end before I humanshaped."

"So what held off the pain?" Lex's voice softened in

wonder. "And what made the babies' pain disappear? I've never seen them happy. Normal. Not in dragon form."

"It's true," one of the women caretakers added. "They were eating without pain. Flying without pain. How is this possible?"

Rion, Lex, Darian, Mendle, and the female caretakers turned curious eyes to Marisa. The women were as beautiful as the men, tall and lean, with high, sculpted cheekbones. Even in rags, they looked regal.

Uncomfortable with the attention, Marisa shrugged. "I don't know what happened. For me, there was no pain—at least not at first. Later, after I calmed the babies, I felt like I was on fire."

"Why didn't she feel pain from the very first moment she dragonshaped?" Lex asked Rion.

"Perhaps she was so worried over the children that she didn't notice the pain until after everyone was safe." Rion spoke slowly.

Lex shook his head. "But the children weren't hurting, either."

Rion rubbed his chin. "It's also possible that since Marisa is capable of group telepathy, her talent shields her from the pain."

Marisa shook her head. "I was still using my telepathy to settle the children right up to the time I humanshaped. And I felt the pain." She shuddered and rubbed her arms. "It was . . . horrible."

Lex's eyes filled with hope. "If we could figure out how you banished the pain, even for a short time, perhaps others could do it, too."

"Do you eat different foods than we do?" a woman asked.

Rion shook his head. "She's been sharing meals with me for the last few days."

"What about a chemical reaction?" Darian suggested. "Hair dye? Or a soap?"

She shrugged, hating to disappoint them. She had no trick to offer. "Perhaps my DNA gives me some immunity. I'm from another world. Earth."

Her statement drew more stares and silence. She was beginning to feel like a tourist attraction.

"She's an offworlder?" One of the women's voices rose in anger. "And we trusted her with our babies?"

"She helped them," Rion said softly.

"She could betray our entire camp." The woman's eyes blazed with hatred. "She could be in league with the Unari."

"The Unari are threatening my world, too," Marisa explained. "I came here to help."

"Or betray us," the woman muttered and walked away in disgust.

While no one else said anything, many people now eyed her suspiciously.

Rion stood and glared down at everyone. "Marisa is a dragonshaper. She's here to help us and has risked her life to do so. Anyone who speaks against her speaks against me. Am I clear?"

Some of his people wouldn't meet his eyes. A few turned and walked away.

"Easy." Marisa placed a hand on his arm. "Let them get used to the idea. They've been through so much. If I were in their shoes, I'd be wary of strangers, too."

Rion swallowed hard. His hands clenched into fists. She sensed him fighting an internal battle.

"What?" she asked.

"Nothing." He wouldn't meet her gaze.

"You promised . . ."

"I didn't promise to ask you to suffer," he growled.

She scowled at him, suddenly aware that he was no longer talking about what people thought of her. "What is it?"

"I don't want to ask—"

"Ask what?" She felt as if she were prying a sword from a stone.

His eyes hardened, even as his lips twisted as if in pain. "If you could dragonshape once more, just for a moment, then tell us if you felt pain, it might help us figure out how to avoid it ourselves."

Marisa took a deep breath and let it out slowly. Before she let fear stop her, Marisa stood and dragonshaped. Her flesh turned to scales. Her eyesight was keen. Instantly every nerve ending burned as if she'd plunged into hell.

She didn't remain a dragon for more than a second before she humanshaped. No one had to ask if she'd been in pain.

Her nerves twitched. She'd borne it for only a moment. She couldn't imagine hours of that unendurable pain, days of that searing agony. She'd rather die than suffer that kind of torture.

"I'm sorry," Lex said with sadness.

"Are you all right?" Rion asked her and slipped his arm around her.

She sagged against him, then slowly straightened. "I will be." She fought to keep her voice steady. "It's not my DNA that gave me temporary immunity. I've failed you. I can't withstand that kind of pain and focus enough to send a message, too."

"No one could." Rion cupped her chin and lifted her head until their eyes locked. "This is not your fault."

She nodded, then leaned against Rion, soaking up his heat. Her nerve endings still tingled with residual bursts of pain. "But unless we figure this out, I can't send a telepathic message. I've come here for nothing. My talent is no good to you if I can't use telepathy."

An awkward silence fell. The women and some men began to drift away.

But Rion's eyes still burned with determination. "Look, you've done what no one else has done. You banished the pain for a little while." He tucked her against his side. "Now that we know it's possible, you've given us hope."

"If you say so."

"We're going to figure out what just happened and duplicate it. And then we're going to use it to save my people."

Slowly, her limbs stopped trembling. She prayed that they wouldn't ask her to dragonshape again. Not tonight. She wasn't up for more pain.

Rion led her to a couch, where she sat. "Perhaps we're not asking the right questions."

"What do you mean?" Lex asked Rion and pulled up a chair. Many of the nursery workers left to care for the children. Others wandered off to their beds. Only Lex, Darian, and Rion stayed.

Rion rubbed her shoulders and neck. "Back on Earth, Marisa was in human form when she unknowingly broadcast to adult dragonshapers and they became agitated." He speared her with an apologetic glance. "This time, when she broadcast again in human form, she made the babies happy and took away their pain."

"Let me see if I understand this." Lex frowned. "When you communicate telepathically to the group, you send emotions along with the message?"

She nodded. "The emotions I send are unintentional, but just like your words convey emotion by their tones, my telepathic messages convey emotions."

"And you're also telepathic with dragons in human form?" Lex asked.

"Yes, but I'm a much stronger telepath after I dragon-shape. When I'm human, the message is weak."

"That's it." Rion's eyes lit with excitement. "When you're human, the message is *weaker*—but the emotions you send are *stronger!*"

Marisa caught his excitement. "And those emotions are disrupting the Tyrannizer?"

A real cousin would wash his hands in blood to keep yours clean.

—ANONYMOUS POET

20

Rion accompanied Marisa to their quarters, his hopes higher than they'd been since they'd arrived. A fire burned in him to make sense out of what Marisa had just done. "Marisa, you told us that you don't consciously send emotions when you send telepathic messages."

"That's true."

"But could you deliberately broadcast your emotions along with a message?" Rion asked, his pulse pounding.

She rubbed her temple. "I don't know. The only time I ever used telepathy in human form was with my brother. And he's been gone for most of the last decade. I'm out of practice." She sighed. "But I'm still not certain your theory's correct. I was happy while helping the baby dragons, but at the end—my emotions didn't stop the pain."

"Maybe you were in dragonshape for so long, the human emotions that protected you faded. And that's when the pain hit."

"Maybe. That would also explain why I had no protection at all the second time I morphed." She sighed. "But even if I could do it again, adults interpret the happiness and joy that come from my passion differently than the babies. Babies eat and play and fly. Adults fight."

Rion had always believed Marisa was special. But who would have thought that sending her human emotions down her telepathic link was the key to preventing the Tyrannizer's pain?

Her talent was awesome. Of course, right now they still had only a theory. One he needed to test.

Rion climbed into bed next to Marisa in their room in Winhaven, but she remained silent. Stiff. Still.

Her breathing told him she wasn't asleep. Her effect on the dragon children obviously had her mind spinning. By now he knew her well enough to know she didn't always see things the same way he did.

He kept his voice low and easy. "What's wrong?"

She spoke slowly, her tone earnest. "In human form, I've affected the dragons twice, both times while we made love. When my mind wasn't on anything but you."

So she was way ahead of him. "Maybe that's the key."

"Huh?" She rolled onto her side and rested her cheek in her hand. In the moonlight that beamed through the window, he could just make out her features. Eyes wide, she wasn't smiling.

"Maybe extreme feelings wrap you in some kind of protective bubble."

She sighed. "I suppose that makes sense. But that doesn't explain why I didn't feel any pain after I first dragonshaped but then it hit me later."

"Perhaps there's a brief after-sex effect."

"An afterglow?" Her mouth twisted. "I hardly think we are the only people on the planet having sex."

"But you may be the only human telepath on the planet."

"I suppose." She sounded tired. "This sounds . . . bizarre."

He kept his tone reasonable. "Suppose we kiss—"

She raised her eyebrows. "You think you're going to get lucky again?"

"A lot of lucky." He grinned. "But while we kiss, try to figure out what you're broadcasting."

She scowled at him. "How will we know if I send anything?"

"Maybe you send automatically," he suggested, hearing her reluctance. "Maybe you can learn to control it. Maybe kissing won't even be necessary eventually—not that I mind kissing you . . ."

"Kissing or making love all the time is a little impractical. Especially for a crown prince—your people might expect you to govern them . . . or something," she teased.

"I know the idea's wacky. But if your skill could save my people . . ."

"You've seen this in a flash?" she asked.

He wanted to lie, but he'd promised he wouldn't. He shook his head. "It's more like a hunch. Or maybe I just need an excuse to kiss you." He slowly leaned toward her, his eyes on hers.

She placed a hand on his chest. "Wait. Suppose I upset the children again?"

"They're in human form now. Besides, you made them happy, remember?"

"Still, some of them could have happily flown into a wall and broken their wings. I think we need a more controlled experiment. Maybe with just one dragon close by and the others far away."

"How far?"

"Damn." She trembled. "On Earth my range was over twenty miles."

"I'll talk to Lex, and we'll think of something."

"What exactly are you going to tell him?" Her tone sharpened, and he realized that although she wanted to help, she was uncomfortable with others knowing what they would attempt.

"I'll say that you need a private place to work on dampening the pain. And we want to make sure the babies don't go wild on us again."

"No specifics?"

"No specifics." His people didn't need to know how Marisa did what she did, not unless she could find a way to teach others. At first, she could try to teach him.

"Good." She licked her bottom lip. "So we're waiting on kissing until tomorrow?"

He tugged her toward him, pleased when she snuggled, but all of a sudden, she jerked away. He frowned. "What?"

"Touching may not be such a good idea, either." Her voice was guarded.

"Why not?"

"Because your touching me creates feelings. And if I start broadcasting . . ."

He groaned. "So I'm not ever going to be able to touch you without everyone within twenty miles knowing exactly how happy I'm making you?"

"Damn." She sat up and drew her knees to her chest. "And what happens if I get angry and broadcast that?"

His heart skipped. "Has that ever happened?"

"Not to my knowledge." She began to shake.

"Hey." He started to touch her, then pulled back and clenched his fingers into fists. "We'll figure this out."

"I damn well hope so."

"Look, when you first dragonshaped, it took awhile to get the hang of telepathic communication, right?"

"Not really. I just used the same communication that Lucan and I always used."

"What about the group telepathy?"

"At first I just did that, too. It's like shouting instead of speaking. But then I learned to narrow down and direct my communication. If there's a group, I don't have to send to everyone. I can pick and choose who will receive."

"Maybe sending emotions works the same way. With practice, you may eventually choose who will receive the emotions you send."

"Maybe." Frustration laced her words. "But how am I going to practice?"

He chuckled. "With your ability to take away pain, there'll be no shortage of volunteers."

She shook her head. "This is so not funny."

"Sorry."

"In the last six months I've been around a lot of dragonshapers. No one's ever picked up my emotions unless I was with you. Not until I kissed you or made love to you. And if you make one crack about having to kiss me for the sake of your country, I'll deck you."

He was smiling inside, but he held out his hands, palms up. "No jokes."

"Good."

He patted the pillow, glad she couldn't see his face in the dark. "Come on. We both need sleep."

THE FLASH WOKE Rion in the middle of the night. One moment he was staring at the ceiling, the next he sucked in his breath.

>*The Holy Grail floated within a glass case. Made of burnished metal, it glowed with an unmistakable inner beauty and a patina that depicted its ancient age.*
>
>*The Holy Grail. A legendary healing cup reputed to be as old as the galaxy.*
>
>*The same Holy Grail Rion had once held in his hands.*
>
>*Four men wearing Unari uniforms stood guard around the case that held the Grail. Behind them were monitors. Rion couldn't read the language. But one screen showed a star map, with a course plotted in.*
>
>*According to the monitor, the ship was part of an armada and heading straight for Honor.*
>
>*Stars. The Unari were escorting the Grail to Honor.*

Rion awakened as the sun came up. His flash last night had left him certain that time was running out for his people. The Unari wouldn't risk bringing the Holy Grail to Honor, not until they'd enslaved every single Honorian.

He left Marisa to sleep and met the rebel foraging party

and Erik at the front entrance. Someone had built a fire in the hall, and the men were drinking hot tea.

"Erik!" Rion stepped into the room. He had no difficulty picking his cousin out of the crowd. They shared the same height, the same dark hair and gray eyes, the same broad shoulders. But there the resemblances ended. Erik was rail thin, with heavy dark circles under his eyes. His skin had been burned by the sun and wind. He had a scar down his neck, but it was his eyes that had changed the most. Rion's fun-loving, luxury-craving cousin had been replaced by a serious and stern man. Rion clapped Erik into a bear hug. "I didn't think I'd see you again."

Erik broke into a warm grin. "They told me you'd come back. With a woman. Knowing you—she's pretty."

"That she is."

"She's an offworlder?" Erik asked.

"What of it?" Rion tried not to bristle.

"Just guard her well. Ever since the Unari invaded, outsiders are not exactly welcome."

Rion introduced himself to the other men, who soon went off to their beds after their night mission. Finally, he and Erik were alone. Rion had dreamed of this meeting, but now that it had arrived, he sensed Erik was uncomfortable and sought to set him at ease by telling his story. He summarized his escape from Honor, the crash on Pendragon, the journey to Earth, then Tor, and back home.

"That's quite a tale. I fear mine is nowhere near as exciting."

"How did you escape the Unari?" Rion asked.

"They kept us weak, starving us of platinum so we couldn't humanshape. But some of the men went without their platinum, so I could . . ."

"Do you know how many times I wished you'd come with me?" Rion shook his head and sighed. "Your staying behind so I could get away . . . I don't know how I'll ever thank you."

"I don't, either," Erik jested, but his eyes didn't smile. "The Unari took over the city in one day. An hour after they landed, they'd installed the Tyrannizer. Chivalri fell in two days. We didn't stand a chance."

"You were part of the slave labor?"

Erik nodded. "The Unari are forcing dragonshapers to build a huge structure. I worked on one wall for three years. It's bad. They only feed the prisoners when they dragonshape. And it's never enough, so they are too weak to humanshape, and remain trapped in slave labor."

"What do you know of the machine?" Rion asked, his voice gentle, his heart heavy. He suspected Erik had suffered much that he wasn't saying. The man was nothing but skin and bones.

"The more you resist obeying Unari orders, the worse the pain."

"You've never seen the Tyrannizer?" Rion asked, and when Erik shook his head, disappointment filled him.

"But I've heard rumors." Erik's eyes turned hard. "It is said that our best warriors are kept in a room with the Tyrannizer. That the Unari torture them and then the machine absorbs their pain and projects it across all of Honor."

Ever since Rion had learned Erik was with the rebels, he'd been counting on his cousin to help plan a revolt. But the Unari had beaten Erik, like everyone else, down to a ghost of his true self.

"I've heard rumors that your father . . ." Erik couldn't meet his gaze.

"They torture him?" Just saying the words hurt.

"It's only rumor," Erik said. "If the Unari find out who you are, they'll turn the countryside upside down until they find you."

"And my mother?"

"She died in the initial takeover, trying to protect the children." Erik's eyes teared. "She was a great lady. Even if she was from Tor."

"Yes." Rion's throat closed with grief. He hadn't grown up in his parents' household, but he'd visited often. He remembered falling and skinning his knee and his mother cleaning it and telling him how brave he was to let her wash it. She'd smelled like violets, and her smile was like sunshine. But her eyes were often sad. She must have loved him very much to have given him up to save his life. Now she was gone.

He told himself that at least she hadn't suffered for three long years. But that fact did nothing to ease the hot ball of anger in his gut.

"They threw her body to the dogs." Erik shuddered, and Rion turned away to hide his tears. "You shouldn't have come back. There's nothing here but starvation, torture, and death."

"We're going to kick the Unari off this world." Rion spoke past the tight ache in his chest, past the huge lump in his throat.

Erik raised eyes that shone with hope. "If you have a plan, count me in."

If you know both yourself and your enemy, you can increase your success in battle.
                    —HONORIAN GENERAL EMERAT

21

As the small group of rebels left Winhaven, Lex cautioned Rion and Marisa, "Stay on guard. If the Unari have learned about our group in Winhaven or our route into the city, they may attack without warning."

Darian took point, Mendle the rear. Lex walked beside Rion and Marisa when the path's width permitted. But often the trail narrowed and forced them to march through the forest single file. They kept a steady pace through the thick trees, and she soon lost sight of Winhaven.

The men obviously knew this forest well. They stopped frequently to fill water bottles from swift-flowing streams. The temperature change from mountains to valleys was more severe than on Earth. Yesterday it had snowed, but today, at the lower altitude, she didn't need a jacket—but this was no pleasure outing. The blaster on her hip reminded her that danger could come from any direction.

Rion had given her a quick lesson. Basically all she had to do was point and shoot. With no safety mechanism, she'd been a little nervous about handling the blaster until she'd understood it took a strong trigger finger to fire bursts of energy.

Their course sloped downhill, and by the time they reached the valley, the sun had risen higher and the temperature had edged up at least ten degrees. She saw no sign of the Unari and was grateful for a chance to stop, take a drink of water, and catch her breath.

Lex pointed to a stone ridge about half a mile away. "That's where we go underground. Be careful to keep your voices low. Sounds can carry long distances here. As far as we know, the Unari aren't aware of our route, but they have spies everywhere."

Rion peered into the distance, and Marisa caught sight of a bird soaring overhead. Merlin had rejoined them.

Rion raised his hand to shield his eyes from the sun. "That's a train tunnel?"

Lex nodded. "Most of the system collapsed after the Unari bombed the transportation system. But with the help of several rebel groups, we've cleared the underground route right into the heart of the city."

"The old trains still work?" Rion asked, his eyes gleaming with interest.

"The Unari appropriated them." Lex gestured them forward and Marisa sensed he was trying to prepare them for what they could expect. "We stole a couple of antigravs—"

"Antigravs?" She frowned at Lex. "Will they prevent us from dragonshaping?"

He shook his head. "Only the Torans modify them that way. We've salvaged doors from bombed houses and antigravs from factories. So we have crude transport platforms to ride on."

"You salvaged doors?" she asked, wondering if Lex was jesting.

"We've had to improvise. And wood is in short supply. They're nothing fancy, but at least we can ride the rest of the way."

The tunnel had no tracks. But waiting for them was a chain of doors, nailed together to make enough seats for their entire group to ride. Headlights shone forward and toward the rear. This primitive train was far superior to anything on Earth. The rebels had fastened antigravs onto one side of the doors, causing the doors to float above the path. As their tiny rebel group sped through the tunnel, wind whipped through her hair. Her eyes teared. But there wasn't much to see. Just lots of dark rock and concrete, with the occasional tree root breaking through.

When the antigravs slowed to a gentle stop inside the tunnel, she jumped to the ground. Gravel crunched under her feet. But that was the last normal sound she heard. The terrible noise of dragons moaning sent fear trickling like ice through her veins.

The sound of wounded animals, tortured souls, screams from thousands of throats raw with agony filled the air. The low moans, the high-pitched whistles, the abject misery turned her stomach, and she swallowed hard.

The horror in Rion's eyes fed her own anger. How dare the Unari do this? They had no right to invade and subjugate Rion's people. No one, absolutely no one, should have to endure the kind of pain that produced those sounds.

The noise rumbled through her, settled into her brain, and took up residence. She no longer wanted to go outside and see what was going on—not when the sounds alone had her knees knocking and her gut churning.

Lex and his men must have heard the broken rumble of tortured dragons many times before, but they were not immune. She could see them gritting their teeth, bracing their shoulders before they exited the tunnel and headed outside.

Marisa couldn't wimp out and remain behind. She forced herself to take deep breaths and slipped her hand into Rion's. She had to be strong—for his sake.

But no amount of courage could prepare her for the sight that met her eyes. From the hillside above the city they had a perfect view of . . . hell.

Dragons flew through the sky, pulling pyramid-sized stones supported by antigravs. Although the stones were weightless, they still had mass, which meant stopping and starting the stones' flight required huge amounts of effort. Dragons flew, placing their bodies between the stones, straining to position the rocks into enormous walls that formed a pit as wide and deep as the eye could see.

Everywhere, dragons worked, suffering under Unari whips. Many sported huge scars where the stones had torn into scales and flesh. Rion had told her of Erik's scar, and she knew he'd worked here, or in a place just like this one. Some dragons had open, oozing wounds. A few were missing limbs, eyes, or parts of their tails. None had the energy to fully spread their wings or fly properly. Their ribs protruded through bony chests. Their wings looked broken, the color a faded puce instead of brilliant purple.

"Half starved, maddened by pain; it's a wonder they can work at all," Marisa said.

Lex sighed. "If the Unari lower the pain levels, our people fight back."

Her throat tightened with tears. She didn't dare let a

sob escape. They had to do something to stop this ghastly display. Anything.

But what was even worse than the dragons' mutilated bodies and starved frames was the utterly defeated look in their golden eyes. She didn't see one spark of hope. As if the Tyrannizer's pain wasn't enough, the Unari had beaten down their spirits, whipping any dragons they deemed slackers with pulsing energy rods that zapped and burned the skin.

The scent of burning scales hit her full-force. For a moment she closed her eyes, but the images had been branded into her mind: tiny babies, their wings stressed almost to the breaking point, flying to deliver mortar to smooth between the gigantic stones. Female and male dragons screaming in shrill bursts when a line broke and giant stones tumbled onto dragons working below— crushing some, the others bellowing death rattles. And the Unari, monsters who looked like ordinary humans, ignored the thrashing injured and forced the remaining dragons to keep building the walls right on top of their dying comrades' bodies.

"Can you send out a message?" Rion said. "Ask the dragons if they know where my father is."

"I can try." Marisa dragged her attention from the horror before her. She had to be strong for Rion and for all these poor souls. Trying to control her breathing, she focused on one simple question. *Where is the king?*

The pain from thousands of minds zapped her.

The next thing she knew, she was lying on the ground, cradled in Rion's arms, her muscles jerking. "Wh-what happened?"

"You passed out," he said. "Are you all right now?"

She nodded. "I'm sorry. I couldn't get through. The backwash of so much pain overpowered me." She pushed to her feet. "I'll try again."

"Not yet."

She recoiled from the sharpness in Rion's voice. "But that's why I'm here."

He shook his head. "I won't risk putting you through that kind of pain again without a better plan. We have to know more about what we're dealing with first."

Although she didn't admit it aloud, she was glad for a reprieve. Echoes of the agony she'd suffered still stung her nerves. She pushed to her feet. "So what do we do now?"

Rion studied the hellish landscape. "We try to figure out what the Unari are doing."

"Maybe they're creating some kind of city," Lex suggested.

"The Unari aren't building a city." Rion's voice was tight, low, and angry.

"If it's not a city, what is it?" Lex asked.

"They're erecting a building to protect the Holy Grail," Rion said.

"What?" His claim drew her attention from the terrible sight. Years ago, her brother had found a map—a star map that located the famous city of Avalon, where King Arthur had enshrined the Grail, not in England, but on another world. Because Lucan hoped the Grail would solve Earth's infertility problem, he had talked the Vesta Corporation into funding his mission to the stars. During his journey, Lucan had found a cure for Earth's infertility problem, but others had wanted the Grail, too. Had the healing cup fallen into the Unari Tribes' possession?

Rion frowned at the Unari building. "This structure's very similar to the obelisk on Avalon that held the Grail. Only it's so much larger, I can't take it all in." He muttered under his breath, "No wonder I couldn't find the Grail."

His words confused her. "But you and Lucan found the Grail, then lost it."

"After I figured out how to use the transporter at Stonehenge," Rion told her, "I returned to Pendragon and searched. The Grail was gone."

Her eyes widened. "When you took me through the Stonehenge portal, it wasn't the first time? You'd used it before?"

"Yes."

She shook her head and sighed. How many more secrets did he have? A dragon howled in agony and shot a chill down her spine: she supposed Rion's keeping some information to himself didn't matter so much in the giant scheme of things.

"If the Unari have the Grail, why wouldn't they keep such a valuable object on their home world?" Marisa asked.

"Lots of reasons," Rion explained. "Historically, the planet that houses the Grail often comes under attack from those who seek to take the healing cup's powers for their own."

"The Unari have enemies who will come for the Grail?" she asked.

"It's very possible that over the centuries the Unari have made more enemies than Honor, Pendragon, and Tor. And the Unari don't care if my people die, or if my world is destroyed. Better for them to fight here—than risk their own people."

"The Holy Grail? It's not a legend?" Lex asked.

"I've held it in my hands." Rion spoke with authority. "I believe this entire structure is being built to house it so the Unari can tap its powers. We have to stop them before they finish and drink from the cup. Because once they place the Grail inside this edifice, they'll become so powerful, we'll never oust them."

Lex scowled. "Is the legend true? That with the Grail in their possession, the Unari armies will not die? That they'll rise again to defeat Honor, Pendragon, Tor, and Earth?"

"We can't let them . . ." Marisa looked at Rion, her heart breaking. Had her brother caused this galaxy-wide disaster? Had the twin she loved found the Grail inadvertently for the Unari?

A muscle ticked in Rion's jaw. "It's up to us to stop the Unari on Honor."

"And to stop them from building, we have to destroy the Tyrannizer," she said.

Rion nodded. "One way or another, we have to find and destroy that machine."

Lex and his men had mostly stayed in the background and out of the conversation. But Darian suddenly tensed, drew his weapon, and hit the dirt, taking Lex to the ground with him.

"By the Goddess," Darian swore. "Floaters."

"Pull back," Lex ordered. "Pull back now."

Seizing the enemy without fighting takes skill.
—SUN TZU

22

Rion had never seen so many floaters. About as wide as a man, the dull black spheres with glowing green eyes swooped toward them with an ominous hum.

Rion grabbed Marisa by the arm and yanked her to the dirt. "Get down."

"What are they?" She flattened her body but watched the sky.

"Floaters. Telemetric remote-controlled transport units monitored by Unari weapons specialists." Lex motioned them back toward the tunnel.

Rion retreated, but a floater placed itself between him and the tunnel. Lex shot it. Rion tried to take another step, but another floater took the other's place.

The men closed in, standing back to back with Marisa in the middle. Rion shot the next one. Marisa looked over his shoulder. "You can't shoot fast enough."

Each time a floater obstructed their retreat, Lex, Rion, or Darian shot it, but each blast wasted precious seconds they didn't have as they waited for the exploding shards to clear before they could retreat once again.

"They don't shoot back?" Marisa asked.

Lex shot one in the sky and it burst into flames. "If their stunner hits you, the blast paralyzes your muscles."

Darian added, "After the floaters capture their victims, the Unari starve them until they're so weak they dragon-shape to eat. Then they feed the dragons only enough to perform slave labor."

Marisa hunkered behind Rion, her voice hard. "We can't let them take us."

Rion agreed. But they would run out of blaster ammo long before the Unari ran out of floaters. "Is there another way out of here besides that tunnel?" Rion asked Lex. He advanced a half step toward the tunnel, looking past the stored equipment to his right and left, but he saw only open land to their sides and the giant hellish building behind them.

"The tunnel's our only way out," Lex confirmed.

They couldn't go forward. They couldn't go back. They couldn't hide.

With floaters surrounding them and more hovering and ready to descend, the rebel group was running out of options. The floaters would capture them within moments.

Marisa gazed longingly at the tunnel. "Can't we just run for it?"

"They're too fast. But we have no other choice." Lex fired at another floater. A beam bounced off the floater and the air sizzled. The floater spun and wobbled. "We have to try for the tunnel. Everybody, let's go."

Every time they damaged a floater, three more swooped down—until the floaters had almost formed a solid wall to block their retreat.

Rion kept hold of Marisa and sidled toward the tunnel. "Try to make the entrance."

They were in trouble, outnumbered, their escape tunnel blocked by a wall of floaters. The rebels tried to shoot their way through. But even if every charge they fired took out a floater, they wouldn't win. The sky was dark with floaters—enough to block out the sun.

Fire.

Fall back.

Fire again.

As a group, they developed a rhythm. Two men shot, the others pulled back. But the floaters were herding them together. Soon the objects would pin them—but still the rebels fired.

The floaters took massive losses. But robotically controlled machines felt no pain, had no fear.

"Lay down your weapons," a mechanical voice ordered.

"Not on your life," Marisa muttered and fired over Rion's shoulder.

When a floater targeted Darian with a yellow light, Rion fired and the machine fell from the sky, taking two other spheres with it, and all three machines shattered. Shards of metal rained down—a few pieces taking out more floaters. The chain reaction had annihilated ten spheres, but one of the shards hit Mendle.

He jerked back with a hiss of pain, then rolled and shot another floater out of the sky. Lex blasted another of the machines that blocked the tunnel, but two more took its place.

Marisa held up a hand and Lex threw her an extra weapon. She fired alongside Rion, muttering fiercely,

"You're just metal. Tin cans." She swiveled and fired again. "Nothing we can't handle."

Rion had never seen her like this. Fierce. Focused. Fighting. And her aim wasn't bad, either.

Rion would fight until his last breath. But he pulled the trigger and his weapon failed to fire. Out of ammo, he swung the blaster like a bat, taking out his anger and frustration on the machines. He dented one but caused little real damage.

"Aim for the sensors. The eyes," Lex shouted.

Darian and Marisa kept shooting. Lex, Mendle, and Rion were reduced to batting practice. Rion glanced over his shoulder. They'd actually gained quite a bit of ground. "Come on. Ten more feet, people. Ten more feet and we'll make the tunnel."

It might as well have been ten miles.

Marisa shouted, "I'm out of power."

"Me, too," Darian added.

Everyone was now kicking and striking the floaters. They smashed sensors, dented the hulls, shattered many of the spheres to bits. And still more came to replace those that had fallen.

"Lay down your weapons," the floaters ordered again, their mechanical voices eerily without emotion.

Dozens of black orbs hemmed in their group. They were going to beat the rebels by smothering them into submission. Marisa fought to Rion's left. Lex to his right. Darian and Mendle had his back.

The floaters kept squeezing them, until Rion couldn't lift his arm for lack of room. Suddenly the sounds of battle ended. The spheres had surrounded them. The floaters had encased them in a metal prison made up of floaters.

"Now what?" Marisa asked, sounding brave and slipping her hand into Rion's.

"Now we wait for the Unari to figure out what to do with us," Mendle spat. "It can take hours."

"Or days," Darian agreed.

Marisa gasped. "Are you saying they'll just leave us standing here, trapped by the floaters until—"

"Until someone in authority feels like dealing with us," Lex answered.

"If we have that long, maybe we can dig our way out," Rion suggested.

"What exactly are we supposed to dig with?" Marisa asked.

"Our toes."

"Sorry, I can't feel my toes. My legs have gone numb. In fact, if they move away, I'm going to fall," Marisa warned him.

He would have liked to tell her he would catch her. But Rion didn't make promises he couldn't keep.

He tried to clench and unclench his fingers. But there was no room. He could barely draw in enough air to breathe. "We haven't been pinned long enough for them to cut off our circulation."

Disarmed and pinned wasn't enough. No, the Unari had to make sure they couldn't move, too? They were thorough bastards. Rion needed a plan to escape. To save Marisa.

But how could he make a plan when his thoughts were slowing? By the Goddess, these floaters weren't just paralyzing his muscles, but his mind. And that was his last bleak thought.

All warfare is based on cunning, guile, and subterfuge.

—LADY OF THE LAKE

23

"O h, yuck," Marisa muttered, trying to see through eyelids crusty with grit. The last thing she remembered was Rion, the floaters, and slowly going unconscious. If she could open her eyes, she might figure out what had happened. From the stench, she guessed she'd fallen into a sewage pit. Her mouth tasted as if she hadn't brushed her teeth in a year. Worse, every muscle in her body ached, not like the flu, more like she'd bruised every bone in a car wreck.

But there were no cars on Honor.

With a groan, she forced open her eyes, then wished she hadn't. She was lying on hard rock—wet, cold rock. No wonder her teeth were chattering. Confused, she gazed up to a blue sky overhead. Not a rain cloud or a floater in sight.

Dully, she turned her aching neck. And her stomach turned inside out. The floater must have dumped her here. She was one of hundreds of prisoners—men, women, and children—all lying at the bottom of . . . where the hell was she?

Straight stone walls climbed skyward around a large open area. Water sluiced down one wall, and the prisoners smarter than she was had had enough sense not to sleep in the runoff.

She shoved to a sitting position, tried to ignore the ice pick stabbing her brain. "Rion?"

"Who are you looking for?" the woman beside her asked, her voice strong.

Surely that robust voice couldn't come from such an emaciated person? The rail-thin woman's collarbones stuck out through the top of her torn shirt. Marisa guessed her age anywhere between twenty and forty. The woman had tied the ripped ends of her shirt together for modesty's sake. Caked in dirt, her hair so slimy the color was undetectable, her nails ragged and torn, she still angled her head to show off a graceful neck. Once her cheekbones would have been beautiful; now the sharp ridges were merely a counterpoint to the dark circles under her eyes, the hollows of her cheeks, and her bruised jaw.

"I'm Marisa."

The woman nodded. "Colleen."

"I was looking for Rion, the man I was with before—"

"You got caught by the floaters?" Colleen guessed.

"Yeah."

"If you have the energy to look, he's probably here. Somewhere." She gestured a bit apathetically. "It's not like anyone is going anywhere."

"Thanks."

Marisa glanced around. Although she ached down

to the marrow of her bones, she still had some strength, if only she could kick her aching muscles into gear. A closer look at the mass of lethargic people around her was enough to shoot her to her feet. Most of them weren't moving. From their gray skin, she guessed either they were very ill . . . or they were no longer breathing.

The wind swirled, and she sucked in a relatively stench-free breath of air. But it was only a tiny reprieve. These people hadn't bathed in days, maybe months. There was no fresh water to drink or bathe in, and in place of a bathroom, there was a trench.

Marisa moved to her right, taking care not to step on anyone. "I need to look for my friend."

"You're better off if you don't," Colleen warned. "It's hard to watch the ones you love die. And everyone here either starves or dragonshapes and becomes a slave."

"I understand." Marisa didn't doubt the truth of Colleen's words. But she had to find Rion. Which meant tamping down the panic that threatened to well up her throat every time she breathed in the stench. Or heard a child moan. Or saw the flies that buzzed around the dead or almost dead.

At first she called out Rion's name as she walked, but she drew too much attention to herself. So she kept a sharp eye out for clothing that wasn't covered in gray grime.

For hours.

For miles.

It was as if the Unari had taken every person in Chivalri and stuck them in this hole. Most of the people stared at her with vacant, listless eyes. There was hardly any talking. Just exhausted whispers. And black despair.

She walked for the rest of the day, until it grew so dark

that she couldn't see well enough to go on without stepping on people. Sliding to the ground, she consoled herself that at least she was dry. But she had yet to come to the far end of the pit. Even worse, she'd walked in only one direction. For all she knew, she should have been walking the other way.

Searching for anyone in this morass of humanity was futile. She should have listened to Colleen. And yet, if Rion was able, she knew he'd be looking for her.

Lips dry and cracked, Marisa yearned for water. Although her stomach rumbled for food, hunger wasn't her major problem. Between the stench and her surroundings, she'd lost her appetite. She should have been grateful. The Unari wouldn't give her food until she dragonshaped, and then they'd force her to work in horrible pain. She understood why it was easier to starve.

"When do we get water?" she asked a woman to her left. Eyes glazed, the woman turned away as if she hadn't heard.

An older man behind her coughed, his hacking dry and weak. Someone by her feet rolled over and began to snore. In a sea of people, Marisa had never felt so alone.

She had no idea where she was—not really. Was this some giant prison? Or a giant grave?

She might survive without food for weeks, but she couldn't go more than a few days without water. Her throat was so dry it hurt to swallow. She tried not to think about her chapped lips, or how dry her eyeballs felt. In fact, she wished she could just sleep and not think about tomorrow.

Get a grip.

She still had her strength. She'd been here less than a

day. Rion and the rebels had to be here somewhere. She would find them. She didn't know how, but tomorrow she would keep looking.

As the sun set and darkness settled in, she found a spot to lie down for the night. A small child curled against Marisa. Since the sun had set, the night air was chilly, and sharing body heat made sense, even with a stranger. Besides, she sensed no malevolence in any of these people. No one had the energy for anything but survival.

Despite her exhaustion, she couldn't sleep. The ground was dry, but it was hard and cold. Sand worked its way under her tunic, into her hair and socks. As an irritant, it was the perfect medium, rough, tiny, and hard. And sand clung to sweaty skin, rubbing patches of flesh raw.

Tomorrow she would have to shake the sand out of her footwear, clothing, and hair. Giving herself something positive to accomplish made her feel better. Sand removal might be a small thing, but . . . she fell asleep thinking about sand.

Marisa opened her eyes. Day two. No Rion. No food. No water. Her tongue had swollen inside her mouth. Her lips were cracked, perhaps bleeding. Exhaustion cycled through her brain, turning off her emotions, her normal curiosity, her energy.

Around her, people stirred. Slowly. The old man kept coughing, the dry hacks terrible to hear. The woman who'd ignored her yesterday had yet to move. The kid who'd snuggled at her back had disappeared.

The first stirring of a breeze had her tipping up her head. She spied a round, dull black ball descending from the sky. Was she already hallucinating? No, it was a floater.

The sphere seemed to be aiming directly for her. Around her, people scooted, backed, and rolled away. Now was not the time to be brave. Marisa backed into the crowd to blend.

But the damn thing followed her.

Coincidence?

Maybe. But she changed her direction, then randomly darted in another. When she glanced up, the floater was still overhead. No way could she outrun it. Or fight it with nothing but her bare hands.

Marisa did the only logical thing she could. She folded her arms over her chest, faced the orb, and waited. "What do you want, you overgrown tin can?"

"It wants you," someone in the crowd muttered.

"What for?" she asked, not really expecting an answer.

"The floaters eat people."

That didn't sound good.

"They like fresh meat."

She'd gotten a whiff of her own stink. She was no longer fresh.

"The newbies always give in to the hunger."

She was swaying on her feet, her legs practically Jell-O. So much for her plan to shake out the sand, to keep looking for Rion.

If she'd had the room, she might have worked up the strength to run. But the crowd ringed her as if she was the only entertainment they'd had that year. Her heart pounded and her adrenaline surged. Perhaps she could kick out one of the machine's six eyes.

The floater hovered about a foot off the ground. She wouldn't wait until it grew teeth. She threw a swift kick at the eye. And was pleased to hear it shatter. The crowd didn't make a sound. The floater didn't stun her. It merely turned a new eye in her direction.

One eye down, five more to go. She lashed out with another kick. Again she smashed it. Four to go. Again the sphere turned.

Kick. Kick. Kick.

Only one to go. "You aren't very smart, are you?" she muttered, taking out the last eye. The floater just hovered, about a foot off the ground. Any moment she expected it to shoot a paralysis beam at her.

Instead, the orb cracked open. She stepped back. The floater had a circular door. Compared to the brightness outside, the interior was shadowed and dark. She couldn't see much at all.

"Get inside, Marisa Roarke."

The tin can knew her name. First and last. She damn well hadn't told anyone here her last name. Come to think of it, she hadn't told Lex's group her last name, either.

"Climb inside," the floater repeated.

Marisa shook her head.

"Climb inside climb inside climb inside climb inside—"

"No way am I climbing into you. Not unless you take me to Rion."

"If that is your order, I will take you to Rion."

Marisa blinked. Was she hearing things? Hallucinating? "You will take me to Rion?"

"Climb inside climb inside climb inside climb inside."

It had to be a trick. But she already knew the floater

wasn't very smart. Perhaps it received orders electronically? If one of those eyes she'd kicked had severed the sphere from its Unari handler, perhaps it was waiting for new orders.

"I order you to find Rion." She didn't expect the machine to follow her orders, but she had to try something to find Rion and get out of this hellhole.

"Rion is on the grid, one thousand two hundred and fifty-three meters south, southwest."

"Fine. I'll climb in. Then you take me to Rion. Do not stop. Do not communicate with anyone else but me."

"Climb inside climb inside climb inside."

She had to be out of her mind. But she climbed into the floater. It was smooth and shiny. There was no seat, but there was enough room that she didn't have to crouch. Once inside, she spied holes in the ceiling where sound came through a speaker.

The door clanged shut behind her. She was now in complete darkness. Inside the bowels of a floater. Trapped. No doubt the people on the ground were sure she'd been eaten—just as they'd predicted.

But so far, no teeth were gnashing on her flesh, no digestive juice was dissolving her skin. With the floater's liftoff, her pulse accelerated.

The machine whisked upward and sideways, flying away in a smooth arc. She prayed the damaged eyes wouldn't cause them to crash.

Think positive. A window would have been nice, air-conditioning better. Most of all, she craved water. She didn't know a throat could be so dry that it hurt to breathe.

"How long until we get there?" Marisa asked.

The floater didn't reply, but she could feel them losing altitude. The orb stopped. Nothing happened.

Now what?

"Open the door," Marisa ordered.

She heard a hiss. Then the door opened.

Marisa looked outside. Her eyes took a few moments to adjust to daylight. The scene outside looked exactly like the one she'd left. Tired and filthy people dressed in stained rags. The same pit.

But then the crowd edged back as a man shouldered his way through the throng. At first her gaze moved on, but something familiar about the man's movement caused her gaze to dart back to him. "Rion?"

"Marisa?" He was covered in sand, his clothing full of mud, his eyes blacker than she'd ever seen. But until she touched him, until she breathed in his scent, she wouldn't believe he was really there. That he was real.

"Wait here," she ordered the floater, then leaped from the tin can and sprinted straight toward Rion. He ran toward her, too. And when they met, he swept her up and embraced her.

"I thought I'd never see you again." His lips crashed down on hers. His arms held her tight. She wound her arms around his neck and pressed herself against his chest.

God. She'd missed him. She'd missed his strength, she'd missed his company, she'd missed his strong arms.

She kept running her hands over his shoulders, down his broad back, needing to touch him to reassure herself he was really here with her. And when she pulled back from their kiss, she could see the relief in his eyes.

She grinned, her first grin since she'd wakened without him. "I can't believe I found you."

"Are you all right?" He set her back on her feet.

"I'm better now." She took his hand and led him over to the floater. She stepped inside, then beckoned for him to join her. "Get in."

Without hesitation, he stepped inside. They barely fit, but she was so glad to see him she wouldn't have cared if it took a can opener to separate them. She wrapped her arms around Rion and reveled once again in the solid feel of him. "I've figured out how to make the floaters give us a ride."

"How?"

"The tin can isn't too smart—"

"Tin can?"

"The floater. After I knocked out all its eyes, it began taking orders from me."

"How did you take out its eyes?"

"I kicked it. When it turned to look at me with a new eye, I kicked it again." She grinned wider. "I must have interrupted its normal processor or communicator. Anyway, the floater obeyed my order to take me to you."

"Why didn't you ask it to take you to freedom?"

"I couldn't leave you behind." In fact, she hadn't thought of anything but finding him.

"Will it take us out of here?" Rion asked.

"I don't know." While the machine couldn't possibly hold more than two of them, she felt compelled to ask, "Where are Lex and his men?"

"I haven't seen them. I don't know how you found me." Rion looked at her with amazement and pride.

"The tin can found you. It might be able to find the others, but we can't carry anyone else on this trip. There's no room." She wrapped her arms around him and pulled him tight against her. "Close the door."

The door shut. Rion squeezed against her, his every muscle tense. As much as she appreciated how good he felt pressed against her, she murmured, "Relax. We won't be able to see a thing until the door opens again."

"Now what?"

"I order you to take us outside the perimeter to the tunnel."

Nothing happened.

"Follow my order," she tried again.

Again, nothing happened. "Why aren't you following my orders?"

It was hot, stuffy, the air growing staler with every breath. She leaned into Rion. "Sorry about this. My orders worked last time."

"Try rephrasing."

"I order you to get us out of here. Now, please." Again, nothing happened. "His circuits must be really fried."

"Or maybe this is a trap."

"I'm sorry," Marisa whispered. "I didn't know we were going to suffocate in here. I thought we could get away."

"It's not your fault."

Yes, it was. Rion wouldn't have gotten in the floater if she hadn't brought it here. He wouldn't have gotten inside if she hadn't asked him to.

They were going to die. And it was all her fault.

Violence is the last resort of the inept.
—HIGH PRIESTESS OF AVALON

24

"D amn. Damn. Damn." With every curse, Marisa kicked the machine or slapped it with her fist. "Do something."

Rion wasn't sure if she was yelling at him or the floater. "You want me to kick it, too?" Before she answered, he slugged the floater with his fist.

The tin can hummed in response. He held his breath. "I think we're moving."

"Way to go." Marisa sounded like she was smiling. "Take us to the tunnel. Don't stop."

"No stop no stop no stop no stop."

"I hope its navigation works better than the voice system." Rion told himself not to get his hopes up. They could run out of air before the sphere landed. Or other floaters could shoot them down. Or they might end up in Unari headquarters.

Rion waited, his arms around Marisa, wishing his back wasn't to the door. He couldn't do a good job protecting her when he was facing the wrong direction. Yet turning around wasn't possible. Not till the door opened.

If it opened. The floater could keep them trapped inside . . . forever.

Finally, he sensed the floater's descent. It stopped. The door didn't open.

"Open door," Marisa ordered.

The door opened and he turned around, squinting against the daylight, hands raised, ready to take on whoever might be there. But they were alone. At the tunnel. He stepped outside.

"It worked." Marisa exited the floater, breathed deeply, and tried to tug him toward the entrance.

But he couldn't go. He couldn't abandon his men. "I have to go back for Lex, Darian, and Mendle."

Marisa spun around, hands on her hips. "That's a bad idea." She ticked off her reasons on her fingers. "One. That floater has loose wires and may not work again. Two. Even if you find them, you may get caught. Three. Since you're the best chance this world has of freeing everyone from the Unari, your life is too valuable to risk."

"I'm not leaving my men behind."

Rion glanced at the floater and thought of a compromise. "I'll get Lex. Then he can go after Mendle and Darian."

"What makes you think that tin can is up to another trip? Or that the Unari won't sense something's wrong and take it in for service or termination? How long do you think you have before they figure out we've escaped?"

"They may never figure it out." Rion spoke calmly, but he couldn't be certain.

Dirty, tired, she stood between him and the floater and tried to push him toward the tunnel. "Everyone inside that pit is one of your people. You can't save them all. And if we can keep our knowledge of how to manipulate the tin cans a secret, we can use that in the final push. You get caught—they'll know what we know. They'll take precautions. We'll lose any advantage we've gained."

"You're right." But he wasn't running away and leaving his men.

Marisa frowned, her expression blank. "You're still going back, aren't you?"

"Yes."

"All right." She took a step back, then another. "Let me show you—" She stepped back into the sphere. "Close door."

He did a double take at the closing door.

Rion lunged, grasped the slick edges. "Marisa," he growled out.

The door began to close. He strained to keep it open.

"You're not going." He wedged his foot into the opening. He was not letting her return to that hellhole.

"I can do this." Marisa pressed her back to the floater, thrust her foot against his chest, and shoved him back.

He lost his precarious foothold, scrambled, and managed to cling by his fingertips to the door's rubber seal. "Not by yourself, you can't." Sweating with effort, he grasped the edge, struggled for a better grip. His muscles burned, but he refused to let go.

But the door began to close. "Marisa!"

The floater tipped. His feet swung wildly over the ground. His fingers slipped. He slid.

"*No.*" He was not going to let her risk her life for him.

The door slammed shut.

He fell to the ground. The floater soared into the sky. She was gone.

He stared at the floater until it became a silver pinpoint in the blue sky. The gut-wrenching fear that hollowed out his stomach was like nothing he'd ever known before. She might not come back. He might not ever see her again.

Resting his hands on his knees, he leaned over to drag breath into his lungs, to dispel the fear that gripped him. What the hell was wrong with him?

The thought of her not coming back . . .

He dragged in another breath. She had to come back.

Dressed in rags, she carried herself like a queen, her tears of torment, the tears of all mankind.
— LADY OF THE LAKE

25

After the floater opened, Marisa looked out into the middle of chaos. Dragons flew everywhere, working, pulling, pounding the giant stones into place with their tails.

If the tin can had stopped in the right place, then the Unari had found a way to make Lex dragonshape.

They'd enslaved him.

Lex didn't yet have broken scales. He also didn't have the massive scars from accidents or Unari whip burns like the rest of the dragonshapers.

But while he looked stronger than the other dragonshapers, from his ponderous movements and the droop of his head, she knew he suffered great pain. All the dragons did.

And no way would he fit into the floater in dragon form. Hadn't Lex told her the Unari kept the dragons so weak they couldn't transform back? A lack of platinum would account for the weakened state of them all.

She didn't want to fail again. But what should she

do? Staying hidden behind the floater, she watched and searched for an opportunity.

The dragons paid no attention to her. She saw no Unari. Lex was placing the huge stones on top of one another. He hadn't looked her way. Didn't seem to know she was there.

Dragons could understand simple human words. Should she talk to him?

Fear of discovery kept her immobile, but nothing changed. No Unari appeared. The dragons kept working, flying, pounding and shoving the giant stones into place. At first she couldn't understand why the weight of the walls didn't cause the stones to fall inward. Then she saw crossbraces and antigravs and advanced engineering that kept the structure strong. Once finished, the site would be a fortress. Practically impenetrable.

Frustrated by the heat, the dust, the lack of water, and most of all by her own indecision, she slid from behind the floater. She walked right up to Lex before he seemed to notice her. Even after he had to have seen her, he kept working. "Lex. You must humanshape."

The dragon moaned.

"Humanshape and I'll get you out of here."

Lex staggered, almost dropping one of the huge stones. At the last second, he slammed it into a precarious position on the wall. The stone teetered. Her stomach tensed as she glanced down to the dragons working five levels below. If this stone fell, many would die.

Lex strained, digging in his massive claws, releasing a strained whistle from his nostrils. The rock steadied.

Had he heard her? Had her words distracted him? Or had he tried to do as she'd asked, but the pain had kicked up another level until he lost concentration? She wasn't certain how the pain controlled the dragons, but she knew that it hurt more when they resisted orders.

Deep in pain, Lex might not not have even heard her words.

If Marisa wanted to get through to him, she'd have to go to a deeper level of consciousness—mind to mind. But once she established a telepathic link, his pain would hit her, too. If she so much as gasped or screamed, she could give herself away. Even worse, if she fainted, as she'd done earlier, she'd be helpless to hide or protect herself.

She gritted her teeth, braced for pain, and focused on Lex. On one message.

Humanshape.

As she fought to form and send the mental message, she opened a direct link to Lex. Pain slammed her like a hundred stinging bees. Like a thousand stab wounds. Like she'd swallowed glass and the sharp edges rubbed acid into her nerves.

Despite her determination to hold on, the link snapped. The terrible agony ended, but the painful backlash took several long moments to fully subside.

God. Tears brimmed in her eyes, and her vision blurred. How did they stand it? There were no words for that kind of torment. Just a few seconds of torture had dropped her to her knees.

Worse, she didn't know if she'd gotten the message to Lex. Groggy, fuzzy-headed, and close to heat stroke, she summoned the strength to try again. A shadow fell over her, blocking out the sun.

Adrenaline failed to kick in. She'd used up her reserve. She'd pushed to the limit, and now she couldn't even focus her vision. Was it the Unari? A dragon? A man? She blinked away the tears, and with sheer willpower alone, she lifted her head.

"Lex." Thank God. He was human again.

"Another hour," he gasped and helped her to her feet, "and I wouldn't have had it in me to break free."

"Let's go. Rion . . . waiting for us." Weak from dehydration and residual pain, they helped each other to the floater, and, bless him, he didn't hesitate to step inside the machine. He didn't ask questions. He simply followed her lead.

"Back to the tunnel," she ordered.

So dizzy she couldn't see straight, she longed to lie down, close her eyes. Rest.

If they hadn't been packed in tight, she would have collapsed. Her mind was fading. With her last breath she whispered, "When we land, order the floater to open the door."

RION SEARCHED THE sky for the tenth time in the last ten minutes. Where was Marisa?

When he finally spied a black dot, he stared so hard that his eyes ached. As the dot grew larger, his hopes rose.

Finally, the floater descended into the clearing, and he had to remind himself to breathe. It was the same floater. The one without eyes. But was Marisa inside? By the Goddess, had she saved Lex?

The door opened with a clang, and Marisa fell out. Lex staggered out, too, just as Rion caught Marisa and scooped her into his arms. Eyes closed, her cheeks flushed an unnatural pink, her body caked with dirt, sand, and dust, she felt light. Hot. Her skin was burning.

He had to bring down her body temperature fast. Before her brain fried.

Rion carried Marisa to where he'd set up the hose. He laid her down in the sand, turned on the spigot, and sprayed cool water over her. But was it too late?

He sat beside Marisa, supporting her with one arm. He used the thumb of his free hand to disperse and spray water straight up, so it could rain down over her.

Lex wobbled toward Marisa and Rion. The man was white. Shaking. That he didn't dive under the water with them revealed his self-control. His concern was for Marisa. "Is she still breathing?"

"Yes. Come under the water with us." Rion gestured Lex to his side, then gathered Marisa into his arms. "There's plenty of water. But drink slowly, or—"

"I understand." Lex tilted back his head, sipped at the water, and began to rinse off the grime, careful to keep the dirty splashes off Marisa.

Rion smoothed Marisa's hair from her face. "Come on, Marisa. Wake up."

"She saved me." Lex's voice was hoarse, choked with emotion. "I don't how she did it, but her mental signal broke through my pain. It was just enough for me to—"

"What?" Rion jerked his attention to Lex. "She didn't find you in human form?"

Lex shook his head, confusion in his eyes. "I figured that's why you sent her. Because of that mental talent of hers. The Unari threatened to kill ten people if I didn't dragonshape . . . And then they made me work on the wall. Thanks to Marisa, I broke free—just barely."

"I didn't send her. I was going back for you, but she tricked me and took my place."

"She took it upon herself to go?" Lex's jaw dropped. "But this isn't her battle. She's not even from Honor."

"She may not have been born here, but her heart is with us. And it may have cost her . . ." Rion swallowed hard.

"When Marisa linked telepathically with me," Lex sighed, "she suffered what I was suffering."

Rion's gut wrenched. "You're certain?"

"After we linked, she dropped to her knees." Lex frowned at Rion. "I owe her my life. If she hadn't come . . . I'd still be there." Face grim, Lex brushed back his wet hair.

"She disobeyed—"

Lex placed a hand on his shoulder. "She risked her life so you wouldn't have to risk yours."

"She saved both of us," Rion admitted. "And I'm afraid it may have killed her."

"You love her?" Lex asked.

"I can't have her."

"You're the future king. You can have what you want."

Rion didn't answer. If only the world were that simple. But if they managed to throw off the Unari domination, he owed it to his people to marry someone from Honor. Someone who could help heal the wounds—not an off-worlder whom they wouldn't understand.

Lex stood. "Tell me how to handle the floater and I'll go get Darian and Mendle."

"If they're in dragonshape . . ."

"I don't think they are," Lex said. "We were separated. Only my group went straight to work."

"You sure you're up to going back?" Rion asked.

"I can do no less for them than Marisa did for me."

Rion nodded and gave Lex the simple instructions to direct the floater.

Lex took one last long, slow drink of water. Then he entered the floater, shut the door, and ascended into the sky.

Rion was now alone with Marisa. He sat with her under the shower, cupping water and tilting it into her mouth, pleased when she swallowed. He fed her water until his fingertips puckered and she refused to take more. Eventually the burning heat in her body eased and she slipped into a natural slumber.

But she mumbled in her sleep. Fretted.

Had her brain suffered any damage during her ordeal? Would she remember what had happened? Would she recognize him?

Once, her eyes opened.

"You look . . . so good," she said, then closed her eyes again.

MARISA AWAKENED TO the distant sounds of dragons in pain. A rumble, a shriek.

It all came back, the floater, her escape. With a groan, she forced open her eyes. Her head rested in Rion's lap. His fingers toyed with her hair. Sweat trickled down his temple over his cheekbone and along his jaw, which sported a sexy dark stubble.

He held water to her lips. "Drink."

She sipped, then sipped some more.

"How do you feel?" he asked.

"Fine."

In the distance, beyond the wall, a dragon bellowed.

Marisa shuddered. "We have to save them. They're in so much pain."

He leaned over her and smoothed a lock of hair behind her ear. "You're in pain, too."

He was clearly worried, but damn, he looked good. Hot. Sexy. Alive.

"Where's the floater?" she asked.

"Lex went back for the others."

"So we're alone." She locked gazes with him. "Make love to me, Rion."

"You're half dead."

"You can bring me back to life," she teased. While there wasn't a woman on the planet that wouldn't be turned on by all that protective male testosterone, she wanted to do more than make love. She gazed at the distant wall, where dragons worked in misery. "And maybe we can test your theory. See if lovemaking can shield them from pain."

His eyes darkened and his voice turned low and husky. "You aren't up to—"

"The only thing that isn't up around here is you." She chuckled and slid her hand over his thigh. "But I know a perfect remedy."

His gaze locked on to hers, and he shot her with a piercing stare that raked her with sizzling heat. His sex pulsed, rock hard. Oh, yeah. Just the mention of love-making and he was good to go.

He'd cleaned himself up, and with his hair still damp and his dark locks curling around his neck, her fingers itched to touch the soft hair, to trace her fingertips along his neck.

She could read the desire in his eyes. Marisa loved having all his intense concentration focused on her. Reaching up, she slid her fingers into his slick, damp hair. Hungry for him, she dragged his head down for a kiss.

His mouth was blistering hot, savage, rough. Ravaging her lips, he plundered her mouth, his five-o'clock shadow soft and erotic. Heat shimmied through her and settled in a hot aching pool between her thighs.

Her reaction was instantaneous. His scent, his kiss, his touch, were primal and elemental, and need raced through her with a ferocity that made her mind swim.

He tasted like torrential rain during an electric storm. She couldn't get enough of his mouth. His touch.

Their mouths fused, and she scraped her palms over his shoulders to his collarbone, then to his muscular pecs, which were crying out for a good stroking. She wanted him. Ached for him. She needed him inside her.

The friction of his hot skin against her palms had her crazy for more of him, and she squirmed to her knees, straddled his thighs.

And kept right on kissing him.

She loved the way he lay back, grabbed her butt, and pulled her tight against his length. Loved the feel of his heartbeat against her ribs. Loved the way he made her feel all hot and feminine.

Rion grabbed her cheeks, splaying his fingers between the seam of her pants, and she almost jumped out of her skin. Damn, he felt good. She was wet, slick, so ready for him she ached with need. Her breath came in long, thick gasps.

Craving for him to take her, she broke the kiss, stood, and unsnapped her pants. Rion sat up and slid his hands onto her hips, and she straddled him, one foot to either side of his knees. He cupped her butt and tugged her forward until his warm breath blew into her soft curls. Her nipples tightened.

She closed her eyes and savored the delicious feel of him dipping his nose into her core and breathing in her scent. In anticipation, moisture seeped between her thighs. After all she'd been through, she wanted this moment to last forever. She ached for this lovemaking to go on and on. And yet, when his breath blew onto her center, she arched and moaned. "That tickles."

"You want me to stop?" he teased, so low and husky an answering tremor rippled through her.

"Don't even think about it."

"That won't be a hardship." He blew again softly, and her toes curled into the warm sand.

She was standing before him naked in the hot sunshine. She'd never felt so vibrant. So alive. So ready for a man.

Rion played his fingertips over the sensitive skin along the insides of her knees and the inner curves of her thighs. Her expectations spiraled as he worked his way up her parted legs, and as he gently stroked the folds of her plump flesh, she trembled for more.

Her every cell tensed as she waited for his lips. When he flicked the tip of his tongue over her sensitive clit, she bit her lip to keep back a scream. But she couldn't contain the tiny coos of pleasure that escaped her throat.

His lips closed over hers. As he laved her with wondrous long strokes, it took all her will to remain still and let the burn pulse through her. When she would have bucked her hips, his hands squeezed her bottom, and his tongue flicked mercilessly, keeping her in place.

She couldn't hold on. She was too close to the edge. He was recklessly driving her over. Her muscles bunched, tightened, clenched, straining for release.

She tried to wait. "I want . . . you . . . inside me," she demanded.

He kept his mouth nibbling on hers. He slipped his fingers between her cheeks, teasing oh-so-sensitive flesh, driving her straight over the edge. She was falling, flailing, gasping, and laughing as she swam in a fiery explosion of stars.

She never even noticed when he changed positions or removed his pants and drew her down onto him. But finally she was free to move her hips. While his teeth captured her nipple and his fingers slid between their bodies to caress her nub, she rode him like a wild woman, her head thrown back, her lips clenched, back arched, and breasts thrust forward. She was beyond thinking, only feeling.

Feeling him slide into her and filling her with delicious friction.

As that feeling built, she never stopped coming. Didn't know one explosion could follow so hot and hard after the other. If he hadn't placed his mouth over hers and swallowed her scream, no doubt the dragons even miles away would have heard her pleasure.

As she slowly came back into herself, she realized he was still hard inside her. With a wicked grin, he flipped their positions until she was on her back, staring at his face silhouetted against blue sky.

And then he began to move again, slowly, sensuously, seductively pumping inside her. The delicious friction had her winding her legs around his waist, hanging on to his shoulders. Her breath came in gasps, and the desire burned anew. And this time when she exploded, he came with her.

Moments later, he tenderly held her head close to his heart.

When she could finally draw a breath and looked up, his gray eyes had gone dark, serious with a gleam of fire. He gazed down at her, his face alight with pleasure. "Listen."

"I don't hear anything."

His grin widened. "Exactly."

"The dragons' pain . . . it's gone?"

"You did it."

He sounded excited, but she sighed. "The pain-free minutes won't last. I should try to send a message."

"Tell them we need to find my father."

Marisa tried. Opened her mind. No pain entered, allowing her to focus on the message. *Where is the king?*

No one answered. She dragonshaped.

Where is the king?

Still, no one answered and she quickly humanshaped.

"It's not working. I'm not getting through." Her heart thudded against his, and she wanted to weep.

She'd failed. "Every time I try to send the message, it slips away. The dragons can't hear me."

Rion cuddled her against him. "At least you've given the dragons a few pain-free minutes. Even the dragons

I can see in the distance are flying with a new strength. And your efforts didn't harm you, either, thank the Goddess."

"But there's a problem. I can't send emotions and a message at the same time. At least not the heavy-duty emotions needed to break through the pain."

Not even his arms around her could soothe her frustration. She'd so badly wanted to help, but for now, she saw no solution. She couldn't help Rion. She couldn't help the dragons. And until she did, she couldn't help Earth.

Use your anger . . . for the greater good.
                                    —LADY OF THE LAKE

26

Lex had returned with Mendle, then gone back for Darian. While Marisa gave the man water, another flash hit Rion.

> *A shining golden machine that reminded him of a computer motherboard, with its circuits and wires embedded with glowing crystals, squatted on a platform.*
>
> *The Tyrannizer?*
>
> *Space itself seemed to ripple in a golden glow around the machine.*
>
> *The scene broadened in scope until Rion could see high rock walls shaped in an octagon. On one wall was a countdown clock, with a date. Two days and two hours left.*
>
> *But it was a countdown until what? Until the Unari finished the structure? Until the Grail arrived?*

Eight dragons stood chained to the walls, and next to each dragon stood a Unari guard holding a whip.

Blood ran from the dragons' every orifice. The dragons were so weak they could barely hold up their heads. Still, they bellowed, throats raw with pain.

Rion's gut roiled. And then he gasped. Sweet Goddess.

One dragon's eyes blazed in fury. Just as he'd feared, the Unari had captured his father.

The countdown clock blinked a new time but added a sinister tagline:

"Two days and two hours until your death."

Rion came out of the flash to find Marisa, Darian, Mendel, and Lex watching him. He felt like the Unari had ripped out his own heart. He'd doubled over from the pain. Crushed by the horror.

Sweet Goddess.

Fighting to control his breathing, he shoved to his feet, squared his shoulders, and began to pace. "The Unari are holding my father and seven other dragonshapers around the Tyrannizer in the palace."

"You're certain?" Lex asked.

"The room had octagon walls, and there are three rooms like that in the palace. I saw a clock ticking down. We have two days to free them. My father has only two days to live."

Rion stared at the rebels. As badly as he wanted to mount an attack right then, they needed more help. The last few days of captivity, on top of years of little sustenance, had taken a toll. Through their shirts, ribs were visible beneath their skin. All the men had gaunt cheekbones. Darian swayed on his feet. When Mendle tried to steady him, both almost toppled over.

They needed more than rest and human food. They needed platinum to strengthen their malnourished bodies.

A cawing Cuttee soared over the wall and drew Rion's gaze to the sky. He shaded his eyes. Beyond the Cuttee, Unari skimmers in fighting formation flew straight at them.

Rion sharpened his voice. "Let's get the hell out of here."

"Run. Run. Run!" Lex shouted.

Rion grabbed Marisa's hand, and together they raced toward the tunnel. The rebels sprinted into the opening and quickly climbed onto the makeshift transport device. Darian fired up the antigravs. And Lex shot them down the tunnel.

Marisa held her hair back with one hand, but tendrils escaped and whipped around her face. "Do you think the Unari saw us?"

"Perhaps it was just a scouting mission," Darian suggested.

Rion and Marisa exchanged a look. Clearly she didn't believe Darian's speculation, either, but both of them said nothing.

Lex frowned and hunched over his door. "This tunnel forms a Y. When we get to the fork, we should split up. Lessen our chances of being spotted."

Rion shook his head. "No. We stay together."

Marisa cocked her head and eyed him. "What are you thinking?"

"We aren't going straight back to camp. We can't risk leading the Unari there."

"What do you suggest?" Lex asked. "A more circuitous route could take days."

"We climb into the mountains and bring back platinum." Despite the flash that had warned him of danger in the mountains, they had to go for food. His people were little more than skin hanging on bones. "To fight the Unari we need to keep up our strength."

"The babies could use nourishment, too," Marisa added. She squeezed Rion's hand and lowered her voice so only he could hear. "I'm sorry about your father. But he's alive."

Rion squeezed her hand back but said nothing. He didn't want to speak of it. Didn't want to think about it. He had to stay focused on a rescue plan.

"Don't you think we've tried to forage for food?" Lex stared at the ground speeding by. "We've sent men into those mountains many times. No one ever comes back."

"Why not?" Rion asked.

Lex shrugged. "The Unari have cut off access to the mountains."

"Oh, God." Marisa tugged on Rion's arm. "Look."

Rion's gut tightened. A Unari skimmer craft barreled down the tunnel, its guns aiming right at them.

"Jump," Rion yelled, leaping off the makeshift train and pulling Marisa with him. His men did the same.

Hanging on to Marisa, Rion landed with a hard thud, protecting her from the worst of the blow. He looked up just in time to watch the skimmer shoot down their makeshift train, which disintegrated in a white flash of light.

The skimmer ripped through the air over their heads.

Rion didn't wait for his ears to stop ringing. Scrambling to his feet, he tugged Marisa up with him.

Her eyes were wide. She had a scrape on her cheek, but she looked otherwise unhurt. "Are they coming back?"

"Probably. We have to get out of here." Rion looked at Lex, who had gotten up much more slowly. "How much farther to the fork?"

"Maybe a mile."

Rion began to run. "I want us there in five minutes."

It took ten. Lex and his men stumbled the last steps, exhaustion on their faces. Marisa breathed heavily, too. No one complained.

"Good job." Rion looked around. This part of the tunnel was overgrown with shrubs and dead trees, plus mounds of dirt from several cave-ins. "Let's rest."

"At least a skimmer can't fly through here," Darian muttered, settling down with his back against a root.

But the Unari could shoot a missile through. Rion kept that thought to himself. He also kept his father's weak condition to himself. No one, not even the Honorian king, would survive such torture for much longer. But neither would these men live if they didn't get them some platinum.

Rion had wanted all of them to go for food, but the men's lack of physical vigor had him reevaluating his position. Lex, Darian, and Mendle could barely walk. Jogging had sucked out the last of their strength.

Rion changed his mind about their staying together. "Lex, you were right. We should split up." These were proud men. And they'd done their best for years under terrible conditions. "After you return to Winhaven, send word for the local rebels to meet me here in two days."

"Yes, sir. We'll take a different route home. But now that the Unari know about this tunnel, we should set the meeting somewhere else."

"Good point. Where would you suggest?" Rion asked.

"Where the Unari wall dams the river and turns its course is a good spot."

"All right. Do what you can to get out word of our plan, and Marisa and I will go for some platinum."

MARISA TRUDGED BESIDE Rion where the path allowed and dropped behind when it narrowed. She hadn't spoken in hours. Instead, she'd saved her strength for walking through the uneven grasslands.

Since the tunnel, she'd seen no sign of pursuit. But Lex had warned them that the Unari had shut down access to platinum in the mountains.

His words echoed in her mind. No one he'd ever sent had returned.

Merlin had joined them on their journey, sometimes keeping them company, often scouting ahead. Marisa's legs ached. Her feet had new calluses. So when Rion halted beside a slow-moving stream, she sat on a boulder, took off her shoes, and checked her feet for damage.

Rion leaned over the stream and drank. "How are you holding up?"

"I'm okay." She rubbed her sore feet. Rion turned and kneeled beside her, took her foot into his hands, and began to knead.

She closed her eyes, tilted back her head to the sun, and enjoyed his strong fingers. "You really are good with your hands."

"That's not all I'm good—" Rion dropped her foot and tackled her.

The air whooshed out of her lungs. His big body covered hers. She gasped in a breath. "What?"

"I heard a tree branch crack. Like someone stepped on it," he whispered.

They were in a grass field. A few shrubs grew along the stream, but she didn't see a tree anywhere. "But there aren't any branches here."

"I know."

Something rustled in the grass. Then she heard a series of snaps, very much like someone stepping on dry tree branches. Her pulse kicked up.

"What is that?" She looked around, but saw nothing out of the ordinary. Nothing but sky, grass, and boulders.

Then Merlin dived out of the sky. Straight at the ground. She lost sight of him in the tall grass, but then he soared upward again, a large snake-like thing dangling from his mouth. "Merlin's found it."

Merlin dropped the creature almost right on top of them. It splattered on the rock.

"Don't move." Rion crawled away from her, and Marisa was happy to stay put.

She did not want to look at alien creepy-crawly things that made snapping noises and that would give her nightmares. It was one thing to know it was there, another to have the image of teeth and dripping venom branded into her brain.

Rion peered at the dead creature. "These snappers are not native to Honor. The Unari must have brought them."

Marisa heard lots more snapping and her stomach clenched. The grass around them swayed with the movements of many creatures. As fear slithered down her spine, she pulled her feet away from the edge of the boulder. "There's more of them out there."

She slipped her shoes back onto her feet. "Should we dragonshape and roast them? Or try to fly away?"

Rion stilled, just for a few seconds, but she recognized that look. He'd just had a flash.

His face hardened, and his eyes filled with shadows. "No dragonshaping. Others have tried. According to Lex, they all failed."

At his hard tone, her heart skipped a few beats. "Then what do we do?"

Rion put his arms around her and his tone was gentle. "I'm sorry I brought you here."

That didn't sound good. Apparently his flash hadn't told him how to escape the snappers.

But they weren't giving up. Rion never gave up. And she hadn't crossed the galaxy to be eaten by alien snakes. Or to let Rion down. There had to be a way.

Marisa turned into his arms and brought him close. As always, she took comfort from his embrace and his manly scent. His rugged face with his five-o'clock shadow and circles under his eyes had become so dear to her. "Yeah, you owe me for bringing me here. But you can make it up to me."

He raised his eyebrow. "How?"

"Kiss me."

"Now?"

"Damn it. These stupid snakes are not going to kill us. They are not going to stop us from getting platinum. Or from saving your people. Kiss me."

Rion's lips came down on hers. And as always, a special awareness of him kicked in. But this time she channeled her emotions.

Even as she held on to Rion, it took so little effort to work up her anger. The Unari had no right to enslave the Honorians. Steal their free will. Destroy the planet.

The bastards didn't care how many people they killed to secure the Holy Grail. But they weren't killing Rion. And they weren't killing her. She would not let that happen.

She burned with rage, and as Rion kissed her, she held on to her fury. Burned and boiled with it. And then she shot it through the grasses telepathically.

Fry, you sons of bitches. Fry.

When she had used up all her anger and sagged, Rion caught her and held her close, his big chest cradling her. He smoothed his fingers into her hair and down her neck. "Marisa, sweetheart, I don't know what you did, but the snappers are gone."

Wearily, she lifted her head. "Thank God. It worked."

"What did you do?"

"I sent them anger."

"While you kissed me?" He cocked his head to one side. "I don't understand."

"Kissing you reminded me how much I want to live." She sucked in a shaky breath. "But I've never done that before. I didn't know if it would work."

Rion tenderly wrapped his hands around her waist. "Did you kill the snappers?"

She shook her head. "My anger chased them away."

"Could you do that to the Unari?"

"I doubt it. Those snappers are a way lower life-form. Their brains are so primitive that they simply feared my anger and slithered away. I couldn't trick intelligent beings like that."

He kissed her forehead, his tone tender. "My people will go to bed with full bellies tonight thanks to you."

"Come on." As much as she'd have enjoyed hugging him some more and basking in his compliments, they had a job to do. She slipped her hand into his. "Let's go get that platinum before those snappers come back."

Marisa and Rion didn't run into any more snappers. But as the elevation steepened, Rion had to help her more and more frequently. When they finally reached a cliff face and she could smell the rich platinum, she was eager to gather the food source and leave before dusk.

Rion had found a sharp, spiked stone, and he used it to dig into the face of the cliff. While he dug, she gathered up the richest portions of platinum and placed them into his backpack.

The concentrated platinum would go a long way toward strengthening his people. But they still needed a way to find the Tyrannizer. Knowing it was inside the palace helped, but without any landmarks, finding the palace itself within the enormous walled structure was no easy task.

The more time they spent searching for the palace, the greater the risk the Unari would catch them. And the higher the chance of failure.

"I have a crazy idea."

Rion kept digging. "Tell me."

She didn't mention that the idea scared her so badly that she almost wished she'd kept it to herself. She didn't mention that she didn't want to stake anyone's life on such a risky idea—never mind the fate of a world. But she couldn't keep silent, either. It was too important.

"Suppose we kick out the sensors on another floater and order the floater to take us to the Tyrannizer? Or to your father? The sphere found you, Lex, and Darian."

She'd half expected him to say her plan was crazy. That it wouldn't work. Or that it was too dangerous. Instead, he kissed her again. "You're brilliant."

"More likely I'm going to get us all killed." Nevertheless, she was pleased with his praise. Pleased because she cared what he thought. Because she wanted him to appreciate all of her. Not just her body, not just her telepathy, but her intelligence, too.

"If Lex can organize the local rebels, we can take over many floaters."

"How many rebels are there nearby?" she asked.

Rion shrugged. "No one knows. But if we move fast and take the Unari by surprise, we might get enough of our people inside floaters to do what must be done."

The hope in his eyes scared her. Because the plan was so iffy. They should have had more intel. But she kept her doubts to herself. "The timing will be critical. For us to have any chance to save the dragons near the Tyrannizer—everyone will have to rebel at the same time."

"I have an idea how to get your telepathy to work." He smiled darkly.

"How?" She'd never seen that particular look on his face, and a shiver went down her spine.

He rested his hands on her shoulders. "We'll go in with a smaller force. And if you and I arrive first—we can deal with the dragons."

Yesterday I struggled to survive. Today I dare to win.
—HONORIAN KING

27

Two days later, word had gone out to the scattered rebel underground. It was time to put their plan into effect.

Everyone had fed on platinum. While one good meal couldn't make up for years of deprivation, full bellies made for high spirits.

The local rebels had come to join their prince in battle. Some had walked day and night to arrive in time. They all carried spears, knives, or throwing axes. Most of all, they joined with the will to fight to the death for their freedom.

Women had joined their men, all of them determined to do whatever they could to help. Camaraderie was high, the mood hushed with grim anxiety. Honorians quietly shared platinum, food, and drink where they'd gathered by the river and waited for the sun to set.

Marisa felt as if she were part of them . . . but not quite accepted. She'd received many stares from the newcomers, a few even hostile. But no one dared outright rudeness.

In time, they might grow to accept her. After all, they shared the dragonshaper heritage. They wanted their freedom and the choice to love and live their lives on their own terms. They were not so different from Marisa. Or was that wishful thinking?

Rion and Erik walked among their people, and Marisa focused on Rion. She'd grown so close to him. Who would have thought she'd fall for a warrior, a politician, an alien, a prince? Despite the rebels' high hopes, she still feared they all stood little chance of living through this day together. Dying together seemed much more likely.

Don't think it.

The team leaders had gathered for instructions from Rion. "When you take out the sensors, don't damage the floaters themselves," he reminded everyone. "And remember, you must order your floater to open and close its doors. Also, if it doesn't accept your first demand to take you where you need to go, don't panic. Just work your way down the list of names I've given you. Hopefully the floaters will recognize one of the names and take us where we intend."

Rion tipped his head to the twilight sky. They'd picked just after sunset as the best time to attack.

Even with the cover of darkness, so much could go wrong.

If the Unari had figured out how the rebels had used the floaters last time, they could have reprogrammed them. Or used them to set a trap.

"Here they come." Rion pointed to the sky. "I see twenty floaters. That means only forty of us can go in the first wave. The rest of you stay hidden." He gestured for them to hide under grass mats. "If one of us goes down, you know what to do."

Marisa held her breath. All hell was about to break loose.

Rion gripped her wrist. "Stay close."

The floaters descended, and Operation Rebellion commenced. Rion swiftly kicked out every single eye on the first floater. She didn't get to touch one sensor. No surprise there. But disabling it seemed too easy.

Light beams from the floaters flared and hissed, hitting many of their targets. Rebels screamed in fear and pain. Several cursed. But no one retreated. When the paralyzers stunned several men and women, other rebels advanced to take the places of those who'd fallen.

The moment the door of their floater opened, Rion lifted her inside. Even with the door open, it was dark. She could still hear the sounds of battle outside.

"Close door," Rion ordered. The door clanged shut. "Take us to Shepherd Jaqard."

"Shepherd Jaqard is not in my memory." The computer spoke in the mechanical voice Marisa remembered from her last trip.

"Take us to the Tyrannizer."

"Tyrannizer is not in my memory bank."

"Take us to the palace," Marisa tried.

"Location unknown."

"Take us to Cavus Prime," Rion demanded.

Marisa held her breath. And waited. The floater hummed, then lifted them into the air.

It had worked! They were on the way.

But Marisa worried that she still hadn't figured out how to simultaneously broadcast emotion and a message telepathically. If she couldn't tell every dragon to rebel at the same time, the revolt would fail. This small rebel force couldn't possibly defeat the Unari. They needed the dragonshapers' help, too.

"Hey." Rion tipped up her chin. "It's going to work."

"You've seen that in a flash?"

"I believe in us."

He always had more faith than she did. And while she adored his confidence, she would have preferred a more tidy plan, one with every step laid out. "But—"

"Let's not waste time talking." His mouth swooped down over hers. His hands closed over her breasts, and his fingers tweaked the nubs.

Oh . . . wow. His fast move took her by surprise, and oddly, the distraction banished most of her fear.

She'd known their lovemaking was an essential part of the plan, and she tried to go with the flow. It was dark. She and Rion were alone. This might be the last time they ever kissed.

She liked kissing Rion. Although she couldn't completely shut out her fear of what would happen once they landed. So in this cocoon of safety, she kissed Rion back, breathed in his scent, reveled in his taste.

When his lips touched hers, maybe it was the adrenaline, but he set off a spark. A deep, aching need. She leaned into him and let her feelings wash over her, accepting that Rion affected her like no other man. Sure, the lovemaking was great, but so were the conversations, the shared glances that so often told her his private thoughts. She liked Rion's sensitive side as much as she was turned on when he went into warrior mode.

Most of all, she liked how he cared about his people.

He didn't set himself apart or above. He considered himself one of them. Their problems were his problems.

Marisa had never felt like this about a man. What was wrong with her? She couldn't have him. She'd repeatedly told herself she couldn't have such strong feelings about him. She was here to help him save these people. Having wonderful sex was not love. She had to control herself. She couldn't get sucked in any deeper. Even if they survived, even if he changed his mind about marrying an outsider, she couldn't stay here. She had to return to Earth to warn her people about the Unari.

She and Rion had no future, period. But that didn't stop her from wanting one.

Rion's kiss had her thoughts swimming and her emotions spinning, but she was still aware of when the floater ceased flying. Rion must have noticed, too, but he didn't rush, giving her one last embrace before finally pulling back.

He whispered, "Ready?"

No. This was the riskiest part of the entire operation. They had no idea what or whom they would face when the door opened. Cavus Prime? The Unari army? Pain-racked dragons with orders to sear them alive? But she'd heard no fear in Rion's question, only solid determination. She could give him no less in return.

"Yes. I'm ready."

Before Rion gave the order for the door to open, something slammed into the floater. The noise almost burst her eardrums. Her elbow banged the side and they wobbled. Her knees buckled. Bright lights flashed. And a painful shock zinged through her.

Suddenly, lights from outside shone through the cracks

in the floater, pinning it in a spotlight. Uh-oh. This was bad. Someone had been expecting them.

She peered through a crack. "There's a squad of Unari out there, weapons raised."

Damn. Damn. Damn. They were outnumbered, outmaneuvered, outgunned. Possibly betrayed.

"Dragonshape," Rion ordered.

Normally, dragonshaping inside a structure was lethal. But a weapon had already shredded a good part of their floater. Her first glimpse through the cracked side had revealed they were inside a large building with an open area big enough to hold dragons, the ceiling high above their heads.

She dragonshaped, her clothes shredding. The floater tore apart like tinfoil. The afterglow from their kiss helped, and at first she felt no pain.

Her sharp dragon vision picked out details. Huge columns that held up a domed ceiling. Polished and slick marble-like silver floors that reflected bursts of light from enemy weapons. Banners bearing the portrait of the Unari leader, Cavus Prime, hung between the columns. Another likeness of his face frescoed the ceiling, his beady eyes black and soulless. Cruel.

Weapons fired and struck her dragon flesh, stinging like the devil.

Beside her, Rion had dragonshaped, too. In full dragon mode his wingspan was cramped. But he was gorgeous, ferocious. Huge. His flesh dark, purple, his eyes flashing a sparkling gold, he roared and shoved her with one giant wing, right out a balcony window.

Fly.

Marisa spread her wings, caught air, and soared. She

expected Rion to do the same, to escape, to fly away with her. But he didn't retreat. He stayed and faced the entire squad of Unari.

No way was she leaving him behind while she flew to safety. She circled and returned to the building. The squad of Unari were firing at Rion, their whips flaring across his scales—while he stomped one to death and razed three more men with one powerful wing. Several Unari had locked their whips on him and fired continuous bursts of light along Rion's tail and shoulders.

Merlin flew out of nowhere and pecked at a Unari's eyes. The man screamed and went down.

Marisa hissed, drawing their attention. And the lash of their whips.

The Unari lashed whips at Rion, Marisa, and one tiny owl. Rion breathed a roar of fire, instantly roasting the Unari alive. Merlin hooted and soared out the window.

Rion had taken out one flank, but the Unari soldiers on his other side took cover behind the columns. Most of their shots went wild. But one sliced Marisa's neck, burning a trail of agony. Turning, she roared, releasing her own fire, blasting one side of the building and felling two Unari. The pain from the whips weakened her, and not just physically. The emotional boost from Rion's kiss was dissipating, replaced by the terrible nerve pain that shot constant agony into every dragon on the planet. Certain she was burning, her very bones on fire, she humanshaped.

Her clothing repaired itself, but she barely noticed. Before she recovered, the Unari dropped a huge net over her, a net of steel, she realized dully. She could no longer dragonshape, not if she wanted to live. If she tried to change, the steel web would cut through her limbs.

Now that they had her, they would starve her until she either died or worked as their slave. She'd rather be dead. She'd known the experience would be terrible, but she hadn't expected to be left a quivering wreck. She could barely lift her head.

But Rion was still fighting. He was twisting and turning, breathing fire at any Unari who dared to peek out from behind a column. She didn't know how Rion could bear the Tyrannizer's agony. But she had to help.

She could not let him die. Not the man she loved.

Damn it, she loved him. There was no more denial. He meant everything to her. Even if she couldn't have him, even if she had to step aside and let an Honorian woman have him, she loved him. Even if she had to return to Earth, she loved him.

Too weak for physical combat, Marisa closed her eyes. She forced herself to think about the many ways she loved him. He was good and kind and brave. He was willing to give his life to save his people. He was the kind of man who inspired others to follow. She remembered Rion's kisses. How good his arms had felt around her. How much she wanted him to hold her. How she longed for his embrace.

Without his touch to help her, she summoned up the glow. She could do this for him. If she could broadcast anger at the snappers, she could broadcast her love for Rion and dull his pain.

She kept her eyes shut, refused to hear the Unari cries of fear or the dragon roars of fury. She reached down deep and thought of Rion caressing her, stroking her. His hands on her breasts. She thought of how badly she longed for his body against hers, inside hers. The wonderful ways he loved her.

She glanced at Rion once and shuddered—a mistake. The Unari had pinned him against a wall, whips striking him in constant flashes of light that arced over his body. The whips alone would reduce any ordinary dragon to its knees, and combined with the Tyrannizer's pain, the agony had to be unbearable.

Rion still refused to humanshape. His eyes glowed golden fire, and he roared in agony, but he didn't surrender.

She squeezed shut her eyes again, slipped her hand between her legs. And she thought of Rion's caresses. His hot kisses.

Rion holding her at night.

Rion making love to her.

Marisa's telepathy kicked in. Suddenly, all of her love and panic and adrenaline connected her mind to Rion's.

She felt his pain, then his terrible agony. *Focus.*

She recalled how his hands felt as they slid sensuously over her shoulders, her back, her buttocks. Ever so slowly, she enhanced her feelings until she and Rion were linked both telepathically and emotionally. Bit by bit, she fed him her glowing passion and squelched his pain.

Through his mind she could see the Unari had lowered another steel net, and it had caught one of his wings. With one massive rear leg, he kicked out a column, then another, and the falling structures crushed five Unari.

The enemy leader, Cavus Prime, a large Unari male who wore shiny armor and a red sash across his chest, marched into the room and commanded his men. His voice was calm, imperious, deadly. "Advance. Use your whips in unison." He tilted his head back, looking not to Rion but to the ceiling. "Bring down more steel nets."

No. She watched in horror as the nets fell, but then they tangled in the broken columns. Rion threw more flames and more men died.

Infuriated at the loss of troops, Cavus, his weapon raised high, charged toward Rion. No man of honor, he tried to take advantage of Rion's weakness.

Marisa gasped in horror. *Do something.*

Working on it, Rion answered, trying to free himself from the netting.

With a savage slash, Cavus sliced the electronic whip across Rion's shoulder, and at the same time he twisted the setting from stun to lethal. One pull of the trigger would shoot heart-stopping pain directly into Rion's nervous system.

Trapped in her own steel netting, Marisa could only watch in terror. *He's going to kill you.*

Not today.

Rion wrenched around, almost tearing his wing from his shoulder. Twisted sideways, he risked burning his own wing as he roared fire at the Unari leader.

One moment the man was flesh and blood, the next there was nothing, not even the scent of burned flesh, just a tiny pile of ashes.

Cavus Prime had been the last Unari in the room. His guards were all dead.

But more would be coming.

Marisa shuddered and finally wriggled out from under the steel net. Rion had won the battle, but she didn't know how badly he'd been injured. He'd used tremendous bursts of energy to dragonshape and breathe fire, energy he would need to recuperate, but he couldn't recharge until he ate more platinum.

Rion humanshaped and staggered toward her, his clothing reassembling. He was covered in cuts and bruises, bleeding in half a dozen places, but the damage appeared superficial, and she breathed easier. Somehow they'd won round one, but there were thousands, maybe tens of thousands, of Unari on Honor, and they would surely be coming after the rebels.

Even as Rion scooped up a Unari weapon, she realized they couldn't keep fighting like this. He might have enough firepower left to destroy a dozen Unari or so. She could defeat only a few herself. Then what?

"I don't know how you took away my pain," he said, "but thank you."

Marisa started to fling herself into his arms, then remembered his injured shoulder. "Are you all right?"

He kicked aside the dead Unari. "So much for the armies of those who hold the Grail never dying in battle." Rion grabbed her wrist and hurried her toward an alcove—as if he knew exactly where he was going.

Head spinning, she stumbled over debris, looked away from the dead bodies.

Marisa called up her research material from the article she'd written so long ago. "According to Earth's legends, the army has to actually drink from the Grail and maintain possession of it to stay immortal."

"Even better." Rion squeezed her hand tighter. "The Unari fleet that's bringing the Grail to Honor has not yet arrived."

"Another flash?" she asked.

He nodded. "They'll be here soon. We have to take back the planet today—or lose our opportunity forever."

"You know where we are?"

"Chivalri Palace. My parents lived here, and as a child I visited often."

They passed a fountain where antigravs made the water flow upward, and the eerie effect gave her the odd feeling that here was yet another trap. It was so quiet she could hear her own breathing.

Adrenaline jangled through her. Where were the rest of the Unari?

At last, rebel reinforcements arrived. Erik, Lex, and dozens of rebels floated in over the balcony. Behind them, more floaters filled the night sky. More rebels had joined them than she'd thought possible.

At least this part of the plan was working. The rebels would secure a perimeter here while she and Rion scouted ahead to search for the Tyrannizer. Rion knew the palace layout, and no one else had her ability to stop the dragon pain. She just prayed Rion had found a way for her to get out a message, too.

They'd come so far. She couldn't fail him. Wouldn't fail him.

Rion took her hand. If he could feel her trembling, he didn't mention it. "Come on."

The one who is worth your tears won't make you cry.

—HIGH PRIESTESS OF AVALON

28

"We need to hide." Cavus Prime and the Unari had appropriated his birthright, but now he looked for strategic advantages in the hallways he'd played in so long ago as a child. "Erik and I used to play games much like your hide-and-seek in this corridor."

Chivalri Palace was huge. As the largest structure in the capital, it spanned ten city blocks. If they had to fight their way through dozens of hallways, they'd not only lose the element of surprise, but sooner or later the Unari might trap them.

The Unari had stripped the royal home of furniture handcrafted by masters, precious works of art that spanned centuries, chandeliers and wall sconces of real gold. In fact, the giant formal greeting room was so bare it could have been used for battle practice.

"Which way?" Marisa asked, stopping at a juncture of two corridors.

Rion tugged her toward the right hallway. "In my flash the Unari kept the Tyrannizer in an octagon room."

"Are there any secret palace tunnels?" Marisa asked.

He shook his head. "Nothing so useful."

"Weapons stashes?"

"We were a peaceful people. Ever since our peace treaty with Tor several centuries ago, we haven't required an army or weapons. We were beyond violence—or so we thought." The damage done here wasn't just physical. His people's belief system had been torn apart. The Unari had destroyed everything.

Except their spirit.

His people lived on, enduring terrible pain and horrible slavery. Courageous rebels were risking their lives to fight back against enormous odds.

Rion chose a hallway lined with closed doors that were once administrative offices. "We have to find the Tyrannizer and knock it out."

And he'd love to find his father. He didn't dare say the words out loud. While he prayed his father still lived, he feared he would be scarred and broken, perhaps insane, from the terrible torture.

"Rion, after you exited the floater and dragonshaped, were you in pain?" Marisa asked.

"Not at first—your powerful kiss on the way here lasted awhile."

"But later the pain hit?" she pressed.

"Yes." He was uncertain how she'd vanquished the pain the second time but was very grateful. "And then you made it go away again."

She avoided his gaze. "You do realize I still can't send a message at the same time as I release my emotions?"

"First things first. Let's find the Tyrannizer." He needed to assess the situation in person. Finding the octagon room before the Unari brought in reinforcements was critical.

They hurried down a long hallway lined with offices. "You're certain the octagon room is in this palace?" she asked.

"I'm not certain. But the Unari invaded Chivalri first. Maybe they chose my country because we were the strongest, or maybe they needed this geographical area because it's large and relatively flat. The weather is good, and the continent is stable, the bedrock deep, which will support those huge walls. Since they came here first and use this palace as their headquarters, I'm betting Cavus Prime kept the center of his control, the Tyrannizer, close by in one of the octagon rooms. It's even possible the Unari will bring the Grail here, too."

"We can't let them keep it," she said.

He nodded. "Even if we have to destroy it."

They hurried through the hallway. He'd forgotten how long the passageways were. "There're three octagon-shaped chambers in Chivalri Palace."

"Three?"

"All are temples to honor the Goddess. The largest one is down this way."

"We can't go near the Tyrannizer without—"

"Making love. I know." As if he could forget. Kissing wouldn't be enough. To banish the pain of everyone on the planet, Marisa would have to be at full telepathic strength.

"SWEET GODDESS." RION turned a corner and skidded to a stop. Two dragonshapers wearing spiked collars stood chained in front of double doors. The slave collars had burned into their scales. Blood ran freely. Their eyes were crazed with pain.

At the sight of Rion and Marisa, the dragons bellowed and shot fire down the corridor. Rion yanked her around a corner and into a room and slammed the door.

The empty office looked much like those he remembered during his father's rule, with one major difference. All the computer systems were gone.

Gut churning, he hefted the Unari weapon he'd confiscated. "I know those dragons."

"They tried to kill us."

"They were once part of the king's elite guard."

"They're insane from the pain. They probably didn't even recognize you."

"I know." His fingers tightened on the weapon. He could barely say the words. "But I wish I didn't have to kill men who taught me how to fish and hunt."

"Maybe you don't have to. Kiss me."

"What?"

"Maybe I can calm them."

He swept Marisa into his arms. Going from passion to danger and back was a difficult transition. But if he could save those crazed dragons . . .

He supposed his ability to function at all was a measure of the partnership that had grown between them. Marisa kept him grounded. He recalled how she'd fought beside him. She'd obliterated several Unari with her dragon fire. Saved him from the pain so he could fight back. Without her, he would have failed.

Marisa was no longer special to him just because of her

talents. She was special to his heart. If she died today, he didn't know if he could go on . . .

Sweet Goddess, keep her safe, he prayed.

Together, they'd come this far. Together, they would see this through.

Losing her . . . was not an option.

Gently, he caressed her cheek, took the time to lock gazes. Stars! She was a beautiful woman, both inside and out. She didn't complain. She didn't back down. She was his equal in every way but physical strength, and she more than made up for that with her intellect and telepathy skills. But it was her heart he cherished most. Her willingness to take on his cause, to risk her life for his people.

They were a team. Fate had been good to him. He was proud to know her. Proud to love her.

He loved her.

He wished he had time to cherish her properly. Time to proclaim his feelings and tell her just how much she meant to him. But their plan depended upon timing and surprise. Conversation would have to wait.

He slipped his hands under her tunic and played with her full breasts. This time, he skimmed his fingers over every part of her quivering flesh except her nipples, letting her anticipate where he'd touch next. When her tongue slipped into his mouth, he wished they had the entire night.

After a few minutes of kissing, his breath grew ragged, his erection ached, and he forced himself to stop and pull down her shirt. Goddess knew, if he kept going, he might simply sink into her soft heat and forget his mission.

He jerked his mouth free. Her eyes were wide and dilated. Clouded as if lost in another world.

He forced himself to talk about the mission. "I have to go."

She just looked at him. Licked her bottom lip. "We are going to do more than kiss, aren't we?"

"Count on it. I'll be back as soon as I can," he murmured. He could barely tear himself from her.

She said nothing to stop him from leaving but closed her hands into fists.

When he headed for the door, cracked it, and saw Lex and Erik waiting outside in the hall, she still hadn't spoken. But the moment Rion slipped through, she was right behind him.

Rion turned back. "I asked you to stay here."

"If we're going to die, I'd rather we were together." She raised her chin. She didn't sound frightened, just determined. "Besides, the safest place for me in this entire building has got to be right next to you."

"But—"

She tensed. "I'm not staying behind."

Lex chuckled softly. Even Erik grinned.

They were about to face the worst the Unari had to offer, and Marisa intended to accompany them. Her courage amazed him. In truth, it was good to know she was beside him. Relatively uninjured. Still breathing.

He glanced around the corner. The two chained dragons leaned against the wall, eyeing them with glazed expressions.

"Kevar. Sugin." Rion stepped in front of them with his weapon held out to one side. "I'm here to free you."

He dropped his weapon to the floor, and unarmed, he

slowly walked forward. The dragons shifted and blew smoke, but they didn't try to roast him again. Progress.

"Easy, guys." Rion kept walking, making his movements slow and deliberate. "You remember me, don't you? I'm Rion. Kevar, you used to take me fishing. And Sugin, you taught me how to sail. I've been away for a long time, but I've come back to free you." Rion strode right up to the dragons and stopped. "I need to use my knife to slice away those locks. Hold still. Easy."

The dragons breathed hard but didn't try to stomp him to death. Praying his words had gotten through, he slid out his knife and placed the blade into the toggle. The lock snapped.

Both dragons stepped forward. Sugin nuzzled him. Rion wanted to stroke him but couldn't find an unbroken scale that wouldn't cause the dragon more pain. "Lex, these men need platinum and to have a doctor see to their wounds."

The dragons shuffled down the hall. Rion picked up his weapon.

Rion braced for danger and kept his voice down to a whisper. "Don't move. Any of you. I want one quick look." He took five steps forward, reached for the door that led into the octagon chamber. And turned the knob.

A dragonshaper's character is his fate.
—KING ARTHUR PENDRAGON

29

R ion opened the door of the octagon chamber, and the
sounds of dragon moans, grunts, hissing, and shrieks
made Marisa flinch. They had found the Tyrannizer. She
peeked over Rion's shoulder to see that the Unari had
chained dragons to shiny golden walls that were now
stained with blood from brutal whippings. In the very
center of the torture chamber, the Tyrannizer whirred in a
constant drone, the air rippling around it.

The Tyrannizer was just as Rion had described from
his vision. About the size of ten men, the torture device
sat on a raised dais, a writhing mass of cold circuitry. Here
was the center of Unari power, the machine that absorbed
the dragons' pain, then broadcast that pain to the world.

Conditions inside the chamber were so disturbing she'd
never forget them. A dragon's shriek curdled her blood.
The room must have been soundproofed to disguise its
location or to avoid upsetting Unari workers. If the sounds
of torture weren't bad enough, the smells of blood and fear
were horrifying. Covering her mouth with her hand, she

stifled a gasp. Looking into that room was like a glimpse into hell. This atrocity had to end.

Rion shut the door, but the terrible memory stayed with her. And the look in Rion's eyes would haunt her for even longer.

Erik slumped against a wall, his shoulders sagging. Head down, he didn't look at anyone.

Lex's complexion had gone ghost white. He, too, turned away and brushed aside a tear. "We have to stop this madness."

"Agreed." Rion's voice cracked. "Gather half the men in this hallway. The others need to find a second entrance around back. Await my signal."

Erik nodded and straightened, squaring his shoulders, visibly steeling himself for battle.

"What signal?" Lex asked.

"You'll know when you hear it." Rion slipped his arm over Marisa's shoulder. "We have work to do."

"I don't know if I can," she whispered as he took her back into the office they'd just left and shut the door behind them. She stood near the door, trying to regroup. They'd been gone less than a minute, but it seemed an eternity. Her stomach wouldn't stop twisting and cramping. If she'd had any food in her, she would have lost it.

Rion drew her farther into the room, away from the door. "If we enter that chamber as men, the Unari will whip the dragons until they breathe fire and burn us. If we enter as dragons, the Tyrannizer's pain will enslave us."

"You think I don't know that?" She crossed her arms over her stomach and rocked back and forth. "Was your father—"

"I don't know. I couldn't see all the dragons." Rion

didn't rush her. God knew, he must want to. Every second they delayed was another second of agony for all his people. Yet he took the time to be gentle. "You and I will help them. But we aren't going to make love only for their sakes. There's something I want you to know."

She could barely focus on his words. She could no longer actually smell the blood, but the stench lingered in her nostrils and the dragon screams resounded in her head.

Rion cupped her chin, lifted her head until their eyes met. His face, deadly serious, wasn't stern or harsh. Oddly, his expression was tender.

"I would have preferred to have told you this while sailing through the Hani Islands, where the sand is warm pink and the water a deep turquoise . . . but I might not get another chance."

"I can't take any more surprises." She didn't want to talk. She didn't want to kiss. Or make love. She wanted to curl up into a ball and sleep. She wanted to forget this waking nightmare.

"I love you."

She jerked her head up in astonishment. "What?"

His expression softened. His eyes warmed. "I love you."

Her mouth dropped open and her eyes widened. Her body and mind were overloaded. Shocked. He'd just said he'd loved her. And every fiber of him vibrated with sincerity.

"I know it's not the right time." He cupped his hands and ran them over her shoulders and up and down her arms, chasing away her chills. "But I wanted you to know . . . in case . . ."

In case they died.

A primal spark kindled. He loved her, and she was so not ready to die. They had to fight back. She had to snap out of her shocked numbness and feed the flame.

But no kiss was going to blanket all the pain in that hellish octagon chamber. Even if she could dull the terrible memory and forget the blood and the screams, even if she could function somewhat normally, she still couldn't broadcast Rion's words—not at the same time as she maintained her glow. She could transmit either emotion or words, but not both.

For his plan to work, they had to take out the Tyrannizer, and the dragons all over Honor had to revolt as one. To do that, she had to do more than stop the pain. She had to send a message, too.

She stood straighter, hands on her hips. "It's time you told me your plan."

"We're going to make love."

"And?" She sensed there was more. A lot more.

"You'll transmit your glow and stop the dragons' pain."

She shook her head. "You know that's not enough. In order for every dragon on Honor to simultaneously revolt as one and turn on their captors, we need to send a worldwide message."

Eyes fierce, Rion shot her a steady gaze. "I'll take care of the message."

"But you aren't telepathic—"

"All dragonshapers are telepathic. When you send out your glow, I'll link my message to it."

"Wait a second. For me to transmit the glow worldwide, I need high-intensity emotion. As close as I can get to orgasm." Marisa scowled. "I have to be human to send that emotion. You have to be in dragon form to be telepathic."

"That's correct."

"But a human and a dragon can't possibly make love. It's anatomically impossible."

"I'm going to dragonshape—but only a little."

"What!" Partial shifting? Was it even possible? A glimmer of what he planned scared her from the top of her head right down to her toes. She looked at him and tried to gauge if he'd lost his mind.

"We'll make love," he explained, "and while you dull the pain, I'll shift some of my cells—just enough so I can tap into my dragon telepathy and tack on my message to your emotional glow. In theory, the dragons' pain will end, and they'll also receive my full attack plan."

"In theory?"

"No one's ever tried a partial shift," Rion admitted. He placed his hands on her shoulders. "But I believe I can hold on long enough to send the message."

He intended to turn into a dragon while they made love. No wonder he hadn't told her his plan. If he couldn't maintain control, he'd morph from human all the way to dragon while he was inside her—and rip her apart.

Oh . . . God.

She wanted to believe he could control a partial shift, but panic threatened to shut her down. She was on the verge of laughing and crying hysterically.

Gunshots fired outside. Men shouted, and skimmers roared off into battle, their engines roaring.

"I don't know if I can do this."

"You can."

"Don't tell me what I can do," she said.

He took both her hands in his. "I'm sorry. I should never have said that. You deserve better."

Marisa pulled her hands from his. "Were you telling me the truth when you said you loved me?"

"Yes."

"If I'm going to risk my life, I have the right to know . . ."

Without hesitation, he swept her against his chest. "I love you so much"—his voice broke—"that if there were a way to send you away to safety right now, I would."

The love gleaming in his eyes proved without doubt that he loved her. She felt the warmth down to her soul.

Rion was counting on her. He needed her. And she wouldn't fail him.

Freeing her arms, she threw away her caution. She ignored the gunshots outside.

Yanking his head down to hers, she nibbled his lip. "Make love to me, Rion."

He peeled off her clothes, and she helped him out of his. At first her nudity made her feel unusually vulnerable. She reminded herself his men outside wouldn't invade their privacy and the Unari didn't know they were here.

Still, when Rion's teeth closed on one nipple, her body didn't respond. She was cold. Naked. In enemy territory. If he noticed her shivering in the chilly air instead of responding fully to his attentions, he didn't mention it.

He simply closed his hands over her breasts and teased her nipple between his teeth. But she was nervous and upset. Thinking that he meant to do a partial dragonshape had her shaking.

What was wrong with her?

The man had said he loved her. They were both naked. He was holding her, touching her. He was the great guy she'd always wanted. But she couldn't get turned on.

The roar of a skimmer crashing made her jump. She could hear men shouting orders, boots stomping.

She was too scared.

Scared of failing. Scared of trusting him. Her throat tightened, and tears welled in her eyes. A sob slid up her throat. She cupped his face and raised his head.

"Rion. I can't."

"What would you like?" He remained calm, no censure in his gaze. "Tell me what to do."

Damn it. She didn't know what to do. Soft lighting, music, and a stiff drink might help. But they didn't have those luxuries.

Rion gathered her close. "It's okay."

Outside, a siren wailed. Even worse, the boots of many men marching their way made her tremble. She had to hurry. She had to get a grip.

The Unari were coming. And she couldn't stop shaking.

Sick at heart, she slid against Rion's heat. "It's not okay. It's not."

Fear is not the natural state of stable people.
                                    —LADY OF THE LAKE

30

M arisa embraced Rion and cried into his broad chest. He moved his hands up and down her back soothingly, making small caresses. He kneaded the knots from her shoulders and massaged the tension from her neck until she finally ran out of tears.

What the hell was wrong with her? She'd just had the mother of all meltdowns. Come unglued. Fallen apart. And she didn't understand it. Marisa had as many self-doubts as the next woman, but she usually had surplus self-control.

She had to calm her raw nerves. In her former career, she'd been under fire several times in the Mideast. She'd gone for days without sleep. She'd been behind enemy lines, even been captured once and had waited in a cell blindfolded for three long days until she'd been saved. But she'd never lost it like this.

What was she so afraid of? She'd looked death in the eye before. Something was wrong. Something was different, almost as if . . . something was altering her perceptions.

She snapped up her head. Looked into Rion's surprised eyes. "That Tyrannizer is getting to me."

He frowned. "I don't understand."

"Maybe it's affecting all humans. Or maybe I'm especially sensitive because of our nearness or my telepathic ability. But it's like depression weighing on me, making me think we can't succeed. Making me afraid."

His eyes narrowed. "You think it's affecting all of us on a subconscious level?" He didn't wait for her answer. "I've always wondered if . . . I thought perhaps my people gave up too easily. I've made excuses for them. I thought it was the starvation, the torture. But Honorians are proud of our freedom. We don't give up." His hands gripped her shoulders. "But even among the rebels, even those farthest from the Tyrannizer, there's a definite lack of spirit."

"It's not just physical pain. That machine piles on gloom and despair, and it steals hope. It may even affect the Unari—without their knowledge."

He frowned. "We need to take out the Tyrannizer, but we can't because we're afraid?"

"Wrong." She grinned. "Now that we know those feelings are false, we can ignore them." At least she hoped she could.

She nibbled on Rion's chest. Concentrated on the pressure of her lips against his warm, smooth flesh. She focused on the pleasure of touch, how sensitive her lips felt, how skimming her tongue over his warm skin increased her craving for more. His scent always made her feel feminine and sexy, and she breathed in deep, relying on her senses. And her memories. He'd told her he loved her, and the knowledge filled her with sizzling need.

Rion was the man she loved. Her true love. This man had returned to save his world. He was willing to risk his life for their freedom. Rion slid his hands over her, skimming her back with slow, smooth strokes, massaging her scalp, tracing the delicate skin at her neck and over her shoulders. He cherished her with his fingers, and she quivered in anticipation.

Damn, he felt good. He always seemed to know exactly what she liked. With one hand he captured both of hers and held them over her head. His mouth found hers, and she closed her eyes, their tongues dancing, the fingers of his free hand playing between her breasts.

He had her stretched out. Pinned. He could take whatever he wished. She just wished he'd hurry up and take.

His exploration with his lips and fingers had her moaning softly. He caressed her breasts with his palms, and with his fingertips he teased her nipples, shooting a direct current straight to her core. Heat seeped and moisture trickled between her thighs. She tried to lift her hips higher and parted her legs.

He stepped between her feet. She could no longer close her legs—not that she wanted to close them. But he wasn't accepting her blatant invitation. And now she'd lost the luxury of squeezing her legs together and applying pressure where she craved it most.

She needed him inside her. But he seemed in no hurry at all.

"More," she whispered between kisses. "More." She needed him to move faster, move lower. Finally, he inched his hand into her curls. She arched her spine, and he cupped her mons, and a delicious flow of warmth washed over her. She moaned into his mouth, trying to get closer. She needed more friction, more stroking, more heat. Every cell in her body tensed.

Waiting.

But he ignored her parted thighs. Kept her mouth too busy for her to speak. His hands stoked, stroked, sensuously teased until she couldn't hold still.

She squirmed, trying to get him to hurry, to let her find release. She was right there, and he had yet to really touch her. She jammed her hips against his hand. But he was staying with slow and easy. Driving her mad.

She ached for fast and hard.

Her breath grew frazzled. She stood on tiptoes trying to lift into his hand, but he kept her right on the edge. Breasts aching, she strained, tensed, waited. If her hands were free, she would have pounded his shoulders, but he had trapped her wrists. His legs kept her from closing her thighs.

She was at his mercy. Open, waiting. He could touch her wherever he wanted, whenever he wanted, however he wanted.

God, how she wanted. Her entire body was sizzling and stressed. Their kiss was hot enough to fuse metal, and the rest of her was melting.

Ever so slowly, he parted her slick folds, slipped a finger inside her. She was so ready, one touch should be enough for her to find sweet release.

But he was too gentle, too slow. She groaned in frustration.

He tapped the center of her nerves. Lightly. Too lightly to do more than wind her tighter. She needed air, tore her mouth from his, and lolled her head back against the wall.

Her entire focus centered on his finger, one tiny pressure point where all her nerve endings joined.

She pulsed in anticipation. But his mouth was now free to lave her nipple, roll the tip between his tongue. Her back against a wall, her breast in his mouth, she could no longer even squirm.

He played her body, drew every cell up so tight that she had to clench her jaw to prevent herself from begging. He was giving her pleasure, pure pleasure. Holding her right on the brink. She couldn't take much more . . .

But waiting felt so damn good. And so damn bad.

She panted. Ached. Despite her determination not to beg, soft words came from her mouth, seemingly of their own accord. "Please. I can't take much more."

"I know." He growled low and husky and went right on doing exactly what he'd been doing. He tapped her clit. She pulsed and throbbed. Panted.

"Again," she demanded.

Ever so slowly, he tapped her again. Her head thrashed from side to side. "Not hard enough. Not long enough."

"I know."

She waited for him to give her what she'd asked for. But he didn't. Instead, he touched her again. So gently, ripples of heat began in her breasts and spiraled outward until she thought she'd expire from the waiting.

Her toes curled, her lips grew numb. Every atom in her body focused on his touch. Which was smooth, soft, gentle.

Her moisture coated his finger. But his touch remained feather light. While he had his finger exactly on the tip of her clit, exactly where she craved, his fingertip made only tiny maddening circles.

"Ah . . . ah . . . Rion. Please. I need you now."

"Mm," he agreed, but he kept his finger caressing her, his teeth biting her nipple, his tongue mimicking his finger.

"I can't . . . oh . . . oh-oh. Ohhhh . . ." She gasped. Her head was spinning. She barely knew what she was saying or doing. Just a little bit more and she would be there. "Please, Rion. Don't make me . . . oh . . . ah . . . don't make me wait."

"I won't," he promised, his voice low and sexy.

Good. He was going to . . . but he wasn't . . . And she grew frantic with the rush of need. Her nipples were so tight, the nubs hard and sensitive, that she panted.

She opened her eyes and stared into his. And gasped. Rion's normally gray irises were shining dragon gold. He still possessed human features, but the flesh on his neck was now dark purple scales. His skin was thicker and tougher, slicker.

But her body was out of control. She couldn't think past the simple recognition that he was dragonshaping, because his fingers between her legs were picking up speed, applying more pressure.

But his progression was still too damn slow. Each time he gave her a tiny stroke of friction, her body adjusted and demanded more.

Sweat glistened on her skin, and her body flushed with heat. The golden gleam from his gaze caressed like fire. Perhaps she was burning up from the inside out. His fingers moved faster, flicked harder.

While their gazes locked, he inserted one finger inside her, and the intimate act shot the most incredible sizzle through her. She strained toward release, but he moved his finger in and out of her way too slowly to do anything more than drive her into a deeper frenzy that left her groping to hang on, her breath raspy, her scales undulating.

"Rion, damn it. I . . . need . . . you."

"Yes."

"I am . . . not . . . freakin' . . . kidding."

He slipped a second finger inside her. His thumb pressed onto her clit. She was going to explode. Just one more flick.

He stopped.

She felt as if she was going to die as all those wonderful sensations stacked up, built. But they didn't break.

She was hanging by one tiny chain that was about to snap.

For a moment, he sucked her breast into his mouth and totally ignored the pending explosion between her parted legs. She felt like she was sizzling, throbbing, panicked with the need for release.

He bit her nipple and sucked away the pain. She gasped in pleasure and frustration. And that's when he telepathically sent his plan for the attack into her mind. Their minds linked. And like two rivers that joined at a fork before merging into the sea, she couldn't tell where her mind stopped and his began.

She could feel her nipple in his mouth. And she could feel his mouth around her nipple. It was like being slammed twice over with sensations. From her side. From his side.

And like a ripple in the water that began with a single pebble and spread outward, his message kept spreading.

Across the palace, across the Unari structure, across Chivalri.

The merging of minds made her oh so much more receptive to pleasure. He no longer had to guess exactly what she wanted. He knew. And still he held back.

Tension bowed her.

Uttering a fierce groan, he released her hands, wrapped his arms around her, and lifted her onto his sex.

With one roaring thrust, he took her. A tiny part of her realized that roar was his signal for the rebel attack to start, but the rest of her was beyond caring. She came apart like a star going supernova, the pleasure expanding and spiraling and widening into an all-encompassing fury.

And the message kept spreading across the ocean.

But he didn't stop pumping and thrusting. And she just kept right on coming. She might have screamed, but Rion kissed her again. Her hands clawed his shoulders, and, frantic, she rode him fast and hard, her body almost mindless. Hot fluid spilled. Hers. His. She was out of control, blazing hot, consumed.

The message spread across the world.

When she glanced at him again, his eyes had lost the golden hue. The scales were gone. Rion was back to human.

And just when she thought she couldn't possibly take more, she exploded one last time.

Marisa must have blacked out for a few seconds, because when she came to, she was fully dressed and in Rion's arms. He was leaning over her, his eyes dark with concern. "Welcome back. Are you okay?"

"That depends."

"On what?"

"It worked, right?"

He grinned. "Yes. Once you dulled the pain, dragon-shapers from every corner of the land responded. The revolution has begun all over the world."

"Then I'm okay." She closed her eyes.

Patriotism is the last refuge of the scoundrel.
                              —SAMUEL JOHNSON

31

At a knock on the door, Rion turned to face the entrance and stepped in front of Marisa. Although the Unari wouldn't knock, he couldn't afford any surprises. "Enter."

Lex strode inside, a blaster tucked into his belt. "You wanted a progress report?"

"Yes." Rion gestured for Lex to shut the door behind him.

"The dragonshapers in the octagon killed the Unari. Our men have cut the last chains from the dragons' necks. Our physicians are tending the dragons."

"My father?" Rion asked.

"We found him." Lex hesitated, then raised his eyes to Rion's and warned, "He's very weak."

Had he been too late? Rion clenched his fists, wished he could kill those torturers all over again. "Where is he? I must go to him."

Marisa placed a hand on his shoulder, slid it down his arm. Just her presence gave him a measure of comfort.

"Doctors have the king in surgery," Lex said.

"What's his exact prognosis?" Rion demanded.

"Not good. I'm sorry. I'll let you know the moment I have any news."

"Thank you." Rion recalled better days. During a visit, his father throwing him into the air and catching him. His father laughing as he'd taught him how to fly a skimmer. His father twirling his mother around the room in an impromptu dance and drawing Rion into their arms.

Rion clasped Marisa against his side. She was always there for him, supporting him, helping him. He wished he had time to sort out their relationship properly, but he had to push aside his personal concerns. His people needed him to stay on top of the rebellion in this critical time. They needed to make certain they took back all of Honor from the Unari—totally obliterated the Tribes, so they wouldn't have even one tiny foothold to use to regroup.

"The rebellion?" Rion asked. "What's going on?"

Lex spoke quietly. "Our people are in full revolt. The Unari are dead or retreating."

Erik knocked on the door and entered. "Rion, we tried to destroy the Tyrannizer, but your owl started attacking us."

"You didn't hurt Merlin, did you?" Marisa charged past Erik and into the octagon chamber.

"We backed off," Erik told Rion.

Lex, Rion, and Erik followed Marisa. Rion caught up to her just as she skidded to a stop.

The Tyrannizer dominated the octagonal space with its rippling golden glow.

"Sir," one of the rebels said, "that bird is defending the machine as if it's his mate. We can't pick up a tool without the owl pecking at our hands."

Marisa stepped close to the bird. "Merlin, what's wrong?"

The owl hooted. She looked at Rion for help. "I don't understand him."

Rion dismissed his men. "Please, leave us."

Everyone filed out until only Marisa, Rion, and Merlin remained. Rion turned around and spoke slowly. "If you can understand me, fly over there." He pointed to the window.

Merlin flew to the window.

"Blink once for yes."

Merlin blinked once.

"Blink twice for no."

Merlin blinked twice.

Rion walked around the Tyrannizer. "Is this machine important?"

Merlin blinked once.

Marisa sighed. "I wish he could tell us why."

"Is the Tyrannizer important to you?" Rion guessed.

Merlin blinked once and hooted once. He flew down, picked up a screwdriver, and dropped it at Rion's feet.

Rion stooped and picked it up. "You want part of the machine? Fine. Tell me which part you want." Rion began tapping the pieces. Every time he did so, Merlin answered no. After several minutes of tapping parts, Rion wiped the sweat off his brow. He still hadn't found the piece Merlin wanted. "Don't worry, little guy, I'm not giving up."

Merlin kept hopping back to the machine. He pecked at a part.

"You want that one?" Rion asked.

Merlin didn't blink.

Marisa frowned. "Maybe he wants you to remove that piece to get the one he wants."

Merlin hooted.

Rion smiled. "Okay, okay." He removed three pieces of the machine, and Merlin kept flapping and hooting, directing him. When Rion touched a long rod engraved with runes, Merlin hooted approval.

Marisa's eyebrows went up. "It looks like . . . but it can't be."

"Can't be what?"

"On Earth, according to Arthurian legend, Merlin had an ancient rune staff that he used to protect King Arthur. I've seen pictures of it."

Rion ran his hand down the staff still embedded in the Tyrannizer. "I've seen this staff in one of my flashes. The Tribes conspired to steal it."

When Rion disengaged the staff from the machine, the machine stopped glowing, the air stopped rippling.

"That staff was the power source," Marisa said.

Rion placed the staff on the floor and stepped back. Merlin carried a bit of crystal, the key he'd found on Tor, in his mouth and swooped with it toward the staff. The moment the owl touched the staff, the bird morphed into a man.

Marisa gasped.

"Merlin?" Rion asked.

"I have gone by that name. I prefer Jordan." The man spoke in a deep voice, full of gravel. Tall, thin, with fierce blue eyes, he stood tall, ignoring his nudity. He picked up the key and pressed it into an indentation in the staff.

"Jordan, I owe you a debt of gratitude. Without you, without the key you found, we wouldn't have even made it back here. My world would not be free." Rion stepped forward. "I've lost count of the times you've saved my life. Is there anything we can do for you?"

Jordan slid his hand down the staff to three additional empty indentations. "I need to find the other keys. Have you heard anything about them?"

"I'm afraid not," Rion answered.

"They were stolen from me." Jordan's eyes burned. He gripped the rune staff so tightly his fingertips turned white. "But you owe me nothing. I've saved your lives. You've saved mine."

Rion nodded.

"You have things under control here," Jordan said. "Don't let the Unari ever come back."

"We won't."

Before Rion could say another word, Jordan tapped the staff on the floor. And vanished.

Eyes wide, Marisa circled the room. "Where'd he go?"

"I have no idea, but somehow I don't think we've seen the last of him."

Erik strode through the door again, his face grim. He swallowed hard. "Your father is out of surgery. King Shepherd's asking for you."

"Thank you." Certain that conveying the message had been difficult for Erik, Rion placed his hand on his cousin's shoulder. After all, Shepherd had raised Erik as his own child. But though uncle and nephew were close, his father had asked for his biological son.

Rion cleared his throat. "How's he doing?"

Erik refused to meet Rion's eyes. "He's not in good shape. We should prepare ourselves. He may not survive."

Lex stepped into the room. "Sir, all Honorians have followed your plan. En masse they've risen up to kill the Unari in a worldwide revolt. Our losses are minimal, but we have many weak refugees to feed. Everyone's hungry."

Rion straightened. "See what food stores the Unari have left us. Make sure the food is equally shared. Move as many people into the palace as it can shelter. Start with the old, the children, and the sick." Rion held out his hand to Marisa but spoke to Erik. "And search for the Grail. If I read my dates wrong and the Unari have left it behind, we need to secure it."

"A few Unari fled through the portal," Erik reported.

"What?" Marisa gasped. "I thought the portal was broken."

"The Unari closed it down so Honorians wouldn't escape. But they opened it again to flee."

"Where did they go?" Rion asked.

Erik scowled and hesitated. Finally he spat out the answer. "Earth. The portal's last coordinates were set for Earth."

"No!" Marisa cried, her eyes wide with horror. "I have to leave, too. Warn my people before the Unari have a chance to set up another Tyrannizer there."

"After she leaves," Erik ranted, "I'd like to blow the damn portal up, so offworlders can never return."

"That portal is necessary to our survival," Rion countered and squeezed Marisa's hand. He understood her need to leave, but he wanted the portal open. Not just so he and Marisa might find a way to be together. Honor needed to rejoin the galactic community. "We must protect the portal at all costs."

Erik glared at Marisa, then Rion. "You can't risk the

welfare of everyone on this planet for her. Outsiders have ruined us. We should be isolating ourselves for our own protection."

"We need that portal so we can ally ourselves with other worlds. We need it for trade, to receive aid while we rebuild. Please, just do as I ask," Rion said, eager to speak with his father. "I must go."

"Of course," Erik agreed, but his eyes narrowed. Clearly, he had more to say, but he backed down for the moment. "I will do as you say."

"Marisa, come with me." Rion swept her down the hallway.

Throughout the last exchange she hadn't said a word, but once they were alone in the hallway, she whispered, "I really can't stay here much longer."

"I know. But you still need proof of the Unari methods of infiltration, and they may have left evidence behind that you can use to convince Earth of the danger." He lowered his voice. "And I doubt they will set up another Tyrannizer on Earth, not without Merlin's staff to power it."

She sighed. "I can't take the chance. They might have other power sources."

"Agreed." Cornering off his emotions, Rion spied Mendle and set the man to the task of searching for anything Marisa could use to prove the Unari were planning to take over Earth. Rion couldn't think about Marisa leaving— not yet. First, he must see his father.

They hurried down the hall, past the octagon chamber. Physicians had set up a triage in spare offices and worked on battle-wounded rebels. In the case of the dragonshapers, the doctors had to clean off filth from years of neglect, before stitching wounds and setting bones.

Rion hesitated outside the room where his father was resting. Marisa kept her hand in his. "Do you want me to wait out here?"

"I'd like him to meet you." He drew her into the room with him.

At the sight of his father's shrunken frame and fierce wounds, Rion had to bite back a gasp. His father had once been as large as Rion, fit and robust. No more. He didn't have an ounce of spare flesh, and his skin was dry and mottled. In three years, he'd aged thirty.

"Father—" Rion's voice broke with emotion.

The king lifted his hand and gestured Rion to him. "My son, I thought I'd lost you."

"And I you." Rion blinked back tears that matched those in his father's eyes. "Father, this is Marisa Roarke from Earth. Her abilities—"

"Helped free us all, thank the Goddess." His father's strength might be waning, but his sharp gray eyes missed nothing. "I thank you, my dear." He coughed and lay back weakly in the bed.

A physician stepped to his side and raised water to his lips. "You must not tax yourself."

"I'm not a fool. I'm just dying." His father waved the man away. "I'll speak one last time with my son. Leave us."

Rion had never understood how his father never raised his voice yet spoke with such authority. The physician bowed and exited. Marisa turned to do the same, but Rion didn't release her hand. "Stay."

His father smiled. "She's your woman?"

"I love her." Rion didn't mince words.

"Good. Marry her soon."

Erik stepped into the room. "Sire, Rion must not wed an alien. We just fought a war with outsiders."

Rion placed his arm around Marisa's shoulders. "Without Marisa's help we would have lost that war."

"Rion himself is only half Honorian," Erik insisted. "If he marries this woman, their children will only be one quarter Honorian. It's unthinkable that such royal blood should be diluted. The people won't stand for it, sire. And we can't afford more strife."

"You overstep. Leave us." The king's sharp gaze nailed Erik. His tone turned steely.

Face red with anger at his dismissal, Erik backed out of the room and shut the door.

"Do you love my son?" Shepherd asked Marisa.

Marisa wrapped her arm around Rion's waist. "Yes, I love him."

"You must follow your hearts."

"And what of Erik's objections?" Rion asked. "He is not the only person in Chivalri who hates everything alien right now."

"A king must do what is best for his people. And if you are not with the woman you love, you cannot lead well."

Was his father right? If Marisa left him, it would be like losing a part of himself. He couldn't imagine an hour going by when he wouldn't think of her. When he wouldn't wonder what she thought. What she was doing.

There was no one he trusted more. No one he loved more. She made him whole. And when their bodies and minds linked, the completion was so total, they were one.

"Our people will enjoy a royal wedding. It will have them looking to the future." The king's gaze settled on

Rion. "I have made many mistakes, but marrying your mother was not one of them. However, perhaps my biggest was sending you away. I saved your life . . . but the cost was so very great." His tone was sad. "When I ordered you and Erik to switch places, I couldn't foresee the consequences."

Rion frowned. "Sir, I don't understand."

"Because I didn't want you to die, I changed history. And because I saved you, a traitor gained power and betrayed us."

Rion had had flashes of a traitor but had never seen his face. "Who's the traitor?" Rion asked.

"I don't know. But the Unari didn't come here by chance. They had inside help." His father closed his eyes for the final time. His chest stopped rising and falling.

Filled with crushing sorrow, Rion leaned over his father and kissed his forehead. He was gone.

"I'm sorry." Tears brimmed in Marisa's eyes. "He loved you very much. He put your life before the welfare of his country."

Had he? Rion couldn't seem to make sense of all that had happened. "Did my father just imply that saving my life caused the Unari invasion?"

Marisa bit her lip. "I think so. And I believe he foresaw the consequences of saving you, but he could not bear to do otherwise."

Rion looked down at his father. The man had loved him enough to send his only son away to be raised by his brother. His father had loved him enough to save his life, to change the future. And his decision might or might not have cost this world dearly.

With a heavy heart, he kissed his father's cheek for the last time. His people had loved him. Rion had loved him.

Mendle knocked on the door and entered. He held a sheaf of papers in his hand.

"This is not a good time," Rion told him.

"You have to see this. Now." Mendle had never spoken to him in such an insistent tone. His posture was urgent, his voice vibrating with tension as he held out the papers.

"What is it?" Rion asked, his heart aching over the tremendous loss of his father.

"We have found documented evidence that proves the Unari intended to keep the Holy Grail in the structure they were constructing."

"Is the Grail here?" Rion asked.

"We don't believe so. But apparently there are beacons on the roof intended to guide those who have the Grail from a world called Pentar to Honor—but the journey was not to be made until the structure was finished."

When Rion didn't say anything, Marisa spoke quietly. "Is there anything else, Mendle?"

"There are also documents with the entire plan to over-run Honor. It's a history of the invasion, sire."

Rion handed the papers to Marisa. "Make copies and take them to Earth. And send a set to Tor."

Marisa scanned the documents. "This should help me convince Earth of the danger. I hope it's enough."

"We're sharing intel with Tor?" Mendle frowned.

"Yes, Tor." Rion pushed down his grief. Mourning his father would have to wait. "More specifically, send the documents to an Enforcer named Drake. You can reach him at the space museum on the rim. I promised that if we found information that might help Tor repel the Unari, we'd share. I want those bastards out of our solar system."

"I will see to it personally, sire."

"Thank you. Hopefully we can prevent what happened here from—"

"Excuse me, lady," Mendle said, his face flushing red before he turned to Rion. "Sire, *you* need to read these papers. Erik's name is in them."

"And?" With a frown, Rion glanced at the papers. Erik's name caught his eye, and he read more carefully before he looked up. "These suggest that my cousin conspired with the Unari. This must be a mistake."

But was it? His father had warned him of a traitor.

Mendle shook his head. "According to these records, the Unari had spies among the Enforcers on Tor. They knew you'd escaped them on Tor, and they had tracked your ship to Honor. The Unari sent an Honorian informant to Winhaven to betray you."

"They sent Erik?" Rion surmised.

Marisa's eyes widened. "He didn't escape?"

"The Unari freed him to spy," Mendle said. "Normally our rebel group is more suspicious, but we were so happy to see one of the royal bloodline had survived, we didn't question his good fortune."

Rion sighed. "Just because the Unari sent him doesn't mean he followed their orders."

Marisa's troubled gaze went to Rion. "When we arrived in the floater, the Unari fired on us *before* the door opened."

Rion dismissed Mendle. He had to face facts. Erik was different from the man he remembered. Harder. More bitter.

But a traitor? How could the man who'd saved Rion's life have betrayed him? It didn't make sense. He and Erik must talk. There had to be some other explanation.

Right now he had so much to do.

He had a country to lead. A father to bury. The possibility of a cousin's betrayal to deal with. And he would also have to say good-bye to Marisa.

At the thought of losing her to Earth, he felt his bones turn to water. His soul cried to go with her. But he wasn't free to do as he wished. His birthright had already cost him a childhood with his real parents, and it might now cost him the woman he loved. But he couldn't compare his own sacrifices to those his people had made to survive.

The rebellion plan had worked. The Unari had been defeated. Woodenly, he embraced Marisa, dropped his head to her hair, and breathed in her scent.

32

Marisa squeezed Rion so hard that if he hadn't been a dragonshaper, she would have broken his ribs. Rion hadn't had time to mourn his father's death, and now he had to deal with the possibility of his cousin's betrayal. And her imminent return to Earth.

She hated leaving Rion in such a mess.

With every atom in her body she wanted to stay. But the Unari had already left for Earth. Just as his people needed him to rebuild and heal, Earth's people needed her to warn them about the Unari intentions.

Rion tipped up her chin. "This is not good-bye."

"But—"

"Shh. We belong together. My father was right. You're meant to be Chivalri's queen. My people will learn to accept you. And come to love you like I do."

Her throat tightened. Perhaps someday . . .

Rion tensed. She thought it due to her lack of a reply, but a guard pushed Erik into the room. "Sire, he resisted when I removed his sidearm."

"Of course I resisted. I'm the king's cousin." Erik straightened, his tone harsh.

"Sire, I found him burning papers. Unari papers."

"I would rid this world of everything and everyone alien." Erik's eyes pierced Marisa's with open hatred.

Rion raised his head, giving the man the benefit of the doubt and speaking as if he hadn't heard the disrespect in Erik's voice. "Would you like time alone with the king?"

"With a dead body? I don't think so." Erik straightened, his back taut. His face was drawn, his eyes wild. "However, I would have liked to have spoken to him one last time."

"I'm sorry." Rion held out his arm to draw Erik into an embrace.

Erik sneered and pulled out a weapon he had hidden up his sleeve, shot the guard, then aimed at Rion. "I could have told Shepherd that all his scheming would do no good. His son will still die."

So it was true. Erik was the traitor.

And even though she shook with fear that Erik might pull the trigger, she could feel the emotional pain rolling off Rion.

Rion might have been hurting, but at the sight of the weapon, he thrust Marisa behind him. "Grief is twisting your—"

"I'm glad he's dead." Erik shook with anger.

Rion made yet another excuse for Erik's behavior and ignored the weapon. "You wanted his suffering to end?"

Erik spoke with bitterness. "Shepherd may have saved you from an assassin, but I've finally found yet another way to be rid of you."

Yet another way? Had Erik tried before? Marisa's

mouth went dry with fear. Just how long had Erik's hatred been festering?

"What are you saying?" Rion took another step closer to Erik.

"You can't believe a word he says," Marisa hissed, unnerved by the way Erik's finger tightened on the trigger. Perhaps if she drew attention to herself, she could buy Rion a little more time.

Frantic, she glanced around the makeshift hospital room for a weapon. But there was nothing besides a bed with the kng's lifeless body, a tray at his side. On the tray was a glass of water.

Erik chuckled. "Ah, so she is intelligent. That makes her all the more dangerous. Maybe I'll shoot her first, so you can watch her die." Erik's laughter sounded forced, his words clearly meant to taunt Rion.

She snatched the glass. It wasn't much of a weapon, but it was all she had.

"By blood right, the throne is mine." Rion took another step closer to Erik.

"My blood is purer than yours. I'm one hundred percent Honorian. You are a half-breed. And now you seek to dilute the royal blood with another alien woman?"

"An alliance with Earth will strengthen us," Rion countered.

"Your mother couldn't bear to lose you, so she convinced your father to alter the future. Another alien interfering in Honorian affairs. If not for her, your father wouldn't have taken a wife and the crown would have been mine." Erik's tone grew petulant. "Now I'm restoring the rightful order."

Erik wasn't making sense. Even if Shepherd hadn't

married a Toran woman, he would have likely taken a wife. Erik still wouldn't have been king. But Marisa didn't argue.

"Erik, you risked your life to save me. You aren't thinking straight right now—"

"Fool. It might have been a mistake to invite the Unari here—"

"What?" Rion's eyes burned into Erik.

Erik shrugged, but he kept the weapon firmly aimed. "The Unari promised they would rid Honor of all outsiders. That I would finally rule. But they didn't keep their word," he muttered. "I was actually happy you didn't die in your escape attempt, that you returned to Chivalri to help rid us of the bastards. Things have worked out. Shepherd's dead. You'll kill yourself in grief and guilt that you left Chivalri when we needed you most. We'll have a triple funeral. First, I'll kill the alien woman—"

Rion lunged. Marisa threw the glass, dived to the floor, and rolled.

Erik ducked the glass and fired.

Instead of striking Erik's head, the glass flew by his ear. But water splashed into his eyes and ruined his aim.

Erik's shot spun Rion around, but momentum carried him forward. The two men grappled for the weapon, and Marisa scrambled out of the way.

Rion released a grunt of pain, and she turned to look over her shoulder. Oh . . . God.

"Rion." There was blood on Rion's chest. So much blood she couldn't see the injury itself. Blood matted his clothing and dripped onto Erik as the two men wrestled across the floor, each trying to aim the weapon at the other.

Fear for Rion made her stomach knot. She had to do something. Help Rion.

"Guards!" she screamed and prayed Rion's men would hear her.

Quick and cunning, Erik tried to knee Rion in the crotch.

Rion twisted his hips to one side and received only a glancing blow.

Even as the men grappled for the weapon, they jammed elbows and knees into each other. At a vicious chop to his ribs, Rion groaned, and he countered with a knee to the kidney. Erik shrieked but kept hold of the weapon. With a jerk, he pulled it free.

Marisa leaped onto Erik's back, wound her arm around his throat, and choked him. Erik's finger tightened on the trigger. She yanked him backward, just as he fired.

With a rising thrust of his arm, Rion knocked Erik's arm upward, and the shot went over his head. Erik bucked Marisa off his back as if she weighed no more than a flea. Tumbling, she slammed into a wall, knocking her head hard.

For a moment, her vision narrowed. The room went black, and stars exploded before her eyes.

Although she couldn't see, she forced her wobbly feet under her and used the wall to balance. Blood on her hand smeared on the wall. It wasn't her blood—but Rion's. By the time she regained an unsteady stance, her vision had cleared. Rion had knocked away Erik's weapon, and it skidded toward her.

She bent to pick it up. But Erik kicked it away, catching her fingers in a brutal blow.

But the pain in her hand was nothing compared to the

pain of watching Rion bleed to death. Blood matted his shirt, made the floor slick as it gathered in pools. She didn't know how he could lose that much blood and still remain conscious, much less fight.

Where were his men? Why wasn't help arriving?

Erik had thrust Rion's head down and trapped it against his belly, his arm wrapped around his neck. She braced for the sound of Erik snapping Rion's neck. But with a roar, Rion shifted into a partial dragonshape. His skin thickened. His muscles grew. His eyes glowed golden.

There wasn't enough room to fully shift. But the extra dragon strength gave Rion the brawn to break Erik's choke hold. As he straightened, Rion rammed the back of his head into Erik's face, shattering Erik's nose in a bone-jarring crunch. Erik fell back against a wall and slumped, his eyes staring sightlessly.

Rion had delivered a deathblow.

But Rion was down, too. Eyes closed, flat on his back, he wasn't moving.

And there was blood. So much blood.

If you honor and serve your people well, they will honor and serve you well.

— KING ARTHUR PENDRAGON

33

Guards and a physician had finally rushed into the room. They'd tried to stabilize Rion, then carried him on a stretcher to a surgery center in the palace where Marisa now waited. The waiting area was much like those in hospitals everywhere, and she paced, unable to sit.

Lex, Mendle, and Darian waited with her. No one spoke, all of them tense.

Sometime around dawn, a doctor came out. Eyes exhausted and lined with dark circles, his hands still covered with blood, he spoke gently. "We repaired the nerve damage and gave the king blood transfusions. The internal bleeding's stopped. Now we wait to see if the blood loss compromised the brain."

He could have brain damage? She swayed on her feet, sank against the wall. "How long until we know?"

"Not until he comes out of the coma."

"And that will be?"

The doctor sighed. "Goddess willing, it will be soon. But you must prepare yourself. He might not ever wake up."

She refused to believe that. She wouldn't think it. No way could she live the rest of her life in a universe that didn't include him. Rion was going to wake up. He was going to survive and lead his country into the future.

Marisa squared her shoulders. "I'd like to see him."

"Come with me." The doctor took her arm and led her through a set of double doors.

Marisa barely recognized Rion. His skin was as pale as the white sheets. Tubes were attached everywhere. Machines that breathed for him pumped and hissed. Careful not to displace the IV in his wrist, she slid her hand into his. So cold. Too cold.

But six hours later, the doctors thought Rion was strong enough to breathe on his own and removed the tube from his throat.

Twelve hours later, Lex brought her food, but she couldn't eat. Aware of the food shortage, she insisted Lex give hers to someone else.

As the door shut behind Lex, Rion opened his eyes. "You must eat."

God, it was good to see him awake.

She grinned in delight, felt like dancing around his bed. Happy tears, the tears she couldn't release earlier, trickled down her cheeks.

Relief lightened her heart. Marisa leaned over him, let him see the joy in her eyes. "It figures you'd wake up to tell me what to do," she teased.

Marisa climbed into the bed and snuggled against him, careful not to damage his tubing or bandages. She needed his touch, needed to feel his heat, to reassure herself that he would be all right.

"How long was I out?"

"Including surgery—almost a day."

Rion held her against his side, his hand tracing a path up and down her arm. She wished she could stay in bed next to him, touching him, talking to him, forever. "I don't know how I'm going to leave you."

"Then stay," he said simply.

"I can't. Now that we have solid evidence of the Unari plan to attack Earth, I have to warn my people."

"I know. But I'd do almost anything to keep you here." He let out a long, husky sigh.

"I should have already left." She nuzzled his side and breathed in his scent. "But I couldn't leave until I knew you'd be all right."

He smiled at her. "I'm glad. But will your people believe you?"

"Some of them will. And perhaps that will be enough to prevent what happened here from reoccurring on Earth."

She propped herself onto her elbow so she could look into his eyes. She wanted to memorize his face, every detail. His specific shade of gray eyes. The pattern of the green flecks in his irises. The shape of his lips.

He reached behind her head, drew her mouth toward his, his voice low and husky. "Promise me one thing."

She lifted her eyebrow. "What's that?"

"You'll come back to marry me?"

A new lump of happiness formed in her throat. "I will, but I don't know how long—"

"However long you take—that's how long I'll wait."

His words bathed her in warmth. "Then yes, I'll marry you, Rion Jaqard."

After hearing her words, he closed his eyes again. When he awakened, she was gone.

Marry a man from Honor and you marry all of Honor.

—HONORIAN PROVERB

34

Marisa's days had been swamped with high-level meetings, but at night she missed Rion so much that when she finally fell into exhausted sleep, she dreamed of him. Dreamed of his arms around her. His kisses. His smiles.

But finally, four weeks later, she'd returned to Honor, and it was better than any dream. Rion had a special guard awaiting her arrival at the Infinity Circle, and they whisked her straight from the transporter into a vehicle.

She had so much to tell him and couldn't wait to hear what had been happening during her absence. The driver, Mendle, opened the door for her. "Welcome home."

Marisa smiled at him. "It's good to see you again."

"Thank you, my lady."

Marisa settled into the seat and gazed out the window.

The moment they left the heavily guarded Infinity Stones and pulled onto a road, she stared in surprise at the crowds of Honorians lining the road. Some waved flags. Many greeted her with smiles.

"What's going on?" she asked Mendle.

"The people are honoring their new queen," he told her.

"They're here for me?" Marisa got a warm hitch in her chest.

Mendle grinned. "You have many people who adore you, my lady. The king has spread the news far and wide of how you risked your life for us. We are most grateful."

Rion was a good man. The best. He had to be working night and day to feed his people, to set up basic emergency services, and to create a new government. And yet he'd still thought of a way to ease her transition. To make her feel welcome—not just to his home but to his world.

"Please, roll down a window so I can wave back."

Mendle hesitated. He spoke gently. "Perhaps you should discuss it with the king."

"There will always be some people who dislike me because I was born on Earth. I won't spend my life hiding."

Marisa rolled down the window and waved. The crowd roared their approval.

MARISA STRODE INTO the room right in the middle of a planning meeting. Rion stood and rushed to embrace her. Damn, she looked good. Wearing a new nanotech jacket that showed off her slender waist and pants that flared wide at the ankles, she was about to set a new style on Chivalri.

Her chestnut hair was shiny and smelled wonderful as he gathered her against him. "What took you so long?"

She chuckled. "I've been a little busy."

"Now that you're here, I'm going to keep you very busy." He kissed her mouth.

She leaned into him, then pulled back, heat rising up her cheeks. "Rion, we have an audience."

"Oh, them." He turned to his advisers. "There are some advantages to being king." With a grin, he dismissed them. "Begone."

The advisers chuckled and began to pack papers into files and briefcases.

"Wait just one minute." She placed her hand on his chest and stepped back. "I have news your advisers will want to hear."

Lex looked at Rion, and he nodded for them to stay. "Before Marisa left Honor, I bestowed her with ambassadorial authority to negotiate with Earth."

"I've set up several trade agreements," Marisa began.

"Trade?" Lex asked, his tone curious. "We have nothing to trade—the Unari destroyed everything."

"Not quite." Marisa gestured to her clothing. "Earth didn't have material that repairs itself after we dragonshape. So I sold Earth the rights to use the nanotechnology."

"And what do we get in return?" Darian asked.

"Food, seed, machinery, generators, and computers, plus tools to start up factories, and the fuel to run them."

"You did great." Rion grinned, his heart light and happy. Not only had she battled the Tyrannizer and helped free his people, her treaty with Earth would help revitalize their economy.

"I may have overstepped my authority a bit," she said with a saucy smile.

Rion raised his eyebrow. "Oh?"

"I also took the liberty of bargaining with my sister-in-law, Cael. She's the High Priestess of Pendragon," she told Rion's advisers. "They were also interested in the nano-technology."

"And what did you get from them?" Rion asked, a smile teasing his lips, pleased at her entrepreneurial spirit.

"A solar electric plant. And telecommunications satellites."

Marisa was making his job easier. Righting his world. Rion's heart swelled with joy that this wonderful woman had agreed to spend the rest of her life with him.

"In addition, both worlds are extending us credit. And Vivianne Blackstone, head of the Vesta Corporation, has agreed to build a spaceship capable of flying to Pentar to retrieve the Holy Grail."

Rion whooped, lifted Marisa by the waist, and kissed her. "You are amazing." He kissed her again, and this time when he flicked his hand for his men to leave, amid much laughter and good-hearted teasing, his team of experts filed out of the room.

Finally he had her alone. Stars, she smelled good. He swept her off her feet and twirled her around. "I'm a lucky man to be holding the sexiest, bravest woman in the solar system, and you have brains, too."

She'd given him so much hope and happiness. He had never felt this way. How could he love her this much? How had he been so lucky to find this woman, a true partner who cared about his world and his people as much as he did, and who loved him, too?

As her hair spun around her face, she stared up into his eyes and he knew they shared something precious and rare. He flashed her a smile. "I can't believe you're really here. Lucan's okay with us?"

"If I'm happy, Lucan's happy. He and Cael sent their congratulations and a wedding gift."

He spun her faster.

She laughed. "You'll make me dizzy."

"I'm going to make you more than dizzy," he promised.

"You already have." Cheeks flushed, eyes sparkling with happiness, she leaned back in his arms as the room spun around them. "We're pregnant."

He stopped spinning and carefully set her down on her feet, then backed up to stare at her. He saw the happy excitement in her eyes, the wonder on her face as her hand fluttered against her stomach as if she could barely believe it herself.

Having a child had been a dream of his for years. But when he'd envisioned the future, he hadn't seen family life. He'd envisioned working to rebuild Honor. The thought of having a family with this woman he adored suddenly seemed like too much good fortune.

For so long he'd been on the run. He'd given up all hope of a normal life. But now . . . now he could have a life, a real family, a future.

Rion's roar of happiness was heard throughout the palace. He kissed her forehead. "I love you." He kissed her cheek. "I love you." He kissed her lips. And after he stole her breath, he kneeled, kissed her belly, and spoke to their unborn child. "And I love you, too."

"Our child will be born in a new era."

"We'll make sure it's a world that doesn't live in fear of slavery. Where people are free and tolerant. Where people don't fear differences but celebrate them."

He stood, and with a tender smile, she wrapped her arms around his neck. "I didn't know I could be so happy."

"Make love to me, Rion."

He tipped up her chin. "I've heard on Earth, it's customary to wait until the wedding night."

Marisa laughed. "It's a little late for that."

"Anticipation will make our wedding night even more special." He winked. "I promise, I'll make the wait worthwhile."

She arched her brow. "In that case, I'll hold you to your promise." Then she lifted her lips for another kiss.

The next day, during the royal wedding, there wasn't a dry eye in the land. The celebration lasted all night. And for a time there was love and peace again on Honor.

BE SURE TO CHECK OUT
THE FIRST THRILLING
ROMANCE IN THE
PENDRAGON LEGACY
SERIES!

•

Please turn this page

for an excerpt from

Lucan

AVAILABLE NOW

The precious myths of our heritage are our way of understanding things greater than ourselves. They are tales of the inexplicable forces that shape our lives and of events that defy explanation. These legends are rooted in the spilling of our lifeblood, in the courage of brave hearts, in the resilience of humanity's tenacious spirit.

—ARTHUR PENDRAGON

PROLOGUE

In the near future

"Slow down, Marisa," Lucan Roarke warned his twin. They were deep inside the cave he'd discovered in the Welsh countryside in the shadow of Cadbury Castle, and his helmet light had settled on a gaping crack in the compacted clay of the cavern's floor. "Don't step on that—"

"What?" Marisa looked back at him just as the ground opened beneath her feet. Falling, she flailed her arms and clawed at the cave wall for a handhold, but the loose earth crumbled beneath her fingertips, and gravity dragged her down through the crevice into the darkness below.

Lucan lunged to grab her, but the unstable earth lurched

and dipped under him, throwing him off balance, and his fingers missed her by inches.

"Marisa!" The sound of splashing water drowned out his cry.

Lucan had brought his sister to Cadbury Castle for a vacation, and he'd been excited to show her this cave—his latest discovery in his quest for the Holy Grail. Although many dismissed the Grail as mythical, his years of exploration and research had convinced him the vessel actually existed.

Lucan peered through the gloom into the chasm, but his helmet light couldn't penetrate the blackness. Even worse, the earthen sides of the hole made a steep vertical descent. Reaching for the heavy-duty flashlight he carried in his back pocket, he yelled, "Marisa? Talk to me, damn it!"

Nothing but silence answered him.

Closing his eyes, Lucan inhaled deeply and concentrated on linking his mind with hers, a telepathic communication the two had shared since they were little.

Marisa. Where are you?

In the water. Help me. I'm cold.

Heart racing, Lucan shone the flashlight into the darkness and spotted her head above the rushing water.

"Lucan. Here." Smart enough not to fight the powerful flow of water that tried to sweep her downstream, Marisa swam for the wall at an angle and clung to a rocky ledge.

"Hang on."

She coughed and sputtered, then shot back, "If I let go, it won't be on purpose. Hurry. It's freezing."

Lucan reached for the rope in his backpack and cursed himself for bringing his sister into the bowels of the cave.

He'd sweet-talked her into coming along, desperate to break her out of her funk. Since her latest miscarriage, she'd been fighting off depression. He'd hoped this excursion would take her mind off her loss, at least for a little while. He hadn't intended to distract her by risking her life and scaring her to death.

He uncoiled the rope, then leaned over the hole to see her lose her grip on the ledge. The current pulled her under. "Marisa!"

A split second later, a pale hand broke through the water and clutched a rock jutting from the wall. She pulled her head and shoulders above the torrent, spat water, and forced her words through shivering lips. "I knew . . . I should have gone . . . to Club Med."

He looped the rope around the biggest boulder within reach. Then he tossed the line down the narrow shaft. "Grab on and I'll book the next flight to Cancún."

Marisa stretched for the rope. And missed. Water surged over her head. Again she swam to the surface, but the current had carried her too far downstream to reach the lifeline.

With no other choice, Lucan jumped into the dark shaft. He fell about twelve feet before frigid water closed over his head and ripped away his glasses. His flesh went numb, but he managed to keep a grip on his waterproof flashlight. His lungs seized and his vision blurred. Forcing his shocked limbs to move, he kicked for the surface. And heard Marisa's scream. Turning around, he swam in the direction he'd last seen her.

Already his teeth chattered. He struggled for breath, and his waterlogged clothing and boots weighed him down. The raging current swept him under, but his concern was for Marisa. She'd been in this icy water too long. Clenching his teeth, he kicked harder until he was finally close enough to grab Marisa's shoulders. They had only minutes to find a way out before hypothermia set in.

He pulled her close. "I've got you."

When she didn't reply, fear poured through his system. Fighting to lift her head above the surface, he shone his light around the cave in search of a shoal or a shallow pool.

Marisa lifted a quaking hand. "There."

Just ahead, the river forked. One side widened, the other narrowed.

Using most of his remaining strength, he steered them toward the wider fork, praying it wouldn't take them deeper underground. His prayers were answered when they rounded a bend and the water leveled out onto a dirt embankment.

He pulled Marisa out of the river, and together they lay on the bank, panting, shivering, and exhausted. When she didn't speak, he aimed the light on her. Her eyes were closed, her face pale, her lips blue. He wrung some of the water from her clothing, then rubbed her limbs with his own freezing hands.

Her eyes fluttered open. "One word . . . about my hair, and I'll s-smack you upside the head."

"You look good in mud."

She slapped at his shoulder but didn't have the strength to land the blow.

He smoothed her hair from her eyes. "Save your strength. I don't want to have to carry you." She needed to walk to keep the hypothermia at bay.

"W-wuss." She crawled up the bank until her back rested against a dirt wall.

Lucan focused on survival. "We've got to get moving or we'll freeze."

"You wrung the water from my clothes. What about you?"

"I'm fine."

"Of course, you're fine. J-just like when y-you were in Namibia and that black mamba bit you?"

"I lived."

"Barely." Marisa took his hand and tried to stand, but her knees buckled. She grabbed the wall behind her for support and it began to collapse on top of them.

Lucan lunged and threw his body over hers, shut his eyes, and prayed they wouldn't be buried alive. Clumps of cold mud cascaded over them and bounced aside.

"You okay?" Lucan asked.

"Oh, now I'm really having f-fun." Marisa spat dirt. "So glad you suggested"—her teeth chattered uncontrollably—"this little vacation."

Lucan shoved to his feet. "Think what a great adventure story you'll have to write."

"I don't want to *be* the story." She rolled her eyes and sighed. "But you love this shit. You're probably getting off on—"

Wow. Her telepathic thought interrupted her words midsentence. And her amazement came through in waves—surprising waves that peaked with astonishment.

"What?" He spun around to see exactly what had shocked her, and he froze. He focused his flashlight on the unearthed urn, hardly believing his eyes or his luck.

The intricate design made dating the piece easy. "It's Tintagel ware."

"Tinta-who?"

"Tintagel ware is an ancient indigenous pottery. Fifth or sixth century. More evidence that Cadbury Castle really was King Arthur's home base."

They both jumped aside as another slice of wall and more pottery crashed down, revealing a hidden room. At the sound of breaking terra-cotta, Lucan winced. An ancient scroll poked from the shards, and he dashed to pull the paper from the muddy earth before the dampness reached it.

Old and fragile, the antiquity had survived in amazing condition. He balanced the flashlight between his shoulder and chin, unfurled his find, and squinted, wishing for his lost glasses.

Marisa peered over his arm, her reporter's curiosity evident. "What is it?"

Lucan stared, his pulse racing in excitement. The astrological map revealed the sun, the earth, planets. And many stars. But what had his heart battering his ribs was the line drawn from Earth to a star far across the galaxy. He was looking at an ancient map of the heavens. His mouth went dry. "This is a star map."

"Why do you sound so surprised? Even the most ancient cultures were into astrology."

"Astronomy," he corrected automatically. "I'm no astronomer, but this looks . . . far too accurate for its time. King Arthur, remember. The age of chivalry."

"Yeah, right."

Lost in thought, he ignored her sarcasm. "This map

has details the Hubble telescope might not pick up, yet it's thousands of years old. It's unbelievable."

"So it's a fake?"

"I'll have to perform tests . . ." He squinted at the map. His gaze moved on to the distant stars and their planets. "Hell."

"What now?"

He pointed to the map. "This moon is named Pendragon."

"Wasn't that King Arthur's last name?"

He nodded and squinted. "And written right under Pendragon is the word *Avalon*."

"Avalon? Is that significant?"

"Avalon was a legendary isle ruled by a Druid priestess called the Lady of the Lake," he answered. "She helped put Arthur on the throne. And according to the stories, Avalon was also where King Arthur left the Holy Grail."

"The Holy Grail?" Disbelief filled her voice.

"The powers of the cup are legendary. If the myths are true, the cup might cure physical ills—cancer, heart attacks, and"—he hesitated before breathing out the word—"sterility."

Though neither his sister nor her husband was officially sterile, like most of Earth's population, they couldn't have children. Her recent miscarriage had been her second in as many years. If the cup truly existed and he could find it, his sister—and hundreds of thousands of others—could finally carry a child to term.

"Throughout the ages," he continued, "many men, including Arthur's own Knights of the Round Table, have searched for Avalon and the Holy Grail. Legendary stories of the Grail's healing properties exist in many cultures, yet no one has found it." He pointed to the small moon on the ancient map. "Maybe that's because Avalon wasn't on Earth."

"You've lost your mind." She sighed, but the catch in her voice exposed her wishful thinking that after all this time despairing, she might be able to hope again.

"A search for the Holy Grail might be the most exciting thing I'll ever do."

"It might also be the last thing you ever do. Didn't you learn your lesson when you went in search of Preah Vihear antiquities?"

"The golden statue of the dancing Shiva I found in the Khmer temple was worth—"

"Ending up in a Cambodian jail?"

"Just a little misunderstanding. We got it squared away."

She cursed under her breath. "You sure you don't have a death wish? Or are you just an adrenaline junky?"

She was only fussing because she loved him, so he ignored her rhetorical questions. Besides, he wasn't the only twin who took calculated risks. As a reporter for the *St. Petersburg Times,* Marisa had placed herself in danger many times. They were some pair. She wanted to report the present to change the future. Until now, he'd believed humanity was headed for extinction and had studied the past because the future looked bleak. But if he could find the Grail, the past just might offer hope for the future.

Marisa sighed. "We need to dig out of here."

He carefully rolled up the parchment and placed it in the dry sample bag he'd pulled from his backpack. Then he shone the light on the broken pottery. Kneeling, he began gathering as many shards as he could carry.

He reached for a particularly large piece, covered in an array of signs and symbols, when he spied daylight glimmering through a tiny opening on the far wall of the hidden room. A way out. "Time to go."

"Now you're in a hurry?"

"Don't you want to find out if this map's authentic?"

She sighed. "I'm more interested in warm, dry clothes."

"Do you realize what we may have found?"

"We? Just you, my brother. Avalon? The Holy Grail? A cure for cancer? The idea is more than crazy. It's nonsense. But knowing you, you'll find a way to follow that map to Avalon."

"If the star map pans out, you'll want first dibs on the story—don't deny it."

"You're a restless, adventure-seeking fool. That stupid map is going to take you straight to outer space."

He could only hope.

As they deny the world, not only in the spirit realm but in the material plane, the world will cease to exist.

—THE LADY OF THE LAKE

1

Eight years later, half a galaxy away

Cael was going to die. Not with the dignity a High Priestess was due. Not even with the respect afforded a physician.

And it was all her own fault. When she'd thought she'd seen her owl, Merlin, flapping frantically in the cooling conduit, she'd foolishly attempted a rescue. That had been mistake number one. Instead of calling maintenance for help, she'd grabbed a ladder, yanked off the outer grid, and crawled into the ductwork. Mistake number two. She'd forgotten to take a flashlight. Mistake number three. And now she was stuck in the dark conduit, half frozen, her hair held firm by the intake valve, her hand caught in the mesh screen meant to keep out rodents.

She'd shouted for help, of course, but no one had heard. With her robes and feet dangling into the hallway, she would have been hard to miss, but her coworkers never came down the hall to the High Priestess's office. Being High Priestess wasn't all it was assumed to be. Yes, she lived in a magnificent residence, free of charge, and her people revered her, even enacting a special law to allow her to be both priestess and healer, but the average Dragonian wouldn't think of stopping by for a chat, never mind asking for her medical opinion.

While she believed her empathic ability was a gift that enabled her to use her healing skills wisely, her people too often looked at it as a curse. A curse that might blast them if they looked at her the wrong way . . . so most preferred not to look at her at all.

To her regret, she'd treated only a few patients since she'd joined the Avalon Project's team of specialists that included astronomers, archaeologists, physicists, engineers, geologists, and computer technicians. Unless they had an emergency, her coworkers preferred other, less daunting healers. And if she didn't turn up for work in the lab tomorrow, she doubted anyone would search for her. They'd assume she was attending to her High Priestess duties.

So she was stuck. Alone as usual.

And Merlin wasn't even here. Mistake number four. Had she imagined that the owl had needed her help? She should have known better. The bird was crafty. He wouldn't fly into a conduit that had no exit. He wouldn't get stuck as she had. It would be just her luck if she died here of dehydration.

"Damn it." She pounded on the metal wall with her free hand and yelled. "Just turn off the cooling coils, hand me a knife, and I'll cut myself free."

No one answered. The suction from the intake valve

threatened to snatch her bald. Again she wrenched her wrist, but the mesh held her fingers in a claw-like grip. Tired, cold, she closed her eyes and dozed.

"Lady?" Someone tugged on her foot.

She awakened with a jerk and almost yanked her hair out by the roots. Teeth chattering, her side numb, she figured she must have been dreaming of rescue.

Then she heard the same deep and sexy yet unrecognizable voice again. "Are you stuck?"

What did he think? That the High Priestess slept here because she liked being frozen into an ice cube? "Please, can you get me out?"

A warm hand grasped her ankle, and an interesting tingle shot up her leg as he tugged.

"Ow! My hair is caught in the intake valve, and my hand got stuck in the mesh when I tried to free myself."

She was about to ask for a pair of scissors or a knife, when she heard the duct metal creak, followed by a thud. Then a man's chest was sliding over her legs. And his movement was tugging up her gown.

Holy Goddess.

She'd never been this close to someone before. No one dared touch the High Priestess.

Yet he'd crawled right into the duct with her and was inching his way past her hips. Both her hearts jolted as if she'd taken a direct electric charge. His heat seeped into her, and the feel of his powerful, rippling male muscles had her biting back a gasp of shock.

It was impossible not to feel the heat pulsing between them. Studying the signs of arousal in a medical book was one thing. Experiencing them was quite another.

The stranger was edging up her body, and her senses

rioted. Never had anything felt this indescribably good. She wished she could see his eyes and his expression. Even her empathic gift was failing her. Her own excitement was preventing her from reading him. Was he enjoying the feel of her as much as she was him? Did he have any idea that her hearts were racing? That her skirt was above her knees?

Ever so slowly, he crawled to her waist and his head slid between her breasts, his warm breath fanning her flesh. His mouth had to be inches from her . . . oh, sweet Goddess.

"The air duct really isn't made for two," he joked.

Her pulse leaped. Her nerves were on fire. "There isn't enough air," she gasped.

"It's fine." He wriggled until his cheek pressed hers, and she could feel the fine growth of a beard one day past a shave. His broad chest warmed her. Her hips nestled his, and she felt him harden against her.

She stiffened. So he wasn't unaffected, and that fact secretly pleased her. Although it shouldn't have.

Apparently not the least embarrassed by his physical reaction, he chuckled, his breath warm and tantalizing in her ear. "Don't worry. It's not like we have enough room in here to get any closer."

She squeezed her eyes tight. "You don't know who I am."

"You feel . . . beautiful." He reached above her head and ran his hand along her hair, his fingers strong and gentle. "I'm going to remove the grate so we don't have to cut your hair."

His muscles flexed, and he popped the vent from the duct. "Now let's free your hand."

He skimmed his other hand up her body, lightly teasing her waist, the side of her breast, her cheek. She sucked in her breath as a ripple of pleasure washed through her.

"I'll be happy to do more of that after I get you out of here," he murmured and ran his fingers up her arm to her trapped wrist. "Hmm. I've got a screwdriver in my back pocket. Think you can reach it?"

She licked her bottom lip and moved her free hand across his firm hip to his curved buttock. Her fingers itched to explore. After all, she had to find his pocket, didn't she?

"Try a little higher, sweetheart," he urged, his voice amused.

"If you want to live, don't call me that," she said in her best High Priestess voice. But instead of sounding authoritative, her tone was breathy and light.

She fumbled her fingers over his buttock, enjoying the hard muscle and the sensuous curve, and finally found and unsnapped the pocket. Oh . . . my. The material inside that pocket was so thin she was almost touching his bare, warm flesh. At the thought, her breasts tingled and, certain he could feel her nipples hardening against him, she flushed.

"What should I call you?" he teased.

She hesitated. If she told him her name, he might not finish freeing her. "I'll introduce myself once we're out of this mess."

"Honey, we're way beyond the need for formal introductions—not when your sexy little hand is grabbing my ass."

She snatched the screwdriver from his pocket. "Got it."

He gave instructions with an easy self-confidence that told her he was enjoying himself. "Reach up my back, over my shoulder, and place the screwdriver into my hand."

She did as he asked and found herself admiring his broad back, the muscular shoulders. She was wrapped around him, and the feel of his hard male body had her trembling. She hadn't known a man could feel so good.

His maleness was erotic, exotic. Exciting. Her blood rushed though her veins with a heat that made her feel more alive than she had since she'd first taken to the skies in flight.

"You're awfully quiet." The rough texture of his words was almost as exciting as his muscles straining over her. "Am I too heavy?"

Too heavy? He was perfect.

She swallowed hard. "How much longer . . ."

"Until we're done unscrewing? Now, there's a question I haven't been asked before." She could hear the grin in his wry tone and was grateful when he changed the subject. "How'd you get stuck in here, anyway?"

Every time he turned the screwdriver, his pecs tensed against her breasts and his erection pressed hot against her thigh.

She tried to distract herself by talking. "I thought I heard a bird trapped in here."

She expected him to tell her she was silly, but he paused in his handiwork. "So you're the adventurous type?"

Was she? She had no idea. From the moment she'd been born, her destiny had been set. The Elders had trained her as High Priestess. It was her duty to perform religious ceremonies, to bless babies, to mediate high-level disputes. But she'd wanted to connect with people, so she'd insisted on becoming a healer, too. That was the reason she worked on the Avalon Project, hoping to find the Holy Grail and cure her world of all illness. Was that the same as adventurous?

He popped out the last screw, and she tugged her hand free. Her fingers landed in his thick, soft hair. "Sorry."

"Don't be. I'm not."

"You might be really sorry—once we get out of here."

"Why's that?" He began to wriggle down her body. "Are you married?"

"I'm never getting married." The High Priestess wasn't allowed to wed. Even if it wasn't forbidden, who would want a woman who had the strength to kill her own mate?

"You have seven big, protective brothers who'll want to beat me up?" he teased.

"There's just me and my two sisters." She couldn't keep the wistfulness from her tone.

"No husband. No brothers. And you don't want to marry. Honey, you're ideal," he said, his tone soft and husky. Finally, he jumped down, and she found herself missing his warmth. Then his strong hands slid up her legs.

"I can get out . . . by myself." She tried to wriggle away but couldn't, of course, with the duct restricting her movements. "Is anyone else there?"

"No one. It's past midnight."

"Thank the Goddess." His large hands almost spanned her waist. He lifted her from the conduit and set her down on her feet. Her skirts dropped to the floor, and she smoothed them while avoiding his gaze.

As the ceremonial robes swished around her legs, her

customary decorum returned. "Thank you. You saved my life. But I won't tell anyone, so please don't worry . . ." She raised her head and met his eyes.

"I'm not worried." Cocking his head to the side, he'd spoken as if he found the idea absurd. He smiled as if he were seeing Cael the woman, not the High Priestess, and it charged her with intense awareness. Of him.

In the dim light she recognized him. Lucan Roarke. The new archaeologist on the team had dark hair, compelling blue eyes, and a sculpted jaw. And he wore glasses. Obviously he needed a new prescription, since he didn't seem to recognize her.

"If anyone learns that you touched me, the State will execute you."

"Really?"

"The only exemptions are during my healing duties or for blessings bestowed in religious ceremonies."

She expected him to back away, tremble, even grovel as others in his position would have. Automatically, she braced for the normal blast of fear, but instead he leaned toward her, his voice seductive. "Lady Cael." Obviously he *did* recognize her. "I wouldn't mind if more than my fate was in your hands."

A LEGEND CONTINUES . . .
PLEASE TURN THIS PAGE
FOR A PREVIEW OF
THE NEXT BOOK IN
SUSAN KEARNEY'S
PASSIONATE
PENDRAGON LEGACY
SERIES!

Jordan

Available in mass market
in March 2010.

1

"Damn it, Jordan. You lied to me." Vivianne Blackstone, CEO of the Vesta Corporation, tapped the incriminating report against her leg and restrained her urge to fling it at Jordan McArthur, her chief engineer. The world was in a total meltdown after learning an ancient enemy had infiltrated Earth's governments and major industries, and Vivianne was determined to keep her *Draco* project safe.

Head throbbing, she stared at the spaceship's complex wiring. The *Draco* had to fly as planned. It had to work out. So much was riding on this venture to find the lost and legendary Holy Grail. Vesta's future. Earth's future. Her future. Everything she'd ever wanted, everyone she'd ever loved, might be lost if this project didn't succeed.

When Jordan didn't respond, she nudged his foot with her shoe. "I'm talking to you."

Lying on the deck with his head halfway through a hatch, Jordan shifted until she could just see his intense blue eyes.

"I heard. How did I lie to you?"

She dropped the papers, but she'd already lost his attention to the ship. He'd wriggled back inside the compartment, pulling another wire to hook into the circuits, no doubt following an electrical schematic that existed only inside his head.

He threaded a wire into a panel box of delicately networked circuits. "Hand me a screwdriver."

Scowling at his back, she slapped the tool into his hand.

"Tell me these findings are wrong," Vivianne demanded.

"What findings?" His profile, rugged and somber, remained utterly still, except for a tiny tick in his jaw that told her he was unhappy she'd interrupted his work. He wouldn't even have a job if not for her—and he would lose it, if he didn't come up with a satisfactory explanation for why his entire résumé had been one big fat lie.

"You've never attended Harvard. Never got your PhD at MIT. Never taught at Cambridge."

"The Phillips-head." He held out his hand again, and this time his voice was laced with impatience. "It's the screwdriver with an X on the tip."

Like she didn't know a Phillips-head when she saw one? While her specialty was communications technology, she'd designed and built her first hydrogen rocket by age twelve. However, when it came to spaceship design, Jordan was the go-to guy.

Despite his doctored résumé, the man knew his aeronautical engineering. From hull design to antigrav wiring, no detail on the *Draco* was too small for Jordan to reengineer and make more efficient.

One of Jordan's engineers spoke over the ship's intercom. "These voltage converter equations can't be right."

"They are," Jordan answered evenly.

"They're frying the circuits." The man's frustration was evident in his tone.

"Sean, you'll find a way to keep them humming. You always do."

"I'm stumped."

"I'll give you a hand as soon as I can."

"Thanks, boss."

"But I'm sure you'll figure it out before then."

Sean chuckled. "I'll do my best."

While this was a side of Jordan she hadn't seen, his encouragement didn't surprise her. But it wasn't his leadership skills that she questioned. Vivianne's gut churned. "Jordan, we really need to talk."

"So talk."

Vivianne paused and considered precisely what to say. She'd already made one mistake by hiring Jordan before he'd been properly vetted. She couldn't afford to make another—like accusing him outright of being a spy.

"As the first hyperspace ship to carry a full crew, the *Draco* has caught the imagination and attention of the masses. Everything we do is headline news, and when the press finds out that my chief engineer falsified his employment application—"

"Damn it, Vivianne, I know what I'm doing."

"To the public, a liar is a liar. And if you lied to get a job, they'll think you've lied about the *Draco* during our press conferences."

"So we don't tell anyone. Problem solved."

Vivianne pinched the bridge of her nose to ease her headache. "But if your lies come to light, you don't just lose your job, you ruin my credibility. My company's reputation. It could crash Vesta's stock."

Jordan threaded one of myriad wires into a nexus of circuitry. "As long as this ship doesn't crash, your stock will be fine."

She could handle the business end. Hell, if she put his picture on the news, the female half of the planet would fall in love at first sight and forgive him anything. Mr. Dark, Tough, and Brilliant's gorgeous face might just sway the general population and perhaps her stockholders, as well.

What she couldn't handle was a traitor.

"What other lies have you told me?" she asked.

"Whatever would get me this job."

"Real inspiring. Why didn't you respond to the memo I sent last week?"

"If I spent all my time reading your memos, how would I get anything done?"

"You've installed miles of wiring that aren't in the specs."

"We're ahead of schedule, so why are you concerned?"

"I suppose you'll say the same about the cancellation of the prototype cosmic-energy converter?"

He merely arched a brow.

She frowned. Before she'd known about his lies, she'd shrugged off his changes to necessary modifications. But could it be more?

In a desperate attempt to suppress her frustration, Vivianne reminded herself how far she'd come. Peering at the *Draco*'s shiny metal, she had difficulty believing they'd built this ship in just over three months. Almost every system was a new design, and while the number of things that could go wrong was literally infinite, she had high hopes for success.

"If the story of your doctored credentials leaks, our client may get cold feet," she explained.

"Chen won't back out." Jordan sounded completely certain.

She didn't bother to keep the exasperation from her voice. "Billionaires willing to buy a spaceship in order to search the galaxy for the Holy Grail aren't a dime a dozen."

Jordan grunted.

"If Chen does back out, I'll have to refund his investment. And with the way you've been spending, not even I have that much credit."

"Down to your last few billion, are you?" Jordan teased without glancing in her direction.

She clenched her fists in irritation. "That's not the point. Maybe we can break the news, spin it in our favor." She pictured an advantageous story. Something like "Genius Engineer Discovered." "Then the article could go on to praise you and some little-known college. I'll have my PR department put together a package."

"Not a good idea."

His blue eyes glittered dangerously, and his response made her uneasy. Something wasn't right. He should be grateful that she was willing to fix the publicity nightmare he'd created. Instead he was acting like a man with something else to hide. But what?

"Do you always make contingencies for contingencies?" he asked.

She snorted. Orphaned at age ten, Vivianne had become a ward of the state. Control became her lifeline. She planned her days from start to finish. She arranged her appointments, both business and personal, to the minute, and any disruption was cause to work twice as hard to get back on schedule. She'd used her obsession to earn herself a first-class education and to build a successful small business into a worldwide conglomerate.

The downside of running a huge company, however, was that she had to rely on others. Brilliant engineers like Jordan didn't give a damn about her minute-to-minute expectations. He got the job done—but he certainly didn't do things her way.

"In your case, I haven't planned enough."

Jordan rubbed his ear and stood, reminding her just how tall and broad he was. But if he was attempting to use his size to intimidate her, he'd learn she didn't back down. He was, after all, her employee.

"What do you want me to do?" he asked. "You have someone else who can build the *Draco* on budget and under deadline?" He didn't wait for her reply. They both knew the answer was no.

"Where *did* you go to school?"

Jordan shrugged. "Here and there."

Her blood pressure shot up ten points, but she did her best to keep her temper under control. "Could you be a little more specific?"

He shot her a nonapologetic smile that was way too charming. "I'm pretty much self-taught."

Hell. She needed more than a damn charming smile to convince her he hadn't been educated on another planet. That he wasn't a spy.

"You don't have a PhD?"

He didn't answer.

Vivianne reminded herself that she'd dealt with many difficult situations in the last few years. She'd funded archaeologist Lucan Roarke's risky mission to a moon named Pendragon to find the Holy Grail. While he hadn't brought back the Grail, he had found a cure for Earth's infertility problem.

Vivianne stared at the scales on the insides of her wrists. Like one-tenth of the population, she could now shapeshift into a dragon and fly.

Too bad the vaccine hadn't increased her intelligence. How could Jordan have fooled her so easily? More importantly, what was he hiding? What else hadn't he told her?

"What about job experience?"

"Nothing verifiable."

"I suppose you fudged the glowing recommendations, too?" Her pulse pounded, and she massaged her aching temple. "Who the hell are you?"

"You might want to take an aspirin—"

"Thank you, *Doctor.*" Her sarcasm escaped unchecked. "Oh, excuse me, you aren't a doctor of anything, are you?"

"I don't need a medical degree to see that your head hurts and you're taking it out on me." His tone was calm, low, and husky, and that she found it sexy irked her even more.

"So now you're a shrink."

He'd barely glanced at her before turning to work on his beloved circuits, but it was so like him to notice details, even her wincing in pain.

Vivianne willed Jordan to turn around. "How did you do it? It's as if you appeared in Barcelona six months ago. Until then, you had no credit. You attended no schools. Even your birth records are fake. I can't find anyone who knew you before you walked into my office to apply for a job."

"And you've never regretted it."

"Until now." Damn him.

"You don't mean that." Jordan shrugged. "You don't regret letting me build you this ship."

Vivianne hadn't built up her company by allowing handsome men to sweet-talk her into trusting them or by ignoring urgent government warnings. Both Vivianne and the Tribes were after the same goal—both wanted the Grail. So it was very possible that the reason her chief engineer had faked his past was because he was a spy— for the Tribes.

Feeling sick to her stomach, Vivianne's tone snapped with authority. "Jordan, put down your tools. You can't work on the *Draco* until security clears you."

In typical Jordan fashion, he kept right on working. "Don't you want to see if the new engine's going to work?"

"We'll straighten that out later." Her temper flared because Jordan knew just how to pique her interest. From the get-go, the engines had been a major issue. It almost broke her heart to know that the *Draco* might never fly now that she was pulling him off the project.

"I'm about ready to test a new power source."

"What are you talking about? What new power source?"

"The Ancient Staff." Jordan reached to a sheath he wore on his belt and drew out an object that resembled a tree branch with symbols carved into the bark. When he flicked his wrist, the rod telescoped and expanded with a metallic click. Extended to five feet, the Ancient Staff gave off an otherworldly shimmer unlike anything Vivianne had ever seen.

The air around the staff glittered like heat reflecting off hot pavement. It was as if the staff folded and compressed the space around it, the eerie effect and haze continuously rippling outward.

She peered at Jordan. The cords in his neck were tight, his broad shoulders tense as if he were bracing for her reaction.

She tried to tamp down a pinch of panic. "Don't move."

He turned to place the staff into position. "The Ancient Staff will supply far more power to the *Draco*'s engines than a cosmic converter."

That staff wasn't in the plans. It hadn't ever been discussed. For all she knew, once he attached the strange power source to the *Draco*, they'd all blow up. Unnerved, she reached for her handheld communicator to call security, but there was no time. It would take only a second for him to snap the Ancient Staff into the housing.

She'd have to stop him herself. "Turn it off."

"The staff doesn't have an off switch."

Vivianne jerked back a step. "Don't attach that thing to my ship."

"It's meant to—"

"I said no." Mouth dry with suspicion, she clamped her hand on his shoulder.

Before she could yank him back, Jordan snapped the rod into place. The anxiety she'd been holding back knotted in her stomach.

But controlling her fear was the least of her worries

as the air around the rod shimmered, then spread up his arm.

"What type of energy is this?" she asked.

"The powerful kind."

"The engines can deal with that kind of power?"

"I hope so."

The energy crawled all the way up his arm and stretched toward her hand. She tried to jerk back, but her body refused to obey her mind. Her feet wouldn't move. Her fingers might as well have been frozen.

Panicked, she watched the glow of energy flow over his shoulder to her hand. Every hair on the back of her neck standing on end, she braced for pain. But when the glowing energy engulfed her fingers and washed up her arm, then sluiced over her body, the tingling sensation somehow banished her headache and expelled her fear.

The effect was instantaneous and undeniable. Her breasts tingled. Her skin flamed as if they'd spent the past fifteen minutes engaging in foreplay rather than arguing over his nonexistent past. She'd always found Jordan attractive, but now it was as if the staff had turned on a switch inside her.

She swallowed thickly. If he was feeling the same effects, he wasn't showing it.

Every centimeter of her skin now was demanding to be stroked. Unwarranted sensations exploded all over her erogenous zones. Her nipples tightened, exquisitely sensitized. The scales on the insides of her arms and legs fluttered. Sweet juice seeped between her thighs.

Drenched in pure lust, she shook her head, trying to clear it. "What the hell is going on?"

"Don't know." Jordan practically growled, as if it took superhuman effort just to speak.

So he felt as totally, inexplicably aroused as she did. Obviously, he wasn't handling it well, either, but that didn't stop desire from rushing through all her senses.

She craved him like a starving dragon needs platinum, yet this could not be. Not without an emotional connection. She didn't do chemistry. She didn't do one-nighters. She didn't crave a man she barely knew.

But there was no fighting or denying the potent passion slamming her. Sexual need burned into her flesh, blazed in her bones, smoldered through her blood, the sensations fiery hot.

If she didn't have sex in the next few seconds, she was certain she would spontaneously combust.

THE DISH

Where authors give you the inside scoop!

From the desk of Susan Kearney

Dear Readers,

I came up with my idea for RION, the second book in the Pendragon Legacy Trilogy, in the usual way. As the sun dipped below the horizon, a time machine landed on the aft deck of my yacht. And another hunky alien, muscles rippling, climbed up the ladder and joined me on the third deck.

Rion.

Damn. How lucky could a girl get? After LUCAN's story, I was filled with excitement at the prospect of hearing about the next installment in the Pendragon Legacy series.

Rion had even arrived at my favorite time of day. As the sun cast slashes of red and streaks of pink across the Gulf of Mexico, the sunlight kissed Rion's skin, accenting his sharp cheekbones. And shadowing his eyes—eyes that really got to me. Eyes that were both kind and hard. Eyes that revealed past heartaches and perhaps a newfound sense of peace.

Did I mention the guy was also hot? From his casual jeans to his open shirt that revealed a ripped chest, he looked more like a treasure hunter than a king from the planet Honor. Between his five o'clock shadow, the dark gleam in his eyes, and the bruise at his temple, he could have just stepped off a battlefield.

And as twilight deepened into darkness, as the waves lapped gently against the hull, Rion told me his story.

He spoke in a sexy rumble. "Lucan said that you're interested in love stories about the future."

"I am." Pulse escalating with excitement, I sipped my wine.

"In the future, my planet will be attacked, my people will be enslaved."

Uh-oh. "But you saved them?" I asked.

"I couldn't do it alone."

"You needed the help of a woman?" I guessed, always a romantic at heart.

"A special woman from planet Earth. In fact, she's Lucan's twin sister."

"Marisa?" Oh, this story sounded exciting. Lucan had told me how his sister had given up a job as a reporter to train dragonshapers. How she'd longed for children of her own. And I could envision the feisty woman with this man. They'd have cute babies . . . "Marisa agreed to help save your world?"

"Not at first." A smile played over Rion's lips. "I had to kidnap her."

Wow. "I'd imagine it took her a while to get over that." While Rion was quite the catch, still . . . he'd kidnapped her. I swallowed hard. Maybe it wasn't so bad. The woman in me told me he'd more than made it up to Marisa. "You mentioned a love story? So she forgave you, right?"

Lucan's face softened. "Marisa, she didn't just help me. She helped my people, too."

"And you made her your queen?"

His eyes sparkled. "First she ran away and almost got herself killed."

"But you saved her?"

He grinned. "We saved each other."

If you'd like to read the story Rion told me, the book is in stores now.

You can reach me at www.susankearney.com.

Enjoy!

Susan Kearney

❤ ❤ ❤ ❤ ❤ ❤ ❤ ❤ ❤ ❤ ❤ ❤ ❤ ❤ ❤

From the desk of Margaret Mallory

Dear Readers,

I love to catch characters on the cusp of change—
on the verge of disaster, falling in love, or just
growing up.

At the start of my current release, KNIGHT OF
PLEASURE, Sir Stephen Carleton is disillusioned,
drinking too much, and going to bed with all the
wrong women. I think we have all known someone
like that—a bright young man with so much poten-
tial that you want to scream or cry when you see
him slipping into a downward spiral and wasting all
that talent. What Stephen needs, of course, is the
right woman. He is at a crossroads—with one foot
on the wrong path—when he meets the no-non-
sense, strong-minded Isobel. She is just the inspira-
tion Stephen needs to step up and become the man
he was meant to be.

If you read my first book, KNIGHT OF DESIRE,
you already know Stephen has a hero's heart beneath all that charm. In that book, he is the hero's
younger brother, an endearing youth of thirteen,
full of gallantry and prone to trouble. By the time I
finished writing KNIGHT OF DESIRE, I was so

attached to Stephen that I simply had to give him his own story.

While I was writing Stephen's story, KNIGHT OF PLEASURE, the same thing happened with Jamie, Stephen's fifteen-year-old nephew: Jamie had to have a book. But Linnet, a young French girl, is such a strong character that she fairly jumped off the page, begging for a leading role. It was not until I tried outlining a book for each of them that I realized these two characters were meant to be together. And so they will be, in KNIGHT OF PASSION. Look out, Jamie, because the fiery Linnet has revenge—not marriage—on her mind.

Now, as I write KNIGHT OF PASSION, I am keeping a close watch on the teenagers who seem to pop up of their own accord in my books. I wonder which one will demand a love story of his own . . . Whoever my next hero and heroine turn out to be, I'm bound to put them on the verge of disaster before I reward them with their happy ending.

I hope you enjoy all three books (so far) in my medieval series, All the King's Men: KNIGHT OF DESIRE, KNIGHT OF PLEASURE, and KNIGHT OF PASSION.

Margaret Mallory

www.margaretmallory.com

Want to know more about romances at Grand Central Publishing and Forever? Get the scoop online!

GRAND CENTRAL PUBLISHING'S ROMANCE HOME PAGE

Visit us at www.hachettebookgroup.com/romance for all the latest news, reviews, and chapter excerpts!

NEW AND UPCOMING TITLES

Each month we feature our new titles and reader favorites.

CONTESTS AND GIVEAWAYS

We give away galleys, autographed copies, and all kinds of fun stuff.

AUTHOR INFO

You'll find bios, articles, and links to personal Web sites for all your favorite authors—and so much more!

THE BUZZ

Sign up for our monthly romance newsletter, and be the first to read all about it!